Born and educate
qualified in comm
School of Printing and Graphic Arts. He has worked for *The Daily Herald*, in advertising, and is currently writing commercials and American television series. His previous and widely acclaimed novels include *Goodbye Piccadilly, Bikini Red North, The Olympic Sleeper,* and *Terminate with Prejudice.*

The Sirens of Autumn

TOM BARLING

SPHERE BOOKS LIMITED
30–32 Gray's Inn Road, London WC1X 8JL

First published in Great Britain by
Sphere Books Ltd 1983

TRADE
MARK

Set in Garamond

Printed and bound in Great Britain by
Cox & Wyman Ltd. Reading

BOOK ONE

CHAPTER ONE

Soldiers of the West Front!
The hour of the most decisive battle of the future of the German nation has come. For 300 years it was the aim of British and French Governments to hinder every workable consolidation of Europe, and above all to keep Germany in weakness and impotence . . .
Soldiers of the Western Front!
With this, the hour has come for you. The battle which begins today will decide the fate of the German nation for the next thousand years.
Do your duty.

Adolf Hitler – Order of the Day 10 May 1940

'All's quiet on the Western Front, but more than a million German soldiers, including nearly all their active divisions, are drawn up ready to strike at a few hours' notice all along the frontiers of Luxembourg, Belgium and Holland.

At any moment these neutral countries may be subjected to an avalanche of steel and fire, and the decision rests in the hands of that morbid being who, to their eternal shame, the German peoples in their bewilderment have worshipped as a god.'

Extract from a wireless broadcast 30 March 1940
Winston Churchill

WAR SEEN ENTERING PHASE OF VIOLENCE

New York Times

ONE: SICHELSCHNITT

'The cut of the sickle'

As dawn broke on 10 May 1940, eight months of 'Phoney War' came to an abrupt and bloody end.

Whilst Churchill breakfasted on bacon, eggs and cigar smoke at the Admiralty, impatiently waiting to be asked to form the next government, and the French Premier, Paul Reynaud, withdrew his resignation and retained General Maurice Gamelin as Commander-in-Chief of the French forces, Adolf Hitler struck.

Protected by a massive Luftwaffe umbrella, the German Panzers rolled into Holland, Belgium and Luxembourg from the Ardennes. Moving at night with doused lights across terrain the French High Command had long considered impassable to armoured vehicles, they smashed across the frontiers at first light, 10 May. Spearheaded by fast-moving tanks, the columns of heavy-supply echelons, flak units, motorised shock-troops and the trailing infantry regiments were seen by General von Blumenritt, Runstedt's Chief of Operations as: ' . . . a giant phalanx; they stretched back for a hundred miles, their rear rank lying fifty miles to the east of the Rhine. Had this mass formation of Panzers been placed in single-file, the tail-end would have been in Königsberg in East Prussia, and the head of the column in Trier'.

In the extreme north, Holland's defensive plan to destroy strategic bridges, flood large areas in the enemy's path and withdraw into 'Fortress Holland', an area between the Zuider Zee and the Rhine, was savagely forestalled by a decisive airborne assault. Commanded by General Student, Germany's 22nd Airborne Division, a force of some 4,000 crack troops, overflew the Dutch frontier to take the three main airfields ringing The Hague, whilst the city itself was heavily strafed from the air. Despite huge losses, Student's force also captured two important bridges over the Maas and cut the tiny Dutch Air Force in half. By the following day it no longer existed.

Groups from the 'Brandenburgers' Battalion failed totally when, dressed in stolen Dutch uniforms, they attempted to seize the bridges at Maastricht and Arnhem. At Gennep their fellows were more successful. There, three 'Dutch policemen' marched a group of 'captured' Germans across the bridge and took the defenders completely by surprise, with the result that the 9th Panzer and part of the 6th Army crossed into Holland almost unopposed.

In Belgium, other 'Brandenburgers' took three of the four bridges at St Vith, an exploit that earned ninety-two of their number the coveted Iron Cross. But even this action was firmly overshadowed by the volunteer sappers of the élite 'Koch Storm Detachment' who took Fort Eban Emael with less than a hundred men, even though the stronghold was manned by over ten times that number, and boasted the largest guns along the vital Albert Canal defensive line.

Trained in secret and knowing all about Eban Emael except its name and location, the sappers boarded their gliders in the pre-dawn dusk and were loosed by their towing Ju-52s at 8,000 feet and left to swoop silently in. Eight of their gliders dropped onto the fort with incredible accuracy, but the one carrying Captain Koch broke its tow line and he landed in a field far from the target. Undaunted, he had himself towed off again and flew back to the fort where his men had destroyed the guns with powerful hollow charges and were busily demoralising the garrison with flamethrower and grenade attacks.

At a stroke, the linchpin of the main Belgian line of defence was breached and its teeth drawn.

To the immediate south, Rommel's rapid advance on the

River Ourthe was halted. Only because the Belgians were ordered to filter away during the night was he able to advance and to provide flanking cover for the main Panzer thrust across the Meuse between Dinant and Sedan.

During the previous day, 9 May, large numbers of Abwehr 'tourists' had pedalled or motorcycled across the Luxembourg border to disrupt telephone communications and secure key road junctions. Their success enabled General Guderian's 1st Panzer Division to race through the Grand Duchy and gain the Belgian border by 0900 hours, 10 May. Here, like the 5th and 7th Panzers north of it, the 1st was seriously delayed by Belgian obstructions and dynamited bridges.

Behind them, on a forty-mile front, one of the largest traffic-jams in history began to develop, and the German ground forces watched the sparkling blue skies overhead with disquiet, waiting for the concerted Allied air-strikes that never came.

The empty skies were not only due to the Luftwaffe's generous attention to the Allied airfields deep within France; much of it was due to the chaotic command structure of the French military, designed as it was to create division and confusion. Firstly, General Gamelin, as Commander-in-Chief of the French Army was responsible for all the armies in the French empire, those manning the German, Italian and Spanish borders as well as the Army Groups within metropolitan France itself; a task this 'ivory tower intellectual' who weighed all military decisions against their impact on his political masters, was hardly cut out for. His *Grand Quartier Général* at Vincennes did not possess a single WT set for fear of 'giving away our position to the enemy', relying instead on runners with written orders; orders that more often than not went astray, were misinterpreted, or worse still, arrived too late for reasonable action.

Command of the battle front between Switzerland and the sea was delegated to General Alphonse Georges, Commander-in-Chief North-East, an officer Gamelin felt personal animus towards, which tainted his objective view of the national crisis just as surely as Chamberlain's distaste for Churchill blinded him to the worth of his many timely warnings of Britain's weakness in the face of Germany's rising military strength and ambition.

Gamelin further exploded his command into rival factions by the creation of yet a third G.H.Q. commanded by General Doumenc, manned by members of Georges's staff, and whose sole function was the issue of carefully polished orders.

Under General Georges, General Billotte had charge of the five armies that were destined to face the German onslaught between the Maginot Line and the Channel. These forces included the 1st, 2nd, 7th and 9th French Armies, and Lord Gort's British Expeditionary Force. The fact that Gort received his directives from Gamelin through Georges, rather than directly from Billotte, points up the convoluted manner of French command. Even the R.A.F. had two heads. Whereas Air Marshal Barratt's Advanced Air Striking Force was directly answerable to Bomber Command in England, it was Lord Gort who commanded the Air Force Component of the B.E.F. Unlike the Luftwaffe, who struck in force where needed, the Allies sent their planes in penny packets to suffer massive losses without measurable success.

The Maginot Line was not to prove impregnable, the Ardennes Forest north of it was not impassable, and the German thrusts into the Low Countries, however monumental, were nothing more than a feinting second front, and not as Gamelin believed, a reworking of the Schlieffen Plan of 1914. More, it was a ploy to draw the mobile Allied forces north and away from the main German assault on the static French defensive line between Dinant and Sedan on the Meuse.

TWO: FRANK

04.30 hours 10 May 1940

Extract from a letter to Lieutenant René de Chambrun from Senator William Borah of Idaho: *Dear René, it looks like a phoney war to a lot of us over here.*

1940: The World in Flames Richard Collier

The soldiers talked to kill the miles as the lorries trundled through the quickening day. The harsh winter had eased through a lingering wet spring, and now, early summer laid mist over the drying French fields. The road from Arras to Béthuen was lined with budding trees.

Frank Cooper drove with Dougie Wayne in the cab beside him. Tosher, Limey and Winkle slept on the ammunition in the back, too bored to smoke or tell each other lies. They had all enlisted as Gunners with the Middlesex Regiment Territorials in 1935. Transferred to the Royal Artillery T.A. the following year, they had been in France since the previous September, and to Frank's jaundiced eye, they were a street gang in khaki. Regular soldiering was bull, boredom and bad food.

Dougie Wayne said: 'What's got four legs and a prick in the middle of its back?'

'A French cavalry horse.' Frank changed down as the truck ahead slowed on a bend. He had cold-shaved and his face stung.

'Correct, Driver-Gunner-Private Cooper. Snouts *up*!' Dougie passed Frank a lit roll-up and they blew smoke at the mist beyond the windscreen. They had caught some sleep in a disused barn heaped with rotten straw and he still felt the cold in his bones. 'I just hope there's a hot breakfast at the other end.'

'What other end? Probably some field of cows in the middle of no place that ain't even got a map-reference. We'll be lucky if we get cold porridge and bully on the same plate, son. Hey up, M.P.s.' Frank dropped into first gear as the convoy halted at an intersection where French cavalry crossed to the north on lathered horses. 'Who's that shower of sherbert then?'

'Ask Limey, he's the expert. Looks like the Seventh to me, General Corap's mob. *La crème de la crème*, mate.'

Frank flicked ash, watching baggage waggons toil past. Dougie always gave his smattering of French a decent accent. *He was like that about some things,* thought Frank, *painful.* 'Oh, yeah, cream? I've seen pikeys down the Caledonian Market with more swank. Just look at Ramon Navarro here.'

A French corporal walked his sweating bay alongside the ammunition convoy to yell at the drivers through the side windows. *'La Drôle de Guerre est finie, mes amis Tommy. Finie.'* He galloped back to the cavalry column, scattering shale.

'What's boiling his potatoes?' asked Frank. The trucks were moving again.

'He said the Phoney War's over. Think there's anything to it?' Dougie gnawed a knuckle.

'Not till I see it plastered over the sports page of the *Daily Mirror*, I don't.' Frank hunched over the driving wheel, out of conversation and bored senseless from following the truck in front. He knew every chip and mud spatter on its tailboard. *Why should those three idle buggers in the back sleep when me and Dougie are grafting for King and sodding Country?* he thought. He drove at a series of potholes in the road and the truck bumped and slewed on spinning tyres. There were yells from the back as Tosher, Winkle and Limey were thrown about by the furious motion. Winkle's white pinched face appeared at the grill. 'Cooper, you're nothing but a bloody bugger.'

Frank grinned over his shoulder. 'Just saved your life, you scrounging berk. Had to take avoiding action. There was a U-boat off the port bow.'

'He's barmy. Bloody barmy,' Winkle complained.

'You've cracked my bum, Frank, mate,' said Limey.

Tosher just groaned.

'Bang goes your Good Fellowship medal,' said Dougie.

'Stopped them from dreaming about grubby things I'll bet,' Frank stifled a yawn. 'They ain't happy without a good grumble. Mark of a good soldier, right? Ain't that right, Driver First-Class, Douglas Wayne?'

Dougie aped Sergeant Tanner's bellow. 'That's for sergeants to know and squaddies like you to ponder on, you nasty soldier.'

'Anything you say, Sarge.'

'Leave it out, you two,' said Winkle. 'Give us a tune, Dougie.'

Dougie played his mouth-organ; sweet versions of tunes he had learned from the old violinist at their favourite bar in Arras. He played well and had taught Frank to accompany him. As the rising sun warmed the cab they unbuttoned their greatcoats.

On the outskirts of Béthuen the convoy turned into a wired compound and halted in line inside the perimeter fence. Shunting rolling stock clanked from the nearby rail-sidings and smoke rose from a field kitchen. Row upon row of petrol cans winked silver in the sun, covered in part by camouflage netting, and men of the Royal Army Service Corps wandered about with towels and shaving tackle.

Tosher, Winkle and Limey dropped from the tailboard to stretch alongside Frank and Dougie as Sergeant Tanner came back from the lead truck and told them to double off for a fifteen-minute break.

'That,' said Dougie, 'sounds like another sun-up to

sundown drive. Do I smell hot food?'

Winkle Watts, a natural scavenger who wore his uniform like a penance, sidled up to Frank. 'Hey, Coop, what my farmer friends couldn't do with some of that petrol,' he said from the side of his mouth. Winkle was incapable of acting directly, he walked and thought in oblique angles, and had 'friends' all over France.

'Nothing inflammable goes on that lorry until we're shot of that ammo. But since you're so keen, Wink, check out the fence. We might get back this way and extra petrol never hurts. Tosher'll nick you some breakfast.' Frank walked Dougie toward the field-kitchen as Winkle lost himself under camouflage netting. 'You ain't still worrying your head about that daft Frenchie and his drole de guerre rubbish are you? Look at Lieutenant Fisher there, sitting in his car and walloping back his tea with his little finger out. He's not worried and he parlez-vous nineteen-to-the-dozen. And Tanner, is he biting his nails? Course not. We're in a different army, son. T.A. odds-and-sods are non-combatants. Sort of padres without the frocks and latin, right?'

Fisher, a lean man with hollow cheeks and a second at Oxford, drew on his mapcase with a greaseproof pencil, marking a route and watched by Sergeant Tanner, a regular close to his pension.

Tosher hefted his rifle, his long face puzzled. 'We carry these don't we?'

'And padres carry crosses. Don't mean they go to a crucifixion every morning.'

'That's bleeding blasphemy,' said Tosher. 'Ain't it?'

'If we weren't keeping radio-silence we might know what was going on,' said Dougie, joining the breakfast line.

'Remember them Royal Corps of Signals blokes we brewed up with last week? The radios ain't even been issued yet.' Frank flicked a dried crumb of something from a tin plate. 'And they reckoned that if the army moved forward all the static lines of communication would be left behind.'

The Corporal Cook said: 'One cob of bread per man. Tinned marmalade, one dollop. Hold out your plates, keep moving, porridge or scrambled egg . . .'

'Which is bleeding which?' Tosher asked under his breath, eyeing the anonymous pap in the steaming pots. 'Oh, one of each, please, Corp?'

' . . . Tinned marmalade, one dollop . . . '

They sat beside their lorry to enjoy the sun and suffer the food. The sky was deep blue and unclouded. A low haze marked the last of the mist.

Winkle came back and ate from the plate Tosher handed him. 'There's ways in everywhere. These R.A.C.s don't know bum from fluff how to patrol a perimeter. Be an easy tickle if we come back. Must be a million gallons here. This is funny old porridge.'

'It's scrambled egg.' Tosher rolled himself a cigarette and tucked it into the corner of his mouth, ignoring the NO SMOKING signs. 'I think . . . '

Frank saw Sergeant Tanner's polished boots stamp close to his own and carefully set his mug of tea on the ground, knowing Tosher had earned them a rocket up the proverbial.

'Bennett, you limping lump of dumb insolence, put that smoke *out!*' Tanner roared. 'On your feet, on your feet, all of you, all of you . . . *Now!*'

A bumblebee droned over the horizon as the Territorials leaped to attention, their backs to the lorry. Part of Tosher's lip stuck to his roll-up as he threw it from him, and a dark crimson bead formed on his mouth. He stared over Tanner's shoulder as the bumblebee came in low from the north, correcting its approach. He picked out the white Luftwaffe crosses on the wings as Tanner shouted hot abuse into his face. A long dark shape tumbled from the grey fuselage and whistled as it fell, wobbling at first, then plummeting in a clean arc.

Bennet, my son, thought Tosher, *you're definitely dead here.*

'Sarge ... ?'

'Shut *up!*'

The first tongue of flame rose from the centre of the silver rows, a lazy lick of brilliant orange that dragged a ball of incandescant dazzle after it, burning a white hole in the sky.

Frank felt the heat of the first concussion tug at his battledress and sear his face as Dougie said something indistinct.

Rolling flame balled outward, growing in intensity as it gathered greasy folds of black smoke.

Frank dropped to the ground, pulling Dougie with him as the sound hit like a hot wall, stealing all the air. A flaming tide of burning petrol blew the field kitchen to nothing. A profound darkness closed in and burning cans fell from the spreading pall of smoke to explode on impact.

Frank threw dirt over his burning sleeve, then tea when it still smouldered, slapping at the thick khaki with his bare hands. *If that Jerry comes back or there are others up there ...* Frank hauled Dougie up into the cab and pushed Tosher toward the tailgate, hoping Winkle knew enough to follow him. Limey was nowhere to be seen. *Knowing that long drink of water, he was off collecting engine numbers or sat on some latrine with a penny Comic Cuts. Well, stuff his luck, one petrol can through the tarpaulin and teddah truck. Teddah us.*

The truck started first time. Sergeant Tanner was up and running down the line of trucks with one of his boots alight. What must have been Lieutenant Fisher was a burning scarecrow scrabbling to climb out of his Alvis. The blackened figure ran blindly into the side of the lead lorry, bounced off shedding sparks and flame and lay still.

Frank ground his truck in a half-circle, turning the wheel to where he thought the entrance might be. Men ran and blinding smoke swept blazing debris in mad dancing whirls, filling the air with a cloying stench.

Dougie was slammed against the side of the cab as a shed loomed on the offside of the truck. Sideswiped, it lost window glass as the frame caved in on a stunned clerk. His eyes and mouth formed three perfect zeroes of fright before he disappeared in a cloud of slashing splinters.

Frank brought the truck square and smashed through the outer fence, uprooting a wooden upright and parting the wire in whipping strands. Then they were out onto the road with burning sludge spattered over the windscreen and bonnet. They jolted down a cinder track and Frank pulled into the lee of a rising bank of earth topped out by burning trees.

Across the way, in the garden of a railway cottage, an old man had frozen in the act of spading over a flower bed. His wife hid her face in her apron. They were both old enough to remember the loss and upheaval of the previous war.

'Boche!' The old man spat at the sky and wiped off his mouth.

Dougie shredded Rizla paper to waste as he tried to build a cigarette. 'All that from one bomb . . .' he shook his head. 'Did you see Lieutenant Fisher . . . he burned like . . . '

'I saw.' Frank shared the cigarette he had rolled with unsteady fingers. If he felt anything other than shock at the speed of the destruction it was a vague, unformed exhilaration, coupled with the memory of his mother drunk on stout in a four-ale bar, podding peas for Sunday dinner and weeping for her lost husband; prodding old Freddy Lucas in the chest and saying: 'Why ain't you dead like my Bert? He done his bit at Wipers before the mustard gas done his chest in. Him burying all them dead horses 'cause he was a navvy and could handle a shovel.' Her bony finger pointing around her glass. 'Why ain't you dead like him?'

Old Freddy rolling his one eye as usual and saying: 'Leave it out, Emma girl. They took me left foot and me right bleeding eye. What more d'yer want?'

'The bleeding rest of you, yer coward. My Frankie won't go to war. He'll never go through what we went through. Look around at the kids today, though. They couldn't stand a Zeppelin attack like us. Cut of cheaper cloth nowadays, ain't they? Well, ain't they?'

'Leave it out, Emma girl ... '

'Yeah, leave it out, Ma,' Frank said aloud. His arm had begun to hurt.

'What say, mate?' said Dougie.

'Nothing.'

The fuel exploded like faulty cylinders in a distant engine as they sat there, unwilling to move or think ahead.

Tosher stood up on the running board with Winkle peering into the cab over his shoulder. Shock gave their faces a smashed look.

'What do we do, Frank?' Tosher's eyebrows had gone.

'Nothing.' Frank watched the old man throw water over the roof of his outhouse as glowing smuts dropped into his garden. A line of trucks appeared in the rear view mirror, emerging from the shimmering smoke like mechanised phantoms. 'Well, Tanner made it out. He bloody would.'

Dougie stirred himself, taking hold. 'He'll know what to do.'

'Oh, *yeah?*' Frank's face was hard with contempt. 'And even if he *don't* we'll follow his tailgate as usual, won't we? When I drove a van on civvie street I at least had a delivery note telling me where I was going. As a T.A. driver I don't get nothing. I just follow the bloke in front. Listen, Lieutenant Fisher only stopped here to ask directions. Our officer was lost, son. Don't that tell you something?'

'Well, he was new on the strength, wasn't he?'

'They all sodding are. We didn't know where that petrol dump was, but Jerry did. He blew it to buggery and swanned off. And us, you lot and me, we've got rifles with no ammo and seven hours on the rifle-range between us. If we're typical of the B.E.F., then God save old England.'

'That's defeatist talk,' said Tosher. 'Ain't it?'

'You want to step down and have a go with belts, Tosh?'

'Only asking, Frank mate.'

'All that petrol at two-bob a gallon. Gone.' Winkle snorted smoke from his nose.

Dougie bit off a giggle of hysteria before it got out of hand.

'Wink, you're a profiteering thoughtless berk.'

'And broke with it,' said Winkle, watching the mounting column of smoke form a huge malignant question-mark and drift toward La Bassée.

Sergeant Tanner leaned from his lorry as it came alongside. 'Back inside, you lot. Follow on, Cooper. We'll pick up the odds and sods at the Deûle Canal Bridge.'

'Prendergast's missing.'

'Likely he'll turn up at the bridge,' said Tanner, nothing in his voice. 'Follow on.'

'Right behind you, Sarge.' Frank watched the convoy roll past then said, 'His bottle's gone. Got any spit, Doug?'

'Some,' Dougie grinned through grime.

'Then give us something on the mouth-organ. Something a bit more cheerful than that old git's face over there.'

The old man stared at the British trucks with watering eyes, his neat hedge black with soot.

'Look hard, Doug. Won't be the last misery you'll see.'

The ammunition convoy rolled north-west.

THREE: FRANK

13.00 hours 10 May 1940

The day browsed under a brilliant sky.

The ammunition convoy was pulled off the road in a small wood, diverted there by a furious major who wanted to hurry his vehicles through the congested junction north of Vieille-Chapelle. Trucks rolled past in dusty column and the basking fields gave off fragrance and birdsong. Tosher brewed tea with radiator water and worried about the missing Limey Prendergast whilst Winkle foraged in a nearby farm and Frank and Dougie lay in dappled sunlight talking of home.

They reminded themselves of Douglas Fairbanks at the Finsbury Park Astoria, of Errol Flynn as *The Sea Hawk* at the Coliseum, Myrna Loy, William Powell and Asta the dog in *The Thin Man* at The Rex, and Tod Slaughter melodramas at fleapit matinees on Sunday afternoons. They talked of saveloys and pease-pudding at the King's Cross coffee-stall when the last bus had gone. Fish-suppers in Caledonian Road, the pretty 'Nippies' at Lyons Corner House, licorice-wood and jawbreaker toffee from Micky Gold 'The Chocolate King' in Upper Street. They showed their dog-eared photographs and talked of their families. An only child, Dougie had two Kodaks of his widowed mother, whilst Frank seemed to be related to half of North London.

'This little darling,' Frank pointed at a small dark woman with an oval face and two small boys, 'is my sister Phyllis. She brought me up really. My ma took to stout and knocking us kids about when the old dad died. There's still a hole in our kitchen door where she just missed braining me with a flat-iron. Funny, when the old man was alive, Ma hated booze. Now she's worse than he ever was. Sober, she'd give you the curtains off the window. Two drinks later she'd be breaking your door down to get them back. Our Phyl always stood up to the old mother for me. And Ma in drink is a tiger on heat.' Frank gulped black sugarless tea and his mouth twisted. 'I hope Winkle liberates some cows' milk.'

'He could find an old brass in a nunnery,' said Dougie.

Frank winked at his sister's picture, 'Language in front of the lady. Sorry, pet.' He buttoned the pictures and his paybook into his blouse pocket and settled himself against a tree. 'Phyllis's husband is a right prune. Nobody's good enough for her, she's a bit special. You should meet someone like her, Dougie mate. Then you'll know your luck's changed.'

Dougie smiled at the sun in the trees and wished he was as close to his mother as Frank was to his sister. A Baptist by conversion and a martyr to mild angina, his mother took brandy in milk with her New Testament and spoke to Dougie through a mongrel bitch with halitosis. She had never kissed him goodnight or comforted him against her bony chest. Frank had taught him street-sense and honed his loneliness into self-reliance.

'More char, Frank?' Tosher held a tea-billy. 'It's stewed, but it's warm and wet.'

'Not without cowjuice, Tosh. Use it to ablute in, you could use a good ablute. Wash up before Sergeant Machlin takes you for one of them black French colonials and has you sand-dancing into the glass-house.'

'Yeah, yeah,' said Tosher, 'very comical. Here, that major that pulled us off the road, know what his outfit was? A bloody mobile bath unit. He pushes ammo off the road for an ablution squad. Daft, this army.'

'Maybe he was in a hurry to wash Hitler's cobblers.'

A passing truck ground into lower gear and a lanky figure dropped from the back. Swinging a kitbag over his shoulder he walked into the trees to take Tosher's tea-billy and drain it.

'Ta, Tosh, I was parched.' Limey Prendergast dropped the kitbag on the grass.

'That ain't your kit, you thieving hound,' said Tosher.

'Nah, won it, didn't I? This snotty officer put me on a lorry after you lot had gone off. It was carrying officers' mess gear, tinned ham and peaches and that, so I sort of adopted some. Got some wine, too. That's one up Winkle's nose, eh?'

'Have a putty medal,' said Frank. 'Hide that kit in the cab before Tanner sniffs it out, Doug. We'll have a sort-out later.' He kicked Limey's boot. 'What happened to you, then?'

Limey had been knocked out by the blast and came to on a stretcher surrounded by burns cases. One of them had been Lieutenant Fisher. 'He'd had it. Seeing him all crisped turned me over, I can tell you.'

They said nothing, secretly glad none of them had been the one who died.

'Where we going then?' asked Limey.

'If you knew you wouldn't go,' said Frank.

'That's mutiny talk ... ain't it?' said Tosher.

Dougie suggested Lille as a destination. 'Any further and we'd be in Belgium.'

'Back to Arras,' said Tosher. 'We always go back to Arras.'

Sergeant Tanner moved down the column, getting the men on the move.

Frank stretched upright. 'Sound the horn for Winkle, Dougie. Can't leave him behind, he's gonna have to win us some maps.'

'He's back here,' Dougie called from the cab. 'With fresh eggs and a billy of milk.'

'Duck eggs,' yelled Winkle. 'And a round of cheese.'

'Arras,' Tosher told Limey as they climbed aboard the truck. 'It's always Arras. Bet you a tanner.'

'He doesn't know his Arras from his elbow.' Frank took the wheel, laughing to lose the image of the burning scarecrow.

The ammunition convoy moved through a constant churn of hot dust and black exhaust fumes. Driving took no conscious thought. Just keep the regulation two-vehicle lengths between your radiator and the truck in front; hating by heart every shake and heave of its tarpaulin, every blemish on its tailgate. Conjure memories of home to save yourself from screaming boredom.

Frank remembered finding short-cuts from Southend to London on the last Saturday of peace. With all major roads into the capital reserved for outgoing evacuation traffic, the many detours made him late, and Phyllis waited with her home packed, ready to move to Hornsey, away from shared squalor and mother.

Racing ahead of the September dusk and the second night of the blackout, Frank reached Islington and turned into Marquess Road just before five. Number 19 was in darkness but Edie Rowley's wind-up gramophone played Harry Lauder from an upper window. Every Saturday, Mr Challis brought a crate of stout to Edie's musical bed. At the height of passion with her undertaker, Edie played *Stars and Stripes Forever*. For Edie Rowley, sex and Sousa went hand in hand.

Frank hammered the knocker until Edie threw up the sash and leaned her bosom on the sill.

'You've missed them, dear. Come up for a glass of stout.' Edie patted frizzed, bleached hair and smiled her fat smile, her face pinker than her nightgown. 'He won't mind, not Arthur.'

'I blasted will.' Mr Challis wound the gramophone without showing himself.

'What about the furniture?'

'Gone, dear. On Bumble's cart. About two o'clock. Tommy had to get back to work, couldn't wait. Phyl took the boys on the tram.'

I bet she bleeding did. Sweat broke out on Frank's nose.

Bumble Hill owned two butcher's shops and the only Railton in the manor, but he kept his horse and cart, and regularly slept in Hercules' stall when his wife threw him out of the house. White-haired and unshaven, his boots permanently crusted in bloody sawdust, Bumble drank with Frank's mother in the *Hope & Anchor*. Worse, Bumble was a gossip. Mrs Cooper would soon know about Phyllis's move and arrive on the doorstep to make trouble.

'There's a jug of mild if you'd rather, dear.'

'No, thanks anyway.' Frank thought of old Bumble saying: 'You can't talk to no motor like you can to a horse. A horse is company.'

'Another time, Edie.'

'If you won't, you won't.' Edie turned sniffy. 'Don't say I didn't offer. All *right. Coming*, Arthur.' She slammed the window and put a military march on the turntable.

Frank stabbed the air with two fingers. Breathing gin and lust, Edie trapped him on the landing one night and had almost smothered him with her chest. *Phyllis is well off out of that rat hole. All the same, Tommy should have waited.* He made Hornsey in fifteen minutes and drew up outside 63

Rathcoole Avenue with rain spotting his windscreen. The door was open and he found his sister in the kitchen, making a fire from tinder and coaldust swept from the cellar floor, drawing it alight with a newspaper held across the grate.

'You didn't wait.'

'Don't *you* start,' snapped Phyllis, seeing the familiar heat in Frank's eyes. 'I've got trouble enough. There isn't a gas mantle in the house, not a scrap of coal. Two back windows are broke, the oven's thick with grease, and Tommy – Tommy's up on the roof putting up an aerial for his wireless.'

'Well where's the furniture?'

'Ask Tommy. Ask Bumble Hill. No beds, no chairs, just that table. If you want to be helpful, see why I can't get no water out of the taps. Tommy says there's a stopcock or something. I don't know, we've never had running water before.'

'I thought he had to be at the Horseshoe Hotel to do his cheffing?'

'He stayed at home to help me,' said Phyllis. 'With wireless.' The newspaper caught alight and she balled it up and dropped it onto the glowing coals. 'Blooming wireless.'

'I'll give him wireless.'

'Nice, now, Frankie. There are times when I think I've got three kids. The two I mothered and the one on the roof.' Phyllis brushed hair from Frank's forehead. 'And looking at you, maybe it's four.' Her head barely reached his chin.

'All right, Phyl. No barneys.'

Frank opened the main cock in the cellar and climbed to find the valve for the loft tank. On his way downstairs he saw Tommy on the flat rear roof, unrolling wire and stapling it to the brickwork. Frank climbed through the landing window and sat on the sill. 'Hello, face-ache.'

'Hold that while I unravel it.' Tommy handed Frank the free end of the wire and backed away along the roof playing out the kinks. 'I've picked up America on this.' Only an inch taller than his wife, Tommy Penny was dark-haired and thin, clever with his hands and an avid card player. 'Great view over the railway sidings, eh?'

'If you like railway sidings.' Frank looked out over the shunting trains and coalyards. *That*, he thought, *is where tonight's fire comes from. A quick nip over the wall, through the allotments, past the stables and into the bunker. There's even sacks and a shovel. Handy.*

In the small back garden, raw earth was heaped over a new Anderson shelter. Beyond it, against the railway wall, was an empty chicken coop.

'I'm getting some Rhode Island Reds ... for the eggs.' Tommy kept backing away, intent on his wire. His left foot caught the edge of the skylight and he hopped backwards off-balance. His leg went through the glass and he subsided onto his rump, firmly jammed in the frame, one leg out along the roof.

Frank choked on a bubble of laughter, hurting his larynx. 'You daft ha'pennyworth of dripping.'

'Don't sit there laughing. Give us a hand.'

Phyllis called from below. Glass had showered into the back bedroom where she stuffed cardboard into the windows. 'What are you boys doing up there?'

'Wireless,' laughed Frank. 'Just wireless.'

'I'm cut bad.' Tommy had gone grey. Blood ran slow and warm down the inside of his thigh. The sky lost focus and danced in an odd red mist. Then he was lying on the kitchen table with Phyllis calling him names and Frank watching her bandage him with malicious laughter in his hard brown eyes.

'It's well after opening time, face-ache. Bumble will be tossing back the rum in some pub with your home parked up outside ... '

Wind gusted rain against the window.

' ... getting rained on.' Frank shut himself up. One of the boys cried fitfully from the front room, tightening Phyllis's mouth. Relenting, he said, 'Don't worry, pet. I'll find Bumble.'

On the doorstep he met Doris and Jack, his sister and brother-in-law. They had moved their furniture upstairs the day before. Doris was a gaunt version of her sister and Jack had been described by Ma Cooper as: 'All hair and barber's rash. All that wool poking through his shirt – looks like he's smuggling bleeding monkeys. Doris should take a lawn-mower to his chest before he cuts her to death.'

Jack shed water from his overcoat. 'Black as tar out there, and she's going on about thunder and lightning.' He jerked his head at Doris who had gone blonde overnight.

'Can't help it.' Doris smoked a furious Weight to calm her fear of thunderstorms.

'Well you can help Phyl.' Frank closed her inside and dragged Jack into the blustery night. They drove towards Islington on sidelights, defying the law.

'Watch it, Frank!' Dougie wrenched the wheel left as the ammunition truck veered to mount a grass verge.

Frank started awake, blinking gritty eyes. The anonymous road passed nondescript fields. They could have been anywhere. Dougie took the wheel and Frank cosied into the corner to dream on …

Lightning sheeted as they knocked at 63.

'Mind where you're splashing.' Phyllis's candle guttered. 'You didn't find him?'

'Sorry, pet.'

'Where's Doris?' asked Jack as lightning illuminated the leaded glass in the front door and stained the sombre passage with brilliant colour.

'In the cupboard under the stairs.'

'Silly mare.'

Frank and Jack laughed like schoolboys when Phyllis saw the horse and cart hitched behind the van. The blown horse steamed in the diminishing rain, shaken by ague.

'You *did* find him. What have you done to Hercules?'

'Nothing. He can't corner for toffees, that's all.' Frank heaved bedsprings down from the tailgate.

'Got some sparks off his shoes at Highbury Corner,' said Jack, carrying a chest of drawers as if it weighed nothing. 'Where's this going?' There were quarts of beer in his coat pockets.

'Back bedroom and God bless you, loves. Tommy's got the kitchen range going, so we can have something hot.' Phyllis hovered between tears and laughter. 'I can't think where Tommy got the coal.'

Twenty minutes later the cart was unloaded and they washed scrambled egg on toast down with beer from jamjars. Tommy limped back from the public telephone, slick with rain.

'The police closed the Horseshoe because of bad blackout,' he said. 'The manager's spitting blood. There was a spot of light on the pavement the size of a halfcrown, that's all. You should have heard him leading off.' Tommy grinned. 'Still, I get paid for the night without turning in.'

'Here, face-ache.' Frank skimmed a fold of paper across the table. 'Bumble Hill's receipt.'

'I knew he'd come,' said Tommy, rubbing his throbbing thigh.

'Leave it out,' said Frank. 'He was never here. He's in the Hen & Chicks as pissed as a pudding. He didn't even know his own name, but he marked that "Paid in Full". Jack even put four quarts of beer on his slate.'

Tommy pulled his ear. 'You took his horse and cart and just left him there?'

Angry sweat broke out on Frank's nose. 'Just like he left your kids and my sister without a pot to piddle in. Never go to strangers when there's family Tommy. Get cottoned to that, my son.'

Tommy reddened; brought up in an orphanage, he had had no family until now.

Frank palmed his nose. 'Bumble'll sober up once he sees

Hercules has gone. Then he'll come looking, right?' His hair shone like oiled butter in the candle light. 'Sunday tomorrow, how about some cards?'

Tommy brightened. 'Solo or brag?'

'Money or matches?' Jack held his stomach. 'I don't think beer goes with scrambled eggs.'

'Brag for money,' said Frank, helping Phyllis clear the table. 'And you two can sub me until I hit a winning tickle. Bumble saved Jack his beer money and Tommy the price of the move. I'm the only one who hasn't earned out of him.'

'Yet,' said Jack, winking solemnly at Tommy who shuffled cards.

'I heard that.' Frank nudged Jack as thunder rolled overhead. 'You'll have to get our Doris trained, you know. All this hiding under the stairs when there's a bit of thunder. What's she gonna be like when the big guns start going off? The railway runs right along the bottom of the garden, and they've got guns mounted on the waggons. Stands to reason they'll bang 'em off in an air-raid.'

'There won't be no flipping war.'

'But if there is?'

'First jack deals,' said Tommy. 'Ante up.'

'Then I'll swop her for Bumble's horse,' said Jack, fishing in his pocket for coppers. 'Hey up, a jack for Jack. My deal.'

Unnoticed, Phyllis went off to bed.

They were still playing when dawn brought Bumble Hill to their door to apologise for leaving his horse behind.

13.00 hours 11 May 1940

To Frank, it was just another fallow field without cows. Somewhere to stop and stretch the stiffness away. To Sergeant Tanner it was a military objective. He stood on the churned turf with his map in his big freckled hands, his upper lip bristling at the co-ordinates marked there as though betrayed.

Light Bren-carriers had criss-crossed the field with raw furrows. Brown patches marked the sites of bell-tents and a freshly-filled latrine trench ran along the hedge. The battery had moved forward recently, leaving Tanner to wonder where. All he had was an empty field and a lot of ignorant drivers.

'Back to Arras, right?' Tosher rubbed circulation back into his buttocks, disappointed when nobody argued or agreed with him. 'Time for a brew-up, Sarge?'

'I'll tell you if and when.' Tanner worried his moustache with a forefinger.

Faint gunfire drawled to the north and tiny black exclamations of smoke drifted in the sky.

'Somebody's copping something,' said Dougie.

'Manoeuvres,' said Winkle, disgusted. There wasn't a building for miles, nowhere to forage.

'Go back to sleep, you useless toerag,' Dougie snorted. 'You snore more sense than you talk.'

'Don't come it with me, Wayne.'

'You and whose army?' Dougie flared.

'Shut it, both of you,' said Frank as he sat on the running board to drowse in the sun. His last Sunday in London had been as golden as this afternoon. He had slept on the kitchen floor under a blanket and woken when young Harry poked a finger into his eye. Frank blew a raspberry against the boy's belly, watching his sister make tea in the scullery. Harry squirmed, glad to have someone to play with.

'Sky, Frank. Throw sky.'

Frank threw the boy into the air and caught him a bare inch from the floor. Held close, Harry smelled of dried apples and shampoo.

'Sky, sky.'

'No more, you chucked up over me last time, Harry

stinkbum.' Frank carried the boy out to Phyllis. 'Where's face-ache?'

'Up and doing instead of snoring the house down. And put your trousers on, walking around like a gypsy.'

'How's his leg? Wonder he didn't cut his bum off the way he dropped through that skylight.'

Phyllis laughed her infectious laugh. 'He'll have a scar. And don't talk like that after all the money Ma saved on your education.'

It was a sour family joke. Frank would have stayed at grammar school if the money had allowed. Or if Ma Cooper had trusted education. 'School,' she believed, 'put ideas in people's heads. Ideas above their station. What's a navvy's son want with education? Won't dig holes faster.' All the same, she had scrubbed doorsteps to buy him plimsolls and a white shirt for the start of the autumn term, though nothing could be done about his patched trousers and darned pullover, or the jeers of his better-off school fellows. Frank fought his tormentors behind the bicycle shed and was caned for it, but it didn't make his scuffed plimsolls into black leather shoes or afford him a jacket. Ability in the classroom and on the playing field could not make up for poverty, so Frank returned to the streets where no toffee-nosed grammar boy dared walk, and joined Sunco Electrical as a van-boy. Instead of History and English Literature he read Zane Grey and Edgar Wallace, and employed his mathematical skill computing cross-doubles and yankees at the bookmakers.

Coins jangled as he pulled on his trousers. 'I took seven and twopence off those two. They'll want their revenge tonight.'

'Cards can wait,' said Phyllis, pouring hot water into a bowl and slapping a bar of carbolic soap into Frank's hand. 'Tommy's re-glazing the windows and Jack's putting up a proper blackout. You can get that wireless working. I'm not messing about with that accumulator, the acid burns holes in my stockings.' Phyllis clattered pots. 'Some music'll cheer us up.'

'It's all organs and hymns on Sundays.'

'Not if you twiddle the knobs a bit. Tommy's picked up America on that set.'

'So he said.' Frank sluiced his face.

'And don't leave soap behind your ears.' Phyllis threw a towel, happily bullying him as usual, making Frank wonder why he never minded. He said: 'I thought you got married to bully somebody else.'

'I can still give you a flip right quick,' Phyllis grinned, watching Frank connect an earth-wire to the cold water pipe beside the kitchen range. 'And it's time you settled down. When you bringing that girl of yours to see me?'

'No chance.' Thinking of marriage brought Frank's nose out in a sweat. The wireless valves glowed and the speaker whined distantly as he sought a station on the dial. Gradually, and building in strength and volume, an announcer introduced the Prime Minister.

'It's talking,' said Phyllis. 'I get enough talking without the wireless joining in.' She drew water and the pipes hammered.

'Hold it down, Phyl.' Frank called up the stairs to Tommy and Jack.

'What's so flipping important?' Jack held his stomach.

'This morning the British Ambassador in Berlin handed the German Government a final Note ... '

Tommy came in, knotting his tie. 'That's Chamberlain.'

' ... stating that unless we heard from them by eleven o'clock that they were prepared at once ... '

'Hello,' said Jack, frowning. 'That is Chamberlain.'

'It's blooming talking.' Phyllis lit the gas under the potatoes and handed young Harry a raw carrot to chew.

' ... to withdraw their troops from Poland a state of war would exist between us. I have to tell you now ... '

Doris wandered in, coughing on a cigarette.

'Swallow it, you daft cow,' said Jack, listening hard.

' ... that no such undertaking has been received and that consequently this country is at war with Germany ... You can

imagine what a bitter blow it is to me that my long struggle to win peace has failed . . .'

'We're in it,' Frank's throat was tight. He watched Tommy make a perfect knot and Jack pull Doris to him, something he never did in public. Phyllis picked Harry up and held the handle of Robert's pram.

The jaded, metallic voice droned on without light or shade, changing the whole world without inflection. '*. . . Up to the last it would have been quite possible to have arranged a peaceful and honourable settlement between Germany and Poland, but Hitler would not have it . . .'*

The dread words swam in Phyllis's mind like dark, serpentine things, making her hold Harry too tightly. Jack looked stoic, too lacking in imagination to see the infinite ramifications. Tommy showed relief. The inevitable had happened and the long waiting was over. At long last words were being replaced by action. Doris saw dark winters racked by storm and wished her mother was there to comb her hair and whisper comfort.

'*. . . It is an evil thing we shall be fighting against – brute force, bad faith, injustice, oppression and persecution – and against them I am certain that the right will prevail.'*

Doris wept and Jack held her close, patting her clumsily. 'Silly old cow, love a good moo, don't you?'

Tommy shook Frank's hand, his mind filled with banners and Elgar's music. For an instant he was Biggles swooping out of the sun. Then, just as suddenly, he was a man late for work. He dropped Frank's hand and lowered his eyes; confronted by Frank's glazed look of intolerance he felt foolish. The heat in the dark pupils was not for him although he had no way of knowing that.

Frank rolled a cigarette, looking at nothing, feeling cheated by the creaking old voice coming through the loudspeaker. That tired old man wasn't the voice of *his* England. There had to be somebody who could put into words what he felt needed saying. Not some actor using flowery grammar from some

Shakespearean text, but a man who could say it with profound simplicity in peoples' English. What that was he did not know, but he knew what it was not.

Seven minutes later the first sirens of the war sounded.

Doris hid in the Anderson shelter and Tommy went off to work. Phyllis told Jack and Frank to get out from under her feet; she had to finish cooking the Sunday roast. She wasn't going to cry in front of them, war or no war.

'The Hope & Anchor?' suggested Jack. 'War's thirsty-making.'

As they crossed the main road an air-raid warden wobbled up on a bicycle and bawled at them through a megaphone.

'You there. Take cover.'

'We are, mate. In the boozer.'

'You can't go in there. Public places are the most vulnerable.' The warden looked at the sky where pigeons flew in circles.

'If there's a bomb with my name on, I'll go with a pint in my hand,' said Jack.

'You. Put that fag out.'

Frank stared. 'That's a blackout precaution, you berk. It's broad daylight.'

'Don't argue. Gas!' The warden pointed at a pillar box. 'What'd you think we paints them yellow for? Lewisite gas detection, that's what for.'

Frank remembered his T.A. training. 'Arsine gas don't burn. It blisters on contact.'

'Don't get funny with me, mate.' The warden dismounted, his overheated face red and wet. 'What's your name?'

'Hitler.' Jack made a fist. 'And he's Ribbentrop.'

A woman with grey hair spilling from under her turban grabbed the warden's arm. 'What's happening, what's happening?'

'Air raid, air raid, take cover.'

'They said they wouldn't use the sirens, they said, didn't

they say?' The woman wore odd slippers.

'That's for drills. This ain't no drill.' The warden glared at Frank. 'Next time I'll take your name.'

'But my cat's run up the chimney. The sirens frighten him.'

'Then take cover.' The flustered warden pedalled off, yelling through his megaphone at a stationary bus.

The bus conductor and driver ordered pints of mild as their passengers milled around finding seats near the free lunch counter. Tommy was at the bar with a light ale.

'They pulled us off the bus and herded us in here,' he said. 'I'm well late for work.'

'You tell my inspector,' said the bus conductor. 'What you think it does to our schedules?'

'One good thing,' said Jack, ordering a rum. 'We got the pub open fifteen minutes early.'

'And we could be stuck here for the duration,' said the bus driver. 'That's my kind of war, eh, Ted?'

'Not if the inspector smells your breath.'

The woman with odd slippers was having hysterics on the pavement.

'She should meet my Doris,' said Jack.

Six pints later they went back to the house where the wireless played light music at full volume. Phyllis was in the front room with the boys and her eyes were swollen.

'Ma's come,' she said. 'She's drunk and she brought ... ' Phyllis shook her head, unable to go on.

'Where's Doris?'

'Still in the shelter I suppose. Unless she's in the kitchen with mother.'

'Silly mare, the all-clear went hours ago,' said Jack, breaking wind behind his hand. He and Frank went into the kitchen, leaving Tommy to comfort Phyllis.

Lying on the step down to the scullery, Mrs Cooper called weakly and obscenely for help. She had fallen on her side and was wedged in the doorway, too fat and breathless to raise herself up.

'God help us, Ma, look at the state of you,' said Frank.

'Don't bleeding touch me. Get me up. I've been calling for hours and nobody come.' Mrs Cooper's hat was on one side of her head and the long green feather in the crown was broken. The imitation cherries bobbed as she swore at her son. 'You bleeding toerag, I only come to bring you your calling-up papers, didn't I? See what happens when I think of my kids? Something's broke in me side. I could've died 'ere for all any bleeder cares.'

Doris called from outside. 'Jack, the door's jammed.'

'Stop shoving. It's jammed against *me*,' muttered Mrs Cooper. 'Daughters, I've shot 'em. And *you*, Frankie,' the eyes like polished raisins locked onto his face, '*you* what was born on Armistice Day. I swore on your head the day I bore you, you wouldn't go to no war. Not like your poor sainted father who coughed himself to death.' She started to cry and tears glistened in the furrows of her plump, angry cheeks. 'Gawd, I hurt.'

'Come on, Ma.' Frank leaned forward to lever the old woman upright. 'Trust you to be the first casualty of the war.'

'I'd give you a clout if I could reach me handbag. Going off to war without a by-your-leave. You never was a son to me.'

When the doctor came he announced the old woman had four broken ribs and must not be moved for several days. She was still in Phyllis's double bed three weeks later.

The sun was lower in the sky when Dougie nudged Frank from his reverie. They were parked in line in a field abandoned by the gun crews they had come to re-supply. A despatch rider brought his motorcycle to a halt beside Sergeant Tanner.

'Movement orders?' Dougie craned to overhear.

'What's he saying, Winkle?'

Winkle had been a tic-tac man and could read lips. 'It ain't back to Arras,' he said. 'Where's Tournai, you know, Frank?'

'Oh, blimey yeah,' said Frank, who didn't.

'We've been there; it's in Belgium,' said Dougie.

'Sod that for a game of soldiers,' said Winkle.

Frank paced the broken earth, sickened by the uncertainty in Sergeant Tanner's face. Away from the confines of barracks or the simple ferries of ammunition from depot to battery, he was lost in indecision, too old at fifty to take command in a fluid situation. The tough old sweat was a shadow in the bright sunlight, his parade-ground hectoring reduced to bluster. His moustache was as wet as his eyes when he ordered the drivers to en-bus.

Frank squinted at the broken smudges of smoke in the northern sky, oddly harmless without accompanying sound. Out there was a fight he wanted to be part of.

CHAPTER TWO

'Only the warmongers think there will be a war. I think there will be a long period of peace.'

Adolf Hitler The Reichstag 30 January 1939

FIRST LORD'S FISHES

A writer in a German newspaper told a new and astonishing story about Mr Churchill. According to him, at the First Lord's 'three luxury castles' there are fishponds containing no fewer than 40,000 fish. 'None may be caught and cooked, as he is anxious to maintain his reputation as a friend of animals.'

The War Illustrated 29 March 1940

THE BROWN SISTERS

A new 'religious' order has arisen in German-occupied Poland. At Katowice the Sisters of Charity have been expelled from their convent, and in their place are the 'Braune Schwestern', who burn candles and perform ceremonials in front of a portrait of Hitler, 'the great saviour of Germany'.

The War Illustrated 29 March 1940

CHRISTOPHER

12 May 1940

2nd Lieutenant Christopher Lutyens heard his batman open the blackout curtains and place a cup of tea beside the bed.

'Morning, Sir. Six o'clock, Sir. Permission to remind you that officers' parade's in twenty-five minutes, Sir. And the *News Chronicle* reckons we're right ready and able to give them Huns a proper drubbing,' said Private Mifflin, laying out Christopher's uniform with just enough care to avoid a reprimand. A twenty-year man with seven left to serve, Mifflin felt it below his dignity to act as servant to a 'duration of hostilities' officer like this one. He wanted a real officer, a regular from the regiment.

'Is the water for shaving hot, Mifflin?'

'Not as you'd rightly call hot, Sir. Something to do with the boiler pipes being furred up and not rightly working with most of the rooms shut off so it won't circulate proper, if you know what I mean, Sir. I hardly do, but that's how it was told me, Sir.' Mifflin left for a smoke below stairs, knowing that a good smack with a hammer would improve the central heating on the upper floors where the officers' bedrooms were, but so long as the radiators kept the Company Office and the pantry warm, who cared? Mifflin did not care for officers.

Outside the hotel window, Weston-super-Mare's seaside architecture, winter gardens, flowerbed clock, sundry haberdasheries, boarding houses and nicknackery shops with their displays of inscribed holiday china boots and windmills, garish embroidered cushions and candy walking-sticks, lay Sunday quiet and wore a distinct out-of-season look; an unlikely place for the Somerset Light Infantry to start its war.

The regiment's illustrious forebears, the 13th Foot, had held the line at Culloden with their officers dead, had denied Jellalabad to the Afghans as earthquakes reduced their fort to rubble, and had repulsed the first charge of Cetewayo's Zulu impis at Ulundi.

Apart from that smattering of history and the fact that the Somersets were trained to march at 140 steps a minute, Christopher was desperately ignorant about the regiment he had joined. Those regular officers he had chanced to meet had kept themselves aloof and had no intention of teaching him their traditional toasts to past gallantry as they dined him over their regimental silver; he was as divorced from their company as an omnibus driver would be from an earl at a masked ball. Save for Neville Charlesworth who tolerated Christopher with an air of superior sufferance, and the professional help from the R.S.M., Christopher felt himself very much alone.

He shaved in lukewarm brown water from a shuddering tap as Mifflin had predicted, and he winced as he seared a razor-nick with a camphor stick. To his mind, the face in the mirror lacked resolution or hardness, so much soapstone that life had not yet etched with character. The smoky blue eyes and fine blond hair were more suited to gliding fresh young ladies around a tea-dance floor than for commanding men; unlike the awful Hatwood.

2nd Lieutenant Percy Hatwood bullied his batman and delighted in abominating recruits on the many route marches with: '*You*, get some guts and initiative *there*.' Hatwood had been a sergeant during the previous war and had been commissioned for this one on the strength of that experience, credentials that Christopher firmly believed had been forged or falsified almost totally. Hatwood's fleshy face was all nose, eyebrows and fat earlobes mottled red by myriad broken blood vessels, and his constantly slitted eyes showed no whites except when he flicked a rare sideways glance. His nose was once described by a visiting brigadier as 'a worm-cast on a bald lawn'. The men called him 'Banana Joe' and hated him with lacklustre venom, too dispirited by excessive training to work up any real emotion about him or the army. They, like Weston-super-Mare, were in stasis for the duration, waiting for peace to restore them to normality.

And Christopher, who nagged them into changing their socks and underwear regularly, and panted just as much as they did over the hills and dales of Somerset, was just another khaki figure with pips who must be saluted when there was no alternative. Just another sodding officer, something to be suffered like sleet or blistered feet; except feet were nursed and he was saluted.

Like his reluctant warriors, Christopher was not deluded by images of Agincourt or the thin red lines so graphically illustrated in the *Boys' Own Paper*; his patriotism shied from battle honours or boasting. Unlike the fevered fervour of 1914, when German shops were burned and dachshunds were stoned in the streets, this war seemed to stumble along in the most apologetic manner.

By falling in Flanders during the Spring Offensive of 1915, Christopher's uncles, Gervaise, Henry and Bertram terminated the dominant male line of their ancient family, leaving their sister, Christopher's mother, heir to the titles and the dwindling family fortune. Broken by grief, she did not survive the winter of 1916, and Christopher's father found himself both widowed and wealthy.

A banker by profession and a misogynist by nature, Basil Lutyens turned the military portraits to the wall and made money. War, in Basil's opinion, was an international conspiracy designed to disrupt honest trade. The pursuit of profit made him a pacifist, just as surely as the sight of Christopher reminded him of his lost wife, Alicia, the only person Basil had ever cared for. His humanity had died with her and Christopher had watched his father's beard grow more silver as the silences between them became more leaden. Like old port, Basil Lutyens hid his fierce heart beneath a thick, dark crust.

Since joining the army, Christopher had not heard from his father and did not expect to. The last communication between them had been an exchange of cards at Christmas. Basil Lutyens' cheap snowscape had been signed in his absence by a secretary.

On his way down to the dining room, Christopher heard Hatwood, Charlesworth and Mason talking over their porridge. Facing them over a typical wartime breakfast depressed him.

Hatwood lifted the cover from a dish and said, 'Good-oh, snotties,' his term for army-issue tinned skinless sausages that were magically pink until cooking bleached them grey and made them taste of disinfected boiled bran. 'I'll have Lutyens' ration if he turns his nose up at them.'

'I think,' said Mason in his clerk's voice, 'the cooks make this mess of pottage from wallpaper paste and old copies of *Sporting Life.*' It was his one joke and he trotted it out every morning.

'Too early for drollery, old man,' said Charlesworth, his stock reply. He was growing a moustache to gain maturity, and beside Hatwood's black pelt it was as slim as a greyhound. Mason tried to grow one for a week and had given up when nobody noticed. Their voices came up the stairs with flinty echoes and Christopher spotted Mifflin listening on the basement flight, a smoking cigarette cupped in his palm. Christopher kicked a step to flush him, preferring not to confront him with a dressing down on an empty stomach. Mifflin disappeared and Hatwood said: 'The new intake's due at 09.00 hours. More raw mothers' boys and clerks to bash into shape.' The last was a barb for Mason who had worked for the water board. 'I want a fighting regiment when I'm made up. Not a shower of shat like this shower of shat.'

'I'm sure we all want that.' Mason rustled a paper huffily.

'Talk's as cheap as newsprint,' sneered Hatwood.

'How very very true,' drawled Charlesworth who despised Hatwood's abrasive crudity. 'Incidentally, may I have a glance at your *Mirror* when you've finished with it? I do like to move my lips when I read the strip cartoons.'

'Is that what I'd call a *remark*, Charlesworth?' asked Hatwood.

'Don't follow you, old man,' said Charlesworth. 'But I do think you might have asked Lutyens before you tucked into his snotties.'

Christopher ducked his head around the mess door. 'Have them by all means, Hatwood. I'll save my appetite for luncheon.'

'Planned to,' said Hatwood, pointing a fork. 'Late on parade, Lutyens. Early bird gets the worm, what?'

'Exactly,' smiled Charlesworth, 'a perfect simile.' He winked at Christopher behind his paper. 'See you at the station later.'

Sergeant-Major Trefoil was already in the hotel banqueting hall they used as the Company Office, his files checked and ready for meeting the nine o'clock train from Taunton. A big and slow man, Trefoil was a patient Trojan without a temper whose voice carried a quarter-mile with the wind behind it. Christopher never hesitated to ask his advice and a guarded trust had built up between them.

'Morning, Mr Lutyens, we've a hundred and eighty men coming in. As billeting officer that's a headache for you.' Trefoil smoothed his red sash. 'According to your list we've only placed ninety-three of the intake.'

'Oh, Lord. I suppose we could bunk the surplus here and at the church hall for now?'

Trefoil sent his Corporal-Clerk for tea. 'You'll have to work yourself up to be a bit firmer with the ladies of the town, Sir. They've got to dance attendance on you, not the other way about.'

'Knowing that doesn't get it done, Sarn't-Major.'

'No,' Trefoil pretended to think then beamed. 'Best we

muster the men here when we've got them off the train, then you and me'll have a trot around the town. I've got a way with ladies.'

Christopher was grateful. Some of the landladies he had met were terrifying. One had trapped him in her parlour and fed him gallons of grey tea as her dress rode up her monumental thighs. Christopher had fled stammering.

'It's the way you handles them without giving them no chance for touching you back.' Trefoil winked solemnly, an immovable rock in a troubled sea. He pointed out where he wanted Christopher's signature on a couple of dozen forms. Christopher signed without reading any of them.

A signals failure down the line had caused delays.

At the railway station, Regimental Sergeant-Major Trefoil pinned arrows along the platform and stationed corporals beside the public toilets and on the footpath. With a fine instinct for blocking escape routes, he had no intention of losing any of the incoming men. Christopher and Charlesworth sat in the Waiting Room in silence until Charlesworth said with suddenness: 'Don't you know the Caldercott family, or did I get that wrong?'

Startled into lying, Christopher said, 'No,' abruptly. Then, stumbling slightly, said: 'I'm not sure that I do.'

Charlesworth shrugged and lit a Craven A. 'I must have misheard.'

'I suppose you must have,' Christopher said lamely as he was plunged back to the last hours of peace when goldcrests and yellowhammers, unaware of the concept of war, exploded from the hedgerows on the road to Herstmonceux. *Of course I know the Caldercott family. Why did I lie? I can still conjure Helen's face in perfect detail any time I care to.*

She had met him in the drive of Martenfall House, her tawny hair disturbed by hard pruning. Incapable of a clumsy move or gesture, Helen had smelled of sun and exertion when Christopher kissed her. Mrs Caldercott put her daughter's natural grace down to artifact rather than to unconscious style, something she patently lacked herself and could not comprehend. And although Mrs Caldercott approved of Christopher's lineage, she cared little for him, seeing him as far too young to be suitable for Helen. Mrs Caldercott meant to match her daughter with a suitable establishment figure over forty with estates, old money and an escutcheon. In her view, sound marriages came from the sensible conjunction of two houses of equal stature and cemented by mutual regard for their social position. That was the route chosen for her by her own parents, and one she heartily subscribed to.

Christopher watched Helen take in his uniform from the corner of his eyes, afraid to look at her directly. He had the crazy idea she would melt in the sunlight. 'I should have told you about the uniform.'

'Yes, you should have.'

They walked in the grounds trailed by a spaniel.

'I didn't know how to. Seeing you seemed easier.'

'For you perhaps. It's something of a shock for me.'

Christopher stuttered when he apologised.

Helen kicked the manicured grass and the spaniel leapt at the scuff as though it were alive. 'Fool.'

'Sorry again.'

'Not *you*, Christopher. Rags.'

'Rags?'

'The dog, you dodo.' Helen walked through an arbour to sit on the dry-stone wall and raised her face to the September sun. 'Mother will be scandalised by us walking here before you've been formally greeted in the house. *And* because you've seen me in my gardening togs. She says I lack all social dignity.'

'That's rot. She doesn't approve of me anyway, so nothing's lost, is it?'

Helen opened one blue eye. 'But will you tell her she talks nonsense?'

Christopher ducked the challenge and thought, *changing your mother's mind would be akin to converting Mohammed to Catholicism. Or striking sparks from an overripened grape.* He said: 'Anything I said would earn blank disapproval.'

'Mother, bless her iron heart, approves of very little, including me.'

'I approve of you.'

Helen smiled like a sunning golden lizard. 'Not too much, I hope.'

'Would that be possible?'

'Pedestals turn my stomach dear dodo.'

There were gold flecks in Helen's eyes. Chips of mica in liquid turquoise. 'I don't want your approval, you darling goat.'

'What then?'

'Your love, my dear. Why can't you say it?'

Because I'm a Lutyens, thought Christopher, back on the slatted railway bench with Charlesworth pretending to doze beside him. *Repressed to hell by upbringing, by the previous generation's mores, by banking and loneliness, by inbuilt singularity based on painful shyness. Making no advances for fear of rejection. That's why, dearest untouchable Helen.* He gnawed the inside of his cheek and prayed he wouldn't stutter. 'Words,' he said stiffly, 'are hard for me. They stick.'

'What? Did you speak, old man?' asked Charlesworth.

'No.' Christopher went back into the garden with clenched fists, his cheeks burning. 'Talking to you is harder than talking to your mother, Helen. And she's impossible.' He threw an idle punch at the rose bower above his head and soft petals showered into Helen's lap. 'You can see what I feel, can't you? Saying it would be . . . inadequate . . . ' He struck the breast of his tunic. 'This feels so right and clean after computing percentums in farthings at the bank. I want to be *this* permanently. A soldier. Not a common usurer like some mediaeval Jew, forced to deal in money because he was denied the right to own land or to trade to make a livelihood. I *need* to know I can soldier as much as I *need* to care for you.' His face blazed. 'Do you *see?*'

Helen said nothing for a long moment. Sunlight burnished her hair and threw hard shadows into the flowerbeds. There was a tiny crescent scar on the flawless grain of her chin and the tiny crumbs of gold in her blue irises were too brilliant to be imperfections.

'I do see, my dear,' Helen said softly. 'All too clearly.'

'There you are.' Henry Caldercott had come up the path. His grey lounge suit matched his carefully groomed hair and moustache. His eyes were as vague as scraps of soft sky. 'Your mother has been calling. Hullo, Lutyens, aren't you taking luncheon with us?'

'It's Christopher, father. And he is.' Helen walked the two men back toward the house, keeping to her father's pace. Since his stroke his right leg dragged slightly.

'Christopher? Aren't you the chap who wants to marry this daughter of mine? That won't do at all, according to Helen's mother. Much like a common buttercup winning the *floribunda exotica* class at the Chelsea Flower Show.'

'A fair simile.' Christopher boiled internally.

Henry Caldercott showed mild surprise. 'Is it? I thought you modern young people dismissed such archaic attitudes with a snap of the fingers. Arranged marriages should have died out with the cream of my generation in France; we seem to have lost the good and retained the intolerable. We English should have swept away the old divisive order like these German Nazis have, but I suppose we're more hidebound than they are. Will there be a war with Germany?'

'Yes,' said Christopher.

'That's forthright enough. Why is he so timid around your mother, Helen?'

'Why are *you*, father?'

'In the garden I have opinions of my own. In the house I am a pacifist.' Mr Caldercott patted Helen's arm. 'Run along and change for luncheon whilst I give Christopher a drink in the jungle. And for the sake of peace, make it something with sleeves?'

Helen promised and went through a French window.

Christopher followed Henry Caldercott into a garden room with glassed sides where tropical plants lived with period furniture. Even with the doors open the humidity was uncomfortable.

Mr Caldercott poured schooners of sherry. 'I suppose the damp will ruin the furniture in time, but the jungle is my one indulgence.' He and Christopher sat under a canopy of fleshy green leaves. 'I knew your father during the twenties. Like me he was a true disciple of Mammon; profitability and penny dividends from morning until night. I thought of Basil Lutyens as a natural dynastic full-stop. Your very existence surprised me, I must say.'

Moisture from the palm fronds spattered Christopher's sleeve and plopped into his overwarm sherry.

'Don't be offended, in describing your father I also describe myself. I don't want my daughter to marry somebody like me, a clod who knows nothing but money-grubbing and the price of rubber on the floor of the exchange.' Mr Caldercott sighed. 'Nor do I want my daughter in mourning before her first child is weaned. My generation has known too many widows, I belong to a time when black crêpe was our national costume.' He sipped breathlessly.

Christopher stood, his face white. 'I only came to say goodbye to Helen, all this is ... ' He stuttered in fury.

'Sit down, you young idiot, don't waste your fire and vinegar on an old man with a cheap watch for a heart. If you let my wife chase you away you won't see Helen again. That will be her choice, not ours. I've been married to a hypotenuse triangle for twenty-seven years, the reason I abhor arranged marriages. There isn't a single curve in her nature. If it wasn't for my jungle and a certain lady in Belgravia I should have dried up and blown away years ago. Now will you sit down?'

Christopher sank onto a couch, disarmed.

'Helen is my daughter, discard to trumps, not a scrap of her mother anywhere, something you should be grateful for. The usual advice to a courting man is: Look to the mother and see the daughter a decade on. Advice I should have followed myself. In Helen's case it doesn't apply.' Henry Caldercott finished his sherry. 'Shall we go in to luncheon?'

Sergeant-Major Trefoil opened the Waiting Room door.

'Fifteen minutes, Mr Lutyens, Mr Charlesworth. There's an empty excursion through first.'

'Thank you, Sarn't-Major.' Christopher eased his buttocks on the hard bench, staring off along the sunlit railway lines to the seaward sky where gulls wheeled, losing himself in the infinite blue, oblivious to the smoke from Charlesworth's Craven A.

The dining room of Martenfall House was decorated in a pretentious mixture of Empire and Tudor styles; mullions and casements shared wall space with an Elizabethan fireplace, tapestries hung beside Versailles mirrors, and alcoves accommodated a modest collection of Graeco-Roman busts. Pliny the Elder, Tacitus and Augustus Caesar watched Christopher dine with blank marble eyes.

Helen's simple black dress hugged and Mrs Caldercott's creation of tucks and frills hung on her gaunt frame like a listless curtain. The other guests were near neighbours who deferred to Mrs Caldercott as the leading social matriarch of their tight community, and were clearly on her 'safe' list. Squire and Mrs Sutherland farmed two-hundred acres near Cowbeech, and Mr Popham was a retired cleric accompanied by his unmarried daughter, a lump of a girl who ran a donkey sanctuary. Christopher heard about the church roof over consommé, the problems of windage during stubble-burning over pressed-duck in aspic, the unwarranted intrusion of evacuees during the entree. None of them used Christian names even though they had known each other for a decade.

'It's bad enough having this fellow Kimber dashing about on his motorcycle,' said Squire Sutherland, 'but he puts tramps up in that shoebox of a chapel of his. That's tantamount to encouraging itinerants into the area. And now that he's Billeting Officer for evacuees, he's even more odious.' He speared a potato and glared at it. 'Broached me on me own threshhold. Said I should house a dozen of them up at The Lodge. I told him, like should go to like – can't go scrambling us all up together. Packed him off to the smallholders and tenants – they've got enough brats of their own, so a few more wouldn't be noticed.'

Mr Popham looked sad. 'It is a time of sacrifice, I suppose.'

'Kimber is a Methodist,' said Miss Popham. 'And since he has this awful evangelical drive, I wonder his bishop doesn't pack him off to Africa or somewhere.'

Squire Sutherland grunted. 'It isn't as if we were truly at war with Germany. Why should we be landed with evacuees from London? Let London take care of Londoners. They'll only be clamouring for fish parlours and picture-palaces if they do come.'

'They should be sent to the seaside resorts, there are plenty of modest hotels with space at the end of the season,' said Mrs Caldercott.

Squire Sutherland swallowed his potato. 'Wish I'd thought of that. What a solution. Have you come across this Kimber, Mr Popham?'

'He did call at The Manse,' Mr Popham dabbed his plump mouth with his napkin. 'And when I explained that an invasion of exuberant youth would send Marigold's donkeys off their feed, he doubted my sincerity and made several unfortunate remarks.'

Mrs Caldercott's fork skidded across her plate. 'Remarks? What kind of remarks?'

'He cast doubt on Daddy's Christianity,' said Marigold Popham. 'He went quite red in the face and raised his voice. I wanted to write to his bishop, but Daddy said we shouldn't.'

Mr Popham looked martyred. 'Distressing. Very.'

'I,' said Mrs Caldercott, 'should have become the billeting officer. Declining was a mistake. You must talk severely to this Kimber, Henry.'

'Billeting officers have no authority to make people take evacuees into their homes, my dear. They can only use persuasion. Kimber was doing that and nothing more.'

Mrs Caldercott's no-colour eyes narrowed. 'Mr Lutyens will drive you over to Kimber's chapel directly after luncheon. Helen and I will compose a letter to the church authorities. Kimber must be removed from the county immediately.'

Henry Caldercott sighed. 'This is a secular matter. Sunday is hardly the day ... '

'It's for the common good. It must be today,' Mrs Caldercott announced, ending argument.

Christopher saw Helen watching him and said: 'My going to see the Reverend Kimber is out of the question.'

'I beg your pardon?' Mrs Caldercott could not have been more surprised if Tacitus had launched into Eskimo Nell.

'As a serving officer under orders, I am not permitted to involve myself in civilian matters. Directive 14, Subsection A/23 of the Defence of the Realm Act 1938 is quite specific on that point. My being in transit complicates the issue even further, that of course is covered by MoD Directive 7745b, Appendix 7b. Your husband, I know, will be familiar with that.'

'So I am, it quite slipped my mind,' Mr Caldercott touched a finger to his temple. 'That also covers ingress onto arable lands, doesn't it? You came up against the army over that one, Sutherland, when they manoeuvred over your land.'

'Not a penny compensation,' said Squire Sutherland.

'How sick-making,' said Christopher with newfound audacity.

'And what do you call this?' asked Mrs Caldercott. 'Isn't taking luncheon with us a *civilian* affair?'

'Actually, that's covered by Victualling in Transit. Much the same as using a hostelry or common inn. I ought to have you sign a chit and pay you in army script, but it is only two shillings I'm afraid.'

'Two ... ' Mrs Caldercott was buffeted by internal winds.

'And you would have to present it in London for payment.'

'I *say*,' said Marigold Popham.

'Typical of the army,' said Squire Sutherland.

Helen made her eyes large. 'You are *clever* to remember all those clauses, Lieutenant Lutyens. How *do* you manage it?'

'No worse than cramming for Latin, Miss Caldercott,' Christopher winked on Mrs Caldercott's blind side. 'Now on foreign duty there are reams of regulations. For example, fraternisation ... '

'Quite so,' snapped Mrs Caldercott. 'Henry, ring for the pudding.'

'Certainly, my dear.'

Carriage doors slammed and steam rolled across the platform as men alighted. Christopher went outside with Charlesworth to watch the N.C.O.s impose discipline on the chaos. Thinking of that rich meal of almost a year before had made Christopher hungry. His stomach bubbled and snarled.

'Pity you missed the snotties,' drawled Charlesworth. 'I thought we'd cut along to the Commodore's Club for luncheon.' He stopped a passing unshaven private. 'How long were you on that train?'

'Yesterday morning, Sir. They shunted us into a siding overnight. No steam and no lights, Sir.'

'Cut along,' Charlesworth shook his head. 'They look more like refugees than soldiers, Lutyens. I don't know that I'm happy to march beside them up the hill, our stock's low enough as it is.'

'Neville, you're a snob.'

'Yes, old boy. To the core.'

As they marched their unkempt men away from the

station, Christopher reflected on the walk he and Helen had enjoyed near Battle Abbey after luncheon with her parents and their awful friends. The autumn air had been warm and the rolling grassland deserted. They climbed the hill where Bishop Odo's men had cut a swathe through King Harold Godwineson's flank and turned the battle in favour of William Duke of Normandy eight hundred years before.

Christopher's more recent verbal victory consumed Helen with giggles of respect. 'Poor mother; and to think I was dreading today.'

'Poor mother, nothing. Poor Lutyens. She won't have me back in a hurry.'

'But she must. Mother's a cardplayer, not a gambler. She plays people like cards and plays to win.'

'Your father swung things my way.'

'Your talk in the jungle must have been very interesting.'

'I like him,' Christopher's shyness came back.

Helen leaned on his arm as they toiled up a slope thick with birch and scrub. 'I hate to see him growing old, but he swears his talent for survival will see him through. Do you have such a talent?'

'I'm coming back, Helen.'

'That had better be a gold-plated promise, darling goat.'

'Only sporting to give your mother her replay.'

Helen sank to the grass and stared into the middle-distance. 'The cream of the English army died here. They had destroyed Harold Hadraada's army at Stamford Bridge only eighteen days before. Then William the Conqueror slaughtered them here. Father used to describe it blow by blow.'

'I'm coming back,' Christopher gripped her shoulders.

'You've made me such a coward.'

'Thanks,' Christopher's temper snapped. 'Stop thinking of yourself. At least your mother is direct in her tartarism, she bullies to get what she wants. You and your father wield your sticks with more subtlety, but they cut just as hard. I'm not a convenient adjunct to your lives and don't intend to be. I'll come back and I want you to be here.'

Helen laughed aloud. 'I do believe I've been told off.' She kissed Christopher hard on the mouth. 'You'll do, Mr Lutyens. You'll do very well.'

Riding on a hot tide of anger Christopher shut her up with his mouth. Breathless, Helen pulled away.

'Am I to be ravished?'

'When *I* choose. Reporting for duty with grass-stains on one's uniform is not done you know.'

'How stuffy of the army. They have regulations for everything.' Helen looped her arm through Christopher's and they walked back to Battle Abbey where a red-headed man with a bad complexion sat astride a motorcycle admiring the Riley.

'Hullo, is this your bus? Miss Caldercott isn't it?'

Helen introduced Christopher to the Reverend Kimber. 'Talking to you is tantamount to treason, according to mother.'

Kimber ran fingers through unruly red hair.

'Your mother taxes the patience of the most Godly. And God knows I'm anything but. I came out here to have a think. Us being in has changed everything, hasn't it?'

'In, in what?' Helen paled, suddenly certain without truly knowing.

'In the war.' Kimber slapped his forehead. 'Your mother don't approve of the wireless, you won't know. We're at war, Chamberlain announced it at eleven this morning.' His Manchester accent thickened with excitement. 'Hey, love, you want to sit?'

'No, take me home please, Christopher.'

We're at war, thought Christopher, *I haven't unpacked, my bag's in the car. I can be back in London by seven, long before dark.* He was closer to the portraits of Gervaise, Henry and Bertram than he had ever been.

'Companeeeee ... *Halt!*'

The men crashed to attention outside the hotel in Weston-super-Mare. Hatwood swished his swagger-stick and walked along the wilting khaki rows frowning into the unshaven faces.

'If they were snotties,' said Charlesworth, 'he'd eat them alive.'

CHAPTER THREE

'To make union with Great Britain
would be fusion with a corpse.'

Marshal Pétain 1940

To Pacifists the proper course
Of conduct is to sit on Force.
For, in their dreams,
Force can't resist,
The well-intentioned Pacifists.

Clarence Day *Thoughts without words*

The one means that wins the easiest
victory over reason: terror and force.

Adolf Hitler *Mein Kampf*

ONE: FRANK

16 May 1940

Sergeant Tanner's lorry led the way.

They had offloaded their shells at a temporary dump that morning and moved along congested roads somewhere on the Franco-Belgian border. Yet another yawning day in convoy; sweating, overtired, lost and indifferent to where they drove and why. They passed knots of loafing Belgian soldiers who wore their defeat like greatcoats, peasants with donkey-carts, French soldiers who gestured at them, some obscenely, others with desperate bonhomie. At road junctions M.P.s kept their vehicles moving no matter where, so long as they kept their particular crossroads clear. The day turned from honey to brass.

Halting and starting, they were overtaken by staff-cars that sent refugees scurrying to the sides of the roads, where they sat in dispirited rows until the need to move away from danger motivated them onward. At one of the many halts Winkle adopted a goat for the milk.

'It's a Billy. A he-goat, you berk. All *they* give is trouble.' Limey Prendergast held his bruised groin as he sat on the verge, butted there by Winkle's find.

'Nobody said, did they?' Winkle gave the goat to an old woman with a pram piled with bundles and watched her hobble off with it tied to her handlebar.

Frank yelled across at the lorries halted alongside.

'Which lot are you, mate?'

'Durham Light Infantry.' A driver ducked out from under his raised bonnet, his ginger hair smeared with oil. 'And me from Shoreditch. Don't make sense, do it? Moved up there when I got hitched to the wife. Nothing doing for carpenters, so I joined this mob. You Terriers?'

'Yeah.'

'Albert Amundsen. The old man was a seaman.' The driver shook hands all around.

'What's the hold-up?' asked Dougie.

Albert mimed masturbation. 'You won't believe it, there's a travelling circus up ahead. Elephants and everything. They give me a poster with a picture of a tiger on it, great striped geezer. Anyway, this sapper major come up and says he wants us all to travel lumped together. In line with proper military discipline, he told our officer. Typical clip-board type, all swank and trousers. Look at this lot, Belgies on the run, old grannies, stray dogs and hungry kids, all mixed up to-flaming-gether.' He spat in the dust. 'Proper military discipline? All *we've* seen is muck-up after fuck-up.'

Dougie passed his Golden Virginia and they all smoked together.

'Thanks, I been smoking French horsedung.' Albert plumed smoke. 'I'm getting so used to being lost I dunno if I'd like being found. Our officer reckons that's Tournai ahead, but I dunno. It all looks the bleeding same after a week behind the wheel.'

They all nodded.

'You're London lads, right?'

'Islington way.'

Albert sighed. 'I miss The Smoke. We come through London on the way through to Dover, only saw it from the window. Choked I was. Still, the Durhams are a good mob to be in. Yours?'

'Handsome,' lied Frank. 'Got any spare maps, cocker?'

'Only for swaps.'

'Dougie,' said Frank, 'get Winkle up here with that vino.' He grinned at Albert. 'Our business manager'll see you get fair trade.'

Winkle slapped his leg when he came up. 'Bloody blimey, old Albert. Frank, me and this git run as kids together. Small world. Come on, son, this vino's got a history, show us your Michelins.'

They walked off chatting and Winkle came back with sheaves of maps.

'You didn't show him no favours then?' said Frank, checking them over before stowing them out of sight.

'Business,' Winkle slurred, 'is business.' He hiccuped wine fumes up into the cab. 'Right?'

The Durham lorry began to move and motors started up all down the line. On the outskirts of town they passed a major with a clipboard who told them to keep closed-up.

'Him and Sergeant Tanner would make lovely dancing

partners,' said Frank, recognising the same air of desperate control. 'Moving us about like toy trains. Another piddle-and-wind merchant.'

On a long bend they glimpsed brightly-painted carts followed by a tank on a half-track. A lion roared above the engine noise.

'Them planes,' Dougie started to say, 'ain't they . . . ' As he thought, 'flying low', their lorry lurched in a sudden wind of flying grit.

Gouts of popping smoke wrenched holes in the trees beside them and threw trunks and boughs bodily into the air. Burning tinder scattered across the road and the lorry lifted in a savage wave of blast.

The sound of Heinkels making a low pass was lost as bomb-bursts ran inexorably down the convoy toward the Territorial vehicles.

In a curious timelessness, Frank cannoned out of the cab and hit the road as flame spurted, ticking up holes in the ground between the running refugees, spinning some of them prone.

The ground heaved as two lorries disintegrated in rosettes of bright flame. Men dropped from tailboards, some running, some dropping. A horse, minus its forelegs, rolled its splintered cart into a ditch. A young woman reached for a distant cloud as her child was shot from her arms, a ragged bundle that lost shape and flopped in smoking ruin.

Frank recoiled, holding his face. Dougie's boot had caught him as he scrabbled past for cover.

Another lorry shook apart with men hurling from it.

Debris smacked down into the road.

Machine-guns stuttered. Whining and ricochetting splinters gouged the milling refugees, peppering them with hot fragments. Glowing shrapnel burned the grass and skittered across the cobbles.

A clutch of bombs straddled the road and blew up in concert.

Frank was paper in a wind; weightless, nameless, helpless. Peace and fear were off in the clouds as he soared in flaring confusion outward and away ...

He scraped across shale and slammed into a tree. Sprawling there under a spinning sky, waiting for his lungs to snatch air, he watched the strange pink bough of the tree above his head spiral into stillness. The severed arm pointed down at him in mute accusation and dripped blood onto his upturned face. Shock drew air into his chest and he smelled burned guncotton and braised flesh. His breath came out as ragged laughter because there was nothing else to do; making the only human sound in the crackling silence.

The arm pointed. Accused.

'Don't blame me, cocker,' he said. 'Blame old piddle-and-wind.'

Dougie pawed Frank's chest for wounds, calling his name.

'Don't dip your bread in my gravy, son,' said Frank. 'Buy your own soup.'

Winkle stood over him, one trouser-leg split from crotch to boot. 'Coop, you gotta be hit. Look at the bleeding blood.' He struck a palm against his right ear. 'Am I talking or what? I'm deaf.'

'If only you was *dumb*.' Frank used Dougie to get to his feet. 'This ain't all mine, it's *his*.' He jerked a thumb at the severed arm, and seeing it, Dougie vomited.

'Don't *you* start.'

Winkle hammered his temple. 'What say, what?'

Sergeant Tanner's lorry was black, twisted metal, burned down to the chassis. Some of the buildings had shattered windows and smoke seeped through the roof tiles.

Then they were hugging the ground as the aircraft made a second pass. The sound clawed the inside of their skulls and started their eyes from their sockets. Squeezing their lids closed behind their knuckles was the only way to hold them in. Each concussion jerked their limbs as they scrabbled to make union with the earth.

A haze of brown smoke rolled in like sudden fog, and

heavy-calibre shells ripped along the column, plunking into canvas and metal and men with dull metallic whacks, keening off as vicious ricochets. Budding boughs crashed down around them and thick dust clogged their nostrils. To breathe they had to snort their noses clear and spit it from their mouths. Their teeth were coated with abrasive talcum that dried their tongues.

Again the quiet. Again the coming back from a long way off.

Limey limped up. 'What do we do?' He was close to tears.

'What we always do, brew up.' Frank bit his mouth, trading manic laughter for fury. 'Check our motor, you daft cowson. This ain't a good place to be. *Move!*'

Limey moved.

Tosher stared at the bodies and the gobbets of flesh in the road, his mouth jerking. *Some of that had to be part of Tanner.* He visualised the mouth and tongue torn from the swollen, angry face, still bawling at him, still threatening charges for slovenly behaviour. Tosher staggered in a half-circle; in motion without going anywhere. Men, blackened by high-explosive, moved past him through drifts of smoke and he warded them off with outstretched arms, wondering how it was he was in this place.

Four white horses trailing their bright red reins and halters galloped out of the fog, hauling the body of a girl behind them. A girl with yellow hair and ballet shoes and no jaw.

Tosher hid his face and walked in his circle.

A man with rolling eyes ran past carrying his arm like a rifle. He came to attention and fell down trying to salute.

The lorry's engine roared when Limey pumped the accelerator. He leaned out to help Frank into the cab and was pushed aside.

'Get Tosher up in back before he screws himself into the ground, Limey. Where's Winkle, for ... ' He punched the dash.

'There,' Dougie took the wheel, shaken wonder in his

voice. 'He never gives up, does he?'

Winkle staggered toward the lorry, laden with clothing and carrying a bottle of wine.

'New uniforms, and I'll bet the bastards fit.' Dougie backed the lorry out of line and reversed into a clearing to make a U-turn.

Winkle took the neck off the bottle with a swipe against the mudguard. 'Albert,' he said, 'won't need this no more.' He hefted the uniforms. 'Or these.' He took a long sloppy swig and wine washed clean trails down his filthy chin. 'To Albert.' He thrust the bottle at Frank.

'To him,' Frank drank and passed the bottle back.

Winkle tossed it into the road where it smashed.

'Get in the back, son.'

Winkle climbed aboard and they drove back the way they had come. Behind them, a wounded elephant trumpeted in wounded rage until somebody found a rifle and ammunition and emptied a clip into his skull.

The major with the clip-board lay on the verge beside a dead alsatian. His mouth was open in frozen surprise and a blotchy red roundel soaked his chest.

Nobody looked at him.

09.00 hours 17 May 1940

Winkle spotted the Fifth Columnist first.

They had travelled south from Tournai and come across the abandoned village at twilight, all of them sleeping in real beds for the first time in weeks. Clothes still hung in wardrobes, disturbed meals lay congealing on their plates and starved caged birds lay dead in their cages. They found two dogs locked in outhouses and a very hungry cat clawed Tosher when he tried to pet it.

Winkle had discovered the profitability of wells. His morning search had yielded two smoked hams, a string-bag of Calvados and a tin-box filled with silver coin. On his way back from the outlying farmhouse he spotted freshly turned earth in a kitchen garden and searched for a spade. Peasants, he had quickly learned, buried things before they fled.

In an outhouse, under some sacking Winkle found a shotgun. The cartridges were in a nailbox, and he plumped two into the breech as protection against stray dogs. Some of those he had come upon were vicious and Winkle was frightened of anything with teeth and hair over three inches long. A guard dog had forced him to leave a safe he was working on and precipitated him into the army one jump ahead of Tall John Law, the reason scavenging came so naturally to him.

Hefting the sack and toting the gun he strolled into the village. A few eggs to go with the ham would make a fine breakfast.

In a house a hundred yards on, Frank regarded himself in a mirror. On the wall were pictures of a retired fireman shaking hands with a mayor, playing a glockenspiel in a band, holding his bride's hand as a young man with the beginning of a belly. Frank shrugged inside the black dress coat and adjusted the blue sash over the white waistcoat. *Ought to give the lads a bit of a laugh. Seeing me dressed up as a dog's dinner. Pity the spats won't button over my army boots. Still, with the topper on ...* He snapped the folding tophat open, sat it on his head and grinned at his reflection. *Not bad*. The soft material was weightless, like down compared to the coarse khaki blouse he had dropped on the bed. The smell of mothballs reminded him of his mother's clothes drawers at home. *Ma used lavender to kill the smell but it never worked. Her bedroom reeked of camphor.*

He wagged a finger at the fireman's portrait. 'You shouldn't be allowed good clobber if you swan off and leave it.' From the bedroom window he could see Tosher lounging in a doorway as he waited for the wood stove he had lit to draw. His face had fallen in on itself since yesterday and he had taken to biting his nails.

He needs a laugh.

Ultra-clean as usual, Dougie was cleaning his brass. Smoke from his cigarette rose without a kink, untroubled by breeze. *He'll come through all right. He's steady.*

There had been gunfire from the north-west around dawn, and later on, the distant sound of tracked vehicles from the north. Nothing close enough to worry about. The war would catch up with them, Frank supposed, and he was ready to do his bit, but right now ... He crept down to the front door. Winkle was coming and he could make all three of them jump. He picked a walking cane from an umbrella stand and waited for Winkle to cover the last few feet.

'What you get, Wink?' asked Tosher.

'Ham. And some of that whatchacallit, cider brandy.'

'Calvados,' said Dougie. 'Any loot?'

'Who me? Nah.' Winkle shared only what was sensible to share. His knapsack was heavy with small precious things he could fence. 'I got this though,' he lifted the shotgun. 'Take care of a few sodding dogs, the bleeders.'

'You couldn't hit Tessie O'Shea with a cannon.' The plump music hall star was Tosher's favourite.

Frank crashed the door open and stepped out, shouting in phoney French.

Winkle dropped his sack and the silver coins spilled. He saw the shouting figure and panic conjured images of nuns in hobnailed boots, priests with machine-pistols under their black frocks. A Fifth Columnist, a disguised German. Without thinking or aiming he pulled both triggers. A window blew inward and the wall above Frank's head grew pits and craters. The double blast sent birds into the air and the butt bruised Winkle's shoulder.

The tophat rolled from the front step and stopped against Winkle's boot. The figure in black had disappeared. Swearing came from the house as the door was kicked closed.

'You've killed him. You've killed Frank,' Tosher chewed his thumbnail to the quick.

Winkle dropped the shotgun. 'That weren't no Frank.'

'Winkle, you ... ' Foul threats came from the fireman's house.

'Who else?' Dougie doubled over himself, shaking with silent laughter. 'He'll kill you front, back and sideways, son.'

Winkle fell on his knees with a wail. 'Ohhh ... *Gawd!*'

'Winkle!'

Tosher's coughing fit sent the pigeons into a second circuit around the village.

TWO: CHRISTOPHER

24 May 1940

On the train to Waterloo, Charlesworth smoked Craven A like a somnabulist and refused to discuss the sudden travel order that precipitated him and Christopher toward London. All he would say over a hurried dawn breakfast was: 'One couldn't bear another second of the abominable Hatwood and his insufferable snotties.'

Days of signing mysterious army documents, notating pay books and counter-signing medical slips for the distracted Medical Officer had made them both testy with the senior N.C.O.s who typed doggedly and pointed out dotted lines for 'the officer's signature', blotting and whisking away reams of buffs and pinks to add them to the formidable filing system that already blocked all daylight from the Company Office. Christopher had finally rebelled when asked to authorise the requisition of two-hundred football bladders and *'Water-Purification Tablets Far-Near-East Tropical. Other Ranks For The Use Of'*.

'But Sergeant Trefoil, *we're* stationed in Weston-super-Mare.'

'And the *regular* Battalions are in India and Gibraltar, Mister Lutyens, sir.'

'Oh.' Crushed, Christopher had signed. The colours of Prince Albert's Own were steeped in honourable blood whilst his own banner remained virginal.

The tabloids sported pictures of refugees on Belgian roads, reported that volunteers of the Local Defence Force, issued with rifles and armbands, roamed the British countryside looking for parachutists. Many of those who had fled to the West Country from London now thought of returning home, fearing an invasion from Eire, convinced it was part of the new Nazi Empire. Some theatres threatened to refuse ladies without gas masks admittance to matinees, and drivers were warned to remove the distributor from their unattended cars, denying their clandestine use to Fifth Columnists and Quislings. The entire populace was being asked to contribute to the war effort; only the home-based army seemed redundant. Bored by the newspapers, Christopher listened to the wheels chant: *Nothing is happening to me, nothing to me, nothing to me*, as they clattered over the points and along the track.

Charlesworth smiled and smoked and remained mute in the taxi to Mallards Club in Long Acre. At the bar he signed for pink gins, a right Christopher had thought reserved for senior members like his father. He drank guiltily, depressed by the grandiose plaster ceiling, the rich rosewood panelling and the richer smell of Cuban tobacco; Charlesworth's cheerful silence, and their being the only members in uniform. At some time during his absence from London that peacetime embargo had been lifted.

'Same again, Baines,' said Charlesworth.

A group wandered in from the dining room and Charlesworth introduced Christopher.

'Knew your father,' said a member who was something in sugar. He was garrulous and florid and cigar ash dusted his waistcoat. He talked of cane sugar derivatives as though they were secret weapons and winked so furiously Christopher thought it was an affliction.

Vasco Cleverly the portrait painter had joined the A.R.P. and talked of interminable teamaking in a sandbagged shelter in the Charing Cross Road. He offered to bring his steel helmet from the cloakroom to show anybody who was interested. Nobody was.

'Same again, Baines. Pink gins for the soldiery.'

Porton Makepiece the novelist thought it high time the Ministry of Labour took the reins of British industry, a move announced that morning, and that now the workforce would be deployed to full effect. 'The days of the selfish celluloid dildo-maker are numbered,' he said, drawing looks of injured surprise from those with interests in such enterprises.

'More port, Baines.'

'A small large brandy, Baines.' Somebody handed Christopher a gin and said, 'Knew your father. Don't suppose he's too taken with all this U-boat menace in the North Sea. Told him there was money in submarines, no reason why they shouldn't carry grain just like ordinary, surface craft. Told him in 1919.' He too had an annoying and disconcerting wink.

'Shouldn't we report to the War House or H.Q. or something?' Christopher asked Charlesworth in a rare lull.

'Plenty of time for that.'

'Knew your Uncle Basil, young Lutyens,' said a man with a red carnation in his buttonhole. 'Must tell you this.'

Recognising rhetoric when he heard it, Christopher nodded through a story about billiards played from horseback that unfolded in surreal jerks.

The others talked about the war in France in tones more usual to the removal of sacred relics from a crumbling tomb. The English Channel sounded as though it had shrunk to the width of the Serpentine.

'First the *Sitzkrieg*, now the *Blitzkrieg*.' Again, Makepiece the novelist was ignored. 'They shall not pass,' he said hopefully.

The man with the red carnation ordered more drinks.

'In the *club*?' Sir Aiden Effingham snapped at Cleverly. 'Saboteurs in the club? Y'hear that, Baines?'

'Wasn't listening, sir,' said Baines.

'Bears out my point exactly. Baines hears only which drink a member orders. A member's private conversation is sacrosanct, like the confessional. A saboteur wouldn't be allowed in the club. Right, Baines?'

'Only if he was signed in by a member, sir.'

'Saboteurs blow things up. It's Fifth Columnists who listen at keyholes,' said Vasco. 'Anyhow, all he would have to do is wait for what he wants to know to be printed in *The Times*.'

'Not possible,' said Charlesworth. '*The Times* never prints anything that is crudely *factual*. The entire point of *The Times*, the very reason for its existence is *never* to expound specific views. One has to know the news in order to understand what it publishes. That is why it is an institution.'

'Well said, Neville.'

Charlesworth inclined his head. 'I'll go further. All knowledge should be printed in dead languages understood only by the scholarly elite.' He caught Christopher's eye with a glance glowing with mischief. 'I drink to an untutored proletariat.'

Makepiece waited for a pause and said: 'Since last year's wine harvest was disrupted by French military manoeuvres, I hope the wine committee has secured a decent quota of this year's claret. I'm told that heavy gunfire sours the wine in the vats.'

'Do bombs have the same effect? How deep are the cellars here? The club has some very fine Bordeaux laid down.'

The group pondered that in silence, unnerved by the prospect of Mallards' liquid assets converted to vinegar by blast.

'Perhaps we should each take a few bottles home.'

'It would take the entire membership a decade to empty the racks. Only a barbarian would suggest swilling vintage wine like cooking sherry. Eh, Vasco?'

'Quite.' Vasco thought it was time for more drinks.

Even on the very threshold of Armageddon, Christopher thought the members of Mallards would always give precedence to proper club etiquette. If the Germans marched down Whitehall tomorrow, the whole of clubland would simply cross to the other side and affect blindness, just as if they had sighted a posse of discredited former members blackballed for cheating at cards.

'Speaking of Italians,' said Makepiece.

'Another time,' Charlesworth led Christopher away. 'Our table is ready.'

They climbed a staircase with a crinoline rail and were shown to their table where Henry Caldercott awaited them. He and Charlesworth shook hands as Christopher looked on, surprised by his own lack of surprise until he recognised how many members had bought him drinks.

'Uncle Henry, you remember Christopher Lutyens.'

'Neville, dear boy, of course. How are you, Christopher?'

'Well, thank you.' Christopher sank into a carved chair and twisted his napkin under the table to keep his hands from making fists. He knew his earlobes burned.

'This young tic is the only one of my wife's nephews I can stomach,' explained Mr Caldercott, 'and only then in small doses.' His vague blue eyes belied his words. He was clearly fond of Charlesworth. 'I thought a decent luncheon might be in order, the fare you two seem to be subsisting on sounds absolutely bloody.' He looked between the two men with a flash of insight. 'We seem to have taken Mr Lutyens by surprise, Neville.'

'Have we, uncle? How splendid.'

'I have missed our chats in the jungle.'

'Thank you,' said Christopher, thinking, *what an inane response. I wish I could melt and soak into the carpet. Try, you idiot.* Nothing came and he sat with lowered eyes as Charlesworth steered the conversation elsewhere. During the fish course Christopher learned that Helen and Charlesworth had grown up virtually in the same crib, that Charlesworths had served with the Somersets since the 13th Foot beat Bonaparte out of Egypt in 1801, and that their brigadier was yet another of Neville's kinsmen. Charlesworth smarted visibly because he had not been allowed to join the 1st Battalion in Gibraltar, and only his distaste for nepotism stopped him asking his uncle the brigadier for the posting directly.

Dining under ochre and pastel cherubs and satyrs attributed to Angelique Kaufman, Christopher progressed from the nut and brine of salmon trout to the dark Arabian flavours of jugged-hare counterpointed by sweet parsnip and curly kale. White Stilton on Bath Olivers accompanied by vintage wines preceded a sorbet that cleansed the palate for brandy and cigars in the Smoking Room where antique clocks tocked and smoke writhed through streamers of oblique afternoon sunlight. The war could have been way off beyond the blue vault of the sky had it not been for a barrage balloon butting about on its retaining wire and Henry Caldercott saying: 'A friend of mine has just returned from Italy where, according to him, mistrust of Hitler's Germany is growing. I suppose our initial funk was almost tolerable, based as it was on the desire for peaceful co-existence with the fascists, but now we are at least awake to the futility of that naïve hope.'

Charlesworth spoke in a gout of smoke. 'Old Musso's army is on the breadline. He'll plump for peace if Hitler lets him. Their tanks are so broken down they haul them into position on lorries. Their cannon dates back to Garibaldi and half the regiments don't have shirts to their backs. Though I do understand their navy and air force are first class. But then, the Italians do have the endearing habit of running. One can always tell an Italian tank from the real thing . . . they're fitted with six reverse gears.'

Henry Caldercott laughed politely. Neville had the ability to bring any conversation full-circle and argue against any point he may have defended only moments before. Silence was a vacuum he filled with contention. 'Listen, you young tic. Drollery is no defence against repression. We shan't win this war with belly-laughs.'

'Mussolini used gas against Haille Selassie's forces in Ethiopia,' said Christopher, finding his tongue at last. 'I saw hundreds of blinded soldiers in Addis Abbaba when I travelled there for the bank. I don't find your comic-opera view of Fascist Italy palatable, Neville.'

Charlesworth changed tack. 'Quite right, Lutyens, old man. He's quite right to chide me, isn't he, Uncle?'

'Christopher has saved me the trouble. He will find as I have that you are all things to all men save when one least expects it. He will discover that soon enough I shouldn't wonder.'

'I already have,' Christopher floated in alcoholic peace.

Henry Caldercott waved away his thanks for a splendid luncheon and when Charlesworth excused himself for a moment said: 'I regret what ... happened between you and my daughter. I am very very sorry.'

'Thank you for that.'

'Can you tell me why things soured between you?'

'No, sir, I can't.'

Henry Caldercott looked suddenly tired. His cigar had died from neglect and his brandy was untouched. He closed his eyes and sank back in the huge club chair. Charlesworth returned and said: 'He's dropped off. Time to fold our tents and creep away. The old boy's become rather frail, I'm afraid.' Outside, he hailed a taxi and gave an address in the East End. 'A duty call to another relative,' he said. 'Bear with me.'

THREE: FRANK

'Out!' yelled the voice in the dream. 'Front and centre.'

Frank came awake as the cab door was ripped open and he stumbled out into a cobbled street biting on a yawn. The brewery doors sagged open and crates of champagne were stacked near the tailboard of the lorry. Winkle, Limey and Tosher stood at attention against the wall with their hands on top of their heads, their faces the yellow of old newsprint. A lance-corporal covered them with a bren-gun.

'Raus, you grubby individual.' A Welsh Guards' sergeant with bandages under his steel helmet pushed Frank against the brick wall. 'Looting, plain and simple.'

'The officer said to ...' Winkle tried to bluff.

'Shut it!'

'Yes, sergeant.'

'Do we shoot 'em, Sarge?' asked the lance-corporal.

'It's Standing Orders,' said the sergeant.

Limey's legs twined as he tried not to urinate.

'Stand-to there.'

'Permission to fall out for a leak?' said Limey.

'Permission denied. I've seen Frenchies as sick as rats on vino looting from their own. Seen Belgies fighting each other to get away. Seen some of ours run too, seen others fight with sod all. But when I see our own looting, that's the bleeding end.' The sergeant lit a Woodbine and scratched his bandage. 'This all of you? You, with the sweaty nose.'

'One more driver ... and the officer,' said Frank. 'They went off for petrol.'

'And you stayed for the champagne.'

'Orders, Sarge.'

'Orders my Aunt Fanny's black cat's arse,' said the lance-corporal. He showed his teeth at the privates with levelled rifles behind him. They all bore the marks of recent action.

'And just where was you going with this champagne?'

'Arras,' said Tosher. 'I think ... '

'Arras? Where the hell have you been? Frankforce pulled out of there yesterday. The Jerries have got it now, what's left of it.'

'We was lost, Sarge.'

Heavy sarcasm puckered the sergeant's forehead. 'And now you've been found, ain't you? Your lucky day I don't think.'

Dougie turned the corner carrying billies of petrol. He stopped when he was challenged.

'Where's your officer, soldier?' snapped the sergeant.

'Dead,' said Dougie, thinking of Lieutenant Fisher.

'How?'

'When the petrol dump was bombed. He got burned up.'

'And where did you get those then?'

'Over there at a pump. There's a charabanc station. I bust the lock and ... '

'Shut it,' the sergeant said wearily. 'That's commandeering, not looting. All right, corporal, get them sorted out with ammo, can't have them leaning on them nice unused rifles like they was shovels. Terriers is only sloppy civilians in khaki.' He leered. 'Until they comes up against the *real* army.'

Frank's nose sweated seriously. The sergeant had the look of a man trying to be dead. *A dead hero taking us along for the ride. Why me, why me, why me ...*

'What's going on, Frank?' Dougie was making two plus two come out as fifteen and threequarters.

'We joined up,' said Frank.

'Shut it,' said the lance-corporal with the bren. 'Maybe you'll wish you *was* shot when I get through with you.'

Tosher believed him implicitly.

FOUR: CHRISTOPHER

The building in Peckham had a grey brick frontage blackened by generations of soot and ornamental cast-iron letters above the portico read: Workhouse For Christian Unfortunates. Reception Centre had been chalked on the huge front door and the exterior notice-board was plastered with religious tracts and Ministry of Information bulletins.

'This is it,' Charlesworth led the way inside and spoke to a woman in W.V.S. uniform at the reception desk. 'Makes our billets seem less spartan, eh?' he said to Christopher as they were asked to wait.

The walls were painted hookers-green and cream and tattered paper signs directed one to Diptheria Inoculation Room 201, to a Cleansing Station in the Annexe, an Infant Care Lecture by Mrs Baldwycke-Smith in the church hall opposite, whilst Infestation Advice was offered in Room 11A. Babies cried in the passages and fitful echoes wailed in the high, vaulted ceilings. Women formed a queue for soup and bread and exchanged listless obscenities in low, grey voices. An old woman in black talked to herself as she knitted a balaclava helmet in brown wool, and a small girl with untidy pigtails read a greasy copy of *Film Fun.* The smell of poor drainage, boiling vegetables and disinfectant assaulted the nostrils.

'Stinks horrible, don't it, Mister?' said the small girl. 'You gets used to it though, dontcha, Gran?'

'No you bleeding don't, Margie girl,' said the old woman, pearling and plaining furiously. 'Ain't right we gotta be here.'

'Don't mind her, she misses the wireless. I like soldiers. You killed any Germans, Mister?'

'A dozen or so,' said Christopher.

'Not as many as my dad I'll bet.'

'I imagine not.'

'Nah, you can't have, he's an hero.' The girl went back to Laurel and Hardy.

The W.V.S. woman sent Charlesworth and Christopher to an office at the end of a long dark passage. Charlesworth entered without knocking and said: 'Hullo, cousin of mine. I've brought someone to meet you. But you know each other, don't you?' He stood aside to let Christopher inside the room.

Helen Caldercott stood behind a desk holding a teapot. She wore a grey tailored suit and a startled expression. The caged canary behind her started to sing.

'I'll be outside if either of you needs me. Which I doubt.' Charlesworth pecked Helen on the cheek and closed himself out of the dingy office.

'I'll throttle him,' Christopher's face burned. 'I'm very sorry to confront you like this. I had no idea.'

'No?'

'No.'

'You stopped writing,' said Helen, and tea dribbled onto her blotter.

'Only because you did.'

'Me?'

'My last few letters were returned marked "gone away".'

'But mother was to forward them to me. I had no idea where you were ... ' Helen banged the teapot down and subsided into her chair. 'Mother.'

Christopher worried the inside of his cheek. 'You mean she deliberately ... ' He could not finish the thought or the sentence.

Helen swallowed with difficulty. 'Would you care for a cup of tea?' she asked lamely.

'I'd like a large whisky and a bloody good swear.'

'I've learned to do that since I've been here. It's been an education in the use of the foul collective noun.' Helen's smile was counterfeit.

'Damn the bloody woman.'

'Too mild by far.'

Christopher crossed the bald carpet on rubbery legs. The tiny room seemed to have expanded a hundredfold. He knocked his knee against the desk in passing and banged his nose on Helen's scalp as he buried his face in her hair. All his joints seemed to hinge the wrong way. He cleared his throat. 'Does the canary come as part of the dowry?'

'They're very useful for detecting gas.'

They bumped noses as Christopher kneeled.

'No marriage is complete without one.'

A tear splashed on Christopher's lip and he tasted salt. Helen's eyes brimmed, too close to his own to have focus. His head was a balloon filled with birdsong.

'You only want me for my canary,' said Helen.

'And your foul collective nouns.'

'We're talking nonsense.'

As their mouths came together they heard Charlesworth say, 'Come back in about fifteen minutes, will you? Miss Caldercott is rather busy at present.'

FIVE: FRANK

The silence screamed.

They lay on the chalky ridge overlooking the sluggish canal and the wide steel bridge. The Welsh Guards held the centre and left flank and Frank lay with Dougie and Tosher on their right. Winkle and Limey were laying dinner plates on the bridge in a random pattern like mines. As they ran back toward the ridge Frank sighted down his Lee-Enfield at them and squeezed off a shot. The sergeant grunted as the hammer fell on an empty chamber.

'Load up, laddie. Let's see if you got the nouse to knock a Jerrie on his arse.'

Frank wiped off his nose. He could hear the German armour beyond the buildings on the far bank and Stukas screamed out of the sky way off to the north-west. The falling bombs rattled around the horizon and across the flat fields like far summer thunder. He thought of another day much like this one when he had rowed Peggy on Regent's Park boating lake on a Bank Holiday. The lions had roared in the zoological gardens, wanting their three o'clock feed and more restive because of the crackling atmosphere. Fat drops of warm rain had plopped into the lake, sending the other pleasure boats scurrying for the landing stage. The shower became a downpour.

Frank rowed on towards one of the artificial islands, his hair plastered to his head, his shirt clinging to his back. Peggy had squealed as her dress became soaked, trying to be a good sport, her long legs curled under her, her new shoes in her lap. On the island they sat under a willow as the rain smashed the placid water into a stew of vapour and dancing dollies. Pearls of water dripped from Peggy's blonde hair and ran into her neckline. Frank wanted her so badly his groin ached. Instead of reaching for her he rolled and smoked a damp cigarette as she ate her sandwiches with sullen apathy, a stranger with a good body and a dullard's eyes. The smoke hung around his head, almost a physical manifestation of her dark mood. She threw pieces of crust to the ducks and sucked her teeth.

Show her a wedding dress or a diamond ring in Bravington's window and watch the light come back to her face, he thought, and a paraphrased nursery rhyme came to him. *What are little girls made of? Confetti and rice, and a ring made of ice, that's what they're made of. Yeah. Kids and kitchens and giving the old man something to grab on a Saturday night after an all-over wash in a tin bath in front of the fire. The rest of the week? Nothing but yawns and early nights with an headache brought on by kids and kitchens and the price of coal.*

Frank grinned at nothing. At least he had made Peggy row

back when the rain stopped; then she had dropped one of her shoes in the lake and he had fished it out with a boathook. The sun had dried their clothes as they walked to the bus-stop through flower beds that steamed, the colours more brilliant in the rainwashed air. They had kept to the grass and avoided the paths. Peggy's shoe had shrunk and she cried on the bus because her stockings were laddered. *Where are the girls who laugh like my sister Phyllis?*

The first German tank halted at the bridge where it was quickly joined by a second and a third. Their blue exhaust formed a veil around their tracks and the guns swivelled in jerks.

And all I've got are ten rounds of .303. They won't even scratch the paint. Do I shoot down the barrel and hope to hit the gunner in the eye? Frank watched the sergeant do nothing but lie prone in the scrubgrass as if he were birdwatching in Cornwall.

If I'd married Peggy Tucker and given her a seeing-to right away we'd be having our second kid around now. I'd have been deferred as a married man with children. I'd be driving my van down Upper Street on my way home for a spot of dinner; a couple of pints with the lads and back home to four legs in a bed. Except Peggy would be as big as a house with one sucking and another coming. And her mother'd be around, boiling nappies and saying I didn't earn enough poppy to waste it on booze. Kids and kitchens and old mother Tucker with her warts and moustache and eyes like wet phlegm; whittering on and turning my Peggy into a carbon-copy of herself. Two big sows with one grunt, sitting there like a hanging jury of two, and me the accused. Nothing bought and cooked fresh, just cheap meat pies and bread sausages, all wind and gristle and tasting of boiled cardboard. Old Mother Tucker the Pie Queen, and her daughter, The Sausage Princess. Frank worked the bolt of his rifle.

The Germans were climbing down from their tanks and

conferred together in low voices, pointing out the phoney mines, full of caution.

They're buying it.

The Welsh Guards sergeant slapped his machine-gun, bringing it to bear. One of the Germans drew a sidearm and a tank commander ordered him to holster it. One shot might set off the charges and they needed the bridge across the canal. All of the crews were out of the tanks and they formed a line, talking and smoking.

They don't look much like the newsreels. Just soldiers in grey rather than khaki, a bit scruffy like us, except they've got the look of blokes who know what they're about. Frank aimed into the middle of them, trying to remember to squeeze and not jerk the trigger.

The machine-gun rattled and the rifle butt jumped against Frank's shoulder. The Germans were going crazy. Like an outing attacked by wasps. Some of them jumped in clumsy dance as they turned for cover. One fell. Another went headlong.

Frank remembered to work the bolt, bringing the trigger alive under his finger. He hit a falling man and fired into the body as it sprawled. An arm flung away and a Mauser skittered through spatters of blood. A running man vaulted through the iron superstructure and went into the canal. Pink ripples formed a bullseye as he sank from sight. A last German leaned against his tank and died on his feet.

And it was over.

'Cease fire!'

The Territorials panted as though they had sprinted uphill in full-pack.

The sergeant started down the slope. 'You and you,' he pointed at Frank and Dougie, 'come with me. Covering fire, corporal.'

'Sah!'

'We did that?' Dougie was a sleepwalker. 'I saw mine go down.'

'Yeah.'

'Shut it,' the sergeant's boot smashed a plate. 'Watch where you're walking.' He turned a body with its face gone. 'Could be you if they're shamming.'

None of them were.

Under the sergeant's direction, Frank and Dougie set the tanks alight and followed him back up the ridge at the double. Ammunition started to explode as they all formed up and marched back to the lorry.

'What now, Sarge?' asked Tosher.

'We hop it, lad. No more ammo. Unless you wanna stay and throw rocks at the bastards. Fancy it, Cooper?'

'Not for all the hot pies in Upper Street,' said Frank.

'Hop to then.'

Looking back as he drove, Frank watched the shells form livid erratic tracery in the eastern sky, banging fretfully like maroons in sea-fog. Ahead, there was nothing but the road. He hoped.

CHAPTER FOUR

I consider victory to be certain if Frenchmen
will show themselves worthy of the great hours
of their history ... We shall conquer the enemy
if first of all we conquer ourselves.

M. Paul Reynaud in the Chamber of Deputies.

There will be no production of the Oberammergau Passion Play in 1940. Many of the actors who take part in it are in the Siegfried Line. The one who would have played Christ is an air raid warden.

War Illustrated 5 January 1940

HITLER WILL BE SHAVED FREE
With an extra-sharp razor

Notice in Stepney Hairdresser's window.

IF YOUR KNEES KNOCK
KNEEL ON THEM

St Laurence Church Notice Board.

ONE

As Saturday 25 May dawned, it became clear to Lord Gort that the Battle of Flanders had reached its turning point. Von Bock's main effort was concentrated on the tottering Belgian forces, and it would only be a matter of hours before he had driven his armour between them and the British, seriously threatening the B.E.F.'s lines of supply and communications; and more importantly, cutting off the only avenue of retreat. Unable now to rely on the French, and knowing his own limited resources negated any possibility of unilateral offensive moves, Gort realistically recognised he must save his force from complete encirclement and destruction. Without consulting London or the French, Gort abandoned Weygand's plan and sent his 5th and 50th Divisions into the gap opening up on his left flank, embittering the French but saving the B.E.F.

When appraised of the true situation in a telegram, Anthony Eden agreed that Gort's only course was to fight his way back to the west where the R.A.F. and the Royal Navy would support the evacuation that must follow, an operation, Gort was warned, he must not discuss with either the French or the Belgians.

In a room that had once housed a dynamo deep beneath the white cliffs of Dover, Vice-Admiral Bertram Ramsay, Flag Officer Dover, gave birth to the plan to bring the B.E.F. home: *Operation Dynamo*.

TWO: FRANK

29 May 1940

Frank had razor blades under his eyelids and his mouth tasted of nothing human. The cab of the lorry smelled of rank khaki and the bitter after-fumes of too many cigarettes. He cleared his throat and jogged Dougie awake to say: 'If there's a soldiering smell, it's socks. Army-issue woollen socks. When they're new they're as soft as young girls and smell like chicken feathers, new sacking, or maybe fresh hay in a stable. Like a raw recruit after his first bath. That's socks.'

Dougie grunted, the sun was rising behind them and they drove after their own long morning shadow.

'First day on parade, socks are warm, dry, friends to your feet. Something honest between you, your boots and blisters. Then after a day of square-bashing, left-right-left-right, about-turn and double-up, they turn on you. They ruck up about your heels and get tucked up around your boot-tongue. They fluff up into tight wads between your toes and snag on your toenails. And the next thing, they've gone into holes and you darn them. But the darn's stronger than the sock and they hole somewhere else. Pretty soon there's more darn than sodding sock and all that holds them together is dried sweat. They come out of your boots as stiff as boards, stinking of hot feet and leather and toe-jam, cheesier than old tarts on a half-a-crown trick. In the morning they're like dead sheep three-days drowned and colder than charity. You need to light a fag to give you the courage to put them on again. And the next night it's worse. They hang on the end of your bed stinking worse than barrels of soured ale. At night, all the socks get together to make fog as thick as soup, just to keep a man from grabbing his eight hours of honest kip. You can't even stand your own socks, let alone your mate's, or his mate's. A hundred socks in a billet, one hundred Tod Slaughters grabbing for your sleep, not killing it clean like with a razor, but slow and nasty, thieving your air, clogging your nostrils with stinking lint. A smell you can see without moonlight. A smell with more body than an Egyptian whore, more horrible ... '

'All *right*. I'll drive,' said Dougie.

'That's British socks, cocker. The smell of soldiery.'

'You been sitting there thinking that up all night?'

'Not all night, just some of it.'

'You're off your rocker. Give us the wheel,' yawned Dougie. 'Where are we?'

'Wormhout, I think. There was some other lorries ahead but they turned off. I just kept west as far as I could figure. There was some flares or something off to the right, might have been big guns. Too far off to know for sure.' Frank put the gear into first, looking for a place to pull over.

'Not here, for chrissake ... ' Dougie gagged behind his hand.

'Blimey, a few socks ... ' Frank broke off, seeing the strange fruit in the hedgerows for the first time. His foot slipped on the clutch.

Bloated horses showed their bellies to the sky and smaller mounds draped over them had vaguely human shapes. Flies clouded over the corpses, giving the bodies an odd crawling life, setting the Territorial's own skin itching.

'It's like a ... film ... '

'You never saw no film like that.' Frank braked, found the clutch and jumped the lorry into second gear. Bloody runs across the road surface had dried to rusty patches; deeper pools were as thick as clots of shellac. Out in a field of clover where a scarecrow stood, a group of refugees had been caught in the open. They lay in a semi-circle around the leaning effigy, as though in perverted homage to an ancient god, almost the same colour as the torn earth they sprawled upon. A small golden dog trotted across the road, his head up and his tail flicking from side to side, his eyes wary as he growled around the meat in his mouth. It was a child's hand.

Frank drove faster than was safe, drifting into bends and accelerating out of them, seeing everything and nothing. Driving because that was what he did best; did automatically. All his life in moments of stress he would drive and drive and drive; getting away, going nowhere except away and away.

A Vickers stuttered ponderously, punctuated by the cough and sneer of an occasional mortar round. A line of anti-aircraft guns pointed their broken barrels at the sky, destroyed by their own gun crews. A burning Signals' lorry sailed sparks into the thatch of a nearby barn and soldiers from many units lolled against the weatherboarding, too dispirited to care about the possibility of fire. An M.P. in shirtsleeves flagged the lorry down.

'You're coming under fire. Back off over there. Into the orchard.'

A barrier had been erected across a bend in the road and was manned by a rifle company. A single Belgian soldier laid barbed wire along a brick wall, his pipe upside down in his mouth. Every now and then he stopped to spit and shake a fist, muttering in fierce Walloon. He ignored the spits of dust coming off the wall, the spiteful *wang* of richochetting German bullets.

'Mad bleeder,' Winkle yelled, dropping from the tailgate. 'Look at that silly cowson, Sarge.'

'Shut it and brew up. Let's see what' up, Corp.'

'Right, Sarge.' The corporal followed the Welsh Guards sergeant up to the barrier in a crouching run. Sniper fire chipped the ground around their boots.

'They're even bleeding dafter than that Belgie.' Winkle sidled up to Frank and Dougie. 'Got a fag?'

'No,' Dougie shared his last cigarette with Frank and they

kept the smoke down as long as possible. 'You heard the sergeant. Brew up.'

'All right, bear's breath.' Winkle drew hot water from the lorry radiator. 'I just ain't cut out for all this bang and bleeding crash.'

Frank pinched Winkle's ear. 'Make a lot of tea, right. Set yourself up over there and offer it around.'

'To all them lot? We ain't got that much.'

'Just do it. And keep your eye on what I'm doing with the lorry, right. Get them all interested in tea. I want them all off the lorry and away, got it?'

Winkle winked. 'We're having it away on our toes, that it?'

'Why don't you go on the wireless and tell everybody?'

'I could fry a few rashers.'

'Yeah, hop it,' Frank let smoke out in a grudging plume and ducked as a mortar round exploded beyond the brick wall. 'Close. They'll have this place bracketted in no time. This *is* daft.'

Dougie picked the dog-end out of the grass. 'How are we gonna do a runner? They've blocked the road west.'

'There's another track the other side of the orchard. Saw a motorbike go down it and have it away toward the coast. That's where we're going,' Frank climbed behind the wheel and let off the handbrake. The lorry rolled down a slope. 'I'll leave you to round our lot up.'

'Where you going, soldier?' The M.P. had his Webley drawn.

'Down there. I've gotta drain the sump and top up with fresh oil. She ain't running nice. The sergeant said to do it.'

'Get on with it then.' The M.P. knew nothing about engines. 'We got a lot of walking wounded we gotta get out.'

Frank made a circle with thumb and forefinger before rolling from sight. 'M.P.s,' he said, 'they're just nosies like the cops back home.' He lifted the side bonnet and pretended to be busy with the engine. Two mortar rounds came in together and the ground jumped under his feet. Dust and smoke swirled through the fruit trees and turned the grass brown. 'Bang bleeding crash. War's a circus of socks and sergeants and *them* trying to separate you from your head.' *One day I'll learn to hate German pilots who shoot at dots on a road. Maybe if they came down for a closer look at what their cannons do they wouldn't be so keen to press the tit. Maybe our R.A.F. boys do the same to theirs? Sitting up above the clouds and dropping shit on them as if they was ants who didn't smoke or laugh or go to the lavatory. Not that I've seen any of our planes. Not that I'd know one of our planes from theirs. Maybe there ain't no R.A.F. like Churchill used to say before he was in Downing Street? Or they're all at the pictures or on their holidays? Leaving us poor odds-and-sods to throw rocks at the Jerries and the Luftwaffe just like that sergeant says. Wouldn't surprise me, not this kiddy. There's just us and women and kiddies, dog's breakfasts all of us if we don't get lucky. I wish I hadn't thought of that dog ...*

Frank went to the back of the lorry and threw the Welsh Guards' kit and weapons out. They made a small, pathetic pile under the plum trees.

Who was it who said: 'A man is what he owns?' Some clever sod who knows what the world's all about – I don't think. A man's what he is, not how much coin he can jangle. I'm worth more than this. I'm in the wrong place at the wrong time, that's all. Those Welsh Guards was trained for this, I wasn't. If I had, it'd be different. I'd have a proper go. Well, maybe one day, eh? Then I'll kill my share of Nazis for King and Empire.

Dougie panted out from under the trees with Limey and Tosher on his heels.

'The sergeant's had it. And the corporal. A mortar hit smack in the middle of the barrier. There was just his boot ... '

'Where's Winkle?'

'Coming. He tried to put a tourniquet on that Belgie's leg. But when he was turned over his gut was all ... '

'Yeah, yeah. There he is,' Frank waved Winkle on. 'Get in, all of you.' He took the wheel. 'The first thing, Dougie, we get us some decent fags.'

'How can you think of fags when those blokes are ... '

'Because it's real, son. Something we can *do*. Understand?'

Dougie's headshake was bewildered. 'No.'

'You will.'

The roar of the engine drowned the calls of the M.P.

THREE: HELEN

Helen combed her hair until it crackled, musing fretfully.

Much as if a new breed of locust had ravaged the capital, things one had taken for granted had disappeared; austerity had swept away frills and ceremony. Only the previous year, one had not needed to be truly wealthy or come from the upper drawer of society to expect a wedding of some circumstance. Now, unless one 'knew' a black-marketeer, almond paste, crystallised fruit, icing sugar or rare lengths of satin or tulle were beyond reach. *Picture Post* had featured a wedding gown of bleached mosquito netting over a bodice and underskirt of reworked Irish linen table napkins and described the bride as 'bravely chic' in the caption.

Helen sat in the tiny dressing room with its gilded baroque mirrors and mulberry walls, giddy from champagne and unwilling to move toward the bedroom where Christopher waited. This, her day of days, had been a whirl of improvised chaos, courtesy of Neville Charlesworth.

He had squared the marriage with County Hall and the War House, paid the five pounds for the special marriage licence, booked the bridal suite at Whyte's Hotel and filled the reception room with all the flowers in Mayfair. The registrar at Caxton Hall had been older than the Cambrian hills, and two Sergeant Cooks had thrown ersatz confetti gleaned from a War Office paper-punch as cavalry drivers from Regent's Park Barracks formed an arch with starting handles. An odd young man attached to one of the new Ministries had photographed the event with a Speed Graphic before scurrying back to his darkroom in the Natural History Museum to develop his film in Ministry of Information chemicals. The champagne was real and vintage even if the three-tier cake had been a confection of plaster and cardboard with a single puny layer of iced sponge for Helen and Christopher to plunge their silver knife into. Mr Caldercott had mistily given his daughter away and Neville had acted as Christopher's best man, jolly and efficient in his own satanic fashion. Still blithely ignorant of her daughter's graceless marriage at a civil ceremony, Helen's mother had been conspicuous by her absence.

Firstly, thought Helen, *mother would bully all the churchmen of her acquaintance, pushing for an annulment on any pretext, then when that failed, she would bombard her solicitors with demands for the same on legal grounds. Poor daddy will take the brunt of her fury; face interminable Arctic silences or screaming fits of recrimination. All that anguish, and for what? This band of gold representing the magic circle of my virginity, snug on my finger, itself the symbol of the phallus; Christopher's right to enter me in the act of conjugal possession.*

Helen regarded herself, her brush still.

I look knowing and know so little. The Japanese have Pillow Books to turn callow virgins into nubile worthies. In Renaissance Italy, senior members of the family attended the first coupling and would display blooded sheets to the populace. There were still villages where that tradition flourished. I wonder how many chickens have died down the centuries to make that symbolic red splash the more imposing? Will we both be clumsy, too ignorant to be good for each other? Will it be brutish thrusts in the darkness, over without kindness? Will it be all show and no substance like that silly cake with its silver paper bells and bakelite bride and groom? Why didn't Christopher make love to me on the grass where Harold's army had died? Will we fail on that ornate hotel bed and roll apart to pretend sleep, each of us withered by shame and inexperience? I don't want that, but what do I want?

Traffic purled from beyond the shuttered windows, breaking Helen's train of thought. She drained the last of the champagne in her glass and wanted more. The bottle was in the ice-bucket on Christopher's side of the bed. She pictured him sitting there, tightening the cord of his dressing gown, fiddling with the lie of his pyjama collar, perhaps wearing a cravat like Ronald Coleman in one of his more romantic roles.

Helen let herself out into the bedroom with a million tiny cartwheels spinning in her stomach. Christopher lay asleep on his back, his lowered eyelashes long enough to make most girls jealous. No cravat, no dressing gown, just striped pyjamas and scuffed leather slippers. Feeling let down in some mysterious way, Helen recharged her glass and perched on the bed, wondering how he was able to sleep when she had been tearing herself apart with awful doubts in her luxurious cubbyhole. She dripped champagne onto his supine face and watched him blink awake.

'Hullo, rotter.' Helen lost the glass somewhere.

'Mrs Lutyens, I presume.'

'I suppose I am.'

'Regrets, Helen?' *What a crass question.*

'Hundreds, you?'

She hasn't frowned, it's all right. 'Thousands,' Christopher touched her face with bed-warmed fingers. 'And none.' The freckles on her breast were shadowed by the flounced neck of her nightgown.

'Me too,' Helen nuzzled his palm and smelled sandalwood shaving cream.

'We will … no, *I'll* probably be … gauche … '

I know that, dodo. Don't look so stricken. 'Yes.'

Christopher stuttered, coughed and said: 'Words … '

'No words, we agreed,' Helen gripped his hand and a knuckle cracked. The dim lighting turned the chairs into fat velvet women and the four-poster was an ark adrift on a dark, carpeted sea. She found the hard rubber buttons of his jacket. There were fine wheaten hairs on his shoulders. His muscles jumped under his skin when she bared his torso and eased her breasts against his chest, hardened nipples against harder muscular silk.

Their mouths conjoined as they kneeled together, overcome by waves of peace and shock; consumed by their first naked embrace; wanting oral, tactile and visual stimulus with equal passion, equal zeal.

They learned from each other as the unseen dusk turned to darkness outside. More bright stars glittered inside their minds than in the high black vault of the May night. Bowing back under Christopher, Helen held herself rigidly in check as he moved inside her, gently at first and then with surer urgency as her limbs softened to embrace him, drawing him closer and deeper. With a suddenness that left them sprawled and breathless they shuddered through a profound release that left them gaping like limp fish in a tidal pool.

Then they lay together and drowsily talked of things eternal as if all their tomorrows would have no reality unless they were composed of nothing but themselves, forever one. Sleep was for lesser mortals, and since parting would come soon enough, sleep would have been a gross denial of what they had found together; almost a blasphemous concept. And as the invisible dawn turned Mayfair to saffron and rose they loved again to the sound of early pedestrian traffic.

FOUR: FRANK

Frank's mood was as savage as the night. Numbed by the constant concussion of German bombs and the sporadic bombardments they had driven through he was consumed by numb fury.

At twilight they had come through Socx where a rabble of drunken French soldiers fought in the streets, lay in their own vomit or sang with linked arms in unsteady crocodiles. What they had not looted they had smashed. They had hauled an old woman's bed into the street and made her dance on it as they sprayed her with wine and beer. Beyond reason, they created fear in others rather than face their own inner funk. Their whistles and catcalls had followed the T.A. lorry until one of them, bolder and drunker than the rest, mounted the running board to yell: 'Run you *bâtards*. As usual, the British fight to the last Frenchman. *Regarde, mes amis*.' He hawked and gobbed into the cab, spattering the windscreen and Dougie's cheek.

Something had torn in Frank's mind. All his pent-up frustration targeted on the jeering face. His forearm smashed the man's nose and toppled him onto the cobbles where he rolled in broken glass. Frank was already reaching for the starting handle, intent on laying it across ribs and legs, one blow not enough.

Dougie held him. 'Leave it out. You'll have them all down on us.'

Frank reared with manic strength. 'I'll crack heads for them.'

Dougie held on and took a painful elbow in the temple. 'Hit *me* then, go on. Then Tosher and Wink and Limey, eh? *Me* first.'

Christ, I already have. I hit Dougie over some mouthy Frog.

The monumental red wind in Frank's mind became an icy gale of reason. Men banged off the bonnet and mudguards as he drove through the mob, twisting down the ruined street, seeing the rabble as one collective face he wanted violently to disfigure any way he could.

They're right. We are running away. But would we if this was our country? If them Germans was coming down Upper Street, I'd not be making some old tart dance on her own bed, liquored up like some bog-Irishman on a three-day bender. None of us would bust up the pubs down the Old Kent Road rather than have a go at the enemy. We'd have a go at 'em with anything that came to hand. He grinned without humour. *Some of the old girls I know down the East End wouldn't think twice about laying their beer jugs over some Nazi's head if he came at them. Just let's get out of this bloody muck-up and then we'll see what we're made of. Let the bastards cross the Channel and climb them white cliffs. Then we'll see.*

Bergues was a graveyard of abandoned vehicles and baggage carts where the French had thrown up a defensive screen. A Coldstream Guards' officer waved the lorry on toward Dunkerque where the night sky was a dull boil of incendiary fires. A bombardment split the darkness like sudden tears in negative.

'At least they're having a go, Frank,' said Dougie.

'It's their sodding country, ain't it?' Frank pointed through the windscreen. 'And we're going over there. It don't look so healthy does it? Worry about us, old son. We're our responsibility. Nobody else rates.'

'They're our allies.'

'Then sod our luck, Dougie. I reckon we're on our own. If we can load up enough loot and drive this waggon across the Channel, we'll be on easy street. With all this shit flying about there ain't gonna be anybody interested in a few clever squaddies helping themselves to what's lying around. We'll go home millionaires, son.'

'If you can't see what's wrong with that, I'm sorry for you.'

'Cheer up, Dougie. Half of it's yours.'

'No.'

'Because I give you a moody dig? Blimey mate, I didn't mean it.'

'I know that. I just don't want to ... rob a grave.' Dougie saw the whole of France as a bleeding corpse torn apart by its own lack of fibre. The advancing Germans were only feasting on carrion already dead from suicide. There were always gleaners after a harvest, always a hungry dog to worry an abandoned carcase. One day, after the last gun had fired, all that would mark this chaos would be a manicured field of neat white crosses and the victor would write the histories in his own image. The loser was never afforded that opportunity... Dougie went to sleep wishing he had the words to explain that to Frank.

Frank whistled through his teeth, thinking that the pubs would be closing back home around then. Tommy would be on his way home after cutting sandwiches and Phyllis would be waiting for him with hot cocoa. The kids would be snug asleep in bed, smelling of Drene and talcum and looking like angels on a memorial stone. The old mother would be tottering out of the Hope & Anchor with her mates and Peggy would be lying asleep with her long legs all the way to the bottom of the bed. *All the way, and me here, needing some of that stuff, smelling like last year's washing with an itch I can't scratch. Just me and the road and a scruffy bunch of soldiers asleep in the back. And if I get back home, who's gonna believe any of this? Nobody with half an alphabet and more than ninepence to the shilling, that's for bloody sure.*

'I can't do it. That officer's bonkers,' Winkle was close to tears. 'All that brandy, them carpets, all that lovely silver plate I liberated. We can't *burn* it.'

'You heard the orders.' Dougie watched smoke from the bombed docks roll in over the burning buildings. 'We burn the lorry.'

Frank kicked an offside wheel and swore long and hard without repeating himself.

Limey and Tosher almost held hands, wondering how much they could carry away.

'If we got sacks,' said Winkle.

'You can't swim with half-a-hundredweight of silver on your back.' Frank wrapped the gold watches and earrings he had taken from a jeweller's in a piece of waterproof cape.

'I can't swim at all. That's why I joined the army.'

'Then you're right out of luck, ain't you.'

'I'm still taking the best stuff. Maybe the brandy or the big silver chalice thing, that's favourite,' said Winkle.

'They're shooting looters, a bloke from the Durhams told me,' Tosher said. 'And them with rifles has got to muster over there.' He waved vaguely toward the outskirts of Dunkerque. 'A defensive perimeter the officer said. I think . . .'

'Think? You think nothing,' Frank sloshed petrol up the side of the lorry. 'No bloody lorry, no bloody rifles, right?'

'You'll get us put on a charge,' said Limey. 'We ought to do something to help.' He held his rifle awkwardly.

'Help ourselves is what we're gonna do,' Frank lit a rag. 'You want anything, grab it now!'

Winkle's knapsack clanked against his leg, heavy with coin. 'Just what I've got.'

'You'll sink. Anybody else?'

Tosher took a bottle of Napoleon brandy and a tin of bully beef.

'Make up your mind, Prendergast,' said Dougie who had half a mind to join him at the barricades.

Limey threw his rifle onto the tailgate. 'Stuff it.'

'Sensible,' said Frank. 'Dougie?'

'Nothing, I told you.'

'Your funeral,' Frank laid the burning rag against the tarpaulin and it leaped alight with a whoosh, forcing him to jump backwards. 'Goodbye millions,' he said bitterly. 'Let's go to sea. All aboard the *Skylark*.'

Bombs fell as they walked through the rubble. In the basement of an hotel they found themselves in a crush of soldiers, most of them walking wounded. A naval officer was doing his best to dress the worst wounds. The man next to Frank was dead, a cigarette still burning between his fingers. The bombing became heavier and lasted all night.

CHAPTER FIVE

In September 1939 the British army was totally unfit to fight a first-class war on the continent of Europe ... Indeed the regular army was unfit to take part in a realistic exercise.

General Montgomery

'The French staff at Dunkirk feel strongly that they are defending Dunkirk for us to evacuate,
which is largely true.'

Captain W.G. Tennant, Senior Naval Officer,
Dunkirk
29 May 1940

Dunkirk is to be left to the Luftwaffe.

Adolf Hitler

FRANK

A series of near misses brought down part of the ceiling and tossed three men to the floor. The door bucked in its frame and plaster dust whitened the press of men. The oil lamps guttered and spilled black smoke into the stink of the cellar. A young sapper wept without waking and a corporal shredded a newspaper as if his life depended on controlling his hands.

'It was you, you two bastards,' accused a signaller.

'Steady, mate,' said Dougie, slapping dust from his mouth organ.

'Steady, nothing. You and him brought them bombs down on us. The Germans can hear you playing those bloody things.' The signaller pointed a finger of a shaking fist.

Glass smashed on an upper floor and rubble fell with a crash and dribbled between the cavity walls. Everybody ducked, coughing in fresh clouds of dust. Frank found himself defending his face from the signaller's raking nails.

'You yellow git,' Frank caught a wrist and butted the signaller in the chin. Dougie pulled him away as he followed up with his boot. They trod on a man lying on a mattress and he bellowed in pain.

The naval officer drew his revolver. 'That's enough.'

Winkle swung his knapsack and knocked the gun to the floor. It got kicked away into the shadows. The young sapper called for his mother.

'Leave it out, sir,' said Winkle. 'We're in different armies together.'

'I'll have you shot,' said the naval officer as if he were still armed, his voice dreamy.

'You're as used up as we are,' said Winkle with rough kindness. 'Just a bit of a lad in a uniform.' He hefted his knapsack. 'I'm for taking my chances outside. What about you, Coop?'

'Oh blimey yeah,' Frank kicked the signaller's boot. 'I'll know you again, cocker. Mark that as fact.' His hands shook with a life of their own when he thrust them into his pockets. 'Lead on, Dougie.'

They hauled the door open and filed up the warped staircase. The reception desk was smashed to kindling under a fallen floor joist and the windows were without glass or shutters. The air was thick with smoke and the smell of escaped gas. The staircase had disappeared and the sky showed through the back wall. Down the street, men of the

Royal Army Service Corps cried openly as they smashed their vehicles with axes. At a crossroads they passed three dead gendarmes lying at attention in a neat row.

'Somebody should do something,' said Tosher. 'Bury them or something.'

'Who is there, Tosh?' asked Winkle. 'There ain't nobody.'

Stukas screamed over the docks where a row of half-demolished warehouses burned unchecked. Out at sea, a warship had keeled over and there were men in the water. Anti-aircraft guns threw covering fire up above the East Mole where a destroyer was taking on men. Naval officers kept the lines of men in order with drawn revolvers as bombs threw up great gouts of water all around them.

'I don't fancy that,' said Frank. *Queuing up to get blown apart with a load of strangers ain't my cup of tea. Twenty-two miles of water between me and home. It might as well be ten-thousand. There are boats out there but they ain't coming in too close, maybe the bottom's too shallow, and it looks a long way to swim. Maybe there are undercurrents, maybe the tide's going out …* 'I'm making for the beaches, do what you like.'

'We've stuck together up to now. We still should,' said Tosher.

'But they're wading out into the sea down there. I can't do that,' said Winkle.

'You're windy enough to float, Wink,' Dougie blew a fanfare on his mouth-organ. 'If you throw that junk away.'

'Ain't junk. Ain't windy.'

'You should see yourself from over here,' said Limey. 'I'm with Frank. You, Tosh?'

'Yeah, I suppose … '

They passed a jetty where soldiers with fixed bayonets held back a mob of French matelots. An officer fired a shot over their heads to scatter them. They held their ground, silent and sullen.

Winkle stopped dead. 'I gotta go to the Mole, Frank mate.'

'Suit yourself,' Frank kept walking.

'Come on, Tosher, Limey,' Winkle pleaded. 'It'll be safer on a big ship. The navy's got guns and there ain't no cover down there on the beach, just miles of nothing.'

'Teddah, Wink,' Frank trudged out onto the sand with Dougie, Tosher and Limey trailing him, counting ships. A paddle-steamer, two destroyers and a few Dutch *schuyts* lay off the beaches. As he watched, the destroyers opened fire on a German shore battery. The shells hurried overhead, racketing like skittles in an infinite alley.

A cheer from the soldiers massed at the water's edge died before gaining any real volume. The khaki lines broke for cover as the sky wailed and hot winds of blast ripped the dunes. Sand jumped in dry spouts as cannon raked the beach.

Frank rolled into a depression thick with marram grass. Stuff fell all around him, stinging the backs of his hands and rapping on his helmet. Through the din he heard wind-chimes. Dizzy from the noise he lay still long after the planes had climbed away, and when he raised his head he found himself staring at silver coins.

'Pennies from heaven.'

The laugh died in his throat and he heard the bulling of wounded men. 'Winkle,' he yelled. 'You stupid basket. You've got yourself killed, you limping great tit.' He climbed to his feet and cast around. Dougie sat up and Tosher and Limey were untangling themselves.

A drift of muddy smoke swept over Frank and his eyes smarted.

A tattered figure stood near a raw crater, his skinny white legs bereft of trousers, his blouse in tatters, his face and hair thick with wet clots of sand. He had lost both boots and one sock and he held a webbing strap in his right hand.

'Wink, that you?' Frank took a step forward. Then another.

'It's all gone,' Winkle said in a stunned voice. He held out the knapsack strap. 'All of it.' Blood ran from his ears.

'Come on, mate,' Tosher held out the brandy.

'It blew away ... like sand,' Winkle told the sky.

Frank caught him as he fell.

*

'If he hadn't followed us ... ' Tosher passed the bottle to Limey.

'Who says he was,' Limey wiped off the neck and took a swallow.

'That's what he's saying over and over. "Stick together mates",' said Tosher, taking the bottle for Frank who tucked a greatcoat around Winkle and brushed drying sand from his blistered face.

'He'll do, won't you, Wink?'

'Handsome,' said Winkle, his one good eye open to the sky. 'Get through the skylight and that safe'll open like a can of beans.'

'Where's *he* at?' asked Limey.

'Somewhere better than here,' Frank drank deeply, wanting to be drunk, knowing it would not happen, watching the tide line as it tumbled in with the wind behind it. *God's truth, I can smell England.*

Dougie played *Clair de Lune* for some Frenchmen on the next dune.

Something banged into the beach fifty yards off and sand made a dry rain.

'Sod, cut myself,' Tosher tried to shave with seawater and a jacknife. His face was raw.

'Leave it out, you look worse than Wink.'

Dougie had stopped playing mid-note.

'Play up, Doug,' Frank passed him the bottle. 'Only some shore battery taking a chancer on hitting something.'

Dougie looked at Frank with blank eyes filmed with something wetter than tears. He coughed blood through his mouth-organ and red bubbles formed in the wooden grid. The hole in his temple was no bigger than a cigarette burn. With a sigh he lay back and went limp. His helmet slipped over his face and dislodged the mouth-organ from his hands. His mouth widened and parted in rictus and he grinned with crimson teeth.

Tosher shook Dougie's thigh and the limp toecaps touched together.

Frank threw Tosher away. 'Don't touch him. None of you.'

The brandy ran to waste in the grass.

Frank unlaced his boots and pulled them off, threw away his helmet and his blouse.

'He's gone doolally tap,' said Tosher, struggling onto an elbow.

'Frank, mate,' Limey saw madness and was frightened by it. 'What are you doing? Stop him, Tosh.'

'You try it.'

Frank was down to his vest and undershorts. He started on Dougie's boots and trousers, stripping him with fast care.

Winkle came out of his doze to watch.

A bomb fell on the beach without exploding, throwing up sand in a silent spurt.

Frank threw the bloody mouth-organ away then retrieved it and tucked it away inside his vest with the waterproof bundle. Oblivious to the incoming rounds he lifted Dougie in his arms and walked toward the sea.

You and me, Dougie mate. We'll make it. I'll swim for both of us until they fish us out or I get us all the way there. You'll see, you'll see.

Unseeing, he passed Coldstream Guards sitting in precise formation, their packs and weapons neatly stacked. A chaplain blessed the men kneeling around his portable altar, his face calm, his hair wild. A rabble of clerks and rear-echelon staff sprawled amongst discarded ammunition boxes. An armed marine told Frank to stop, threatening to shoot. Frank stumbled around a stack of iron rations and kept going.

The surf chilled his feet and a swill of oil blackened his thighs. A corpse rolled against him in a sodden embrace then drew away, rolling on a wave. Water swilled around his chest and bore Dougie up. Frank faced the beach and swam on his back, his hands supporting Dougie's head. The beach receded and the cold underswell tugged at his burden. He bumped through driftwood and stinking slicks of oil.

Going home, Dougie mate. Going home.

Then there was just the sea and a great rolling silence.

Drowning is easy.

The sky went away and he was wrapped in wet green fogs. They tasted of brine and boundless olive depths tempted him to sink deeper. His expelled breath threw out rolling ovoids in regular streams and they spiralled up to a surface he could no longer see. Then the bubbles were small beads trickling aimlessly from his mouth and the constriction in his chest became a vice. His temples hammered in crimson mist. All he must do was become part of the sea, simply by letting it take him.

The sea was infinite. It reached all the shores of the world in continuous ebb and flow, eating at chalk and coral and basalt from Java to the Pillars of Hercules. It was all the real world. One day it would reclaim all the continents, so why not go along with what was irrevocable? Breathe it in and be forever part of the great saline swill of immortality?

Think of Dougie.

He was up in a flail of spray and taking air and water into his mouth. He coughed and gagged and sank and kicked and was up again with panic making him try for life for both of them. An oar slapped down near his face and he tried to snag it with his teeth. His hands were full of something heavy he must save from something. What and why confused him.

He was hooked by the hair until a wave took him. The vastness of water rolled him deep again and he had no strength to kick.

Then he was up and spewing over a gunwale with his naked buttocks shamefully in the air. He was hauled inboard and he drooled a teacupful of brine over a seaboot as his face hit varnished decking. The cold raised welts on his limbs as a blanket enveloped him. Oil gave him the sheen of polished coal. He was as black as a beaten minstrel.

'This other bloke's had it, skipper.'

'Float him off then, lad. Don't want him fouling the prop.' The voice was as thick as shag tobacco and softened by Devon brogue.

I went to Devon for a week with Dougie. We cycled and ate cream teas and drank our first pints of cider under a hedge as our knees turned red from sun and wind; too pissed to ride back to the lodgings.

'Dougie, you all right, mate?'

'Pass him below, Jack. God knows how many others we can pack aboard. Hook that rubber boat in there. Make yourself useful.'

Frank was stood up and supported. He found the waterproof packet as he was helped along a companionway. 'I got these watches. You can have them from Dougie. I got to take the earrings for my Peg.'

'You keep 'em, mate. No profit in this for no one.'

Frank slumped on a slatted seat and slept with his head in another man's lap, too exhausted to be seasick.

CHAPTER SIX

WHITE RAJAH GIVES BRITAIN $470,000
London 4 June (A.P.) Sir Charles Vyner Brooke, the white Rajah of Sarawak, now visiting in England, has given 1,000,000 Malayan dollars, (about $470,000) to the British Government as a contribution toward war expenses, it was announced today.

The Sun, New York, 4 June 1940

Last night the French Admiralty and the British War Office announced that Dunkirk had now been abandoned by the Allies after the most remarkable withdrawal in military history.
In the House of Commons during the afternoon Mr Churchill declared that no fewer than 335,000 British and French troops had been evacuated from the port.
B.E.F. losses were: 30,000 killed, wounded and missing; 1,000 guns and all transport and armoured vehicles lost.

News Chronicle Wednesday, 5 June 1940

SCHOLARSHIPS NOT BATTLESHIPS

Slogan on American Youth Congress Banner.

ONE: HELEN

24 June 1940

Parting took the bright colour from the day.

The special troop train let off steam and the station pigeons made their startled circuit of the iron rafters. Young men in suits, flannels or hard-wearing corduroy, their belongings variously packed in cricket bags, paper parcels or battered suitcases milled about on the concourse, resolved, confused, frightened or numbed. Many of them had never before been more than a mile from their homes except for a day excursion to Southend or Canvey Island for whelks and a boat-ride around the pier. Some mumbled goodbyes to mothers, new wives or girlfriends, others punched their workmates on the arm, yet others boarded the train without a backward glance, leaving nothing behind.

A girl looked mistily into the eyes of a man she had met only the night before, more enamoured of bidding farewell to an acolyte warrior than feeling affection for the youth himself. She and her many sisters were new phenomena of this peoples' war and would be seen haunting points of departure from Glasgow to Portsmouth, deluded that their fond farewells were as patriotic as making munitions or working the land. These sisters of mercy would never join the Civil Defence organisations to drive ambulances, buses or mobile canteens. They would give solace in rented rooms, drink last toasts to safe return and having waved the train or boat from sight would go in search of another gunner, pilot or submariner, the object of their previous affection forgotten, his identity as ephemeral as their may-fly emotions.

A guard jostled Helen against Christopher, too full of his

own self-importance to apologise. Invasion and war from the air may threaten, gas and bombing attacks on the civil population may be inevitable, along with cardboard coffins for the dead and food rationing for the embattled survivors, but for him, nothing mattered except to make the trains run on time. He slammed doors with his eyes on his railway watch.

'Write soon, darling dodo,' said Helen, boldly kissing Christopher's chin, unafraid of public display.

Christopher became shy, conscious of a slight cockney grinning at him over his wife's shoulder, a baby in his arms and a small boy clinging to his leg.

'S'all right, guv. I'm gonna kiss mine. Ain't I, Phyl?'

'Don't cheek the officer, Tommy,' said Phyllis as young Harry shot his father with a wooden gun.

'Ain't got me yet, girl. Not until I report at the other end,' Tommy gave Phyllis a round, smacking kiss. 'And don't lose your platform tickets, don't want them catching you for another threepence.'

'And you take care.'

'All aboard now, soldier,' said the guard, unrolling his flag.

'That uniform don't put you in my army,' Tommy snapped in a flash of temper.

'But you're in mine. Get entrained,' ordered Sergeant Trefoil, snapping a salute at Christopher. 'Good morning, sir. We've got the full complement, we can board when you're ready. I'll see to the stragglers.' He jerked his head at Tommy who entered a carriage and disappeared behind a slamming door.

'Carry on, Sarn't Major,' Christopher waited until Trefoil had marched off before giving Helen a small package. 'Open this when you get back home. And please, not before.'

'Only if you'll promise to write reams of letters.' The lump in Helen's throat could not be swallowed and she was unable to return Neville Charlesworth's comic wave.

'I'll start one on the train.'

'Then I solemnly promise. Go away now please.'

Christopher climbed into the luggage van and a last door slammed. The guard swung up and blew his whistle. The train jerked into motion and slid slowly away to the west. The passing windows winked with sunlight as they passed and all too soon the rear buffers were receding along the track to disappear around the bend in the platform.

Twenty-one days of honeymoon leave were over.

Helen drifted towards the exit with other saddened relatives and friends, far too distracted by her own melancholic thoughts to be aware of their grief. Waterloo Station had no bustle, no cheerful noise; a new grim resolve had silenced paper boy and traveller alike.

On the hoardings, Friday night was still Amami night, Dennis Compton brushed his Brylcreemed hair, a Waterman's pen wrote peaceful calligraphy and a drummer boy promoted household dyes as if France still stood and all was right with the Empire and the Pax Brittanica. It took little imagination to believe there were no U-boats in the North Sea; that the Norwegian fiasco had not brought down the Chamberlain government and drawn Churchill out of the political wilderness; that foreign aliens were not incarcerated on the Isle of Man or crammed into Brixton Prison; that Mussolini's declaration of war had not caused the disappearance of several famous Italian restaurateurs from Mayfair; that no official pamphlets warned the populace not to leave their homes in flight for fear of being machine-gunned from the air like the Belgians and Dutch.

Helen wandered into the station cafeteria and ordered a pot of tea to ease her aching throat. Beaverbrook was bullying the Air Ministry into making aeroplanes whilst his *Daily Express* proclaimed that any schoolboy who could bowl a cricket ball could throw a grenade with equal ease, a concept that horrified Helen. She would cheerfully impale a German on her hatpin, but children combatting tanks ...

'Excuse me, Madam, but that lady is trying to attract your

attention,' said the waitress, setting down a tray.

Helen frowned through the window at the dark young woman with two children who scratched on the glass and beckoned.

'I don't know her.'

'Seems to know you, dear.'

Helen went outside and said, 'Yes?'

'I couldn't come inside with the boys and the pram and all. Sorry to bring you out, their tea's not all that hot to start with, made in an urn like it is.'

'Yes, but what do you want?' Helen wondered if the woman was begging or selling lucky white heather.

'I had terrible trouble catching you up. Couldn't rush with the pram all folded and the boys being so heavy. It's like running for the last bus.'

'I still don't see.' Helen wondered if she should give the woman sixpence or call a policeman.

'I saw you with your young man and I think he give you this,' Phyllis held out the small package. 'It fell out your pocket when you give in your ticket. I was gonna give it to the porter but you can't be careful enough these days, steal the pennies from a blind man some of them.' Phyllis Penny's face shone with exertion. 'It is yours?'

Helen said it was. 'Would half-a-crown be enough?'

'Don't be daft, love. Honesty don't rate pay,' Phyllis was annoyed and sickened. *Some people put a price on everything as if doing right could be paid for like a loaf of bread. The toffee-nosed cow ought to think herself lucky my Tommy ain't here to give her what for. Still, what d'you expect from them that's got? Nothing but snotty looks down their noses. As if pride comes in packages for them that can pay for it.*

Helen saw the blush of anger and recognised she had been insulting, however unwittingly. 'Look, this is very precious to me, and I thank you. Truly.'

'That's all right.' *Hope it keeps fine for you.*

'Let me give you something. For the children.'

'I can take care of them.' *Bet you've never scrubbed a floor or done a day's turn behind a bar. Them hands never lifted anything heavier than a bar of scented soap.*

'You surely won't refuse a cup of tea? Please, I'll take the little one.' Helen saw her smile melt the frown.

'A five-minute sit-down would be nice.'

'I'm Helen Lutyens, that was my husband on the station.'

'That was my Tommy. I'm Phyllis Penny.'

'How do you do?'

'Nice enough, thanks.'

Between them they got the children and the pram grouped around a table. Helen ordered fresh tea and scones.

'I promised not to open this until I got home,' said Helen.

'We all do that, love, I mean Mrs Lutyens. I've never had the patience myself. I'd have had that opened as soon as I had my hands to myself. Not that I've had much in the way of presents. My Tommy don't go in for it much. He pays the rent on time and don't drink his money away like some, but giving don't come easy to an orphan. I suppose it comes of never being given nothing in the home where he was. Anyway, the money don't always run to it, does it?' Phyllis bit off what she was going to add along with a piece of scone.

'No it doesn't. You needn't look so surprised, I work in a reception centre in Peckham run by the W.V.S. Some of the women there have very little indeed. Some of my friends spend more money on cosmetics than those women have to keep a family.'

'Hold the cup properly, Harry. Don't dribble it down yourself,' said Phyllis. She told Helen she had been in service before marrying. 'What do you do down at this place in Peckham? If it ain't rude to ask?'

'Help with rehousing problems, get the children medical care, keep the place clean. That sort of thing.'

'What, scrub out?'

'Sometimes.'

'Blind old Riley. Sorry, language.'

'I've heard worse than that.'

'You would in Peckham. And you an officer's wife.'

And therefore on the right hand of God? 'Christopher, my husband, is only a second lieutenant.'

'That's still an officer. You ain't ... well, what I'd expect.'

'No.'

'And you shouldn't do it. There's others who can and should. If you can't keep yourself clean, you shouldn't expect someone else to do it for you. And not a lady like yourself.'

'I don't mind.'

'Well you should. Dirt goes to dirt like money goes to money. And old dirt ain't old money, it don't smell sweet. You could catch something excruciating down there. A lady like yourself wouldn't have no resistance to it. Mongrels don't get sick, do they? It's only them highly-strung pedigree dogs that gets ill.'

How old is she, thought Helen, *twenty-two or so? She has two children to keep on nothing whilst her husband is in the army, and here she is worrying her head about me. There's spirit in those brown eyes, and mischief without malice. Good humour bubbles out of her.* She said: 'I'm stronger than I look.'

And prettier than Vivien Leigh or Bette Davis or any of them stars in Gainsborough pictures that me and Frankie and Tommy used to go and see. But Frankie and Dougie and his other mates ain't been heard of since we gave up Dunkirk.

'Are you all right, Mrs Penny?' Helen touched Phyllis's cold hand.

'Just tired. Seeing Tommy off has been a bit of a rush,' Phyllis finished her tea. 'But this won't buy the baby a new bonnet. I got to get these children home on the bus before they start playing up.'

'Let's share a taxi, shall we?'

'What, to Hornsey? That'd cost at least five bob. I can do it on the bus and get change from a shilling.'

Helen gathered the pram and the baby. 'My treat, come

along.' She made for the taxi rank before Phyllis could protest further.

TWO: FRANK

Frank and Winkle caught the London train.

As the Kentish countryside ran past the carriage windows, more rolling than Belgium and more varied in aspect than France, Winkle talked about how he, Tosher and Limey had got away from Dunkirk aboard a minesweeper and been separated at Folkestone. He did not mention Dougie Wayne.

Frank dozed, saying nothing. Transferring from the motor-cruiser to the destroyer was a distant muddle, and when he slept the screams of Stukas and men came from Dougie's bloody mouth. The dock at Dover had moved under his feet like a rolling ship as he queued for sweet tea, five cigarettes and a twopenny bar of chocolate.

Ferried by bus to a military hospital he was issued with over-large boots and a uniform made for an obese giant. The wards housed the sobbers and the silent, the burned, the sightless and the limbless, those with awareness and those without. During the day he walked in the grounds and watched dogfights out over the sea, cheering the Hurricanes on like prizefighters in an aerial arena. At night, when the shore-batteries exchanged fire with incoming bombers and sleep eluded him, he bulled his boots to glass and brewed tea for those patients who could drink it. He joked with the nurses and held his tongue around the doctors who examined him for lung damage. He had swallowed a lot of crude oil.

On his last morning, as he awaited his release from hospital and fourteen-days 'disembarkation leave', Winkle came in on a stretcher to be discharged from the army as medically unfit. He was profoundly deaf in one ear and the retina of his left eye was detached. For Winkle 'active duty' was over and he thought he might even warrant a disability pension.

They had their first pint of English beer at London Bridge Station and parted at the Underground without regret or a backward glance.

Winkle already thought of the army in the past tense. His future was to be abandoned houses ripe for burglary, scrap metals and black market food, forged petrol, food and clothing coupons. German bombing and constant blackout would only increase his chances of operating in the massive disruption that must come. He pledged the watches he had lifted from Frank at a pawn shop in Bethnal Green and was gloriously drunk by closing time.

The world had shrunk in Frank's absence.

The cobbled streets were meaner, the terraces built for pygmies. The pubs were dark and smelled of stale ale. Flurries of soot blew across the pavements and swirled up as shuddering trams passed with electric whines. He could taste it in the air, smell it on the wind, see it tainting the summer sky, dulling the blue to violet-grey. It discoloured paint and grimed brick, streaked the hoardings and got into his eyes. The trees were black with it.

On the bus to Hornsey he lit a cigarette and tasted soot. He read: *Penalty For Spitting £5.* He had forgotten bronchitis was the English disease and his throat ached as the bus passed the Gas, Light & Coke Company where the permanent fog of gases smelled and tasted of copper and rotten eggs. The pickle factory stank of sweetness and the old soap factory still stood in a cloying pall.

It was marvellous.

A group of girls had a skipping rope stretched across Rathcoole Avenue and let it down to allow a coalcart to pass. An old woman holystoned her doorstep, her gasmask case jiggling against her huge buttocks, and next door, a woman in a hairnet cleaned her windows with paraffin and newspaper, carefully avoiding the crisscrossed sticky paper. One of the skipping girls yelled: 'Ginger, you're barmy. Went and joined the army.'

The others took up the chorus and Frank threw a halfpenny to see them scramble for it; deciding how best to spend it would occupy the rest of their afternoon. A shared sherbert dab, a quarter of dolly mixtures, some liquorice wood, a bag of batter crackling ... the possibilities were infinite.

'Hey, mister. You're still barmy.' Giggling, they ran off to the shops.

Frank pulled the keystring from the letter-box and let himself into 63. The same brown roses repeated down the hall, the same tan linoleum was threadbare in the same places, the leaded glass galleon in the front door glowed with the same brilliance. Sandy the neutered cat yawned at him from the bannister rail as he breathed the house in. The floors had been waxed with lavender Cardinal and the grates had been blackened with Zebo. A heavy wash had been boiled up in the copper and fried bread and bacon faintly lingered. The smell of home.

Frank silently opened the door of the back kitchen. Phyllis sat staring at a cold cup of tea, her eyes puffed from crying. She had lit a rare cigarette and it burned to ash in her saucer. Disquieted by this show of emotion, Frank slammed the door to make Phyllis jump. His sister was a smiler, always capable and cheerful. Not some wailing drab like Doris or the old mother.

'God, Christ and Christmas,' Phyllis reared in her chair. 'You'll turn my milk to camel's water.' Then, 'Frankie?' And louder: 'FRANKIE?'

'There's only one of me, Phyllis Ena.'

'What're you doing here? I mean you're *here*.'

'Oh blimey, yeah. At least put the kettle on instead of letting your jaw drop.'

Phyllis pulled Frank's face down and kissed him soundly.

'Leave off. You'll make me all soggy.'

'We all thought you was, you know, missing. Mrs Wayne got a telegram about her Dougie and we didn't know what to think.'

'Well you do now.' *Don't talk about him. Not yet. And not now.*

'Have you seen mother? Or that young lady of yours?'

'You first as always. Where's that tea?'

'You go out in the garden. The boys are out there playing. They'll be glad to see you with Tommy gone.'

'He's gone and upped and left you?'

'No, twerp. In the army. Went down to Somerset with the infantry this morning. Now go on, I'll bring the tea out.'

Frank sat in an old deckchair by a bed of lupins. Pullets clucked in the chicken run and a light plane drowsed overhead. Harry was astride the Anderson shelter drifting dust through his fingers and Robert blew bubbles in his pram. High pillows of cloud formed faces like a cumulus Mount Rushmore.

Phyllis set a tray down on an old stone sink and they washed slabs of seedy cake down with strong tea.

'Nothing like home-brewed.' Phyllis had sluiced her face and dabbed powder on her shiny nose.

'How'll you manage?'

'Like always. Harry, come off that shelter before you fall on the marrows.' Phyllis refilled their cups.

'On fifteen bob a week.'

'If we have to.'

'Tommy could have got deferred.'

'He wanted to go, pleased as Punch when he got through the medical A1. Said that proved all them other doctors was wrong.'

'But they said he had consumption, Phyl.'

'Can't have if he passed the army medical, can he?'

Frank wiped the sweat from the bridge of his nose. *Can't he? Army doctors take you ten at a time, make you pee in bottles, cough when they tap your chest, bend over for a look up your jaxie, give you a quick short-arm inspection, and if you've got the right number of eyes and kneecaps, you're in. Tommy hobbling over assault courses and shoving bayonets into straw dummies? Taking orders? Christ, they'll murder the poor sod before dinner time.*

'Anyway, it's called tuberculosis now,' said Phyllis.

'They only call it that so they can charge you in guineas.'

Harry toddled down the path and climbed into Frank's lap.

'Sky, Frank.'

'He remembers you. Must be a good year since you went to France.'

'Still two-penn'orth of dripping. Mind my tea you little toerag. He's spilled it all down me. No he ain't, the little ... ' Frank swung the boy out at arm's length. 'He's wet all over me.'

'That's very lucky,' Phyllis said gravely, hiding a smile. 'Like pigeons hitting you on the head.'

'He's bigger and wetter than any sodding pigeon. Here, take him.'

'Come inside and I'll sponge you off.'

In the kitchen Frank wrapped himself in a towel as Phyllis swabbed his trousers.

'Was it bad in France?'

'Not so bad.'

'I'm sorry about, you know, Dougie ... ' Phyllis bit her lip at the sudden agony in her brother's eyes. 'Sorry if ... '

'Yeah. There's nothing to tell, Phyl.'

Unaccountably, Phyllis found she was angry. 'All *right*. Go out in the sun. You'll dry off quicker out there. I'll bring these out and hang them up on the line. *Don't* talk if you don't want to.'

'Is there any beer?'

'No. Nor port or brandy or porter. Talking's all we've *got*.'

'Well, I don't want none.'

'Suit yourself, dogs do,' Phyllis spat on the flatiron, her

back turned, her shoulders quivering. *I only wanted to help, that's all. Just talk and ... help ...* There were no adequate words.

Frank fished the fold of waterproof cape from his blouse. 'I want you to have these. They'll maybe fetch a few bob when you need it.' He found himself looking at five lead washers and the small pair of gold earrings. 'The bloody biter bit.'

'I suppose you nicked them from a French plumber.'

'Someone's idea of a joke,' said Frank and went back outside to find Winkle's face in a bank of cloud, one eye winking in fluffy white humour. 'And I know whose.'

BOOK TWO

CHAPTER ONE

Underestimating the enemy, England now knows, is one of the first milestones on the road which leads to Vichy.

Mollie Panter-Downs *New Yorker*

A gas-mask cardboard container, picked up in a Suffolk village street, was found to contain: Some knitting, a ball of wool, a powder compact, lipstick, a mirror, a handkerchief, some letters, a folder containing snapshots, chocolate – and the gas-mask.

War Illustrated

'The Battle for Britain is about to begin. Members of the R.A.F., the fate of generations lies in your hands.'

Air Chief Marshal Dowding, 8 August 1940

The only defence is in offence, which means you have to kill more women and children more quickly than the enemy if you want to save yourselves.

Stanley, Earl Baldwin

ONE:

Spitfire Summer.

By the end of June the Germans were in Paris and had occupied the Channel Islands, the civil population of Gibraltar had been evacuated to Britain, which was already a haven for many dispossessed French, Belgians and Poles, leading Fascists and anti-Semites were safely locked away in Brixton Prison, their foul organisations outlawed, their racist publications banned. Warnings about careless talk costing lives plastered buses and hoardings and food rationing began to bite. The South Coast was a rat's maze of barbed-wire and concrete pillboxes where whole towns were deserted and even bathing huts filled with pebbles were manned by riflemen.

As July blazed toward August, the Luftwaffe turned their attention from shipping in the Straits of Dover to coastal targets, moving further inland with every raid. They attacked the vital radar stations and the seven R.A.F. Sector Stations guarding London. They bombed Manston, Tangmere and West Malling aerodromes, and during an attack on Portsmouth Harbour, Goering learned just how vulnerable his Stukas were against the Hurricane and Spitfire. Designed as infantry support planes they were sitting targets for the R.A.F. who shot them out of the air with consummate ease. Forced to withdraw the Stukas, Goering lost the use of a third of his bomber force at a stroke.

Because of its stringent training the R.A.F. was short of pilots rather than planes, and constant sorties against the incoming raiders took their toll on men who fell asleep the moment they landed, too tired to eat, to drink or remember how to write, sleepwalkers whose reactions were honed by excessive adrenalin and exhaustion. They flew and fought and flew again.

Hitler's *Führer Directive No. 16.* issued 16 July 1940 read as follows: 'As England in spite of the hopelessness of her military position has so far shown herself unwilling to come to any compromise, I have decided to begin to prepare for, and if necessary to carry out, an invasion of England.'

Most of the population of Britain would have argued with him over their 'helplessness'.

Armed with staves, clubs, pikes, duck guns, the odd shotgun and the even rarer rifle, men of the Home Guard looked to the sky from field, farm, factory and town for parachutists, ready to fight the invader with anything to hand.

Men and women learned to make and throw Molotov cocktails at German tanks, learned that Lewisite gas smelled of geraniums, manned anti-aircraft guns, joined the Auxiliary Fire Service, became air-raid wardens, dug for victory by turning their lawns into vegetable gardens, contributed their sixpences to Spitfire Funds, and patriotically invested in National Savings and War Bonds.

It was their war and they planned to win it or go down fighting. After Dunkirk, and relieved to have no allies to let them down, they wanted leadership from people with ability rather than breeding, wanted the truth rather than pleasant fiction, expected attrition and prepared for it.

Churchill struck the right chord when he told Hugh Dalton: 'The public will stand everything except optimism'.

TWO: TOMMY

17 August 1940

He could hardly hold the pencil to write.

The hands that had filleted sole with deft skill, sliced ham and smoked-salmon as thinly as paper tissues were swollen and calloused from bayonet drill and scalded from boiling rifle parts.

Like the rest of A Company, Tommy had mastered one-hundred-and-forty steps a minute on the parade ground, but running on sand slicked by summer rain with full-pack, gas respirator and his rifle at high-port had blistered his feet, torn his abdominal muscles and made his calves painful to the touch. Tommy sat with his feet in an enamel bowl of salt and vinegar and thought Lieutenant 'Banana Joe' Hatwood was a first-class bastard.

'Hate the enemy,' Hatwood had yelled as the platoon toiled up the crumbling slope toward the target dummies on their gibbet. 'Give it to 'em hot and hard. You, Penny, get some guts and initiative there.' On the march back to Weston-super-Mare he had said: 'Every man but Penny is out of step. On the command ... *change*. Not you, Penny.'

As thunder muttered out at sea and rain chuckled in the eaves of his billet, Tommy wrote:

Dear Phyl,

I'm posting this in town so it doesn't go through the company censor. One of the lad's letters home was all blue-pencilled out but for his wife's name and address. We think it was Banana Joe but that don't change it. I'm all right and I don't want you to worry your head so long as you and the boys are O.K. The army is just like the home I was in. The same rules and regulations, but the food isn't much cop. I've bought myself a decent cup, plate and knife and fork and keep it as clean as I can. A lot of the lads just swill theirs under the cold tap and wonder why they get bellyaches.

I've started a canteen for the lads in the church hall, mostly sandwiches and fritters made from bully beef and the bit of batter I whip up. They seem to like it and I make the odd few coppers from it.

The lads all miss their families, the married ones most of all. A few of us thought we'd have our wives down for a weekend in three weeks time. We've all been saving what we can which isn't all that much on sixpence a day. I sold my camera to a beach photographer for £3.10/-. It should have fetched more but there wasn't nobody else interested and who had that kind of poppy. The woman at the hotel says she'll put you up full-board for five shillings. I've got that much and I enclose enough for the train fare down. I suppose Doris will have the boys?

I have to do guard duty and it gets us all down. One of the regulars called Mifflin says if you become batman to one of the officers you don't have to do sentry go. I'd do it like a shot but the only one who needs a batman is Banana Joe and I don't fancy being his dogsbody. He's got it in for me in a big way as it is. He put his last batman on a charge for some piddling reason so he'd do worse to me if he had the chance.

That Lt. Lutyens is decent as officers go. He doesn't have that smell under his nose all the time like Banana Joe and Lt. Charlesworth. I'm glad you saw his Mrs in London and she got you home by cab. I'd thank him personal but you don't just go up to an officer and talk to him. We're dirt and they're the darlings. I asked Mifflin if he'd do a swop for being batman to Lt. Lutyens but he said not for all the fags in the N.A.A.F.I.

We went on a night manoeuvre last week and ate out of

tins in the dark. Could have been cold cabbage for all we could tell, and the landladies here cook nothing but stews of gristle and dumplings which is why I do the canteen for the lads.

I'm getting fitter though. Basic training was hard, but most of the lads feel better for going through it, not that they would again, not for anything. Sometimes when I'm not aching all over I feel like I could push over a bus.

I wish I was home with you and the boys. I think I'd rather peel a mountain of spuds all day, every day, instead of doing sentry go at night. Shouting 'who goes there?' at seagulls and stray dogs ain't what I joined up for. Soldiering is boredom and being broke.

Write soon, Phyl, I miss you a lot.

Love, Tommy.

He addressed, stamped and sealed the envelope with a lick before realising he had not mentioned Frank's safe return from France. Phyllis had written about the impromptu party she had thrown for him, and how all had gone well until Emma Cooper had arrived drunk to reclaim her mangle.

She would. Any excuse to make trouble. Tommy visualised the rented piano coming through the window and Mr Mason the pianist playing all night for three halfcrowns and all the beer he could drink; Frank and Jack draining the last dregs from the barrel through a stocking and dancing with their trousers rolled up, singing all the old songs, playing the mouth organ and the spoons, and horsing around with all the old ladies in the street who sat in singing rows with their gills of ale. Then the cards coming out for brag and poker, the coins clinking on the green baize as blind-bidding moved the luck around the table.

And here's me in an attic room with whitewashed walls, an iron bed with musical springs, a bare blue bulb in the ceiling, no wireless, no books and nobody to talk to. And I'm not standing around in a pub, dawdling over a pint of cider to make it last. Money don't come that easy I can throw it away on suchlike, not if I want to bring Phyl down for the odd weekend. I miss her daft chatter and her snug little body next to me. I even like listening to her breathe in her sleep. The times I used to wake up scared in the home and think everybody was dead because I couldn't hear them breathing in the other dormitories. And this is lonelier than them days ever was. Tommy yawned at his feet, miserable in his isolation, aware of boots hurrying up the uncarpeted stairs.

Private Mifflin came in without knocking.

'Caught you playing with yourself, have I?'

'What's up, Miff?'

'Up? Everything's up. Get your boots on and report to the Company Office chop-chop. Don't leave nothing, we ain't coming back.'

'Where we going, Miff?' Tommy towelled off his swollen feet.

'China, for an egg and spoon race, right?'

'Invasion, Miff?'

'I'm a batman, not the Chief-of-bleeding-Staff, how would I know? We're pulling out for Portland Bill, and those that miss the trucks will have to leg it all the way. So be warned.'

'That's over sixty miles.'

'Good at geography, are you? Nobody argues with Sergeant-Major-bleeding-Trefoil when he says hop to, and that goes for "Banana Joe" Hatwood as well, though he'd flaming well like to.'

'He'd argue with the garden gate.' Tommy stuffed his kitbag full and pulled the drawstring. 'Ready, Miff.'

'Then cut along. And save me a place on the lorry. My kit's in the hotel basement, know where it is?'

'Where you brew up and have a quiet smoke.'

'Right.' Private Mifflin led the way down to the street where they were lashed by windborne rain. Cloud boiled in from Bridgewater Bay and thunder clattered like dropped pots. Searchlights played on the lowering western sky and they could hear the sea tumbling onto the foreshore. 'This weather should keep Jerry at home.' He buttoned his greatcoat and disappeared into the gloom.

Tommy hurried to the Company Office, reported himself present and went down the back stairs to the batman's cubby-hole. There were several kitbags piled in a corner and he turned them to read the names stencilled there. He found Mifflin's and hauled it out. The drawstring was loose and the clothes disturbed.

'Somebody's got sticky fingers,' Tommy said aloud, wondering who to inform. Miff always had tobacco and chocolate and sold single cigarettes to those without.

'What the devil are you doing there?'

Tommy turned to find Lieutenant Hatwood in the doorway, his face livid. 'Collecting kit, Sir.'

'Helping yourself more like. Stand still.'

'No, Sir ... '

'Stand *still*. I could never abide a thief.' Hatwood called Sergeant Trefoil and he came down with Lieutenant Lutyens hard on his heels.

'Mr Hatwood?'

'Place this man under close arrest. I caught him going through the batman's kit.'

'No, Sir, I was copping Mifflin's ... ' Tommy was dizzy with rage. 'I never thieved nothing in my life.' The small room was suddenly airless and claustrophobic and he was back in the assembly hall where the headmaster birched a boy before the whole school for stealing apples. He had vomited then and been made to clean it from the floor as the other boys tittered behind their hands. The humiliation had made Tommy ill for a month. Sergeant Trefoil was telling him to turn out his pockets and Hatwood had his letter and was making up a further charge. Then Mifflin was there checking his kit for missing articles.

'Nothing's missing, Sir.' Mifflin's face was a blank page.

'You always have cigarettes, I've seen them,' said Hatwood.

'Have you, Sir?'

'Don't be insolent.'

'No, Sir, sorry, Sir. But I had no cigarettes, and nothing's missing, *Sir!*'

'I'm not satisfied.'

'Sir, I asked Private Penny to collect my kit. That's what he was doing, Sir.' Mifflin kept his eyes on Lieutenant Lutyens, willing him to see the injustice of the situation.

'You're absolutely certain, Mifflin?' asked Christopher.

'Yes, Mr Lutyens, I am.'

'I think that settles that,' said Trefoil. 'This man is in your section, Mr Lutyens. I suppose you'd like to handle the matter of the letter not going through the company censor?'

'Now look here, Lutyens . . . ' Hatwood blustered.

'Were you planning to post this without showing it to me first, Penny? It has been sealed.'

Tommy could not talk. The room was all shadows.

'Permission to speak, Sir,' said Mifflin.

'Well?'

'Penny was writing that letter when I went to his billet. I think the rain got to it and wet the glue on the envelope.'

'Indeed.' Christopher tried not to smile.

'Raining very hard, Sir.'

'I had noticed.' The letter was bone-dry and Christopher knew a transparent lie when he heard one. He did not like Mifflin, but he knew he must protect both men to save Penny from Hatwood's specious accusations.

Trefoil made a show of looking at his watch. 'Excuse me, Gentlemen. It's past the time we should have enbussed the men.'

'They can wait,' said Hatwood.

'Brigade wouldn't like that, Sir.'

'Nor would H.Q. Division. It is an Immediate Action Directive,' said Christopher, taking his cue. 'I'll keep this letter, Penny. Is there anything in it you wish to tell me about before I open and censor it?'

'No, Sir.'

'Very well, carry on then, Sarn't-Major. Unless Mr Hatwood wishes to give you a direct order to delay our departure?'

Hatwood's stubby forefinger explored his inner ear. 'No.'

'Right you two, outside.' Sergeant Trefoil doubled Mifflin and Tommy up the stairs as Hatwood's voice rose in angry protest. In the foyer Trefoil stopped them both to say, 'Walk soft, lads. I've heard some baldfaced balls in this girls' finishing school, but *that* little demonstration of the mendacious art takes the ship's biscuit. Mifflin, you lie like a vicar's parrot.'

'Thank you, Sarge.'

'You've got two of His Majesty's officers shouting the odds down there. Try it again and your feet won't touch. I'll personally see you both in the glasshouse. Do I make myself clear?'

'Sir.'

'Sah!'

Trefoil slapped his pace-stick against his palm. 'Go away.'

On the lorry Tommy said: 'But somebody *had* been through your kit, Miff.'

Mifflin passed Woodbines. 'I know it.' He blew moody smoke.

'It wasn't me, Miff.'

'No,' Mifflin's voice was dreamy in the stormy darkness. 'But somebody got lucky tonight. Just keep your eyes peeled for three Navy Issue tins of Player's Navy Cut and five bars of Cadbury's.'

'A hundred-and-fifty Players? Bloody blimey.'

'Keep away from Hatwood, Tommy, both of us should. And know this, there ain't but one of five faces who could have had my gear away.' Sheet lightning illuminated Mifflin's hard, furious eyes. 'And I'll find him.'

The lashing rain made further talk impossible.

THREE: CHRISTOPHER

Nobody had heard of them at Portland Bill.

A coast guard directed Christopher to the Naval Station where a Chief Petty Officer abandoned his fish supper to telephone the nearby Black Wood Army Camp. The Duty Officer there was doing his rounds, and when he came on the line during the false dawn he made it very plain that he had been given no instructions about the 7th Battalion's arrival. There were no barracks available until the new wings were completed because the civilian contractors were hampered by a lack of timber. He could offer no messing facilities or ablutions, the cookhouse was only a square of concrete and the drainage system existed only on paper. He himself lived under canvas and messed with the 'wavy-navy boys' when he could, otherwise he motorcycled into Weymouth and ate at an hotel at his own expense. He was very sorry.

Christopher did not tell him he was the only officer who had arrived. 'You're sorry. I've got men spread out from Blackmoor to the Bill. Have you ever tried to transport seven-hundred men from Somerset to Dorset at night in filthy weather, on shielded lights and without a solitary signpost to show the way? Do you know how many ditches there are between here and there?'

'I've found a few of them myself, old boy. Try it on a motorcycle.'

'Thank you, no. Look, check your incomings again, will you? There must be a signal from Command or Brigade.'

The droll voice said: 'Last week I was landed with a bolshy mob of Royal Green Jackets and some Poles. They beetled off with half the stores and all my transport. Now I've got an even bolshier lot of Durhams who came from Dunkerque, and they, old boy, do nothing but hold farting contests and run around in the nude. Even the Military Police won't come inside the perimeter to chastise them. Your problems are therefore low on my list of priorities, much as I sympathise. Why not do what I do, leave it all to your N.C.O.s and generate enough paperwork to cover yourself? Good luck.' The line went dead and no amount of jiggling helped restore the connection.

Christopher trudged back to the trucks with a case of begged bully beef, a packet of dried egg and a pound of tea. Sea fog came in from Chesil Beach and Portland Harbour was a peach lozenge where toy frigates rode at anchor. Maverick sunlight made the long incoming swell into glittering silver snakes skimmed by herring gulls. Their screams climbed the headland of greensand and scrub as though torn from their throats by the brown coils of barbed-wire.

Mifflin detached himself from the men squatting at the roadside and saluted as Christopher came up with the rations.

'Think you can do something with this, Mifflin?' Christopher felt and sounded jaded.

'Yessir, reckon so. Penny's a bit of a cook. I think we can come up with some sort of a fry-up. There's ninety of us in the three trucks, what's the ration to be?'

'See they all get something. The others will have to make their own arrangements when they arrive.' Christopher wandered to the cliff edge and sat on a slab of Portland stone. Staring out to sea he was deaf to the men's banter and blind to the magnificence of the view. He had half-known the confrontation with Hatwood would come, but was still shaken by the raw venom of the man when he had blocked the door of the batmen's pantry, pointing his stub of a finger, the red scrawl of veins on his cheeks suffused with blood.

'I should knock your block off, Lutyens. No officer backs an enlisted man against a fellow officer. Get this, your money and manners mean nothing nowadays. It's men like me who'll wield the big stick, not draper's assistants like Mason or half-baked amateurs like you and God-Almighty-Charlesworth.' The finger had prodded Christopher's chest. 'Get. My. Meaning.'

How did I keep my temper? Outwardly at least? Inside I churned and mashed his silly face into raw meat. Broke his limbs with punches and kicks. And all the while my voice came out as coolly as water from an iced jug. 'Your threats are as empty as your head, Hatwood. You are a silly, boorish disgrace to your uniform and I would hesitate to employ you as a cinema commissionaire. You are dull and unpleasant and you smell unwashed. You don't even have the wit to be stupid. The men despise you and I find you despicable. Do you really imagine you can gain any semblance of respect by getting yourself called "Banana Joe", by insulting the men like the corporal you undoubtedly once were? If you threaten me again I shall report you for "conduct unbecoming" to Brigade immediately. Also, it may interest you to know that I agree with the consensus of opinion, you *are* serving in the wrong army. Have you considered crossing the Channel to offer your services there? Now, kindly stand aside and allow me to pass.'

'Who calls me that? Who, damn you, who?'

Christopher passed into the stairwell on watery legs. 'Why not ask the brigadier what *he* calls you?' was his parting shot before ascending to the clean, rainwashed night.

'Mr Lutyens? I brought you this, Sir.' Private Penny held a billy of tea and a plate of frittered beef surrounded by scrambled eggs. 'You can use my irons to eat. I'll use a spoon.'

'How on earth did you cream the tea?'

'Condensed milk, Sir. Miff ... Private Mifflin had a tin stashed.'

'I can imagine he would. All right, Penny, thank you.' Christopher started to eat, knowing the men watched him covertly. They had filled oil-drums with sand doused with petrol and lit them to make a field kitchen. When he had finished, Mifflin collected his plate.

'All right, Sir?'

'Ambrosia.'

'Is that good, Miff?' Penny asked in a loud whisper.

'Tommy lad, with officers you never can tell.'

An hour later a despatch rider brought them the order to return to Weston-super-Mare. Charlesworth and Mason did not appear until the following day, and without Hatwood. Their lorry had hit a tree in the dark and Hatwood had broken ribs. By one of the mysteries of coincidence, tinned sausages disappeared from the menu to be replaced by tinned rolled bacon. Even odder to Christopher's mind, was Mifflin's offer to take charge of Hatwood's effects whilst he was in hospital, and his insistence on accompanying the recovery crew when they went to retrieve the crashed lorry.

'After all, Sir. Your gear's there too. Don't want that to go missing, do we?'

That night, Christopher learned the reason for Mifflin's puzzling behaviour. Passing the batmen's pantry on his way to the file store in the basement he saw Mifflin sewing horsehairs through loose cigarettes as Penny carefully repacked them in Player's tins. Hatwood's duffle-bag was on the floor between them.

Mifflin turned a doctored cigarette. 'Who says there ain't a God, Tommy? I reckon it was His divine hand that crashed that lorry so I could get into Hatwood's duffle. Every time Banana Joe lights one of these he'll do himself a mischief, the thieving basket.'

'Pity you can't do nothing about the chocolate, Miff?'

'Can't I just.' Mifflin held out a small vial of liquid. 'Observe, my cockney-sparrow. This is something special I borrowed from the M.O. Phenolthalein, or to you, squitter juice. We unwrap the chocolate very carefully, paint a few drops of this over every bar and rewrap the buggers. When he scoffs one he'll be on the po for forty-eight hours. Be like being shunted up the jaxie by a lorry-load of laxatives.'

'What if he offers it around to the other officers?'

'Not his style, sharing, is it? No, Joe's for the high jump.' Smothered laughter followed Christopher up the stairs.

FOUR: FRANK

24 August 1940

A creeping barrage of rain swept in over the fields and drove the soldiers to shelter in a barn. Water sheeted from the roof and a lake of ochre water began to form in the lane, its surface in constant dance. A grey veil of vapour rose to merge with the lowering sky, silencing the crows in the elms. Their fatigues smeared with clay, the soldiers were as sullen as the cigarette smoke around their heads.

'Don't they grow nothing but potatoes in East Anglia?' Limey threw a King Edward at Tosher.

'Yeah,' said Frank, 'rain.' He let water out of his boot.

'You'd think the War Office would give us something better to do than digging potatoes.'

'Because we're veterans? Did our bit in France? Leave it out.' Frank wrung water from a sock and found a hole with his finger. 'I've even got spuds in these.'

Tosher lit a moody cigarette. 'Hiring us out to farmers ain't legal. Is it?'

Limey picked straw from a bale. 'Take it up with the officer.'

'Leave it out. Officers don't talk to squaddies. Here, did you hear about them Royal Artillery blokes picking beets over Ipswich way? They burned their tents and mutinied.'

'Who told you that load of toffee?'

'That bloke from Signals. He said . . .' A potato hit Tosher on the ear. 'Watch it, Prendergast.'

'Watch it yourself.'

Frank unlaced his second boot. 'You'll be getting your news from blackbirds and foxes next. A little bird told me ...' he mimicked. 'According to you, Tosher, the Jerries have landed at Dover twice and the Luftwaffe are operating out of the Royal Sussex Flying Club. And who was it who heard church bells and thought the invasion had started? And who was it ran out in the middle of the night right smack into a cow with a bell around its neck and half-killed it with a shovel? Lord Haw Haw ain't your aunt or something, is he?'

'They do look alike, Frank mate,' said Limey.

'You know you're right, Limey my son. Here, Tosh, show us your left profile,' and he pushed Tosher's jaw to one side.

'Get off.' Tosher's cigarette fell and died in a puddle. 'Now look what you've gone and made me do.'

'Pardon us for breathing, did you do that, Frank?'

'Not me. You want me to say three Hail-Marys because you've got wanker's wrists, Tosher darling?' Frank blew derisory kisses. 'Tosher Bennett the cow-killer.'

'Oh-bleeding-lé,' sneered Limey. 'I'm hungry. When's that food waggon come around?'

'Half-past Wednesday. Who cares? It'll be cold potato pie and that maiden's water they call tea.' Frank walked to the barn door to watch dancing dollies smash the clay to yellow soup.

'If you can't take a joke you shouldn't have joined up,' said Limey.

'He's changed. Even when Frank laughs it sounds, you know, hard.' Tosher stamped the sodden cigarette to paste, still haunted by the sight of Frank walking into the sea with Dougie Wayne's body. 'And he don't play the mouth organ no more since then. You'd think it was him died at Dunkirk.'

'Maybe he did.' Limey remembered his own crawl down the beach with Tosher and Winkle, edging along on their buttocks for fear of being shot for running for the shallows. The long wait in the water as the rising tide came up around his neck and supporting Winkle as men in full pack drowned trying to keep their rifles dry. Then the longboat edging in and being hauled aboard one at a time, and the mad major who almost swamped the boat as he broke from the line to save himself, seeing the naval lieutenant shoot him in the head, throwing him back into the sea in a long spurt of blood. And rowing away in an oily chop as a soldier holding a puppy and a French doll sang the same line of a hymn over and over until Winkle hit him with a baling can. Rowing through bodies and burning pools of oil to the destroyer under tow from a tug and standing on deck with hundreds of other men who marked time on the spot because the fires below turned the steel plates cherry red. 'Maybe we all did,' he said.

Frank watched the bullnosed Morris slew in from the main road and negotiate the rutted lane in clouds of spray. 'We've got company,' he said.

A captain in a yellow waterproof cape and the farmer got out of the car and came into the barn. Nobody moved or took any notice.

'Who's in charge here?' demanded the captain.

'I've got the stripe,' said Frank, hating the shiny boots and the plump well-groomed face.

'Sir,' said the captain. 'Name and number.'

'Cooper, F.W. Six-two-oh-two-four-five-two, Sir.'

The farmer scratched his crotch and reset his tartan hat. 'Why aren't your men out in the fields?'

'Because it's pissing with rain.'

'Don't be insubordinate, Lance-Corporal. I want these men back in the fields immediately.'

'Then tell 'em yourself. I won't until we're issued with proper wet-weather gear like you've got, and when we get proper food and billets. Those huts are wet, cold and lice-ridden. The last hot food we had was three days ago . . . Sir.' Frank deliberately spat into the rain.

'Order the men outside at once and I'll overlook your insolence.'

'Overlook what you like. You want them out, you tell 'em.'

Frank sat on a bale of straw and wiggled his naked toes. 'All I know is, I ain't going.'

'You're under arrest. You two,' the captain pointed at Limey and Tosher. 'Take this man's boots and uniform and lock him in the loft. The rest of you men, outside.'

'We got to do it, Frank,' said Tosher.

'Then do it,' Frank peeled off his wet blouse and threw it down. When he stepped out of his trousers he was naked from the waist down.

'Where's your underwear?' snapped the captain.

'In my kitbag. I like to keep something dry to sleep in. Oh yeah, *Sir*,' Frank winked at Limey. 'You want the shirt too?'

'Leave his shirt,' the captain tugged a sideburn. 'Get him out of my sight.'

As he climbed the ladder to the loft Frank waggled his buttocks in Tosher's face. Somebody turned a laugh into a cough. From the barred window Frank watched the men straggle out into the field and wished he had kept his tobacco tin and papers. The Morris U-turned and drove away and he was alone with the mice and the rain.

There are thousands of good blokes in German PoW camps, thousands of others manuring French fields with their rotting bones and who knows how many like Dougie who ended up as fish food? All for what? So some prune of a captain can treat squaddies like black field hands in some Civil War Hollywood flick? A smooth mother's boy with shiny boots who never saw the business end of a Jerry bayonet except in war pictures, who's got nothing but rank and not enough brains to know when he's out of order. And look at that scarecrow. It's even got an umbrella. More than those poor sods have working around him. Frank let out a long breath and grinned. He pulled his jacknife from his shirt pocket and chopped at the wooden frame around the window bars. 'Can't catch me,' he hummed, 'I'm the gingerbread man.'

As dusk fell he climbed through the window and dropped to the ground. A dog barked from several fields away and stars gleamed through the thinning cloud as he made his way to the scarecrow and patted its turnip head. The hat and coat fitted well but the trousers needed to be rolled up. He carried the broken shoes and the umbrella up to the road and padded towards Ipswich under a clear sky.

Going home, Dougie, mate. Going home.

Frank walked into the Booking Hall of Ipswich Station and bought a platform ticket with his last coin. He had added a cardboard collar to his wardrobe and the man in the Ticket Office called him 'Vicar'. The last train to London was already in the station and Frank got into a No Smoking compartment, reasoning that most servicemen would avoid travelling in it. As the train jerked into motion a young airman climbed in and plonked himself down opposite Frank. He had acne, bad teeth and halitosis, and introduced himself as Norbert Norris.

'The Reverend Jellicoe,' Frank improvised.

'Toc-H do sterling work, don't you agree?' said Airman Norris. 'I'm a member of the Christian Circle.'

Frank nodded in the dim blue light, hiding his bare ankles behind the umbrella. 'Good,' he said, 'very good.'

'I know all the churches around the airbase. I sketch as a hobby and churches are my favourite subject. Is your church Saxon or Norman? I'd very much like to come to one of your services.'

'No church. Just back from Africa.' *I did have to get lumbered with a budding holy-roller. My luck in a nutshell.* 'Can't talk, bad throat.'

'Then you're a Methodist. Are you going to Exeter Hall?'

Frank shook his head. 'Sorry, throat.' He coughed and leaned back to feign sleep. The carriage was warm and his clothes were drying. The airman ate a bag of toffees with his mouth open, his foul breath gusting in Frank's face. Frank slept until Liverpool Street when Norris woke him with a gentle shake. They stepped down onto the darkened station where a woman with two suitcases and three small children struggled toward the barrier.

'Here, let us help you, madam.' Frank picked up the suitcases. 'Airman Norris will take your little ones,' and without waiting, he strode away down the platform. At the barrier he said, 'My wife and son have the tickets.'

'Right-oh, Vicar.'

By the time Norris and the woman reached the ticket collector, Frank had abandoned the suitcases and disappeared; gone in search of Winkle.

FIVE: HELEN

'Just off down the chippy, ducks,' Mrs Tolliver said around the office door. 'Me and Margie-girl. Want a nice bit of roe if I can get it?'

The idea of battered fish made Helen nauseous. 'What you eat, your baby will grow on,' the doctor in Chelsea Walk had said, and more cheerfully added: 'Still, early days yet. Congratulations, Mrs Lutyens.'

'Thank you, no.' Helen signed the final form and initialled the last file. It was finally over. All the Reception Centre's temporary charges had been relocated in suitable accommodation with the notable exception of Mrs Tolliver and Margie-girl who would be off to Chislehurst in the morning, courtesy of the Salvation Army.

'You don't eat proper,' Mrs Tolliver slammed off to brave the blackout.

Helen would miss the irascible old woman and her dishevelled grand-daughter; not so Peckham, or the looming Gothic workhouse with its noisome archaic plumbing, gaunt dormitories, cellars and corridors. The building was more coldly inhospitable than any of the haunted mansions described by Wheatley or Poe in the books she had read by torchlight under the bedclothes at boarding school. The local authorities could have it back with the greatest of pleasure. Helen was heartily tired of the obdurate and the foolish, the losers who liked it that way; the women who refused to grasp the concepts of basic hygiene or what constituted a balanced diet for their offspring. She had seen children with lice-ridden hair, with rickets, with skin diseases that marked them as permanently as smallpox, with rotten teeth and poisoned gums, wrapped in goose grease and brown paper, without underwear, socks or shoes, permanently snivelling, always hungry. Much of the time Helen felt she had been catapulted into the previous century, where grinding poverty was the norm and mindless squalor a simple fact of life.

Helen stacked her files and changed her canary's water before covering his cage for the night. The cramped office had been an island of sanity for so long, that she knew she would think fondly of it. She smoothed her skirt over her still flat stomach and gently touched her swelling breasts, and resolved to write to Christopher before she went to bed. Since she felt ambivalent about her pregnancy she had no idea what his reaction might be to the prospect of fatherhood. He might grin and look foolish, he might stutter and become clumsy, or would he hate the whole idea of his wife swelling up like a dirigible? As she stood there musing, sirens started up from South of the river, closely echoed by those nearer; overlapping wails of mechanical banshees, mourning louder and nearer until they were all around her. The canary fluttered under his cover and let out a single, plaintive cheep. Helen was deafened by monumental sound.

Then the wall bulged and the window blew in. Helen was skidded across the floor and the heavy desk jumped to trap her against the filing cabinets. The light failed and the falling ceiling plunged Helen into dark oblivion.

SIX: FRANK

'Wink's a mate of yours, is he?' the publican asked around a cigar.

'Yeah.'

'Down on your luck?'

'I ain't Rothschild. Just got invalided out.'

The publican wrote on a cigarette packet. 'Try there, say I sent you, Albert from the Fox & Grapes.'

'Is he still flogging watches?'

'Cheese now, last week it was Argentine beef. Tell him to drop in some time, know what I mean?' The wink broadcast confidentiality.

'Got you.'

The club in Peckham High Street was a cellar where men diced on a threadbare snooker table and beer was served from a pile of crates. A man in a collarless shirt that barely met over his stomach walked Frank into a corner.

'How do I know you're a mate of Winkle's?'

'We served in the cake together. I'm Frank, he'll have mentioned me.'

'Frank what?'

'Just Frank.'

'No last name, eh? Like most around here. Have an ale.'

'It'll have to be on Winkle's slate, I'm boracic.'

'No slate, you'll have to go thirsty.'

'Winkle won't like that.'

'He'll lump it then, won't he?'

'Your funeral, fatty.' Frank took a cigarette from an opened pack and lit it with the fat man's matches.

'Got more front than Woolworth's, ain't you?' The fat man pushed a light ale forward. 'Handy are you? Or is your mouth the biggest thing about you?'

'Me? I'm a pussy-cat. A darling.' Frank swallowed warm ale, light headed from hunger. 'And you carry two cut throats behind your braces. I don't fancy smiling with a second mouth.'

'Don't miss much, do you?'

'Cats don't.'

'Member of the Gee-Oh-Dees, are you?'

Frank finished the ale. 'The what?'

'Grand Order of Deserters, sticks out a mile. I'm Nobby, stick around.' The fat man went to the telephone and spoke briefly before listening for several moments. He rang off and came back to open another bottle. 'Drink that while you wait to be looked at.'

'By Winkle?'

'Maybe,' Nobby's unshaven chins shook with silent mirth. 'Might be the M.P.s.'

Somebody yelled 'Snakes eyes' and money changed hands amid groans and whistles.

'Look at the state of you.' Winkle came out from behind a floral curtain, resplendent in charcoal grey and a black homburg, a carnation in his buttonhole.

'And you look like a pox doctor's clerk.'

'He's into you for two ales,' said Nobby. 'Half-a-crown.'

'Daylight robbery.' Winkle threw Nobby a coin. 'Bloody sirens are going again. Can't go out there for a bit. You done a runner, Frank?'

'Maybe. Where can we talk?'

'Here, we're all mates.'

'Some friendlier than others though, eh?' Frank sucked an eyetooth and picked a fleck of tobacco from his tongue. 'Just you and me, Wink. Without your minders.' He jerked his head at the two stolid men at Winkle's elbows.

'So long as it's friendly.'

'Oh blimey, yeah. Through here?' Frank held the curtain aside until Winkle walked through into a passage at the bottom of a flight of stairs leading up to street level. 'You owe me, Wink.'

'How d'you make that out?' Winkle hooked a thumb behind a lapel.

The toerag's got a razor hooked back there. 'Five watches at a tenner a time. A round fifty.' Frank watched Winkle's hands and eyes.

'I'll do you a favour, Frankie my son. How would you like to be on the strength, part of the firm? You've seen the rubbish I got minding me. Blimey, one of them got himself nicked for stealing railings. Sawed 'em down and carted them off on a pushcart. The old bill had him banged up before he'd gone ten yards. Fifteen quid a week, five times what you earned driving a waggon.'

'That's a lot of poppy, Wink,' Frank said, making fists and holding one out. 'And I'd earn it with these.'

'Just the odd moody dig now and again.' Winkle slapped Frank on the shoulder and his eyes grew big and misty before he folded over himself. Frank's fist had taken all the breath out of his stomach. His razor clattered to the floor and Frank kicked it away before taking Winkle's wallet.

'Ten white fivers,' Frank hauled Winkle to his feet. 'Now, you and me'll take a little walk.'

'You've hurt me bad, you . . .'

Frank pushed Winkle up the stairs ahead of him. 'Save your breath.'

Winkle fumbled for a key and cracked the door. The passage light went out automatically.

'Nice touch.'

Winkle protested as he was backed into the street, a dark shadow against the starlit August night.

'Forget all this, I want you on the strength, straight Frankie.'

'You would have laced me lovely if I'd said yes. Come off it, Wink. Just walk.'

They both heard the bomb-vane whistle and were

prostrate before the public house across the street lost its roof and upper brickwork in a harsh violet burst of concussion. Tile and brick hurtled across the narrow street and the lamp housing sheered from a gas standard to smash down between them. Winkle rose in a crouch as a secondary blast rocked the street and he flew away. Incendiaries clattered down to roll in the frosting of powdered glass before flaring, alight, to brighten the street with phosphorescent glare.

Frank staggered upright and held onto the topless gaslamp. Where he had lain was a perfect outline of himself on the pavement. The club door had blown in and Winkle lay halfway down the stairs, his arms waving weakly.

'Done it again, the baskets done it again ... ' Winkle's suit was coated in plaster and crumbs of glass. A thick veil of dust rolled from the curtained doorway and men coughed and swore and stumbled in the darkness.

Frank walked along a pavement that pitched and yawed in a windless gale. His ragged clothes were too heavy and scattered glass made the surface treacherous as he ducked past the radiant heat from the demolished pub. Liquor bottles exploded in the bar and the engraved glass danced in firelight.

Keep walking, Frank told himself, *keep walking ...*

The street got cooler and normality returned for a while. At an intersection he paused, deciding which way to go. Bells rang several streets away where fire licked the sky.

'Mister, hey, mister,' a small girl with an opened bag of chips clutched Frank's sleeve. 'Gran says come, mister.'

'Where?'

'Over here, ducks,' an old woman in black hobbled up. 'We can't get in the door and she's in there. It all come down on her.'

'What about the fire brigade ... ?'

'I dunno, do I? They got the telephone box too. Come *on*!'

Frank stumbled over rubble that had spilled across the road. The old workhouse had lost much of its fascia and the pitched roof had dropped into the void and hung over the pavement like a vast shattered chevron. The huge front doors were jammed together in the warped stone opening.

'She's in there, down past that window. It's an office.'

'All right, Ma. Stand back and I'll have a go.'

'Here, I got a torch. You can't light no matches – I can smell bleeding gas.'

'You and me both, Ma.' Frank unscrewed the torch and took the tissue paper out of it. The beam was still weak but it would have to serve. Frank inched out along a fallen beam and jumped to catch a window sill, hung there and hauled himself up and over. The interior floor had buckled and fallen masonry had punched holes through to the cellars where water from a ruptured main seeped through the vaulting. The roof creaked and snapped as it settled and slate tiles ground together like fretting teeth.

'Here goes nothing.' Frank lowered himself over the sill and dropped onto a wooden floor. Dust rattled and the floor timbers groaned. A fallen steel joist had smashed the reception desk to kindling and blocked most of the passage to the rear of the building. Frank climbed over it and kicked a way through the rubble piled there. His torch picked out the door of the office and he gingerly opened it to sidle inside.

Something fluttered under a dusty cloth when the light beam passed across it and Frank found the canary in a buckled cage. He set the cage outside the door and began heaving joists out of the window. The woman lay on her side in a foetal curl, the leg of a desk jammed into her stomach. There was blood on the torn and dusty stockings and the tumble of hair stirred from erratic breath.

Belling and the unmistakable throb of a fire appliance came from the street.

'Just in time to be too late,' Frank said aloud, inching the huge desk aside. It snagged against a broken board and his back muscles cracked as he lifted it over the obstruction. He was drenched with sweat and dust tickled his nose, stinging his eyes. He got a hand under the limp neck and brought the lolling head up into his shoulder. Then, lifting her legs, he brought the woman off the floor as slowly as his strength allowed.

The air was hot and the smell of gas grew stronger as he backed into the passage and hooked the birdcage with a little finger.

The floor vibrated under his feet from a fresh fall of masonry, and as he inched back toward the window, slate fragments dropped with soft plops onto the heaped scales of wall plaster.

An ornate helmet showed against the oblong of stars and a torch beam momentarily blinded him before sweeping away to light the floor. A ladder swung through the window and made a solid footing. Frank backed into it and walked upward, leaning heavily against the solid rungs. A second ladder had been lashed to the first and Frank felt himself guided onto it. A fireman took the birdcage and Frank descended to firm ground.

'Is she alive?' Mrs Tolliver pushed a warden aside.

'Oh blimey yeah.'

'The baby,' murmured Helen.

'There ain't no one in there. No babies, she's raving, poor girl.'

'If you're sure, missus.'

The burden was lifted from Frank's arms and he sank onto a broken wall as Helen Lutyens was laid on a stretcher and carried to an ambulance.

'Thank gawd they got her out, Margie-girl.'

'Yeah, but gran, where're we gonna sleep tonight?'

'What do it matter? Just thank your cotton socks we wasn't in there.' Mrs Tolliver cast around for Frank, remembering her torch. 'Wouldn't you know it, he's gone off with it. Ain't that typical of people today?'

The All Clear sounded as Frank walked towards the all-night bus stop.

SEVEN: CHRISTOPHER

The Brigadier fiddled with his monocle whilst Hatwood lumbered to a chair, easing himself down onto it as if the padded leatherette was stuffed with chipped glass.

To Brigadier Marchbayne-Cleverley the fellow seemed to favour his buttocks rather than his strapped ribs, and the thought of sodomy crossed his precise and ordered mind. He had recently presided at a Court Martial where like charges had been proven against a fellow who had looked a lot like this Hatwood. The Brigadier knew very little about these 'Duration of Hostilities' junior officers and their conscripted soldiers, and was inclined to remain incurious so far as he was able. His nephew Neville Charlesworth was sound enough and he spoke highly of young Lutyens, but Mason and Hatwood were cuts of cheaper cloth. Mason's hair was far too long at the nape and he said 'Right-oh' rather than 'Yes, sir'. And hadn't Hatwood contrived to fall from a stationary lorry during the Movement Exercise? Dipsomania crossed the Brigadier's mind.

He screwed his monocle into his good left eye (shrapnel on the Somme had gouged bone from the brow of his myopic right one and made wearing an eyeglass painful), and in doing so reduced the Company Office to unfocussed shades of gentle brown. He would make a point of having a word with the Medical Officer before he left for oysters and turbot at the Commodore's Club. Hatwood was quite red in the face and would not sit still. The Brigadier added worms to sodomy and dipsomania.

'Coastal Defences – that's us,' he said, 'are now on constant Red Alert. When I say "Cromwell" you'll all know what I mean. Apart from one officer and ninety men, none of your force reached your objective on time. *He* knows who *he* is, so I have no need to mention *him* by *name*. That's a "well done", by the way. The rest of you were not up to snuff. If I were the enemy I'd be delighted. I'm *not* the enemy, though some of you will begin to believe so. All of you will submit written reasons for your failure, in longhand, in triplicate, in no more than a thousand words and no less than seven-hundred. I may even read them.' The Brigadier listened for sniggers and heard none.

He thought, *humourless bunch*, and said: 'Several such exercises are being laid on in the near future. When the balloon goes up you will be ready, see to it. It shouldn't matter to you that we are caught up in shuffle and change, countermanded orders or "Integration movements" or "expedient imperatives" whatever they are; you know no different, unlike myself who is used to brigade routine, and have been all my serving life.' *That's telling them, they ought to be damned pleased I'm confiding in them, they ought to know the pressures of senior command.* 'Some of you,' the Brigadier glared directly at the squirming khaki smudge that was Hatwood, 'need some opening medicine. Well, these exercises should supply the right dose. Carry on.' And he left them sitting in a ring.

'I think we have just been dressed down,' said Charlesworth. 'Brickbats from the Brigadier.'

'What's "Cromwell"?' asked Mason.

'The codeword for Invasion,' said Christopher, closely watching Hatwood who was trying to reach the door without parting his legs. 'Are you all right, Joe?'

'Tired, s'all . . . '

'That's what comes of being treated by the R.A.F. quacks. A thousand words on failure? Great Harry. And you've no reason for that look of simpering pleasure, Christopher. I expect you to help me write my hundred lines.'

'Of course.'

'What's so blasted funny?' Charlesworth demanded.

'Help Hatwood with the door, will you, Mason?' Christopher sounded strangled.

'Right oh.'

Christopher's soaring laughter followed Hatwood out of the Company Office and chased him up to the first floor lavatory. The Brigadier heard it as he questioned the M.O., a slight, balding captain who blushed readily.

'I blame the R.A.F. treatment,' he said. 'Hatwood thought he was urinating blood and brought me a sample.' He produced a bottle of shocking pink liquid.

'And that's it?'

'That it is.'

'Damned rum to my mind. Is that a manifestation of unnatural sexual practices?'

'His urine is alkaline, that explains the colour. It could only be brought about by the ingestion of a certain medicament.'

'So, he is an alky. Thought so. Keep me closely informed, Doc. I want to know about his drinking habits, bottle-a-day man, know the type. I'll have no dipsos on my strength.'

'That isn't what I meant,' said the M.O.

'Natural for you to defend the man. Hippocratic oath, doctor, patient, all that ethical mumbo-jumbo. Quite understand. Keep this under your hat and keep me posted. Carry on, Doc,' the Brigadier walked out to his car and drove away.

'I seem to have given him quite the wrong impression,' the M.O. said to the empty dispensary. The Hungarian who had formulated Phenolthalien in 1900 had a lot to answer for to his mind. He resolved to write a strong letter of rebuke to his counterpart at the R.A.F. base. The M.O.'s pen scratched late into the night.

Mifflin and Penny came to attention as Christopher appeared in the batmen's pantry, warily trying to read his mood with their eyes front.

'Mr Hatwood is indisposed and will need a batman. I think

it's time one was forthcoming from the ranks.'

The soldiers remained silent.

'A volunteer,' prompted Christopher.

Silence.

'I'm returning your letter, Penny. My advice would be to destroy it and confine your future observations to topics of general interest. *Not* discuss personalities, especially those of your superiors. I should put you on a fizzer. Company punishment would be the least you would earn if this libel was published. Do you understand?'

'Sir.'

'I'm looking for an improvement in general attitude from both of you. Voluntarily or otherwise. Clear?'

'Permission to speak, Sir?'

'Well?'

'Private Penny was just informing me he would be glad to volunteer as Mr Hatwood's servant, Sir. Just until he's better, that is, Sir.'

'I thought he might have.'

'Sir.'

'And he will prove useful I'm sure. Unfortunately, certain toxic elements must be kept from Mr Hatwood's diet. That will take a more experienced man. Somebody like yourself, Mifflin. I think you understand me.'

'Sadly, Sir. Yessir.'

'We'll start the new regime immediately. You know where Mr Hatwood's room is, and on the way, you can make certain Penny knows how I like my cocoa. Good night.'

'How did he know?' asked Tommy.

Mifflin tapped his temple. 'The old third eye, Tommy son. And I didn't think he had it in him. You've fallen on your feet there. As for me,' he released a long breath with puffed cheeks, 'I got my work cut out.'

EIGHT: FRANK

Phyllis's wireless described the first bombs on London as a 'nuisance raid' and added that casualties were 'light'. It was not then known that the German raiders had missed their target in the Home Counties and had jettisoned their bombs on London by mistake and in direct contradiction of Hitler's policy to leave the capital and civilian targets strictly alone. In his bunker, Churchill was already drafting an 'Action This Day' directive to Bomber Command for a retaliatory raid against Berlin.

Frank sipped hot saccharined tea. 'At one place you could read a newspaper by the fires. There was a hole you could drop a bus down, and a whole lot of trolleybus wires had come down.' He did not mention the incident at the workhouse.

'You're as brown as a pot. You're all covered in brickdust.' Phyllis had lit the copper and a tin bath of water heated on the stove. 'You'll need a good long soak to get all that off.'

Frank's elbow left a brown ring on the American cloth. 'Heard from Tommy?'

'Never mind Tommy. You've done a runner.'

'Nah, compassionate leave. I missed your pease pudding and faggots.'

'All leave's stopped, even I know that.'

'Know more than I do then, don't you?'

'Always did and always will. Now get them clothes off while I pour you a bath in front of the fire.'

'Leave it, I'll do it myself.' Frank died for a cigarette.

'Listen, you. Don't get all coy with me. I've wiped your nose all your life and kissed your bum when you was a baby more times than you've earned pennies. Get all hard-nosed with who you like, drink all the breweries dry and get yourself in dutch with the army. That's all you've ever done, find trouble where it don't exist. But don't think you can come it with me. Ever.' Phyllis ruffled Frank's dusty hair and clipped his ear. 'Waking me up in the middle of the night with your knocking. Thought you was the warden. He fined a woman down the street five bob in the magistrate's court for showing a light.'

'It's always them as haven't got it gets lumbered.'

'Saying it don't change it, Frankie. It's the way of things. And this war won't turn things about. Them as has it will keep it, and us? We'll get by as we always does. Maybe them Comm'nists got it right some of the time, but that's still only talk and this ain't Russia, so get stripped off.'

As Frank soaked, Phyllis brought him Tommy's suit and a white shirt, and an hour later he was in Finsbury, waiting for Peggy Tucker to leave her house for work.

CHAPTER TWO

The Home Office has invented
this little verse:
'Wavering sound:
Go to ground.
Steady blast:
Raiders passed.
If rattles you hear:
Gas you must fear.
But if handbells you hear:
Then all is clear.

The War Weekly

Do not believe the tale the milkman tells;
No troops have mutinied at Potters Bar.
Nor are there submarines at Tunbridge Wells.
The B.B.C. will warn us when there are.

A.P. Herbert

The announcements of the first air-raid deaths are beginning to appear in the morning papers. No mention is made of the cause of death, but the conventional phrase 'very suddenly' is always used. Thousands of men, women and children are scheduled to die very suddenly, without any particular notice being taken of them in the obituary columns.

Mollie Panter-Downs *New Yorker*

ONE: FRANK

Hot sarsparilla permeated the length of Chapel Street Market where costers yelled their undercut prices at the women who queued for eels and bread, sausages that were already more bread than meat; argued the price of sheep's hearts and tripe and agonised over what to use their shilling's-worth of ration points on. The wireless shop was loud with Gracie Fields and Carroll Gibbons, Big Morrie 'The China King' Dutch-auctioned plaster Alsations and wind-swept girls with Afghans, totters sold second-hand clothes from doorways, and a crippled veteran of the Gallipoli campaign ground tunes from a barrel-organ as his niece passed the hat. 'Prince Poobah', an Indian from Mauritius, promoted medicines he claimed could cure anything from scrofula to obesity, white powders that were 'instant death' to the cockroach and bedbug, and the curtain stalls offered little but rolls of net and blackout material. Anything in demand was 'under the counter' and only the favoured could purchase them, with the result that most stalls were devoid of their pre-war displays of fruit, vegetables, rabbits and eggs. The lowly and coveted onion had disappeared for the duration.

Frank watched for policemen as he walked Peggy through to the factory where she worked, half-listening as she gossiped about the other girls on the assembly line, whittering on as if nothing had changed or ever would. At the factory gate, Frank gave Peggy the earrings.

'Are they real?' She held them up to her lobes.

'Oh blimey yeah.'

'They ought to go with a ring. You know, third finger?'

'Pigs should fly and turn kosher.' Frank admired Peggy's skin and wished her mind was as flawless.

'It's, well, not right accepting a gift of gold without some sort of ... arrangement. What will I tell mother?'

'Tell her nothing. There's nothing to tell.'

'All right, bear's breath. It's just the talk. You know what they're like round here. All talk and no drawers.' Peggy coloured up. 'You make me talk like that, you and your sister.'

'Leave Phyl out of it. I got to go.'

'Don't take it like that. You know what I mean... you both talk ... free.'

'Free country, right? And it beats wearing iron knickers and thinking Queen Victoria's still on the throne like your old mother does, *and* looking like she's smelling drains all the time.'

'She don't neither. Mother likes to keep standards.'

'She likes to keep you indoors and unmarried so she can cop your wages every Friday and has someone about she can nag. You want that, have it. My old mother may take a drink and eff and blind on the beer, but sober, she'd give you the curtains off the window and the po from under the bed. Yours just sniffs and complains when somebody else's cat walks across her bit of garden. Nothing's right for her, is it?'

'You spoil everything. Even giving me these,' Peggy said, knowing things were going wrong again, and unable to change the course of the conversation. The factory hooter blew and she stepped through the gate. 'You know they dock an hour's pay for every five minutes we're late. I've gotta go. See you tonight?'

'I'll see.'

'I want to, honest.'

'Yeah, but I'm not coming in. You be on the doorstep ready at half-six.'

'But she'll want to see you, she'll have to know where we're going. You know how she is.'

'Doorstep half-past six.'

'Just come in and say hello.'

And smell the wintergreen she rubs in her chest? Listen to her clocks tick and tread on the newspaper because she don't want her lino dirtied by my boots? Put up with her asking me my collar size and my laundry number as she sits in that creaky rocker like unclaimed bagwash, her eyes as mean as dried spit on a kerb? Not this kiddie. 'I'll think about it.'

Peggy's smile was brilliant and a little smug. 'See you,' she ran for the entrance to clock on, turned and waved, and lost herself in a press of women.

'Oh blimey yeah,' *and I'd better get more than my hand held in the back row of the Odeon tonight.* Frank shook his head and rolled Golden Virginia into a Green Rizla. *I don't get it, every time she opens her mouth she gets up my nose, but the old family jewels get all tight when I look at her and getting my breath ain't so easy. Like looking at a winning racehorse or a greyhound romping home at fifty-to-one and me with a fiver riding on it. Better than a goal at Highbury as the whistle blows, better than meat and potatoes and Yorkshire pudding as light as a virgin's sigh after ten pints down the boozer. But it don't make sense all the same.* He puzzled over his dilemma as he walked to Caledonian Road and took the tram to the Archway. A 41 bus dropped him outside the Hope & Anchor and he found his mother at the bar with a gill of stout.

'Early for you, ma.'

Emma Cooper sniffed. 'So you've come to see me have yer? I thought you thought I was dead and gorn. Didn't they teach you to write down that school?'

'Wasn't there long enough, was I? A pint here, John. Anyway, the army don't let us write when we want to.' Frank paid the crosseyed barman in small change. 'Drink up, ma, and have the other half.'

'I'll have a port and lemon to keep out the cold.'

'What, in August?'

'There's cold and cold. Wait till you get some years on you, you'll see.' Emma drained her stout and patted her hat, a cloche of a particularly vivid green. 'Here's me working behind this bar most nights to make ends meet. Not that I ought to with grown children and all. That sister of yours don't give me nothing now she's married that Tommy.'

'How can she with two kids and just army pay to live on? All you gotta worry about is you. Never thought of you as a whiner, ma.' Frank winked at Johnny across the mahogany bar.

'Who's whining, you cheeky toerag? You'll get a flip right quick, however big you are. All I want's my rights. It ain't easy being a widow alone. I brung you lot up on nothing, and that's what I get from you, nothing.' Emma drooped in a show of self-pity, her faded yellow eyes on her drink. 'When you going back? I only got the one ration book.'

'I've only just got here and already you want to know when I'm off.' Frank laid a ten shilling note on the bar. 'Here, get us something a bit nice for dinner. And don't go drinking it.'

Emma's smile formed fleshy dumplings either side of her mouth. 'There's my lovely boy. I knew you'd come across.'

'Course you did.' Frank drained his bitter. 'I'm just going down the house to get a pair of slacks and a clean shirt.'

'You'll be lucky, I moved.'

'What again? Where now?'

'Down the road, Cannon Road. Had to didn't I? The landlord tried to stitch me up over the rent. He got my handbag up the side of his head. The hand-barrow cost me five bob. Daylight robbery.' Emma rummaged in her oversized bag and Frank glimpsed an alarm clock amongst the handkerchiefs, string and bottles of salts and lavender water. 'Here's your ticket for your stuff.'

'You pawned my clothes?'

'Could have got lost in the move, couldn't they? This way I knew they was safe. Won't cost you but a few shillings.'

'Welcome home, Frankie,' said Frank. 'It's like being mothered by a fairground roundabout. Give us another, John.'

'Don't get out of your pram. Self, self, self. That's you and your sister all over. No thought for your mother.'

'I suppose Doris has kicked in, has she? She earns good wages and there's only her and Jack. She ought to have seen you all right.'

'Jack's a big eater, great hairy sod. He eats all she earns, she'd help out if she could.'

'Course she would. I don't think.'

'Doris is a good girl. Always stands her round.'

'Good customer,' said crosseyed John.

'When you learn to see straight I'll listen to your bent opinions.'

'Hoighty-bleeding-toity. Pay up and drink up.'

'Don't start on John, Frankie Cooper. Getting all sweaty-nosed over nothing.' Emma patted John's tattooed wrist. 'You pay no mind, ducks.'

Frank slapped coins on the counter. 'That's right, John. You listen to the old mother. She knows best.' He finished his beer in three long swallows. 'See you around, ma.'

'Off down West with some flighty baggage I s'pose? Not a thought for your own mother, no.'

'You'd pawn me if you could. Teddah.' Frank paused outside long enough to hear his mother order another port and lemon. The ten shillings would never see the inside of a butcher's. Frank shrugged and walked back to Rathcoole Avenue, whistling. He was arrested by the military police twenty minutes later.

TWO: CHRISTOPHER

'This is not a drill,' the Brigadier shouted down the telephone.

Sergeant Trefoil dropped the receiver in its cradle.

'Corporal, where are the officers?'

'At breakfast, Sarn't Major.'

'Present my compliments and ask them to come immediately. Some clown's sighted a submarine in the Bristol Channel. Don't shout it about, right?' Trefoil telephoned the armoury and told them to stand by with rifles and live ammunition. 'I know you've only got a hundred rifles, and yes I know I need a requisition from Brigade. Ah, Mr Hatwood, feeling better, sir?'

'Middling.' Banana Joe was the colour of old, crusted porridge. 'A submarine?'

'And troop transports ... *they* say at Brigade.'

'It's another bally drill,' said Mason.

'The Brigadier said not.'

'Oh, righty ho.'

Hatwood held his stomach and a chairback. 'Tell the police to sound the sirens, Trefoil. We'll muster the men at the school hall. What about transport?'

'Brigade's sending lorries from Lulsgate.'

'That'll take what, an hour?' Christopher looked at his watch and the office clock.

'Forty minutes at the outside.'

'The Germans could be ashore by then. Look, B Company's already mustered for map-reading. I'll commandeer a bus and get them moving. Where to, Trefoil?'

'All I've got's the Bristol Channel, Mr Lutyens.'

'All right,' said Christopher, 'I'll make for Portishead Point.'

Trefoil grunted approval.

Hatwood tapped the wallmap. 'I'll flank you at Redcliff Bay. Mason can take King Road to the north.'

'Right ho.'

'Signals should send a radio truck, and what about the Home Guard?'

'Brigade says it's our show, Sir.'

'Better make it a good one then.' Hatwood kneaded his midriff.

'Look here, Joe. You still aren't a hundred per cent. Why

not control communications from here?' Christopher suggested.

'You'd like that, wouldn't you, *Mr* Lutyens, eh? Grab off all the recognition and make me the lame duck?' Hatwood snarled. 'I'm going and don't get in my way.'

'As you wish.' Christopher turned his back, his face flushed. 'Come along, Mason. And please don't say ...'

'Right oh.'

'Dear *God*.'

'Cheer up, old man. Action at last, eh?'

'What's up, Christopher?' Charlesworth wandered in sipping tea.

'Tell you on the way. We're commandeering a bus.'

'What splendid fun. May I sit by the driver and ring the bell?'

'Charlesworth, you're a fool.'

'Yes, dear boy. As you wish, too pretty a day to squabble.'

The tide had retreated from the mudflats at the mouth of the Severn and seabirds wheeled over a sea of dull brown hummocks washed by lazy outfalls of ochre water. Wales was a long green sprawl on the far horizon and Cardiff was a grey pall of industrial smoke. There were no columns of men struggling ashore; any Germans making such an attempt would have foundered a mile from the beach.

'And Englishmen abed will think themselves accursed they were not here,' Charlesworth misquoted. 'Hardly worth old Hatwood's time threatening that bumptious armoury clerk with his revolver, was it?'

'What about my bus?' demanded the conductor. 'There'll be hell to pay back at the depot.'

'If the fool had accepted a direct order from Brigade over the telephone to release the arms, Hatwood wouldn't have needed to fire into the ceiling. We could hardly repel an invasion with our bare hands.'

'Fifty men on a thirty-two seater is against company

regulations, it's all going in my report to head office.'

Charlesworth poked at the scrubgrass with his swagger stick as a flying boat made a slow circuit of the bay. 'What is that dreadful smell?'

'Ozone?'

'There's a dead cow caught up in the barbed wire,' said the conductor. 'That all the army's good for, killing innocent animals. Your blokes ought to bring it up and bury it decent.'

'With full military honours. Go and punch tickets or whatever it is you do.'

'I'll punch your ticket, officer or no officer. I was at Wipers in the first lot. That was real war, not like this caper.'

'One can't choose his war, you offensive clod. Go away.'

'I will. And I'll take my bus with me.'

'And my men will cheerfully shoot you if you try. What do we do now, Neville? We have no orders to withdraw.'

'I suppose we could deploy the men. Have them dig in.'

'We brought no entrenching tools.'

'They have their bayonets.'

'The ground is rock hard, we'd have to hose it down before it would turn.'

'We could organise a bucket chain for seawater.'

'We have no buckets, and would you go tramping through all that mud?'

'I take your point, old man.'

'And this is the modern army,' the conductor went back to the bus and sat on the boarding step.

'Is that Mason's group down there along the point?'

'I do believe it is. And isn't that the Brig's car?'

'Good lord, yes. And it's coming this way.'

'Spread the men out, Neville. One every ten yards with their rifles at the aim. I'll go down and see what he wants.'

'Best let me go. You're better with the men than me.' Charlesworth went down the track before Christopher could argue. The Brigadier's car bumped up towards him and he saluted smartly as it came alongside him.

'Stand easy, Neville. No sign of the Hun, what?'

'None, Brigadier.'

'What's that awful stench?'

'A dead cow.'

'Somebody should bury it. Is Lutyens with you?'

'Yes, Uncle, he is.'

'You're particular friends, aren't you?'

'Yes.'

'Then you'll want to be the one to tell him. His wife's been injured in a bombing raid. He must go to her of course. Isn't she family in some distant way?'

'Your niece, my cousin,' Charlesworth said around a thickening tongue. 'How badly is Helen ... '

'Pretty poorly off. Take Lutyens to the station in my car. I'll take your bus. I've put Moxon in charge, Hatwood looks to have been drinking. Can't abide the fellow.'

'It's Mason actually.'

'Hatwood's the drinker. You see to Lutyens, I'll see to the cow. Can't let you accompany him to London. Need you here. Incidentally, Neville, congrats. You and Lutyens have been made up to First Lieutenants. Odd how good and bad tidings travel in tandem, what?'

'Yes ... yes it is.'

'Gad what a stench.' Brigadier Marchbayne-Cleverley sniffed emotionally. 'Cousin, eh?' The sun formed a golden halo around his polished boots as he stared out over the mudflats. 'The tide's on the turn. We've had our retreats, now it's all forward.'

'Yes,' said Charlesworth without understanding.

THREE: HELEN

There was pain and drifting.

There was bustle and astringents and crisp white linens beyond her closed lids, gurneys moved along corridors and women spoke with hushed clarity to men whose baritones were clipped and decisive, a world apart yet paralleling her own. The bed held her in thrall, both comforting and restrictive. Sometimes there was sunlight on the cream wall; other darker times, shadows and dim blue light.

Adrift in medication she saw parades of faces, some scrubbed and wholesome and efficient; others familiar, lined and concerned. One of them was very dear to her and she loved it when it hovered over her, missing it desperately in the dark times when she was alone and the parallel world slept. Once she watched the dear face sleep in the chair beside the bed, the long lowered lashes throwing spiked shadows down the tanned, freckled cheeks. His name would be very dear to her when she remembered it. All in good time ...

The gaunt woman who was her mother in that previous time came to block out some of the cream wall with bouquets and clacked knitting needles as she kept vigil. And father, grey and calm, would talk of things dimly remembered in the hope she would respond. The need to try made her melancholy.

In the quiet languorous times the cockpit of her mind was scented by sundried grass and summer flowers. When pain scalded her into screaming spasm she was pursued by King Harold's English dead until a plunging needle gave her dreamless peace.

And as she slept she mended.

CHAPTER THREE

'In England they're filled with curiosity and keep asking, "Why doesn't he come?".
Be calm. Be calm. He's coming! He's coming! When the British Air Force drops two or three thousand kilograms of bombs, then we will in one night drop 150, 250, 300 or 400 thousand kilograms. When they declare that they will increase their attacks on our cities, then we will raze their cities to the ground. We will stop the handiwork of these night air pirates, so help us God!'

Adolf Hitler

When that man is dead and gone ...
Some fine day the news will flash,
Satan with a small moustache
Is asleep beneath the tomb.

Popular song.

'Hitler's tree reaches as high as the sky – but it grows only towards ruin.'

Benito Mussolini

ONE: FRANK

1 September 1940

'Right, the M.O.'s passed you fit for punishment and duty. None of you's got the clap, mother's milk on your lips or queer-corns on your backsides. That means you're mine.'

Five naked men stood to attention in the cold tiled room. The high barred window cut the sunlight into yellow stripes and laid them across the concrete floor, bright without warmth.

'You are no longer soldiers. You are prisoners. Prisoners are not *men*. They have no rights. *You* have no rights. Like nuns we're a silent order. Prisoners do not talk. Ever.'

Frank felt goosebumps grow on his limbs.

'Everything here is done at the double. You eat, work, think, march and defecate at the double.' The Provost-Marshal had white hair, a pencil moustache and a baton he slapped against his palm. Frank had a dark blue bruise across his ribs and a long welt on his upper thigh. He had been slow climbing from the Black Maria. The Scot on his right bled from the nose. He had 'fallen' when the escort had run him across the square.

'We like hard men here. There are two kinds of hard men. Those who take all we hand out and love it. And those who don't take stick from nobody. Which kind are you, I wonder?' The Provost-Marshal walked the line staring into their faces, his eyes like peeled eggs with blue yolks. 'Hard men are my meat.'

The thin soldier on Frank's left tried not to weep. His knees were raw from kneeling on concrete with a sandbag held above his head. He had sat on his cot without permission.

'You are alone. The man next to you doesn't exist. He is deaf and mute. *You* are deaf and mute. You only hear orders and you obey them immediately without question.'

A nerve jumped in Frank's cheek. Cooling sweat found the razor nick in his shaven scalp.

A tattooed prisoner swayed until a baton in the kidneys straightened him up with a muffled gasp.

'Talking earns you bread and water. Anyone with a dirty cell gets bread and water. A second infraction of the rules earns you water. Not just to drink either.' The Provost-Marshal tasted his words like game meat. 'Show them, Staff.'

Frank was smashed against the wall by a solid jet of water from the fire hose. It played down the line, bowling the men over like skittles.

'Stand still there.'

Gasping and frozen, the prisoners reformed their line.

'Outside. At the double.'

The prisoners ran down the corridor and out into the square.

'Ten circuits. Commence.'

'Knees up there,' bawled a Staff Sergeant.

The Scot took a baton jab to the buttocks.

'Knees *up*!'

The fifth man was flabby and he waddled as fast as he could.

'Don't look at me. Eyes front.'

Frank ran behind the thin man. His bare feet pounded on gravel and he counted each burning footfall. There were four-hundred and twelve paces to the circuit and blood seeped between his toes when they were finally ordered to halt.

'You run like fairies. Have we got any girls amongst us? Wear high heels do we? Right, left *turn*. Left *turn*. Left *turn*. Stamp those heels there. *Stamp*.'

A cleaver chopped meat and the thin soldier lay prostrate.

'Stand still.'

'Atten … hut!'

Frank stopped himself from helping the man on the ground.

'Wise,' the Provost-Marshal's face was close to Frank's. 'He don't exist. There's only you, right?' the baton rested against his shrunken penis. 'Act the comedian and I'll have you jumping through hoops of fire.'

The sky revolved in both directions and came together behind the Provost-Marshal's head. The fine hairs on the nape of his neck shone like spun silver. Frank bit the inside of his cheek, willing himself not to nod or speak. *Think of beer with the bubbles rising into a head of froth. Think of Hampstead on a Bank Holiday when the fairground music drifts over the courting couples on the grass. Think of Peggy's legs under her skirt and the double jut of softness under her starched blouse. Think of Phyllis's shepherd's pie.* The face and the pressure on his manhood went away and there was just the boundary wall to look at.

'Inside. At the double.'

The cold building closed around them and they were herded into a shower room where they scrubbed off with lye soap under lukewarm jets. Blood and gravel washed down the sluice with the carbolic suds.

'We like our hard men to be clean.'

They dressed in coarse denim and the tattooed prisoner tore a nail on the hard rubber buttons. The boots they were issued were thick with dubbin.

'Double up. One, two ...'

Out in the yard they were lined up beside a concrete pit filled with red water.

'This is your playpen, hard men. Here's where you learn hard ways. Show 'em, Staff!'

'Sah!'

The Staff Sergeant pulled a rusted dustbin from the water.

'There's one for each prisoner. You clean them with wire wool and razor blades until they look like this,' the Provost-Marshal struck his baton against a shining, highly polished dustbin. 'That's inside and out. Shiny as a new pin. Right, get started.'

Frank's dustbin was almost thin enough to poke a finger through, it had been polished and rerusted so many times. *Twenty-eight days of this,* he thought. *Twenty-eight days and nights.*

The thin soldier still lay where he had fallen when they were paraded for a midday meal. Nobody looked at him as they doubled into the mess hall where the other prisoners ran on the spot in a queue.

'Mark time at the double.'

'Halt!'

Highly polished boots crashed in unison.

'Serve the meal, Staff.'

Cabbage soup was slopped in their billy trays, then a dollop of grey mashed potato alive with eyes, a cob of dry bread and a scoop of lentil pap. The metal tables were bolted to the floor and there were no chairs.

'On the command, kneel ... *kneel!*'

They ate at the kneel in enforced silence with greasy bakelite spoons and watched by the Messing Staff who made certain no shoulders drooped, no mouths moved in conversation. Several prisoners received whacks to the soles of their boots.

Doubled outside, they sluiced off the billy trays under a cold standpipe and cleaned off the grease in a sand tray.

'You four stand still. Company, right-turn. Double!'

Frank saw that the thin soldier had disappeared. There was a smear of blood and mucus where he had lain. The other prisoners were shrugging on backpacks filled with house-bricks and taking sandbags from a pile. They formed up, doubling on the spot, the sandbags above their heads.

'Now you new hard men. Now you earn the victuals His Majesty was pleased to feed you. Double them off, Staff.'

'Sah!'

Doubled back to the concrete pit they worked on the dustbins. Their knuckles cracked and rustflakes got into the cuts. Their palms blistered and stung when they burst. Batons prodded them when they flagged and the sun slowly crossed the sky to fall into the west.

'Work party, stop ... *work!*'

Frank straightened wearily, thinking of eels and mash and hot parsley sauce.

'On the spot-double. Loosen up there. Swing them legs. Knee yourselves in the chin. One, two, one, two. Ace, King, Queen, Jack. Hup two three ...'

They ran on the spot for fifteen minutes before being

doubled to their cells in A Block.

'Now it's boots,' said the Staff Sergeant. 'I want 'em shining. Dirty boots earn a Number One Diet. Bread and water. You ain't got matches so you can't burn 'em shiny. Elbow grease is the way. No hot spoons and other barrack tricks. Just spit and polish. Right, fall to.'

Crosslegged on the floor they buffed away for three hours. Stood to attention they were given mugs of unsweetened cocoa made with water. Nobody's boots were good enough for the Provost-Marshal.

'Four o'clock reveille for these prisoners, Staff. No breakfast.'

'Sah!'

'Lights out in five minutes. Right, bang 'em up.'

'In cells – march. One, two, halt!'

The cell held a steel cot and a china pot. There was a single blanket, the thin mattress stank of naptha and there was no pillow.

The doors clanged shut.

Frank's muscles trembled and his kneecaps jerked with a life of their own. His head throbbed and the cell rippled. He had to sit on the cot to undress. Sleep would not come. Huddled under the coarse blanket, Frank heard the thin soldier cry out for his father.

'Talking earns water,' bawled the Duty Staff. 'Take him down, Staff.'

'No, Christ, please, please ...'

Think of yourself, son. There's only you. Only you ...

The racketing screams became clanging bells, bringing Frank into a new day.

The prisoners shaved with a shared dull razor under strict supervision and worked on their boots. The stiff denim cut at Frank's crotch and he feared he would have an ulcer there before long.

'Your boots are filthy, hard man,' the Staff Sergeant told the thin soldier who had slept all night in wet clothes.

'Number One Diet. Punishment Block for you. The rest of you, double off.'

Frank, the Scot, Tweedledum and the tattooed man ran into the dawn with empty stomachs.

'Get them knees up. Wet them shirts there. Let's see some sweat and pluck.'

Their highly polished boots grew a patina of dust.

'Double, double, double. Right, draw backpacks and sandbags.'

They sweated around the parade ground until noon.

It was Sunday. After a church service there was Spam floating in the soup and tea instead of water. It was the last day any of them saw meat in the glass-house.

On the third day Tweedledum clutched his throat and fell forward into the rusty water. He had vomited up his breakfast during the morning drill and been hosed down for it before they made him clean up the mess with his own toothbrush. Nobody moved as air caught in his blouse and rolled him on his back. Thick streaks of rust plastered his face and ran into his gaping mouth. His lips were as grey as scars. The bloated head rolled under water and Tweedledum's trousers ballooned, raising his boots above the thick red scum.

The thin soldier refused to notice as he assiduously scrubbed at his dustbin. The Scot watched the Staff Sergeant to see what he would do and the tattooed man half-straightened, his fists working his arm muscles.

'Nobody told you to move,' smoke from the Staff's cigarette drifted into the tattooed man's face.

Frank's dustbin shook as he gripped it too hard.

The daft basket's gonna lip the screw, maybe give him a moody dig. If he starts he won't be able to stop. Hitting a Staff earns you a rope's end and ten years. Killing one earns you burial inside the glass-house walls. But somebody's got to do something, don't they? Just don't let it be me.

'He couldn't sink if he tried. More front on him than Mae West. Working our ticket are we, lard-arse?' The Staff's cigarette butt hissed as it hit the viscous water and floated near Tweedledum's head.

The smell from the last drift of smoke haunted Frank's palate, almost sexual in its intensity. He had not smoked since they charged him, more days ago than he cared to recall.

Silence makes your brain into mush. When you talk you know you're here. You can hear yourself being alive. If you talk it's punishment. If you just look like you want to it's dumb insolence. There are no winners here, even the screws double everywhere like we do. We're all in the glass-house, and there's no way out except in a pine box or when they've made you into a toy soldier with mashed spuds for brains, only anxious to jump-doggy-jump for any bastard with rank.

But I still wouldn't have gone out into that potato field.

But how long before I will, with a smart salute and a click of the heels and a sunny, 'Yes please, sir. Kiss your dirty socks if it wouldn't be a privilege, sir'? Don't look at the fat man in the water. Watch the tin brighten as you scrub. Only you, remember?

The clang of the Staff's baton on the dustbin brought Frank back into the yard.

'I'm talking to you. Stand still.'

Frank blinked at the Staff.

'You, haul him out.'

Frank had to think twice before he understood. He waded out into the water and caught the seat of Tweedledum's trousers, turning him face up. The sound he made was like singing under water.

Phyllis had said the old dad had made a noise like that at the end. I never knew him, more's the pity.

'You with the snake and the fat lady on your forearm. Help get lard-arse landed. You, you Highland Queen, get his legs.'

They hauled the fat prisoner onto the concrete and Frank started to loosen his collar.

'Leave him you no-hope bastard. Have him away to the M.O. at the double.'

We can't, Staff. He's too big, too wet, too flabby to get a good hold of. Can't you see?

'You're all runners, hard men. Good at having it away on your toes, right? Now double away or your feet won't touch on your way to Punishment Block,' bawled the Staff, rapping his baton at their heels.

Frank dug his nails into slippery denim, heaving the slack chest up against his own. *Get his legs, Jock. Before we all go a purler and end in a heap.* His boots struck sparks as he loped forward, willing them all towards the main blockhouse. The Scot and the tattooed man had a thick thigh apiece and their necks were corded with effort as they managed a clumsy gallop. The fat head banged against Frank's chin and the underwater singing came in weak jerks as the big soft ribcage rose and fell inside his arms. *He's got dugs like an old fat cow. This ain't a man's chest, you could carve hamfat from it.*

'Halt. Stand still!' The Staff snapped a salute at the Provost-Marshal and slammed to attention.

'What's this, Staff? A holiday camp obstacle race? Are my hard men having a go for the packet of fags on the prizes shelf?'

'Passed out, sir. Fell in the pit.'

'Working his ticket, is he? Wants a sugar-tit to suck on in a nice soft hospital bed, does he? Have Mother Goose read to him?'

Pale vomit trailed over Frank's sleeve in a harsh hiccup. Tweedledum's scalp was old putty under the fouled hair. Only his earlobes had colour, a fleshy purple.

The Staff said nothing. There were roundels of sweat under his armpits.

'Stand him up, hard men. Let's see this slacker.'

The thick thighs were lowered and they rolled under the wet denim as the flaccid legs buckled. Frank staggered under the weight of the big torso before releasing his grip, fearing he would sit down with the fat man, sure it would earn him a punishment demerit. Tweedledum's head cracked against the gravel and the jaw gaped.

'Rust poisoning, is it? Or does he want to be a Red Indian? We don't go in for amateur theatricals here, do we, Staff?' The Provost-Marshal was enjoying himself at the prisoners' expense.

'No, sir.'

'No, Staff, and it's no grinning matter. All right, give this hard man to the vet. Maybe he'll decide he's a red setter and send him over the obstacle course in full pack to see him wag his tail. Double him away, hard men.'

The outer surgery had green lino, cream walls and was thick with iodine fumes. The prisoners propped Tweedledum on a hard chair and held him upright with the flat of their palms until orderlies came for him.

'One away to you, Staff. M.O.'s Parade toot-sweet.'

'Not 'til the M.O. signs an Intake Docket. He's still yours 'til then, Staff.' An orderly peeled back an eyelid and touched a finger against the fat neck. 'Get the M.O., Staff,' he told his partner.

'Sick, is he?'

'Sick?' The orderly closed the grey eyelids. 'Not any more, he's dead.'

'That's an officer's decision, not yours,' said the Staff.

'Order him to double then, see where it gets you.'

The Staff nibbled his lower lip. 'Outside, hard men. Double.'

In the lee of the Punishment Block he halted the prisoners and lit cigarettes for them. 'Anybody see anything they shouldn't?'

The prisoners smoked in silence.

'The Provo'll want to know, so tell me first.'

Silence.

Frank held the fragrant Virginia smoke in his lungs, warily leaking it through his teeth. *You run him at the double carrying all that lard and a sandbag above his head, giving him a baton across his backside when he couldn't keep up, and you ask us did we see anything? We're tarbabies, mister. We don't say nothing.*

The tattooed man ate smoke hungrily, nothing in his face. The Scot could have been contemplating a pint in a Gorbals pub or allowing his thoughts to drift with loch water.

'He'll want to know if you have any complaints against his staff. Any niggles you might wanna pass on if you get through the gates at the end of your glass-house bird.'

'No, Staff,' said the tattooed man.

'You?'

'I'll not greet,' said the Scot, adding, 'Staff,' in a hurrying gout of smoke.

'Your second time with us, eh, Highland Queen. You know how it goes with us. And you, hard man?'

Frank laid ash into his palm and shook his head.

'I'll hear from you, Mister,' said the Staff.

Frank looked him in the eye. 'No, Staff.' His voice sounded as weak as an atrophied muscle.

'Drop your butts in the sluice. Right, double outside.'

The thin soldier did not look up from his dustbin when they returned to the pit. His eyes were sly and bright. He was the only one with clean boots.

He's learning, thought Frank. *No, he's learned.*

TWO: HELEN

7 September 1940

The watery autumn sun cast shadows from the plain trees through the hospital window where they dappled the ceiling with shifting patterns of light and dark. Helen concentrated on finding images there, to block out what was happening to her body. Each time the wind shook the leaves in dance she found new things. An old, bent man became a rabbit with a wrinkled nose, a rhinoceros butted a dinosaur and a bird hovered on the light globe as girls jumped a rope.

Salt, mustard, vinegar, pepper. I skipped like that to make my pigtails bob and slap my shoulders like plaited hawsers. Green memories as soaring as birds on a thermal. Slashing at cow parsley with a stick in a bowered lane where wild horseradish, docks and nettles bobbed in the hedgerows, as mysterious and tropical as the imagination could make them before hunger took me home for tea in the nursery with nanny.

'All over, Mrs Lutyens.'

The probing fingers withdrew and Helen brought her thighs together with a light slap. He had touched her more intimately than her husband and his sleek professionalism made no difference to the profound revulsion she felt, nor could she rid herself of the growing notion that he had branded her in some undefined yet indelible manner. The thought was both compelling and revolting. His clinical internal examination would abide and survive all the bath oil and scented soap in Harrods.

I do not like thee Doctor Fell ...

'I am extremely pleased with you,' the surgeon said. 'You're a remarkably resilient young woman.' He wore latex finger stalls like obscene little hats.

As Helen sat up on the bed to tie her robe he dropped them into a soiled-dressing bag and scrubbed his hands white over the sink.

The reason why I cannot tell ...

The surgeon towelled off and patted a sideburn; straightened his university tie in the mirror.

Do you know why I dislike you, sleek surgeon? With your glossy hair and the dimple in your cheek deep enough to bury a thimble in? You violated me without a second thought, with the arrogance of a Norman Warlord bedding a Saxon shepherdess on her wedding eve, claiming his ancient and inalienable right as Lord Protector of her bridegroom's villeinage. Does the Hippocratic Oath give you the rights of a conqueror? A German bombardier took the embryo of my baby and you have invaded me with your antiseptic rubberised fingers. Has your sterile touch scoured away my fertility as surely as your surgery saved my life? I need to know, but not from you.

The surgeon smiled over his half-glasses. 'I'm sure you have a thousand questions, Mrs Lutyens.' He sat in the chair where Christopher had slept and crossed an ankle neatly. 'Most women would rather be kept in ignorance of what is happening inside them, I think you are more sensible than that.'

Don't patronise me, sleek surgeon. Who is it who has kept us on pedestals and in ignorance? Who taught us to blush and vapour at the thought of anything as indelicate as physical functions? Don't confuse honest shyness with prudery, you goat of a man. Society's sexual mores are more hidebound than any class barrier mankind has erected. My mother is a lifelong subscriber, so I know. She had to let nanny tell me what was happening to me when I had my first period at fourteen. She poured tea for her circle of friends and left me frightened and blubbing in my room with poor unmarried nanny trying to make me understand with her limited vocabulary and her even more profound ignorance. We all learn somehow, but not from you.

'Your monthly cycle will be erratic for a while, but it will settle down, and you'll menstruate as regularly as you did before your injury. You'll make babies in time. You have a lovely pelvic arch.'

'Have I?' *You make me sound like a fine example of chemical architecture. I shall giggle or weep if you keep this up.*

'I've had a word with your husband. He understands there will have to be a period of abstinence from the physical side of your marriage. Conjugation over the next several weeks would be harmful. He's a splendid chap and understood.'

Helen nodded, biting on laughter. *Conjugation. Now making love is an inflected form of a latin verb. You silly, pompous man. I feel so much better, perhaps I should thank you after all?*

'Christopher would,' she said.

'I've written to your general practitioner, of course. But any problems, any at all, please don't hesitate to contact me here.'

'You mean ...?' *Does he mean ...*

'Yes,' the surgeon's smile widened to show big irregular teeth. 'You can go home if you wish.'

'Today?'

'Today. Your husband is outside. I'm sure you would like to brush your hair and put on a lick of make-up before I send him through?'

'Yes, yes I should.' *How do you know such things are important? Or are you patting the little lady on the head? Keeping up your patient's morale so she'll remain compliant and spread the gospel according to the medical profession. Trust thy surgeon for he will make us all well.*

'Thank you,' said Helen.

The surgeon stood in the doorway and leaf shadows danced on his face. 'For what? You're the one who got well. I'm only a poor mechanic. I wish all my patients had your will to survive. Take plenty of bedrest if you tire, my last direct order.'

Helen promised. 'And I shan't dance on top of a grand piano, not for a while at least.'

'I thought that sort of thing went out with the flapper and syncopated melodies. Goodbye, Mrs Lutyens,' and the surgeon was gone.

'I think I misjudged you,' Helen said aloud, half-sorry she had thought so ill of him. 'Now you hag, let's have you looking attractive for darling Christopher.' She stuck her tongue out at her reflection in the mirror above the sink and made a face at her limp hair. 'Rats' tails and tangles. I'm so thin in the face. Poor Christopher. No bedroom romps and this morning-after-the-night-before face.' She pinched her cheeks to make them blush and began painting her mouth with the palest lipstick she possessed, anxious not to look as though her face had bled to death to redden her lips.

The taxi sped towards Bethnal Green and Christopher said: 'I hope you approve of the house.'

'But how did you know I wanted to stay in the East End?'

'You talked of nothing else when you were under sedation. All I had to do was listen. The W.V.S. want you back when you're well enough, and I thought I'd organise things so that you were on the spot. If you do change your mind ... well, I can easily find you somewhere to stay in Somerset, near me.'

'I ought to do that, like a dutiful wife.'

'No, you've set your heart on being here at the heart of things. And I don't know where they'll send me, and probably at a moment's notice.'

Helen squeezed Christopher's hand. 'Darling dodo,' she said, still seeing him in her hospital room with flowers and chocolates and the new outdoor coat he had brought in for her. It was thick tailored Scotch tweed and had a wonderful high collar. She had twirled in it with sheer exuberance, only to make herself sick and dizzy. She wore it now and was comforted by its weight and warmth. 'How did you manage to buy it without clothing coupons?'

'I met this awful chap in a pub who gloried in the name of Winkle. If his lapels had been wider, any strong wind would have carried him away. It's probably black market, I hope you don't mind?'

'It might even be stolen, how delicious,' Helen did not mind. 'You know, this is a terrible waste of a taxi.'

'You mean I should have brought you by bus?'

'No, you darling clod. Taxi. Boy and girl?' Helen snapped her fingers. 'Does nothing occur to you?'

Christopher looked haunted. 'I thought ...'

'Christopher Lutyens, if you don't kiss me immediately, I shall get out and walk.' Later, breathless, she said, 'How long before you have to go back?' She wiped lipstick from his mouth with her handkerchief.

'Let's not talk about it.'

'I'd rather. We've lost so much time and that precious commodity has a way of running out on us. I don't want to waste a second of our being together.'

'Forty-eight hours, Helen. Brigade's been awfully decent and I can't cut up about it.'

'I shall thank the Brigadier in a long letter. The old duffer is awfully sweet, but very absent-minded when it came to the girls in the family. He would insist on calling me Neville. Once, on my birthday, he bought me a box of toy soldiers and some icing-sugar regimental badges. Neville was as sick as a parrot. He got a fishing rod and some rather threadbare butterflies in a display case.'

'That would put his nose out of joint.'

'He is a prima-donna, isn't he? But I do adore him. You?'

'He's been a brick.' Christopher relived the shock of hearing about Helen's ordeal with the ripe smell of putrefaction in his nostrils. The interminable drive down country lanes and the slow train journey to the capital, unable to see out of the windows because of the thick protective webbing glued to them; unable to read in the dim blue light and listening to the wheels repeating: Helen is dead, Helen is dead ... 'Sorry, what?'

'This is it, guv'nor.' There was three and ninepence on the clock.

Christopher paid off the cab and walked Helen into the small square of redbrick houses with odd turreted roofs and eaves. A small boy in ragged trousers and braces over a grimy vest bowled a hoop around the central garden. The iron railings had gone for scrap to help the war effort. Christopher knocked at a peeling door and it was thrown open by a woman in rusty black who grinned toothlessly.

'Welcome home, missus.'

'Mrs Tolliver, but you're supposed to be in Chislehurst!' said Helen.

'Never you mind that, ducks. Here, Mr L., you get her into the front room and I'll bring a nice pot of tea through. Give us them bags, you see to yourself.'

Margie-girl waved from the kitchen. 'Hello, Miss. Mr L. bought me new ribbons and 'e says we can have a cat.'

'Christopher.' Helen was escorted into a small living room furnished with her few pieces and some she did not recognise. She sat in an overstuffed chair when Christopher had taken her coat. 'Christopher explain.'

'First tea.' Mrs Tolliver brought a tray in and sat herself down to pour. 'I'll sit with yer, cause it's yer first day back, after that, me and Margie-girl got our own rooms upstairs, and we'll see yer all right, no fussing, right, Mr L.?'

'Quite right.'

'Here, no sugar, the way you likes it. Good thing with rationing. Means we got a bit spare for baking and Christmas and that,' said Mrs Tolliver in her fierce, direct way, trying not to cry. 'We'll get you back up to scratch, see we don't. When we seen you brought outta that building all scratched up and . . . well, fair broke our hearts, me and Margie, and we swore then we'd do right by yer. We got a safe basement. Mr L. had workmen put iron bars all up the walls and round the ceiling when he seen how the shelter out back was full of water, so we'll be all right whatever bleeding Hitler does, pardon my French.'

'I hope you approve,' said Christopher as Mrs Tolliver leaned to light his cigarette. 'It seemed so right.'

Helen blinked back tears. 'Yes. But what about Chislehurst?'

'You can have my share. You had to sing an hymn just to get a slice of bread and a bowl of gravy, and the rules! They had an 'undred a day and double on Sundays. The Sally Ann may be God's army, but they ain't mine or Maggie's. Huns who pray, that's what they are.'

Helen's laugh rang like silver on crystal and then she was crying, her teacup dribbling into her saucer. Christopher held her, his own eyes prickling uncomfortably.

'Had to 'appen,' said Mrs Tolliver. 'Coming home always does that.' She drank tea with her little finger cocked. 'You're happy, ain't you, ducks?'

Helen choked and sniffed. 'You'll never know how much.'

'Told yer, didn't I?' Mrs Tolliver stood up. 'How about a nice hot bath? Me and Margie-girl shared our reg'lation five inches of water, so you got ten coming. I'll run it now, you ring if'n yer wants anything.'

Helen held Christopher close to whisper: 'Fifteen inches. If we shared, dodo.'

'Mrs Tolliver would not approve.'

'Poo. She'll think you're supervising the invalid. And we are married.' Helen flicked Christopher's nose with a forefinger. 'And I should like to see you without that damned uniform for a change.'

Christopher unbuckled his Sam Brown. 'Very well, you hussy. I suppose I must humour the patient, mustn't I?'

'Outrageously and constantly, dodo.'

'You know we can't actually ... '

Helen held Christopher's face. 'But I can make *you* happy. My contribution to our forty-eight hours and this darling house.'

'Helen ... '

'I know, dodo. I know.'

THREE

For the first time in days the skies were cloudless over Southern England and Fighter Command awaited the Luftwaffe's arrival. During the early afternoon coastal radar began picking up large concentrations of bombers with their fighter escorts crossing the Channel towards Kent and Surrey. Expecting massive raids on their airfields and installations, the R.A.F. squadrons scrambled every available Hurricane and Spitfire, but the German formations overflew Biggin Hill, Kenley and West Malling to turn along the Thames Estuary towards the London Docks. Wave after wave of Dorniers and Heinkels laid down massive patterns of incendiaries on dockland and the East End of London. Huge fires began to rage and the Fire Service fought them with grim determination. The Luftwaffe had changed their tactics and their prime target was the civilian population of London. It was the first day of a Blitz that was to continue unabated for nine months ...

FOUR: PHYLLIS

Far, faint thunder made Phyllis look up from her ironing.

She thought first of Harry and Robert and then of her washing hanging out to dry in the garden. She hurried outside, where her bedsheets hung in bright sunlight, and touched them to her face, inhaling their freshness. Harry sat on the Anderson shelter making dust pies with a bucket and spade and Robert slept in his pram. The sky was clear and yet the thunder persisted to the east of Uplands Hill, counterpointing the clank of shunting rolling stock and the lazy croon of the Rhode Island Reds in their chicken run.

'And you lot can lay eggs as soon as you like,' Phyllis scolded, 'the money you cost me in food and grit.'

Doris leaned from her kitchen window. 'Funny weather, Phyl.' She watched the sky anxiously.

'That's all we need,' Phyllis muttered. 'You hiding yourself in a cupboard at the first sign of a drop of thunder. You frighten the boys with your moaning and carrying on. I'm not having them getting as daft as you are.'

'What, ducks?'

'Nothing.'

Fluffy contrails marked the flawless blue vault, random scribbles of high-flying aircraft. Doris's upturned face was as bleached as her hair.

'That's not thunder. It's bombs.' Doris turned to call Jack before slamming her window closed.

'I'll give you bombs.' Phyllis gathered her washing without haste, too cross about being inconvenienced to feel frightened. *Doris could be scared for everbody. Jack ought to put her across his knee.*

In overlapping sequence, sirens sounded from the eastern boroughs to be drowned by the local one on the Police Station roof. Doris came out into the garden.

'Come on, Jack. You going down the shelter, Phyl?'

'Stop pulling at me. I don't want my sheets dragging in the dirt.'

'But it's a raid.'

'I don't care if it's half-time at Arsenal. Don't truck up my washing,' said Phyllis, thinking: *and you could do with being a bit more houseproud instead of worrying about your plucked eyebrows and your stocking seams. Without make-up you look like a startled chicken about to lay a bloody egg, which is more than that lazy lot down the end of the garden do. I reckon those sirens put them off laying. And Harry's got himself dirty, he's as black as coal, he'll have to be washed before he goes down the shelter. Blooming silly war, sirens going at all hours of the day and night and we've never even seen a bomb over this way, not that I can complain about that. Harry can't be that black, surely?*

Doris hopped from foot to foot, close to babbling.

'Hurry up, Jack. They're coming, they're coming, and you got to see if there's spiders down the shelter ...'

'And sex them I s'pose?' Jack scratched his chest, 'before I put 'em out of their misery. Give us your washing, Phyl. You get the kids down.'

Jack may be a plodder, but at least he don't get aereated like some. 'Harry Penny, what have you done to yourself?' Phyllis reached to lift her son down. His whole body was alive with insect life. They crawled in his hair and eyes and into his open mouth. 'You've sat in an ants' nest, you poor love. That calls for a strip-down wash in the sink.'

'Not now, you can't, not now ...'

'He can't go down the shelter like that. Don't be dafter than you usually are, Doris May.' Phyllis held Harry at arm's length as she walked him into the scullery and stood him on the draining board.

'Mind they don't eat him,' said Jack, listening to the sirens wind down into an eerie silence. The drone of aircraft came in light, monotonous waves and the windows rattled from distant concussions. 'Somebody's catching a packet. I'll get her and Robert down the shelter. Don't take all day, Phyl.'

'Hitler can get along without me for a bit, I'm sure,' said Phyllis, reassured by Jack's hand on her shoulder. 'You go on, love.' She shook Harry's clothes over the sink and watched ants wash down with the running water. Harry spat them from his mouth and refused to cry.

'I'm a big boy,' he said.

'Mummy's little soldier, that's you.'

'Is ants Germans?'

'No love, they're on our side, much good may they do us,' Phyllis felt her stomach heave as the sashes moved in their frames. 'Now, let's get them socks off before they nibble your toes.'

'Bang,' said Harry. 'Is God moving his furniture?'

'That's right, that's what he's doing.' *If there was a God this wouldn't be happening. Men start wars and women have to suffer it. I hope I don't get buried and can't reach the children. Come on, God. Send them planes elsewhere. Anywhere. Not here, not here ... I'd smoke if I thought I could keep one in my mouth.* 'There's a nice clean boy. Let's go and see Uncle Jack in the shelter, shall we?'

As Phyllis crossed the garden her hair seemed to scrape the sky.

Not here, anywhere but here ...

FIVE: CHRISTOPHER

Helen's mouth moved with his shuddering contractions and she held him until he limply withdrew.

'There, dodo, there ... '

Christopher knew she would taste of salt and peppermint

if he kissed her. Instinct stayed him. She had given unselfishly and wanted nothing back.

'That was ... ' he sought a word.

'Natural?'

'Yes.'

Borrowed light from a chink in the bedroom curtains touched the crown of her head, hiding her lazy smile in backlit shadow. The fine grain of her shoulders glowed with pale fire and glistened with dampness. Helen's hands rested on Christopher's hips, keeping the memory of her recent attentions alive through her fingertips. She ran a nail along his thigh and brushed her moist lips against his neck.

Christopher lit two cigarettes and passed one up. 'You weren't taught that at Roedean.'

Smoke wreathed in the dusty shaft of sunlight.

'The netball mistress believed in cold showers and gooseberry bushes. I once had a crush on our dorm captain, but she knew less than I did. Aren't you glad, dodo?'

'Very. I'm jealous of anybody you share anything with. Ever.'

'I'm glad.'

'Good.'

'Don't look so fierce, you'll give me the giggles. And when you frown you get a deep hole between your eyebrows. Most unbecoming.' Helen snuggled and her right breast lay heavily on Christopher's pectoral.

'You must be tired. Why don't you take a nap?'

'Not whilst you're here, dodo. I'll sleep when you've gone.'

'But I like to hold you when you're sleeping.'

'Well, I shan't indulge you. Not that way anyway.'

'Hussy.'

'Yes, isn't it delicious?' Helen stifled a yawn. 'I won't sleep forever and ever and ever.'

'I'm sleepy.'

'Then sleep, you laggard. Men have no endurance. It's inbreeding that does it. Out of uniform you've all got clay feet.'

'And you know all about such things?'

'Women are older than time, only men are born young

enough to be gauche and spotty and callow. But you wouldn't know that, you're only a man, poor dodo.'

'I'll learn to live with that.'

Helen kissed Christopher's wrist and ash dusted the counterpane. 'See you do. You and I will make beautiful babies, you'll see.'

'Your mind bounces about more erratically than a shuttlecock.'

'Bouncy, bouncy,' Helen moved her breast against Christopher's chest. 'You hate it, don't you?'

'I'm not capable of such a monumental lie, darling girl.'

'Honest Luytens, doyen of the dodos.'

Christopher covered Helen's mouth. 'What's that?'

'Sirens? An air-raid in daylight?' Helen leaned up on an elbow and breathed smoke at the drawn curtains. 'They're coming closer. We'd best go down to the celler.'

'Do we have to? It's so comfortable ... '

The curtains shook themselves and swept out from the rail in a straight line and a window pane snapped across with a dry crack. A small pyramid of glass dropped on the lino and a profound roar shook the house on its foundations. The bed swung aside and rucked the carpet as it swung into the wall. Christopher tasted sulphur and saline. He had bitten his tongue. A blast of air stirred the leaves of the aspidistra and the curtains slowly settled against the window.

Christopher got a foot to the floor and wrapped Helen in the counterpane as he scooped her off the bed. She weighed nothing as he waded through glue across a tilted floor, his sense of balance impaired by blast and fear for his wife's safety. The door opened too slowly and he banged a deltoid on the architrave. Helen snatched his dressing gown from behind the door before it slammed of its own accord. In the hallway, Mrs Tolliver was holding onto the banister rail as she tried to put on a slipper one-handed. Margie-girl held a rag doll and forgot to walk downstairs when she saw Christopher's nakedness. Her mouth formed a big O of awe.

A million tin trays ground against the roof as slates slid over the eaves.

Christopher heard himself shout orders as he bore into

Mrs Tolliver, forcing her down towards the cellar. A picture of hollihocks in an English garden swung on the wall like a pendulum before it jumped from its hook and bounced down the stairs ahead of Margie-girl. A portrait of Uncle Bertram turned itself to the wall with a flip and a bowl of artificial flowers grinned into two pieces, scattering the silk blooms across the floor. There was a strong gagging smell of sewage and mortar on the lower landing where the manhole cover had jumped from its housing.

Christopher pushed the girl and the woman into the cellar and closed the steel door with his back, plunging them all into darkness.

Christ, I'm erect again. I thought funk had the opposite effect. Where's that gown? Christopher set Helen down and felt for it. His hand encountered Helen's midriff and upper thigh.

'The light's here somewhere.' Mrs Tolliver's sensible heel ground on Christopher's instep.

'Here,' Helen thrust the gown into Christopher's hand.

The world's falling apart above street level and here am I worrying about being unclothed. Christopher covered himself and pulled the lightcord. The 25-watt lamp cast shadows as it swung on its flex. Margie-girl's knuckles were in her mouth and she mewed around her fist until her grandmother moved in beside her and held her against her ample chest. The ground jumped as though struck by gigantic stone fists and tearing whistles came shrieking through the walls. *You never hear the one that kills you.* Christopher sat on the bunk bed next to the shivering Helen.

'Cold?'

Helen's smile was a dead grimace. 'Actually no. I'm terrified.'

'Not much longer, darling.'

They bowed together as a near miss rocked their shelter.

'Not much longer …'

Mrs Tolliver sang in a cracked voice and stroked Margie-girl's hair. '… the old Jerusalem's dead …'

'Not much longer ... '

The light flickered, dimmed and went out. They stayed in darkness until the All Clear sounded two hours later.

SIX: JACK

Young Harry sat on Phyllis's lap, his eyes fixed and dreamy as he struggled to stay awake whilst his brother slept, his eyes drooping and flaring with each wave of aircraft. The monotonous drone of engines was as pernicious as the tart fog from Doris's chain-smoked Senior Service. She pecked away at them, her arm clamped around Jack's biceps, her bony thigh pressed against his. Jack waved smoke away from Robert's sleeping face and said: 'Go outside if you got to eat nicotine all the time. It ain't hardly fair to the kids.'

'Just 'cause you don't smoke. You know the panel doctor said I got nerves.'

'And you'll do anything to prove him right, that it?'

'Give over, Jack, love.'

'Flipping give over, you'd get on a saint's nerves.'

'It's all right, Jack. Can't be much longer, can it?' said Phyllis. 'They look to be passing us over.'

'Don't say that. You're tempting fate,' Doris lit a fresh cigarette from her stub.

'And what're you tempting?' Jack said, feeling his slow anger rising like a rock from the sea. *You selfish, silly bitch. Why I stay with you is a mystery. No wonder your husband Johnny left you and went north. Now he's doing time in Durham Jail and thinks he's well off out of the Smoke away from you. Before we met, him and me drank in the Hen & Chicks and he told me he hid his money in his shirt-tails to keep you from finding it. I know I'm big and hairy and slow, and your pissy old mother thinks I'm King Kong unchained. Maybe I am, but I ought to get better than you. Look at Phyl there, your sister, and she's got more in her little finger than you've got in your whole skinny carcases. When she cooks it tastes of something. And when she takes care of a problem she takes care of it. She don't poodle about over a dozen light ales and hope it'll go away with her hangover. She gets on with life and looks like she's enjoying it. If I only had the words I'd take her off that Tommy and give her the time she deserves. And in bed she wouldn't be all self, self, self. I have to go down on my hands and knees for a bit of comfort on a Saturday night, and then it's over for you before I've got rightly settled down to it. Before I know it, you've rolled over, you're patting your curlers and reaching for another fag, with me lying there still up and strong and feeling all unnecessary with nowhere to go with it. We live together but this ain't living. Living in sin, don't make me chuckle?*

'Meaning what?' said Doris, ready to squabble to take her mind off her fear.

'Meaning you'll cough yourself to death before you're forty.'

'We live a long time in our family.'

A sunflare lit the interior of the shelter and the garden made an upward heave. The double crash came with a punch of warmed air. A second and a third brought the smell of cats and geraniums, then the stink of burning mulch.

'That was close, close ... '

'Up the road.' Jack tasted tar on his tongue and smelled gas. The droning aircraft retreated into the distance and they heard wind in the lupins and lime trees.

'I'm going for a look-see. It's time I was off anyway. Blimey, it's half-five,' Jack shook off Doris's grip.

'You can't leave us.'

'Got to. It's time I clocked on. We're s'posed to report the moment there's an incident. An air-raid to you. Well, I'm going now.' He paused in the doorway. 'You want anything from the house?'

'No.'

'Mind how you go, Jack, the All-Clear hasn't gone yet,' Phyllis rocked Harry backwards and forwards.

'Never worry, Phyl. I can see the smoke from here. They dropped the other side of the main road.' He winked and his right eye disappeared as his thick eyebrow descended. 'They can't get me, I'm wearing me magic bicycle clips.'

'Smells like they've hit a sewer,' said Doris.

'Knowing you you've spilled your scent in your lap. Teddah,' and Jack was gone.

'He never says nothing nice. Never,' pouted Doris.

'What man ever does?' asked Phyllis. 'Tommy wouldn't know a compliment if he fell over one.'

'It don't matter for you so much. You're married with kids. It's over for you.'

'Don't start on me, Doris May. So what if you're barren. Means you get all the fun without the responsibility. Kids would kill you.'

'And you're my *sister*.'

'If you can't be true to your own, you can't be true to no one, right?'

'You've got a mouth like a knife.'

'And you've got a bum like a pair of scissors. I wonder Jack don't cut himself giving you a squeeze. Put some flesh on you and come again.'

Standing outside, Jack grinned at the sky. *That Phyllis is a prize rucker,* he thought. *She can go through my pockets anytime.* He cycled towards the depot with sirens mourning all around him.

SEVEN: CHRISTOPHER

The house was normal apart from the smell of drains, a cracked ceiling and the broken window.

'At least we've still got gas.' Mrs Tolliver filled a kettle and lit the stove, firmly convinced than an infusion of *Thea sinensis* was the universal panacea for all the ills in the world. She cut a doorstep of bread and smeared it with precious jam for Margie-girl. 'There lambie-love, get that down yer.'

'She's tired out.' Helen smoothed a straggle of mousy hair from the girl's round forehead.

'Tired ain't dead and there's the blessing. Be dark soon, hope the lights come back on.'

'Can we still 'ave a cat, Miss?'

'We can have a cat.'

'Well he wouldn't take kindly to this milk.' Mrs Tolliver turned the bottle upside down. 'Curdled, and it was fresh delivered this morning.'

Christopher knotted his tie as he came into the kitchen. 'Must have been the blast.'

'I hopes you likes black tea then, Mr L. We've only got a small tin of condensed milk and I was saving that for a rainy day.'

'I'll go to the corner shop. If it's still standing,' Christopher said. 'I want some cigarettes.'

'He'll only have them rotten Turf or Airman, and they'll be under the counter.'

'Don't go, we'll have lemon tea,' Helen tried to keep her voice steady.

'Now when did we last see a lemon, ducks?' asked Mrs Tolliver.

'One sometimes forgets.'

'I know. Why don't you tuck up in bed and I'll bring your tea up, eh?'

'They got bananas down the greengrocers.' Margie-girl licked sticky fingers.

'They're plaster. For show, child. Hard to make kids understand.' Mrs Tolliver turned the gas down low. 'You get off, Mr L. We'll be all right.'

Christopher hurried into the street and stopped dead. Roof slates were scattered along the pavement and the big elm in the square had been toppled. It lay beside a deep crater big enough to drop a family saloon into. A woman swept glass into the gutter and two small boys searched for shrapnel. An old coster trundled a barrow past the square and as Christopher passed him he said: 'They got the Drum & Monkey. And the church and the flats. They wouldn't let me down our road. Nothing but rubble.' He patted the shivering black and white mongrel that lay in his barrow. 'Gyp got out but nobody else. It's all gone. All gone ... '

Christopher offered him his last cigarette.

'Don't use 'em. And where was your lot, eh? Where's your guns? They said they wouldn't get through no how. Well, that's a flipping whopper, and no mistake. Get out of it, you khaki ponce,' the coster spat onto the ground and heaved his barrow into motion. 'Come on, Gyp. Don't need nobody. It's all bleeding gorn ... '

Christopher realised he had heard no anti-aircraft fire during the air-raid. He picked his way over a demolished wall that had been blown into the street and came upon a tangle of water-hoses. Firemen stood around their fire appliances watching a row of shops burn. There was no pressure in the hydrant. The musical instruments in a pawn shop window made a surreal jigsaw against the flames within, and the torso of a tailor's dummy had been thrown up onto a window ledge, its 30/- ticket still pinned to its chest. Where the corner grocery had been was a gaping hole where a ruptured gas main belched flame.

Christopher stood at the hastily erected cordon and stared at the devastation, hardly recognising the location he had come to know well over the preceding days. There were corpses on the opposite pavement. Somebody had hastily covered them with what was to hand, a shop roller-blind, a run of bloody curtain and some cardboard.

'Stand back there, squire.' A warden in a filthy coverall carrying a folded deckchair ducked under the cordon and walked towards the line of bodies. On the bright striped deckchair lay a three-month-old baby. 'You looking for somebody? Best go down the wardens' post or the Town Hall later.'

'I came out for milk.'

The warden looked over the tiny corpse at Christopher without the need to speak. His eyes said it all.

'She's *going!*'

The façade of the pawn shop toppled into the road, scattering blazing timber and smoking brick amongst the dodging firemen.

Christopher turned away.

'That's it, chum. Leave it to us,' yelled the warden. 'Just give it to the bastards hot and hard when it's our turn. You hear me?'

Back at the house, Christopher stood in the hall and trembled for a millenium of seconds, shaken by a new and intense hatred, swamped by an ugly passion for revenge. *My child dead in the womb. My Helen only a block away from being torn to fragments. Margie-girl dead on stinking rubble, her sticky thumb clamped in a dead mouth. When it's our turn ... this war is no honourable cavalry charge in bright uniform on brave horses, sabre against pike, man against man.* As he stood there the sirens began to revolve air through their fans, building in pitch. When he opened his clenched fists his fingernails had left deep crescents in his sweating palms. The letter-box flap jiggled as high-explosive dropped three streets away.

In the shelter Mrs Tolliver sang her coster's lament for a dead donkey. '... the old Jerusalem's dead ... '

Helen took Christopher's hand, and as the steel door closed the electric light was miraculously restored. Mrs Tolliver's bun had slipped and a hairpin brushed her shoulder.

'Sing up, Mr L. They won't get us down.'

'No,' Christopher said with force. 'They won't.'

'She found the port,' Helen whispered. 'We've all had some.'

'Then pass it to the left,' Christopher's laugh was an angry bark. 'Form is everything.'

EIGHT: JACK

With darkness came the searchlights and the Luftwaffe squadrons.

The Gas Company lorry bumped over rubble at London Bridge and ran east towards the red hot sky. The Thames was a wide orange glitter where coal barges and lighters burned like funeral arks. Jack glimpsed a fireboat pumping water over them before the dark waterfront buildings closed in around them.

'Where're we supposed to go?' asked the driver, his upper lip coated with a frost of sweat. 'I ain't never been this far before.'

'Follow the flipping fire, you berk,' said Jack. 'It's flipping big enough, even for a tosspot berk like you.' Jack's size kept the driver silent, he had seen Jack bend horseshoes until they snapped without so much as a grunt. 'I can see to read the *Daily Worker's* racing tips, so you can find Paget's Wharf I reckon,' Jack added, turning the screw on the bourgeois twit of a driver who never voted or had an opinion on anything but the comic page in the *Daily Mirror. About time you thought of something more than seeing Jane's legs or whether or not you get two packets of salt in your Smith's crisps. Come the revolution, brother, you'll be mining salt, see if that don't wake your ideas up. There's more to life than gas pipes and poncing your wages back off your mother after you've done your lot at Harringay Greyhound Track.*

A fire appliance came out of nowhere and raced past the Tower of London. The ancient and sooty stone towers were starkly outlined against the burning warehouses on the Docks.

'There you go, schoolboy's dream, follow him. He knows what he's at.' *Look at that, the whole world's alight. This is too big to be scared of. You can feel the heat from here. There used to be workers' cottages along this stretch, now there's nothing.*

The Gas Company lorry went beneath a run of intersecting viaducts and swerved to avoid the fire appliance which had halted on the cobbled approach to a wharf. The spice warehouses blazed from end to end and cinnamon and cloves burned on the rolling updraught, scenting the wall of scurrying flame with all the fragrances of Arabia. Auxiliary firemen directed their hoses into the heart of the fire where the jetting water turned to steam, adding white vapour clouds to the hugely lit night sky.

'Where's Nero? He'd have loved fiddling to this,' said Jack.

'Who?' The driver was mesmerised by the conflagration.

Jack sneezed and his eyes smarted and prickled. Breathing the oxygen-starved air made him light-headed. Whirling orange motes fell all around the lorry and the firemen were retreating with their hands over their faces.

'Back out,' gasped Jack, his throat raw and burned. 'It's pepper. Burning pepper. Back off before it blinds us.'

The driver reversed and drove away under the viaducts. The orange light followed them along the black brick tunnels and out into an area of flattened buildings. Heavy Duty Rescue teams picked their way across a smoking sprawl of toppled brick and twisted girders that had been houses, stables and a manufactory. The skeleton of girders formed a rigid cat's cradle above the digging men. An old Chinese woman in a torn pink nightgown held the leg of a chair and a moquette cushion, all that remained of her home.

'Smell it?' said Jack, jumping to the ground. 'Gas. There's a ruptured main somewhere.' He made a mental plan of where the pipes would have lain as he worked out the building line. Kicking through the debris he found the manhole and levered it open. Blast had torn a hole beneath the broken pipe and coal gas billowed up at him. His hair stood away from his scalp. The fumes would be seeping into the debris and if there was anybody trapped in the cellars they would not last long.

'Bring the tools, Ken.'

The driver wandered over and handed Jack his tool bag when he had climbed into the manhole. He had to stand on the pipe and brace a knee against the crumbling masonry. The beam of his torch was lost in darkness when he flashed it down the hole. *One slip, Jack my lad, and it's Australia for you.* He heaved at the valve lever, using all his strength. It shifted slightly, then stuck fast, warped by blast.

'Get me some rags. I'll have to whack it. And damp them down, don't want no sparks.'

'Standard practice ... ' said Ken.

'Balls, you Turk. This whole lot'll go up without a good whack. You want my toe up your backside?'

'There's no water, Jack mate.'

'Then use the tea in your flask.' Jack's back muscles bunched under his soaking shirt. The lever turned another inch. *Come on, cockalorum, turn for Uncle Jack.*

Ken handed Jack a coverall leg. 'Waste of good tea.'

Jack wrapped it around the lever and hefted his hammer. 'You can squeeze it out into your mug when I've done. Your mother's tea tastes like oily rags anyway. Here goes *nothing!*' He gave the lever a smart rap and a course of bricks fell into the void. There was a slow count of ten before they hit the bottom, splashing into water.

Ken flinched. 'My old ma won't like that remark.'

Jack knew he was breathing too much gas, his legs were filled with air, his thoughts were oddly scrambled. 'What's that got to do with the price of pencil boxes? I wonder if they have them in Waltzing-Matilda land?' He struck down with the hammer twice more. His boot slipped and he smacked a forearm down on the metal lip of the manhole, gaping for air as his heel sought purchase on the pipe, greasy with London clay.

'Come up, you've gone blue.'

'One more whack. No pipe ever beat Jack Day.' The hammer was as heavy as his eyelids. Jack beat at the lever unrhythmically, hard-pressed to remember why he was doing this. Then he was lying on his back and hot unsweetened tea was dribbling into his mouth. The rubble under his back spun in eccentric circles as his eyes and the sky revolved in the opposite direction. The night was all fire and his head ached. 'I don't take sugar.'

'Saccharine. Drink it down, you heavy great lummox. I've put my back out 'auling you out of that 'ole. It all but fell in and us with it.'

'Cosy way to go if you can't swim,' Jack leaned up on an elbow. 'Did I do it?'

'I dunno, I s'pose. Yeah, you did it. Now get yourself straight.'

'I'm all right, cocker.' Jack stood up and looked into the hole. The manhole had gone in a slide of subsidence, leaving the pipe unsupported. 'Haul out a "Danger" sign, Ken. Then we'd better get on. There's gonna be a lot more like this.'

'Standard practice is to go back and write a report,' said Ken.

Jack's big hand reached out and crushed the driver's shoulder.

'Say "standard practice" once more and the hospital will be extracting your vaccum flask from your sit-upon. Got it?'

'Okay, okay ... '

The old Chinese woman talked to herself in musical Cantonese and the rescue workers were bringing two children out of a gap beneath a concrete coping stone.

'Call that "standard practice" do you?' Jack stumped back to the van and closed his tools away. They had worked on fourteen different incidents before dawn sent the Luftwaffe back to France.

NINE: TOMMY

The lorry found the right gear and trundled away with the relieved sentry. Tommy stood easy, cursing his luck, watching nightfall approach. The dusk came in with the tide and late seabirds homed in on the foreshore for a supper of crustacea.

The breakwater hooked out into the sea like a crooked stone thumb before doglegging back to protect the inner lee of the dock where a fast merchantman lay hove-to for a gunnery refit. Her upperwork rolled with the incoming water, a multiple fret against the peach and salmon and umber sunset. Giant cranes were skeletal storks in the dying glare. The rising offshore wind tugged at the skirt of Tommy's greatcoat, mourning in the gantries like ululating widows.

Private Mifflin had broken the news over a Woodbine.

'Hatwood's got you on the sentry roster. No point kicking, Tommy. A servant without an officer to bat for is a supernumary in any army.'

'But there's thousands of others to do sentry-go, hanging about doing eff-all but grow earwax.'

'You're kicking, Tom. Told you not to.'

'Wouldn't you?'

'What, trade a nice peaceful sentry box for Banana Joe's sweet ways? Wouldn't I just.' Mufflin had been run ragged by Hatwood's attempts to ingratiate himself with the brigadier by his smart turnout. 'All that brasswork, he shines like a Brighton whore on the club circuit. Have some of that, cocker.'

The point was made and Tommy drew an Enfield and five rounds.

Phyllis would have nappies in soak and be ironing or mending with the wireless on to kill the silence. Saturday night was always better than midweek when it was mostly Sandy McPherson on the organ or news broadcasts that said nothing. She had never learned to tune in for Kate Smith and the big bands they played on that Schenectady radio station.

She might even be playing cards with Doris and Jack if they wasn't down the boozer. How Jack wasn't in the army was a mystery. Him and his gas pipes and how the Bolshevik system was the way of the future and the King should be thrown out in favour of a Praesidium. Nobody's gonna bring down the Royal Family while I've got a bullet up the spout. If a man wants change he makes it for himself with his own two hands and his God given wit, not as one of a crowd being told how to think and vote.

When I get out of the army I'll never work for another guvnor. I'll have my own business. People got to eat and food's where the money is. Maybe a cafe with a tea urn and penny busters made fresh every day, nice crusty rolls filled with fresh brawn or German sausage, sardines and cress on toast for a penny-ha'penny; a set shilling luncheon of soup, meat and two veg, a sweet and coffee. There's money in that, and it's nothing more than me and Phyl did when we worked at Peel's Hotel in Fleet Street. The till never stopped ringing. The customers got value for money, and we lived on what was over the day after. They'll never get me eating stale food again, never.

Had enough of that when they chucked me out of the home when I was fourteen and I went looking for my mother. All I had was five shillings and the last address she had worked at. I found it near Barking Steps in a mean alley where women and girls loaded sacks onto totters' carts, yelled at by an old Jew with a beard as long as a wet week. He gave me two minutes of his time.

Ma had died seven weeks before and had been buried by the parish. She had a lung complaint and the hemp dust from sackmaking didn't help. It went with the job and who could choose how to earn a crust? Go to the cemetery, all you'll find is a numbered lot, no names. Forget it, live your life. Here's sixpence, eat in good health. I can still hear that coin ringing on the cobbles when I threw it away. I hated that bugger of a Jew, maybe I still do. He stood there looking sad when I walked away.

The woman in Records of Births & Deaths at Poplar Town Hall told me I had a maternal aunt in Canning Town. The house in Fox Street, Canning Town was next door to a workhouse, and Aunt Mary had four daughters so she couldn't take me in straight off. I got a room in Brixton and swept out a toolmaking shop in Denmark Street for sixteen shillings a week. With eight bob a week rent, bus fares and a shilling for the electric light, I lived on bread, suet and tea until it came out of my ears and I had to quit. On a building site I caught pneumonia for the third time and got fired because I was slow and coughed a lot. I went home to Aunt Mary with no money and stole the bread the people in the workhouse put out on the window sill for the birds.

'Happy days, I don't think.'

Tommy sloped arms and marched a square to keep his circulation going. The wind was chill and his feet were as hard as potatoes inside his boots. It was dark now and stars showed. The afterglow on the sea was the blue of bonfire smoke.

Tommy presented arms for something to do and the bayonet lodged itself into the wooden lintel of the sentry box. As he pulled it free he found himself laughing aloud. *I don't know an Heinkel from my orifice, how am I supposed to know what to shoot at? Blimey, in this darkness I wouldn't know friends from foe either. It's dark and cold and lonely and I feel a right prune standing here while the Navy boys are slugging back the pink gins in their wardrooms.* Tommy warmed himself thinking of Phyllis.

A cold draught brought us together. She told me off for

making one with my Oxford bags when I walked up and down the bar and sent shivers up her short skirt. The next minute she told me I could take her to the cinema and buy her a fish supper afterwards. When I told her she was forward, she said Queen Victoria was dead and she was alive and you was only young once and she wanted some fun before her teeth fell out and men went to the moon which wouldn't happen. Always did have a way of turning things around, did Phyl.

Tommy watched a fat moon turn the night to hard monochrome as wisps of fast cloud progressed past its cratered face. *Don't bring no Jerries over, Mr Moon, leave them with the Vichy bastards who gave their country away to the Nazis. They deserve each other.*

Tommy made himself comfortable in the sentry box and worked on staying awake, more concerned about a spot inspection by Banana Joe than seeing parachute canopies in the moonlight.

TEN: FRANK

The week slogged on and it was Sunday again.

In the chapel he learned to talk to the other prisoners by changing the words of the hymn when the patrolling Staffs were out of earshot.

'Oh God our help in ages past ... '

'The screws got an accidental death verdict over Tweedledum, la, la, lal, lah, lah, lah ... '

'Our hope in years to come ... '

'The lucky basket's out of it now ... nicking butter from the Officers' Mess should have been Company Punishment ... not the glass-house, la, lal, lal, lah ... '

'London got plastered yesterday ... the East End's still burning ... rivers of fire ... got the docks at Rotherhithe ...

thousands of Jerry planes . . . thousands of dead . . . thousands . . . '

Phyllis and the kids. Peggy under a pile of rubble. I've got to get out of here. Only way is with a clean nose. Play the toy soldier. No trading snout with the barons. No clever-clever. Just do my bird, hop-to smartish when the Staffs holler and earn my way out. Only way.

'My lesson today is from the Book of Matthew . . . '

Speak up, vicar mate. I'm listening . . .

CHAPTER FOUR

'They had one bomb on Aylesbury, a near miss, and they're still talking about it.'

Visiting London Housewife.

Shops became a favourite symbol of defiance. Big and small, they had their windows blown out. The West End stores would erect painted wooden fronts with only tiny panes of glass to replace them; the little fruiterers and grocers would often do without any glass at all. The impromptu signs became favourite blitz jokes. 'MORE OPEN THAN USUAL' was a common one. 'BLAST!' was the most laconic. One pub advertised, 'OUR WINDOWS ARE GONE BUT OUR SPIRITS ARE EXCELLENT. COME IN AND TRY THEM.'

Angus Calder *The People's War.*

'The individual's reaction to the sound of falling bombs cannot be described. The moan of stark terror and suspense cannot be encompassed by words, no more can the sense of relief when you realise that you weren't where that one fell.'

Ed Murrow.

ONE: PHYLLIS

17 October 1940.

Autumn turned to winter as the train chugged toward the West Country. Gales had stripped the trees of leaves and hoar frost covered the fields like powdered glass. Phyllis held the boys close to her in the unheated carriage and shivered in her thin coat, already homesick for London. Tommy's letter had read:

> ... so it looks like we're settled here for a long while in Weston-super-Mare. You'll like the bungalow I found for you and the boys. With the billeting money and what I make out of the canteen we can just do it, and being together will be worth it, you'll see ...

So we shall. Phyllis held Harry's legs as he stood on the seat to look out of the window.

'Where all the houses, Pillis?' asked Harry.

'In the towns.'

'What are towns?'

'Where the houses are.'

'Oh.' Satisfied with the answer, Harry watched telegraph poles strobe past wreathed in engine steam, wondering how the engine made the fields all white and why the seagulls sounded so cross when they had all those trees to play in. If he could fly he would never come in for tea or go to bed just because it was dark. If he was a bird he could lay his own breakfast eggs and the farmer would give him bread and butter soldiers to dip in them. 'Do birds drop bombs, Pillis?'

'No, ducks.'

'Not even German birds?'

'No.'

'I'm a train,' Harry pointed to his clouding breath.

'That's nice.'

'Are German planes birds with engines?'

'No, love.'

'One made me do naughties.'

'You're still my brave soldier,' said Phyllis. The Messerschmitt had strafed the road when they were shopping and the cannon shells had blown holes in the grey brick of the Gas Company boundary wall ten feet from where they had cowered. Harry had messed his pants in fright, and cried more over soiling himself than the prospect of being hurt. His young pride still smarted and he whimpered in his sleep every night, his hands clamped over his tiny manhood.

'Don't like naughties, Pillis.'

'It won't happen again, love. You'll have other boys to play with and there'll be sand and you can paddle in the sea.' Phyllis held the sturdy legs too tightly and Harry squirmed. *I swear you'll never hear another bomb or watch the ceiling move from near misses. You won't see the dead under blankets laid in rows like they were outside the cinema in Holloway. You'll live to see real fireworks, not crane to see tracers and chandelier flares from the shelter door during a raid.* Phyllis lit a cigarette and blew smoke. She had picked the habit up from Doris.

'Now you're a train,' said Harry. 'Me blow out the match.'

'That's a big blow.'

'One day I'll be big and blow out the sun.'

'Then we'd live in the dark.'

'Oh.' Harry thought and said, 'Won't then. Germans live in the dark.'

Phyllis came close to tears. 'One day they won't, love.'

'I know. Frank kill them all with his gun. And Tom.'

'That's right, love.' *How can I tell him otherwise?*

'Why is there night?'

'So we know when to sleep.'

'If there wasn't night there wouldn't be Germans.'

'Sit down now, we're coming into a station.' Phyllis reached the suitcase from the rack as the train drew into Weston-super-Mare.

'Bang,' said Harry. 'When Frank tired I'll hold his gun. I'm a big boy.' On the platform Harry tugged at the first soldier he saw. 'Are you my Daddy?'

The private grinned. 'If that's your mum I wouldn't mind. Help you with your case, love?'

'My husband'd give you an argument and put you back in your pram,' said Phyllis.

'Forget it, Son. Never could abide a rucker. Got one of me own in London.'

'Then you ought to know better.' Phyllis saw Tommy weaving towards her through the crowd and instinctively knew there was something wrong. He looked strong and fit and shorter than she remembered, and his eyes had that tight, hooded and 'How am I going to explain this?' look. He gathered Phyllis and kissed her.

'Get in there, mate,' the private boarded the train.

'Who's he?' asked Tommy, reddening.

'My daddy,' said Harry.

'Never mind him, what's up, Tommy?'

'Give us your case and the baby, let's get a cuppa.'

'Tommy ... '

In the cafeteria they sat over watery tea and cold metal chairs.

'Well?'

'Banana-bloody-Joe, that's what's happened. Since when have you smoked, Phyl?'

'Since my water broke, and watch your tongue in front of the kids.'

'I haven't got the bungalow. Banana Joe took it for his wife. Pulled rank on me,' Tommy lit a Woodbine. 'And she ain't even his wife as far as Miff can figure. He got a look at the files. Hatwood was married but she took off long ago for some Frenchman when he was stationed in British Somaliland. Anyway, he took the bungalow. I only found out this morning.'

'What about your officer? Won't he do nothing?'

'What can he do? I can't go to him over this.'

'Bloody officers. All smiles when it suits, but it don't last. They kick you without changing expression. I'd hit him where Maggie wears the beads, right up the throat. There's not a train back to London 'til seven tonight. It'd be two in the morning before I got the kids back. We'll have to find something else, that's all.'

'The billeting officer says there's a Reception Centre in one of the hotels,' said Tommy. 'It's only a step down the road.'

'Old Nick's on his bike today and no mistake,' said Phyllis. 'You'd think we had enough trouble with Hitler without our own turning against us. There ought to be changes, Tommy.' She pushed her untouched tea away. 'Come on.'

The hotel was stone and slate and peeling paint. The flower beds had been given over to cultivating vegetables and abandoned rows of sprouts had gone to seed, yellowed by frost. Women squabbled in the foyer and their children ran wild amongst apple cores and torn newspaper. Upstairs, the dormitories stank of urine and body odour, and the lavatory overflowed onto the floor. Phyllis said nothing until they were back in the street, then it was a single cryptic: 'No!'

'What then?'

'God gave us legs and busfare. I want the boys to see the sea.'

On the bus to Brean Sands Phyllis spotted a sign advertising a chalet for rent.

'Ring the bell.'

'But we paid to the end of the line.'

'I'll owe you the fourpence. Ring the bell.'

They walked back to a small bungalow set in a neat garden with an orchard to one side. A thin woman answered the door and she smiled at the children through half-glasses, slouching to disguise her height.

Blimey, thought Tommy, *with that flowered dress she looks like rambling roses on a trellis. Must take her brain an hour to tell her feet what to do.*

'We only let the chalet during the summer. But I'll show you if you like, hang on, I'll get the keys.' As they followed a path down to the sands she introduced herself as Mrs Wormold. 'Hubby' was a retired chemist and older than she was, but very considerate. The chalet was white weatherboard with sky-blue sashes and door. 'The wind blows here something shocking,' she said, letting them inside. 'In the summer it's nice and we charge fifteen-shillings a week.'

There were two bedrooms, a kitchenette with a Calor stove and a living-dining area with a folding table. Windborne sand rattled against the windows and the sea glittered like wet sequins.

'It would do us a real turn,' said Phyllis.

Harry held Mrs Wormold's skirt, peering up at her. 'Why are you so long? I got chickens but they couldn't come on the train. They didn't have tickets.'

'What a shame. What were you thinking of paying, Mrs . . . ?'

'Eleven shillings. And it's Mrs Penny.' Phyllis gave a resumé of their disappointment over the bungalow and the conditions in the Reception Centre. 'I haven't seen my husband for five months, 'til today, that is.' She found herself blushing as if she had admitted to sex mania. 'The boys hardly know him.' *I hardly know him.*

Mrs Wormold melted visibly. 'Let me talk to hubby and we'll see.' She was back within fifteen minutes. 'For twelve shillings I'll throw in gas and electric light, but you'll have to supply your own bedding.'

'Pay Mrs Wormold, Tommy. We're home, boys.'

'Come up to the house, hubby wants you to have a bite of lunch with us. I'm sure we'll all get along wonderfully,' said Mrs Wormold.

'Who says there ain't a God, Tommy,' Phyllis whispered on

the path, taking and squeezing his arm.

'What's God?' said Harry.

TWO: HELEN

The square was tawdry in the grey morning light. Workmen cleared the rubble from what had been Christopher Wren's most easterly church. The building next to it had lost its entire stone fascia and exposed its beams and lath-and-plaster undercladding as obscenely as a naked corpse blown from the grave bares its rotting bones. The smell of wet burning wood, of ruptured sewers and the small, mean stink of escaped domestic gas was the new abiding odour of London, and smelled worse when it rained.

The staring desolation had its lighter sights, but even they had palled for Helen. Lavatories and baths hanging from their soil pipes three storeys up, or wardrobes standing confidently on a single joist, and bottles of milk on the doorstep of a house that had miraculously disappeared in a yellow spurt of high-explosives no longer amused. Everybody had a bomb story, and Helen wore a badge that read: 'I have a bomb story too!'

Each morning, the lines of the dispossessed outside the Reception Centre in Bethnal Green grew longer. Some of them had lost everything for the second or third time, and billeting them in an area where there were less and less houses and more and more bombed sites consumed most of Helen's time. More often than not she fell asleep over her books in the small hours of the morning and existed for most of the working week on less than six hours sleep a night. Had the peace-time assessment of casualties been correct, her life would have been easier, but since they were wildly overestimated, and the survivors many, their problems became more acute as winter advanced.

The petty tyrants at the Town Hall were the bane of Helen's life. Their obsession with neat paperwork and their insistence on applying the divisive 'means' test to those unfortunates who went to them for financial help to become rehoused, blinded their codified minds to the single salient fact that the funds they administered belonged to the homeless by right, and that they were not running a workhouse charity for social misfits. It surprised Helen not at all that the bulk of the independently spirited East Enders would have nothing to do with the penny-pinching bureaucrats who dispensed these monies as though every coin was largesse from their own pockets. One official had rudely called Helen a Communist when she agitated on behalf of a one-legged First War veteran whose papers had vapourised with his cottage.

Many people had trudged into Epping Forest and sat down beneath the old oaks, too dispirited to seek proper shelter or to travel further. One Essex mayor had flatly refused to accommodate 'these strangers' in his suburban borough, anxious not to alienate those of his wealthy constituents who thought the presence of these unwelcome unfortunates would blight their fair estates.

Many others, more fearful of the indiscriminate bombing, travelled to the Chislehurst Caves where they eked out a troglodyte existence in the dripping and humid atmosphere. The deeper London Underground stations were solid with people who staked out their 'pitches' on the platforms before noon every day, oblivious to the rush-hour traffic, preferring the crush and squalor of the tunnels to the official street shelters with their noisy community singing and blatant public courting.

Stray cats grew wild and crafty, ratting and mousing through the new wastelands of Stepney, Bow and Rotherhithe; abandoned by their bombed-out or evacuated owners, they scavenged as avidly as their wild brothers. And like them, gangs of children, used to roaming the streets and stealing from market stalls to implement their penny dinner money, plagued the elderly in the street shelters with their dicing and their sublime disregard for public order. This new lost generation of innocents, made anarchic by the lack of filial guidance and official disregard, were as much casualties as those who had died. And yet they flourished like grubby individualistic weeds, as much at home on the bombed sites and in ruined houses as the purple stands of Canadian willow that grew amongst the bricks and rubble on the acres of waste ground.

With gas, electric and water supplies disrupted by bombing or unavailable due to official power cuts, people learned to live with dirt. Bathing once a week was fast becoming a luxury, and there were several old women in Helen's ward who had not changed their clothes since September for fear of being caught naked during an air-raid. To cover their mounting rankness they doused themselves in wintergreen embrocation, the fumes of which in an overcrowded and badly ventilated shelter were almost as offensive as their unchecked perspiration.

Helen picked her way through a litter of broken glass, glad of her thick tweed coat because of the chill wind. The trolley-bus wires were down again and there was no transport to the Reception Centre. She had spent much of the night at the refuge beneath the railway arches at Tilbury in Stepney. Although an officially adopted shelter, the rambling intersecting labyrinth of cellars and vaults was a shameful example of how people were required to huddle together in foul conditions for company and protection during the constant nightly alerts. The Borough Council had adopted the complex as a public shelter for three-thousand people. But because it was well known in the neighbouring districts, and had been since the Zeppelin raids of the previous war, Helen calculated she had shared the refuge with at least fifteen-thousand men, women and children.

Lack of proper sanitation meant toddlers slept beside piles of human ordure on unswept floors that ran with urine and the trodden paste of discarded food, paper and cigarette butts. Nursing mothers exposed their breasts for their infants, quite unconcerned that Lascars played cards, an Indian family ate with their fingers, an eightpenny prostitute favoured a client, and a group of black sailors danced to an accordion, all within touching distance of them. It was as if an impromptu crêche had been set down in the middle of several street parties whose conflicting revels hammered against the crusted vaulting, drowning out the sounds of railway traffic, the ubiquitous drone of bombers and the brawling concussions of land mines and 1,000 lb bombs.

To Helen, at first sight, it was a massive bacchanal held by men and women and under-aged minors, desperately filling what might possibly be their last hours with lusty singing and drunken dancing, eyes overly bright and glazed with bottled ale, unmusical voices raised to screen the sounds of destruction and sudden death; the bawdy ballad against the massive monotony of the incoming Dornier 17Zs' 1,000 horse-power Bramo Fafnir radial engines.

And yet, and yet ... thought Helen, *there's an underlying strength here, a will to survive with gaiety even under these reduced conditions. Despite the hot and foetid air redolent with faeces and unwashed limbs; the knowledge that their already mauled district would most certainly be further reduced when they emerged blinking into another day, they carried on without the benefit of the barest trappings of hearth and home, hot food or basic medicine, clean linen or freedom from head-lice, impetigo or child-killing diptheria.*

Perhaps, she thought, *now that the poor had been bombed out of their private neglected poverty and been precipitated into the public gaze of such shelters, however badly-off the lack of proper amenities made them, their plight was in the open for all to see, and a programme of medical and social care must be forthcoming. Fine speeches and parochial charities headed up by people like my mother in their flowered hats and finery would no longer do; and general practitioners could no longer treat their patients from the lower orders with less regard than veterinaries had for the sheep they treated for footrot. Damn it, these people have spirit and their taproot vitality must no longer be thrown on the scrapheap, dismissed and forgotten as they were.*

But even thinking such things, Helen still suffered a still, small voice deep within her that repeated over and over, *class traitor, class traitor.*

Oh, mother, there's just enough of you in me to give me pause in this headlong flight into the bottom of a thousand pits of others' despair. You'd change things in your own convenient image without crossing any emotional borders, without chopping holes in the palisade defending your glossy and pampered ghetto. Daddy might understand what I'm doing, perhaps better than I. Even darling dodo Christopher gives me my head in the name of affection without true regard for what I've learned to see here ...

Helen halted on the corner of Brick Lane, surprised to see the milling crowds, thinking she had come upon a public meeting or an impromptu street market. People were setting up shop wherever they found convenient, and nowadays an orange box on a kitchen chair under an umbrella served when one's shop or stall had been reduced to kindling.

'Mrs L, Mrs L ... ' Mrs Tolliver came out of the press, her pink face pinker than usual. 'They're all for us. What're gonna do wiv 'em all, they're all over like cock-bleeding-roaches.'

Helen calmed her, feeling her own anxiety rise. 'Those people have come to us for ... aid?' She shook her head and a thick lock of hair escaped from her collar to flutter across her face. She brushed it aside. 'There must be several hundreds ...'

'More,' Mrs Tolliver was positive.

Helen let out a long cloud of white breath. 'Once more unto that *very* crowded beach ... '

'When you talk, you know, lahdie-posh you lose me.'

'Shakespeare was a country boy.'

'Who?'

'Never mind, come along.'

They pushed their way into the Reception Centre, and by eight o'clock that evening, they and their volunteer helpers had served one thousand five hundred meals and twenty-two thousand cups of tea.

THREE: PHYLLIS

Phyllis tucked the boys into the narrow cot and looked down at them fondly. They had fallen asleep the moment their heads touched the pillow, unworried by the sandy wind rattling the window frames. The quiet was almost unnerving and the hush of the sea reminded her of trams on cobbles. One of her neighbours had evacuated to Dorset for three short weeks and returned to say: 'One more day of trees and hills and I would have eaten the buttons off me shoes. Not a picture palace for miles, and when I asked the woman next door when the whelk barrow came round she just stared at me. Give me bombs and sirens so long as there's a chance of a bowl of tripe and faggots on a Saturday night.'

Phyllis looked out at the miles of sand where the pilings of the breakwaters had been worn to jagged stumps by years of water-action. *Dull and safe,* she thought. *Old Rudolph Valentino would have felt at home here, galloping up and down with a girl thrown across his saddle. But he'd have to watch himself on the barbed-wire they've strung all along the dunes below the road. Do himself a nasty mischief if he fell off into that, gaucho boots or no gaucho boots. Nobody for miles except Mrs Wormold and her slow old hubby. Just me and the boys and Tommy when he can get away. Still, I can go into Weston-super-Mare once a week to draw me army money from the Post Office, and Bristol can't be all that far away by bus. I'll meet other service wives there and maybe make friends. Won't be too bad.*

And there's Mrs Wormold, although her pie crust could use some work. My Tommy did well getting it down, seeing how fussy he is about his food. The first time I took him home to the old mother she rucked him for cutting the fat off his gammon. 'That's the best part,' she said. 'Where all the goodness is. No wonder you're all scaffolding and no brickwork. Give it here,' and she made her chin all greasy eating it. Ma wouldn't last through the morning down here. If there ain't a pub in singing distance she's not happy. Now who's this?

Two figures came over a dune. A stout woman with a brown cheerful face and hair as dark as a gypsy's crow, leaned into the wind as she dragged a small boy towards the chalet.

'Say you're London and make my day,' she shouted. 'Come on, Stanley, this wind makes you cry gallons.' She slapped her huge bosom. 'Gets up his bronchials something shocking, don't it, Stanley?'

'Come in out of the cold,' said Phyllis.

'Ta.' The woman flopped into a chair and held Stanley to her. 'Name's Sissie Ackerman. London-Jewish and proud of it. You?'

'Just London.' Phyllis introduced herself.

'Then we'll get along. I'm down the beach in a boat. You come around anytime. Bit different from the Old Kent Road, eh?'

'A bit. I'll put the kettle on.'

'A cuppa tea'll go down a treat. You save your rations though, this air gives you all kind of appetites. I weighed less than a wet kipper when I come here two months ago,' Sissy softened the lie with an infectious laugh. 'Still, my man likes his money's worth, and he gets it. I had my eye on this place when I first come here. But her up there, old beanpole, took against Stanley 'cause of his cough. And us being kosher. Don't look so shocked, Phyl. They don't like strangers around here in the usual way, let alone people like us.'

'Mrs Wormold was nice to us and the boys.'

Sissy smiled broadly. 'So who could take exception to a nice Church of England girl like yourself?'

'Not everybody's like ... that, Sissie.'

'Enough are and we can live with it. There's enough enemies with this war going on without we should go looking for more. Don't sniff, Stanley. Use your handkerchief.'

'Ain't got one.'

'And don't say ain't. It ain't polite.'

The two women giggled with their heads together.

'Sissie, you're a tonic.'

'I know, I can't wait to hear what I'm going to say next. Me and the English language, two strangers in the same bed,' said Sissie.

A sharp crack clattered on the wind and chased itself down the beach.

'What was that?'

'Shooting. The army does it sometimes.'

'Should we look?'

Before they could move, Tommy came through the door, tripping over himself in his hurry. Grotesquely fat and bright red from running, he made for the main bedroom. His rifle banged into the architrave before he threw it onto the bed springs. 'You haven't seen me,' he gasped, winded. 'Go see if I got it.'

'Got what?' asked Phyllis.

'The rabbit of course.'

'What's he talking about, rabbit?' asked Sissie.

'Tommy, this is Sissie Ackerman.'

'Never mind that. Don't let no-one in. And see about the rabbit.'

'What rabbit?'

'The one I shot.'

'Where did you get a bullet? And why are you so fat all of a sudden?'

'Blankets from the billet. Miff got them for me. Six of 'em, you won't be cold now.'

'I'll go,' Sissie offered.

'Watch out for the officer. I didn't know he was there until he started shouting.'

'He's worse than my Asa,' said Sissie, 'and he'll do anything for the crack. Stay here, Stanley. Do as you're told and stop your sniffing.'

'We'll both go,' said Phyllis.

'And don't pick your nose, Stanley, you'll dig a hole in your brain. No wonder the kids at school call you silversleeves. He's all cold and sniffles.'

Stanley sat with his hands in his pockets. 'Yes, ma.'

'And don't go drinking nothing,' Sissie buttoned her coat. 'He drinks things.'

'Will you two get on with it?'

'We're gone.' Phyllis and Sissie climbed a dune to the scrubland below the road and Sissie's laugh streamed with her breath. An officer and a sergeant quartered the ground.

'What now, Sissie?'

'Bold is as bold does. Hey there,' Sissie called.

'Ladies,' the major tipped his hat. 'Did you see who fired that shot? He can't have got far.' He held a rabbit by the ears.

'You what?' said Sissie. 'You lot shouldn't be shooting here. There's women and children living hereabouts. Shocking the way they carry on, ain't it, Phyl?'

'Shocking.'

'They nearly galloped over me and Stanley last week. Fixed bayonets and everything. They should be chasing Hitler, not us civils. I'll report this to someone, see if I don't.'

'This is a war zone, madam,' said the major.

'And what's that make me? The Queen of Sheba's maiden aunt?'

'Did you or did you not see who fired that shot?'

'Not. But he'll get the edge of my tongue if I do, right, Phyl?'

'Right, Sissie. Miles of beach and you have to choose here to bang away with your guns. My two boys are asleep down there, you know. We didn't leave the bombing to be shot at by our own.'

'Are you service wives?' asked the major with suspicion.

'And proud of it,' said Sissie. 'What're you going to do with that rabbit?'

'Are either of your husbands with you?'

'Mine was taken prisoner in France,' Sissie lied. 'And this lady hasn't heard from hers since he was posted missing in Norway.'

'Now, about that rabbit,' said Phyllis. 'Make a lovely stew for the children. First bit of fresh meat the children will've seen in months.' She wiped tears from her eyes and allowed her lip to tremble.

'Ah,' the major coughed behind his glove. 'Anything, Sergeant?'

'No sign of anyone, Sir.' The sergeant eyed the rabbit and his head moved almost imperceptibly toward the two women. 'Must have made off along the road. But we've denied him his kill, Sir.'

Sissie stared at the rabbit and the major seemed to see it for the first time. 'Perhaps,' he said, 'you ladies would accept this rabbit with the compliments of the Durham Light Infantry.'

'Hear that, Phyl. What a *mench*.'

'A real gentleman,' said Phyllis. 'One of the old school.'

The major swelled visibly as he handed the corpse across with a gallant salute. 'Ladies ... '

'Come on, Phyl. Watch you don't get blood on your frock.'

Back in the chalet they dissolved into helpless laughter.

'Ladies ... ' Phyllis threw a comic salute. 'The Queen of Sheba ... '

'Right through the eye,' said Tommy. He had found some string and a cork to make a drawstring to clean the bore of his

Lee Enfield. 'It's all right for you two, whittering away there like a couple of dafties. If they'd caught me I'd be on a fizzer.'

'Yeah, but how do we skin this thing?' Sissie's laugh set Phyllis off again.

Tommy looked sourly at them. 'And I caught your Stanley drinking Dettol.'

'Honestly, he's into everything. Last week it was soapy water.' Sissie sobered with difficulty. 'The time before it was lighter fuel. He said he wanted to be a fire-eater.'

'It'll be dark soon. I'll creep off then.' Tommy cleaned his rifle, disliking both mother and child for spoiling his first chance of being alone with his wife.

FOUR: FRANK

Transit Camp 3 (North) was set in dark Cumberland woodland and covered eight acres. The rows of Nissen huts were camouflaged and the complex was surrounded by a double fence of rigid steel mesh topped with four strands of barbed-wire. R.A.F. dogs patrolled the perimeter between the fences and enabled the commandant to boast that he had never lost a man A.W.O.L.

Tosher Bennett lay on his cot in Hut 12 Section 4 reading a copy of *London Opinion*, his lips moving over the longer words. Opposite him, Limey Prendergast memorised infantile jokes from the comic section of the Scottish *Sunday Post*. His only copy of a James Hadley Chase novel was out on loan at a penny a time and he was seriously considering copying it out in longhand to double his income.

Their unit had been posted four times in five weeks, each time at an hour's notice, and each time further north. They had been issued with both arctic and tropical gear only to have it withdrawn again. They had been promised courses on gunnery, map-reading, endurance and motor-maintenence, none of which materialised. They had all heard the Padre's lecture on British birds many times and they kept book on how many times he tugged his earlobe during the course of his rambling dissertation. They were paraded for P.T. and tested for swimming proficiency and underwent medical inspections only marginally more stringent than that the short-arm variety. They were inoculated and vaccinated, called to general quarters at irregular hours, paraded and marched and paraded again for no other reason than there was nothing else for them to do. It was the old army runaround and they were all heartily browned-off with it.

'What d'you bet it's Spam fritters for dinner?' said Tosher.

'No bet,' Limey turned to the *Oor Wullie* strip. 'It's always Spam fritters.'

'Not always.'

'Always.'

'Bet.'

'If you'll bet me you can spell disestablishmentarianism.'

'No bet,' said Tosher. 'Clever clogs.'

'Bottle gone?' asked Limey.

'It's in the oven right at the back,' somebody said, dropping his kit.

'And who pulled your string?' Tosher turned on the stranger, ready to direct his belligerence at anybody.

'Want a go with belts, do we?' the soft chuckle struck a familiar chord.

Limey came off his cot, the jokes forgotten. 'Frank?'

'That's me,' said Frank. The hut was just another hut that smelled of soldiers, ballsealed floors, metal polish, boots and hot wool. The train journey under escort had been tiring, cold and long. 'Which is my pit then?'

'Since when did you ask? Take which one you want, Frank mate. Don't he look good, Tosh?'

'Yeah.' Tosher thought Frank had lost weight. His face was thinner and the cropped hair aged him. A new scar pushed his left eyebrow out of alignment, giving him a one-eyed frown. 'Who give you that?' Tosher asked before he could stop himself.

'It comes with graduation. Like earning a stripe.' Frank bounced on cotsprings. He had spent the previous night in the Tote booth of a racecourse where the escort corporal had taunted him by blowing cigarette smoke in his face. Frank blanked off his temper, something that came as second nature now. 'This place looks like a rest cure.'

'It's better than some we've suffered,' Limey lit and passed cigarettes. 'You've missed some darlings since you been gone.'

'I've had my share,' said Frank. The other men in the hut were watching him with undisguised curiosity. One of them wandered over to stand behind him, his thumbs in his belt.

'This your famous criminal, Bennett?' he asked. He was all freckles and spiky red hair.

Frank said nothing. *There's always one barracks bully-boy who thinks he's Jack the Lad on roller skates. This one's all neck and no forehead. What ain't muscled is tattooed, and the rest grows hair.*

'What's that to you, Taggart?' said Tosher.

Taggart tucked his small dimpled chin into his thick neck and gave the hut a tight grin. 'I like to sort out the glass-house monkeys, don't I? Like to see they don't pollute the air with the funny old notions. This is my hut and I like it run my way.'

Limey blew uneasy smoke. 'Leave it out, Taggart. No one's asked you over here. Go get snotty with the recruits. They're more your mark.'

'Funny-cuts here is sitting on that pit like he owns it. And the really funny thing is I've had my eye on it for myself. So, do us a favour, have your girlfriend move.'

'Don't bite, Frank,' said Tosher. 'Giving him a moody won't just earn you Company Punishment, right?'

Frank grinned into his lap. 'So, Ginger wants this pit does he?'

'Don't you "Ginger" me. If Taggart wants a pit it's his,' said Taggart.

Frank kept his smile. 'Then have it, Ginger. Shift down one, Tosh.'

Taggart snapped fingers. 'Stay where you are, Bennett. I won't have no criminal bedding down next to me. They learns nasty habits in the glass-house, don't they? Like walking in their sleep and not keeping their lily-white hands to themselves.' Taggart tapped Frank's shoulder with a thick finger. 'You're a Shirley Temple, ain't you, Frankie boy?'

'Me?'

'You,' again the finger prodded.

I didn't see the boot that tripped me. Or the baton that laid my eye open when I fell in the glass-house passage on the last morning. A finger ain't a baton, and this ginger berk is just that, a pushy tit without the brains to come in out of the rain. Don't let him push you back inside. Frank turned his hands over to look at his hardened palms. 'Oh blimey yeah,' he said.

'Talk's cheap, Taggart, but you're cheaper,' said Limey, seeing Frank's ears burn as his eyes turned to black glass.

'Wait your turn, Prendergast. I'll get to you soon enough,' Taggart rolled his shoulders and bared stained teeth.

Frank stood abruptly, his back turned towards Taggart who stepped back and raised his fists. Frank ignored him, his eyes on Limey. 'Leave it out, mate. And you, Tosher. He'd murder you.'

'But Frank ...'

'You heard,' Frank threw his kitbag onto another cot and went to stand by it. 'Satisfied?'

Taggart preened himself. 'I'm watching you, criminal. You just remember that.'

'Oh blimey yeah.' Frank picked a scale of loose skin from his clenched knuckles, unwilling to look into the redhead's face. *Taggart's hair is the colour of rusted dustbins*, he thought, lying down to face the wall. *And I've barked my knuckles on too many of them to worry about one more. Give me time, Taggart, and I'll shine you up so you won't know yourself. Time, Taggart, time ...*

'Game of cards, Frank?' said Tosher. 'Brag or something?'

Frank did not respond.

'Shirley Temple's sulking,' Taggart laughed. 'Somebody hurt his feelings.' He lay on the cot he had won and showed off his wide chest and flat stomach.

'What about cribbage?'

'Leave him, Tosh. Can't you see he's flaked out?' Limey picked up his newspaper.

Tosher leaned in to whisper, 'He hasn't lost his bottle, has he?'

'Nah,' Limey said doubtfully. 'Course not ... '

FIVE: HELEN

The small man stood in front of Helen's desk, his busy eyes on her tweed coat as he toyed with a cigarette to show off his oyster wristwatch and gold cufflinks. 'Well I'm blowed, Missus,' he said, 'small world and there's a fact.'

Helen waited for the All Clear to wind down. Or was it another Alert? They came and went with such rapidity she lost track. She was so tired, that there wasn't a smile left in her world, and this man offended her with his cocky bravado, wide lapels and snap-brimmed trilby. He even had a handkerchief hanging from his top pocket, and she would not have been surprised if it had been spotted. He could have been one of those loathsome spivs who sold platform space on the Underground for half-a-crown a time, or a member of a racecourse gang. Lord knows, Helen had met enough of those twilight characters. His whole manner and appearance said Black Market as he grinned his 'something for nothing' grin. He even had a gold tooth and two-tone Oxford shoes.

'Small world and getting smaller,'– he did not flinch when a near-miss shook the windows. He cocked his head, 'Delayed action, you can always tell.'

'We haven't met before,' said Helen.

'But I knows you. Come from a long line of fortune tellers, didn't I? No, straight up, Missus, it's your coat. Spotted it straight off. Nice goods if I do say so myself, none of your ten-and-a-tanner Woolworth's shmutter. I always thought you W.V.S. ladies wore red and green uniforms. Course, if you had I wouldn't have known yer.'

'Look, whatever your name is, it is after midnight and I'm far too tired to ramble through convolute conversation with a man who clearly . . . '

'Earns out of stuff what nobody else can get, right? Don't try insulting me, Missus, I'm too ignorant to take the rise. It was me who flogged that coat to your husband.'

'Then your name is something fishy like Hake or Whelk.'

'Very good, Missus, I like a smart lass. Winkle Greenland, at your service. You want it, I'll get it.'

'This is a Rest Centre, not a street market.'

'Dead right, go to the top of the class. Pick any prize on the top shelf. And that's why you're in such a gawd-help-us mess.'

'Mr Greenland . . . '

'Hear me out, Missus. It's right what they say about you W.V.S., the ladies who never say no. I thought you was all ladies who come down here to swank over the lower classes. But I met that Lady Reading, saw her scrubbing out without batting an eye when the office in Pimlico got bombed. Set me thinking that did. And what you done for old Charlie Pinchbeck. Him with the one leg and them down the Town Hall giving him the elbow when he asked for relief. Well, you sorted them out double-quick. And you brung that swanky doctor down here to help out. Well, that's worth a lot to Winkle Greenland, and yours truly pays what's owing.'

'The W.V.S. is a voluntary organisation, Mr Greenland.'

'Blimey, I know that don't I? Who's offering a pocketful of

sovereigns? Did I mention money?' Winkle perched on the corner of Helen's desk and wagged a finger. 'Look, lady, I know what you think I am, and you're right. But that don't mean a tealeaf like me can't see when a favour's overdue. You're one side of the law fence and I'm the other, but you ladies have got as much aggravation from them as runs things as I have, right? Okay then, what them down the Town Hall won't give you we will.'

'You're offering to sell us Black Market off-ration goods?'

'When did you last get offered a packet of pins instead of a farthing change? When did you last see a decent bit of knicker elastic or a length of dress material that ain't been made-over twice before?'

'Ages, but I still don't follow ... '

'I duck and dive about, don't I? Do a bit of trading. Well, sometimes I fall over a bit of gear that's embarrassing. That's what I'm talking about, ain't it? You take it off me hands, right?'

'And no questions asked, is that it?'

'There's my smart lass.'

'Thank you, no.'

Winkle's frown was as black as his tie. 'And I thought you was brighter than a 25-watt bulb. You ain't got the glimmer of a nightlight. I ain't selling, I'm giving. A donation to charity like.'

'Nevertheless I cannot accept.'

'You can't refuse. I'm giving you this stuff because you and your lot are fair. You'll see it goes where it's most needed. You ain't gonna stand by and see people go without when you got the means to do something about it.'

'That's blackmail, emotional blackmail,' said Helen, ready to slap Winkle's face.

'So what? You ain't so much different to me. You wearing that tweed coat proves that, so don't come on so high and mighty. Here, have these on the house.' Winkle opened a brown paper bag and rolled oranges onto the desktop. 'There, your actuals, not that bottled stuff. 'He swung his leg to the floor. 'That coat puts you my side of the law, and it ain't so long ago they was hanging kids of nine and ten for nicking a loaf of bread. Most of us have had to steal to get by. Don't make it right, don't mean you has to like me, but it do mean you ain't got the right to elbow my offer.'

Helen found herself weighing responsibility against morality, the law against expediency, and wished she was not so incredibly tired.

'There's one stipulation of course,' said Winkle. 'Nobody's to know where the stuff comes from, right? I want your word on that.'

'Because it's stolen?'

'No, and it ain't. I can't have it getting about that I'm giving freemans away when I can sell it for a good few sovs. Blimey, I'd be a laughing-stock. The whole manor'd be saying Winkle Greenland's gone soft. I'd have every face in the East End moving in on my patch.' Winkle's whole body sang with tension, and Helen saw the feral animal under the surface.

'Mr Greenland, I really can't see my way clear . . . '

Mrs Tolliver burst in, her hands covered in soapsuds. 'Mrs L., Mrs L., there's a bloke outside who wants to know where he's to unload a whole chest of tea, umpteen boxes of margarine, and would you believe it, a sack of double-knit wool.'

'Wool?' said Helen.

'Prewar stock,' said Winkle.

'And Irish linen. In bolts. Think of the things we can make with *them*.'

Winkle grinned through cigarette smoke. 'Turn it down, why don't yer?'

Mrs Tolliver turned on him. 'Turn it down? There's thousands crying out for stuff like that. You're looking for a right-hander, cocker. Who is he, Mrs L?'

'Me?' grinned Winkle. 'I ain't nobody. See you, Missus,' and he sauntered out leaving a thin veil of Player's smoke in the room.

'You shouldn't truck with sherberts like that,' said Mrs

Tolliver. 'You're too free-and-easy sometimes.'

'Am I?' Helen mused. 'Am I really?'

'Yus,' Mrs Tolliver said firmly. 'Too easy by half-and-half again.'

'Hmmm,' said Helen, feeling the nap of her coat.

SIX: FRANK

The overhead light snapped on.

'Stand by your beds!'

Groaning and coughing they stumbled out of their beds to blink awake on the cold floor. A sergeant and a corporal marched the length of the hut shouting at the tardy.

'On your *feet*. You nasty little soldier, get yourself erect and leave your family jewels alone. You'll be asking for married quarters next.'

'You! Get that nasty thing covered up. You may frighten your mother but you don't frighten me. Put it under the cold tap, you fairy.'

'Stand up! Stand still! I've seen more life under a cabbage leaf . . . '

'What's up, Sarge?'

'Shut your hole. Stand still. Stand straight.'

It's three o'clock in the morning, they can't want us out on the dustbins now. What did I do wrong? Frank remembered where he was. He snapped to attention, his thumbs down his trouser seams.

'Well, we got one soldier,' said the corporal. 'Atten . . . *hut!*'

'Right, you're all going on a nice little outing to the seaside. I want you outside, shaved, sober, hands off your cocks in full pack and ready to travel in . . . ' the sergeant looked at his watch, 'seven minutes. Late on parade earns my boot smartly up where the sun don't shine. Hop to!'

'You heard the sergeant. *Move!*'

On the windswept parade ground they were loaded aboard lorries flanked by motorcycle outriders.

'In tens forward ... board!'

'Greece, it's got to be. Give the bubbles a hand with the Eyetalians ... '

'Nah. Them Greeks can handle the Eyeties one hand tied.'

'Africa?'

'Benghazi?'

'Who?'

'Egypt, you ignorant berk.'

'That's Libya, berk y'self ... '

'The Eyeties are there too.'

'They won't send us abroad with the invasion coming.'

'What bleeding invasion? A dollar says it's the Med.'

'Yeah, kick old Musso off his Lake of Peace.'

'Could be the Med ... '

'Could be Wigan Pier for all we know.'

'More probably potato picking ... here, who threw that?'

'Could be London, burying the dead ... they say there's thousands unburied and the rats ... '

'Shut up there. Get enbussed. No smoking!'

'What d'you think, Frank mate?'

'Why ask me? You're the experts.'

'That's it, criminal, butter wouldn't melt in your cakehole.'

Keep it up, Taggart ...

'Wherever, it's gotta be against the Eye-bleeding-ties ...'

'Oh blimey yeah,' said Frank.

CHAPTER FIVE

S.S. Standartenführer Dr Franz Six, prepared to take up headquarters in London, to implement the rounding up of all persons ranging from Churchill to Nöel Coward on a 2,700-name black list. 'My dear,' Rebecca West, also prominent on the list, commented dryly to Coward, 'the people we would have been seen dead with.'

1940: The World in Flames Richard Collier.

ONE: CHRISTOPHER

24 December 1940.

The hotel room was small, primrose yellow and had chintz curtains at the tall windows. The fireplace was filled with red silver paper and a note on the wall apologised for the lack of coal to heat the guest rooms. Frost coated the panes with white surreal flora, an entwining silver bouquet of frozen flowers.

'I haven't felt my feet since London,' said Helen.

'I still can't believe you're here.' Christopher lined Helen's luggage up beside the double bed, shivering inside his greatcoat. 'How did you manage it?'

'Not another word until we're in bed. And not because of *that*,' said Helen. 'It's the warmest place.' They snuggled under the counterpane fully clothed and Christopher drew the cork of a bottle of red wine.

'It's Algerian and quite filthy. I couldn't tell you the unit had been posted, everything seems to be hush-hush nowadays. Seeing you in uniform is disconcerting.'

'It opens doors, dodo. Without it I should still be wandering about Weston-super-Mare like some of the other abandoned war-wives. They'll have a miserable Christmas. A splendidly horsey woman in the W.V.S. found me at the station and drove me all the way here in her bullnosed Morris. She must have used up most of her petrol ration, but she refused to take a penny for her trouble. I did manage to get her to take some bobbins of thread and needles for her sewing group, though.'

'That seems very little.'

'They're like gold dust, dodo. Her group makes camouflage netting and she says it's the filthiest job imaginable. The hemp dust gets into everything, even her underwear.'

'Mentioning the unmentionable isn't polite, darling girl.'

'This isn't polite company, we're married.'

Christopher touched the tip of Helen's nose. 'Just please remember not to be so forthright if we meet up with any of our set.'

'Pooh, I'm not yet completely debauched.'

'You do look tired.'

'I'll perk up once this awful wine gets to work, you'll see. I have four days with my husband and that makes me one of the lucky ones. I say, you do have leave, don't you? You won't be rushing all over Portland with barbed-wire for Christmas?'

'I'll turn and turn about with Hatwood and Mason. Charlesworth may put in an appearance at some time. He's rather smitten by a lady friend in Weymouth. He keeps her rather a secret, and I suspect he has crossed the class barrier and is ashamed of himself.'

'Is she a tart, Christopher?'

'Heavens above, I hope not! I rather think she's married though.'

'Wicked old Neville. How things change, dodo. A year ago I should have been thoroughly shocked, but the odd liaisons I've come across in the W.V.S. make anything Neville might do pale into utter insignificance. D'you know, one of my mothers has four children and all by different fathers? She hasn't the foggiest who fathered the fourth. When I asked her about it, she said: "I dunno, Miss. It was in a shelter and it was dark and I didn't like to ask."' Helen aped the Kennington whine perfectly. 'She's rather a pet and not very bright, but she adores those children.' She snuggled into Christopher's shoulder. 'Four whole days, a lifetime. With things so uncertain it's silly to make plans. It's more important to enjoy what one has now, and what *we* have is *us*.'

'A touch more Algerian plonk?'

'Yes. After a couple of swallows it sort of numbs the tongue and tastes marginally less like spirits of salts. And I can feel my toes coming back to life. How about you?'

'You'd be surprised what I can feel coming alive.'

'Beast. And you chide me for talking baldly. I've a good mind to take my presents away unwrapped.'

'My present's already unwrapped.'

'Beastlier and beastlier.'

'Come here please.'

'Don't make me spill my ghastly wine. It'd probably eat its way through the bedding and springs all the way to the floor ... mmm ...'

'Warmer?'

'Much. There's a lot to be said for immediacy. We've probably committed a treasonable act. Isn't doing it in uniform against King's Regulations?'

'Half the British Army's guilty in that case. More wine?'

'No, it's varnished my throat. Two coats of shellac at least. Do they have any real drinks at the bar, dodo?'

'Some esoteric liqueurs and some gin I think.'

'Let's go down and get some then. I need to talk to the landlady about my surprise anyway. Tomorrow's luncheon menu reads like a railway buffet's. Yuk.'

'What are all those parcels?'

'Never you mind, dodo. But, I do have a turkey!'

'Great heavens, how did you manage that?'

'Influence with a rather murky character called Winkle. That man can lay his hands on almost anything.'

'At a price, I imagine, *if* that's the chap I'm thinking of.'

'Don't frown, dodo, you'll get worry lines.'

'But Helen . . . '

'Pooh, what's the good of money when there's hardly anything to spend it on? And the only butcher left near the Rest Centre is a bad-tempered old fascist who bullies his customers. His sausages are all sawdust and wood-shavings, and even Mrs Tolliver quails before him. Can you imagine how tired I am of having shopkeepers saying, "Don't you know there's a war on?", when I ask for something they don't have?' Helen rebuttoned her blouse and checked her stockings for runs. 'I'm strong enough to stand the sight of dead women and children. Something stops me from seeing them as people any more. I concern myself with the live ones, and I love them all; the lost, the old, the apathetic and the hysterical. Even the ungrateful ones who swear at us because "them" at the Town Hall and "that man" Hitler are too remote. We don't even mind the drunks, men, women or minors, who hurl abuse because it's the only crutch they have left. There are enough strong and funny ones to keep us cheerful. What I mind are the little things we used to take for granted. Like pearl buttons and the twists of coloured silk that have disappeared from the shelves. Seasonal fruits like apples and cherries, punnets of fat red strawberries. I mind washing with rough soap in cold water that stinks of chlorine. I mind wearing patched and darned underthings for days when I used to change every day, twice if there was an evening dance or we went to the theatre. Small things, dodo, very small, very precious lost things.' Helen plumped the pillow with her fist.

'Razor blades,' said Christopher. 'Fresh shellfish. An hors-d'oeuvre as well as an entree. Food that doesn't look and taste as though it had been reconstituted from old newspapers and engine-oil.'

'Were we terribly pampered, Christopher? Am I awful to miss such things?'

'It would be unnatural not to miss them. Neville's main complaint is that his wine merchant can only supply half his usual order, and mostly with Australian brews. Let's put it all from our minds, shall we?' Christopher smoothed Helen's forehead with a gentle thumb. 'Look who's getting worry lines.'

'I'm all right, dodo, really. This is Christmas. Our Christmas together, and I'm not going to waste it being weepy and silly. Do you remember those highly-coloured illuminated advertising signs in Trafalgar Square and Piccadilly Circus, and how vulgar we considered them? How I should like to see them back again. It's so sad to see Landseer's lions sandbagged and to have Eros in a bombproofed cellar, his fountain covered in hoardings advertising war bonds. People care about and notice such things, and the newspapers make all kinds of fuss if one of the West End stores loses a few panes of glass, and yet *nothing* is said about the hundreds of small businesses that have been bombed flat. Nobody cares that their owners have lost everything and that they won't get a farthing compensation. Nothing. The very people who are suffering the most, who are Royalists to the core and are truly patriotic, are being ignored in the most callous manner.'

'Talk if it helps, but you can't take the conscience of the world on your shoulders, darling girl.'

'How can I make you understand?'

'I'm afraid you can't. No more than I understand why I'm piddle-balling about here at Portland Bill when the local Home Guard could do what I'm doing with half the effort. Don't you think I should like to be released from this duty to do something worthwhile? You at least have been doing some good, even if you think it isn't enough.'

'It isn't.'

'But it's more than I've achieved, my darling.'

'Is it, dodo, is it really?'

'I'd trade places with you tomorrow. Wavell's Australians have taken 30,000 Italian prisoners in Egypt and have advanced into Libya. The Greeks are knocking seven kinds of hell out of Mussolini in Albania, and I'm sitting here with my highly-trained men guarding the Navy who doesn't need defending. My chaps may not be regular army, but they're keen to have a crack at something. Anything.'

Helen looked grave, 'You sound bitter. I'm very selfish, thinking of myself when you're so ... wasted.'

'Not you,' Christopher shook himself from his melancholy.

'Yes I am, and I'm going to be more selfish. Just for four lovely days.'

'Good, that means I get indulged too.'

'Unmercifully.'

'Promises, promises ... '

'You'll see. Now, let's go and make the landlady's eyes pop with my glorious fat turkey. Or does she think of herself as an hotelier?'

'Hotelier probably. Her Cheltenham ladies have given her airs of grandeur. By the way, is it a cock or a hen bird?'

'Does it matter?'

Christopher kept a straight face. 'If turkeys follow the general rule of jelly-babies, you get more meat with a cock bird.'

'That,' said Helen, 'is a fowl remark.'

'Ouch,' said Christopher, 'I suppose a bad pun is better than no pun at all.'

'Infinitely. And it's lovely to see you laugh, dodo.'

'Then I shall grin like a baboon all through luncheon.'

They went down to the lounge bar hand in hand to drink gin and bitters.

TWO: NEVILLE

Twenty-three miles to the west of Lyme Regis, Neville Charlesworth watched the woman undress in front of a spitting coal fire, her sturdy naked back flickering with fitful orange light. Her brassiere strap had left red weals on her shoulders and her calves were slightly chapped. Champagne had made her giggly and coy. She laid her skirt across a chair and wriggled out of her petticoat, exposing her dimpled buttocks.

'I can't stay all night, Neville,' she said. 'Ro might get leave from Oswestry. I shall have to get home in case he does.'

'A wife's duty, my dear Rosalind. And who wouldn't cross rivers of fire to enjoy your ample pulchitrude?' Charlesworth said drearily, thinking, *the matron Rosalind, she of the carnal appetites and collector of glass animals, married to Roland Pepper, soldier and lush. Roland couldn't get an erection with the aid of a scaffold. He'll arrive drunk, kill a bottle of whatever is going, paw you ineptly and snore into your bosom whilst you dream of embracing some matinee idol. Rosalind, thy name is disaster, but you salve what ails me.*

'Don't say wife so loudly. Somebody might be listening. Honestly, you don't give a jot for my reputation, do you?'

'Your reputation is what attracted me to you in the first place.'

'Are you being cross, Nev?'

'I? Never with you, buxom lady. Come, drown me in mammarial plenty. You have the most magnificent bosom this side of the Chilterns.'

'You're awful. I need a dictionary to keep up with you. They are quite good, aren't they? Considering I'm almost thirty.' Rosalind drew her shoulders back to bring her breasts erect. 'Only as far as the Chilterns?'

'That's as far as my travel warrants have taken me. Should I quest further for comparison's sake when I have you here?'

'I'd be jealous. Do you love me, Nev?'

Call me Nev again, you mindless bitch and I'll bite off your nipples and feed them to the cat. I'm drunker than I thought. But not drunk enough not to know what a crass idiot I am, allowing my glands to precipitate me into a sordid affair with a silly tart like you, Rosalind Pepper. 'My adoration is boundless.'

'Adoration isn't love. I may not be clever like you, but I know semantics when I hear them.'

'You do own a dictionary, you brilliant besom.'

'The full Oxford, all twenty-five volumes. Just be kind, Nev. Don't be clever with me. It hurts.'

'Uncle Neville will feed you cream from the pitcher and stroke your pretty fur as you purr into my lap. Is that kind enough for you?' Charlesworth edged onto a cold part of the bed to allow Rosalind to swing in beside him. Her cold limbs twined around him and he was immediately aroused.

'More or less.' Rosalind's plump hand ran along his thigh.

'Is it more or is it less?'

'I don't want to talk any more.'

'You always talk when we're like this.'

'Not with my mouth full.'

'Abandoned creature.'

'You love it ... don't you ... don't you? ... '

'God rot me, yes.'

'And that, and that?'

'All that.'

'Then love me back a little, Nev.' Rosalind straddled him to press her heavy breasts against his face. 'Love them.'

She tastes of talcum and lavender. Was she this voracious with Roland during the early part of their marriage? Is she seeing him when she's like this with me, seeing him in that earlier time without his beer-belly and yellowed hair? His breath sweet and his body hard against her? Does she roll the years as easily as she draws me up inside her? Am I a cypher to her as she is to me? Give her something of yourself, Charlesworth, or all this is nothing but mechanical easement between strangers, four legs in a bed and minds at opposite ends of different universes. To despise her you must first despise yourself, clever lieutenant, and you can't do that without losing more than you can ever afford.

'Love me, love me ...'

'My name is Neville. Neville, Rosalind, Neville ...'

'Yes, Neville, yes ...'

Why does that make it different? Charlesworth moved her onto her back in a slow roll of breasts.

'Neville ...'

Her breath in my face is a multiple pant of loss, as angry as the slap of our locked thighs. I can make it tender, I can. There, she's opening up like a folded flower, she senses the change in me. Move with her, not against her, find rhythm. Pace her. The poor bitch can't help it if she isn't who I really want and can't have. First cousins don't marry. Nature played a monstrous trick there, monstrous, monstrous ...

'Neville, you do, you do ...'

'Of course.' *Climb with me into the stratosphere, you poor lost and lonely bitch. Tense your lush body, arch your back and buck us both to the dark beyond the stars where we can both forget who and what we are. Leave your lost drunkard behind. Help me to lose the images of what might have been with the girl I shared a playpen with, made sandcastles beside, sat with under Christmas trees on Boxing Days when childhood and childish love went on forever ...*

'Stay with me, Neville, don't leave now ...'

'I'm here, Rosalind.'

'Together, together, together ...'

Explosion and melting quiet. Over the mountains of the moon with a thudding heart to where shared hot musk perfumed the skin. The long, quiet coming back into the mundane room with its hotel decor. The leaden borrowed light on the counterpane and her outflung arm. The second hand of her tiny watch ticking in inexorable circles. Her slackly opened mouth as wet as fresh wet paint. Ah, but Helen, it isn't you.

'Neville?' Rosalind's voice had a burr to it.

'Yes?'

'You *care*, you truly *care*. I could cry for happiness.'

'I'd rather we cried for champagne.'

'Don't withdraw, not yet. Stay there. Please let it last a short while longer.'

'That's no hardship, you delicious baggage.'

Rosalind found Charlesworth's mouth with a moist hand. 'No jokes, not yet.'

'No,' *that would destroy the little I gave us both.*

'Thank you.'

Thank you, brave lieutenant, thank you. You cuckold my husband beautifully. It's unfair of me to be irritated by her gratitude, but I am, damn me to hell. I'm not some doorman to be thanked and tipped with a silver gratuity, dismissed like some menial with a gracious bob of the head. I ought to knee her in the stomach and watch her face change to mud as pain takes her breath. 'You're entirely welcome, Mrs Pepper.'

'You're trying to spoil it.'

'Thirst does that to a man who has slaked another thirst.'

'Don't, Neville.' Rosalind's thighs slackened and she moved to bite her fist.

She's such a pathetic creature. 'I apologise. I speak before I think. We both talk too much.'

'Yes?'

'And don't drink enough. Let us toast this moment in bubbly, my treasure, for tomorrow is the day of Roland. Your warrior husband returns to check the locks on your chastity belt.'

'Are you jealous of Roland? Are you?'

'Insanely, woman of my dreams. Pour wine upon yourself and let me kiss you dry.'

Rosalind giggled with misted eyes. 'You do care.'

Charlesworth thought of Helen with Christopher and despair made him laugh aloud. 'You'll never know how much.'

'You must tell me often.'

Charlesworth looked through the windows with unseeing eyes. 'There aren't enough words in the world,' he said. 'But there is enough champagne.'

'I don't understand.'

No, nor never you shall. 'Pour the libation, pretty one,' *for you'll never know that I may wake up some blessed tomorrow and find myself free of her. But that's self-delusion, Neville my lad, and well you know it. You may think of her happiness selflessly during the sane daylight hours, but on those chill midnight vigils when sleep is elusive and you conjure her out of the darkness – almost make her a tactile entity, you aren't anything more than a rampant male seeking her body for your own. Then you'd kill Lutyens for her. Instead you kill glass soldiers filled with tincture of amber. Enough whisky to bring dreamless sleep and form a barrier between you and the lives of others, like Rosalind and Roland and Hatwood and Mason and the Brigadier and on and on and on ...* 'World without end,' he said aloud, making it a toast.

'To us, Neville? Forever?'

'You'll tire of me soon enough. If Tyrone Power walked in on us you'd leap on him with a low moan and forget I was here.'

'That's only silly fantasy. All women like men like that to dream about, but they don't expect to even meet them – or would want to. We should all know our dreams have limitations.'

'Should we now?' Charlesworth drained his glass, suddenly thoroughly tired of the whole affair.

'Why does your face change so fast? One moment you're all sharp jokes, the next ... bang, you're in a bad sulk.'

'Gentlemen never sulk. That's for tarts and the lower orders. Pass the champagne.'

'You're cross then. You can admit that much. Sour grapes.'

'Champagne, Rosalind. Don't stretch your limited cerebellum in the pursuit of convenient truth. You'll lose.'

Rosalind bit her plump lower lip. 'You mean don't be clever, don't you?'

'I mean, don't *try* to be clever.'

'How can I get to know you if we don't talk about ... things?'

Know me, you cretinous doxie? Us forever? In five years you'll have a dozen chins and an arse as big as Stonehenge. No man could penetrate your thighs without a crowbar and a road-map. Even Roland will look at you with the disgust he usually saves for his own bloated features when he sees them in his shaving mirror.

'Don't laugh like that. It's ... ghoulish. You give me the shivers.'

'Then pour the champagne and see if you can't coax some hot water from that Edwardian abortion this hotel describes as a bathroom.'

'You really are a bastard, aren't you?' said Rosalind.

'And don't you love it.'

'I suppose I must.' Rosalind rolled from the bed and padded through the adjoining door. As water ran and the pipes knocked, Charlesworth heard her crying into a towel.

'And the compliments of the season,' he said, toasting his alter-ego in the dressing table mirror. 'Now you have to be kind to her again.' He drank without pleasure. 'But who'll be kind to you?' he asked his reversed image.

Helen.

THREE: PHYLLIS

Hoar frost had transformed the breakwaters into the outer walls of some magical ice palace haunting the leaden overcast. Row upon crystal row, they ran into the sea where frozen surf had bearded the uprights with icicles and grime had formed silver spurs on the barbed wire. The beach glittered like yellow sugar and the hard clumps of marram grass in the sparkling dunes were unmoving white spears despite a brisk wind from the sea.

Harry stamped as he walked, breaking the crust to leave perfect footprints in the sand and breathed hard to see his breath cloud before the breeze broke it into scribbles of vapour. Phyllis carried Robert against her face, blind to the beauty about her, anxious to get her sons out of the bitter cold. The walk from her chalet to Sissie's boat was a long one and her thin topcoat was no protection.

Sissie's overturned fishing boat was no longer a dark wooden whale beached by the storm. The carvel hull was as white as wedding cake and the smoke from the steel chimney stack ran in whipping black strands speckled by sparks. The small lagoon outside her back door was iced over and the yellow light from her two small windows shone like bright flags of welcome. The outhouse was a lonely white sentinel, its pitched roof forming a chevron of frost against the soiled grey sky.

Phyllis thought of hot tea as she trudged on. The Champion Dairy float had brought her muffins with her milk and orange juice, and wonder of wonders, a half-chicken for Christmas dinner. She had sewn it up with thread and stuffed it with breadcrumbs and sage. It would have been lovely to have Tommy home on leave, but that would have meant smaller portions all round. Doris had written to say that she and Jack were well and that she had not been able to get hold of any white meat at all. Being childless, they hadn't enough points to qualify. *What she didn't say,* thought Phyllis, *is that she only bought scrag end and offal at the best of times, and no butcher was going to put anything by for a bad customer like that. Blimey, I don't remember the last time I saw a bit of liver or kidneys. The only offal you see nowadays is sheep or ox hearts, and they took a year to cook up tender. The boys won't touch them neither, nor that jam I tried to make with carrots and potatoes. The Ministry of Food have got some funny ideas on what you can do with less than nothing. Fed it to Mrs Wormold's chickens in the end. At least she gave me a couple or three eggs for it and the chickens pecked it all up, bless 'em.*

Sissie wore a turban when she opened her door.

'Oh, Phyl, am I glad to see you.'

'What's up, pet?' Phyllis leaned on the door and forced the latch home. 'You look upset.'

'That ain't the half of it,' Sissie wagged a finger at Stanley. 'That little bleeder got paint all over me one good tablecloth. Said he wanted to make a flag like *Swallows and Amazons*. That's what comes of giving kids books. Gives 'em bloody silly ideas. And he's made all my potatoes into animals with matchsticks and things. Said he read about *that* in a book too.'

'You can take the matches out.'

'Not when he's painted them all with red nail varnish, can I?'

'Oh, Stanley, you need your ear clipped,' said Phyllis.

'Already have,' Stanley sniffed sulkily. 'S'er fault we ain't having Christmas like you lot.'

'No Christmas, Sissie?' Phyllis was appalled.

'He'd have had presents, wouldn't have left him out of that. We just wouldn't celebrate it, that's all.'

'Because you're not . . .'

'Not Christian, right?'

'Bet they got jelly and crackers,' said Stanley.

'Listen to him belly-ache. In London it wouldn't have mattered so much with all the family around and such. But here.' Sissie wiped at a spilled tear. 'It's getting to me, being alone. Here, where's my manners? I'll make tea.'

'Sissie's crying,' said Harry, patting her substantial thigh. 'Smile Sissie. Be a big boy.'

'Bless him, the little *mench*.'

Phyllis sat at the rickety table with Robert on her lap. 'It gets us all down at times, Sissie love.'

'I can't have Asa seeing me like this if he gets leave. I'm a sight.'

'Yeah, show her, Ma,' said Stanley.

Sissie mimed a blow, 'You'll get such a hit.'

'You do and I'll drink something.'

'More of your *chutzpah* and I'll knock you into next week.'

'I'm going for a walk,' said Stanley. He put on his coat and went out into the wind.

'Such a burden,' Sissie sighed, warming the teapot. 'If his father was here, though God forbid he should see me like this.' She undid her turban and dared Phyllis to laugh. Her hair was no longer black and lustrous. The crown was white-blonde and tufted and her bangs hung in streaked varicoloured strands.

Phyllis's laughter startled the baby on her lap. 'Sissie, what have you done to yourself?'

'Asa said he likes blondes, so I bleached it.'

'Didn't you read the instructions on the box?'

'What box? I used ordinary bleach.'

'It wasn't peroxide? Oh, Sissie, you must have burned yourself.'

'I did. What do I do?'

'First things first,' said Phyllis. 'Don't waste that water on tea. We got to wash your scalp and get all that filth off it. Then have a go with the scissors. Can't have you looking like the last of the Mohicans.'

An hour later, Sissie looked at herself in a looking-glass. Phyllis had given her a short pageboy with nail scissors and a razor. Henna had turned her hair an odd reddish pink. 'I look like a fat elf,' Sissie said. 'Me and the turban don't part company from now on.'

As they drank tea and Sissie began to cheer up, Stanley came in with his face purple and contorted. He had drunk paraffin.

Harry and Robert cried in sympathy as he vomited into the sink.

'Some Christmas,' said Sissie as they waited for the doctor.

'I told you I'd drink something,' said Stanley.

'If you'd died your father would have killed you,' said Phyllis.

'He don't care. Nobody cares . . .'

'It's the war,' said Sissie. 'This bleeding war.'

FOUR: FRANK

The horizon dipped and turned in a lazy figure-of-eight motion as the troopship rolled with the swell, beating against wind and tide. The sky was rose-madder and a thick white cloud ran from the tip of Gibraltar, spun out on the warm wind from the North African coast.

Frank held the rail, his feet braced as the ship gathered itself to plough into a dark green trough. Spray was a clean rain on his face and he breathed the fresh ozone blowing in at him, grateful that it threw the shipboard smells away from him. Motion sickness had swept through the ship in the Bay of Biscay and the fire hoses were in constant use, sluicing vomit from the decks. Men sprawled everywhere, most of them too wretched to move. The conditions below decks were awful. The heads overflowed and vomit slopped and swilled in the companionways, ran in the scuppers and crusted the lower gangways.

The ship put its nose down, shuddered and came up in a long slow surge with spume hissing away from the creaming bow-wave. The wind smelled of hot desert, of wadis and palms and Frank wondered how a camel smelled or if he would see Riff forts and Bedouin tribesmen similar to the ones he had read about in *Boy's Own Paper* and seen at the pictures.

Tosher staggered in beside Frank. As the horizon shifted he closed his eyes and swayed. 'How do you do it, Frank mate? You ain't chucked up once.'

'It's the way you think, Tosh.' Frank put Tosher's hands on the rail. 'Think of something else.'

'What, for gawd-help-us-sake?'

'Christmas at home. Your old mum basting a turkey. All the fruit on the sideboard. Brazil nuts and dates and tangerines in the best cut-glass bowl. A big fat plum pudding stuffed with lucky silver joeys simmering away on the stove. A bit of mistletoe over the kitchen door so you can kiss the girls when they don't expect it. Lashings of custard and hot mince pies. Having a wish when the old mother sets light to the brandy she's poured over the pud and you hoping to get a silver joey without swallowing it. Going back for second helpings after loosening your belt. Lovely.'

The thought of rich food, of any food, turned Tosher's stomach. 'Leave it out ... '

'And for Boxing Day breakfast, a nice bit of fatty pork and crackling, fried eggs and a bleeding great doorstep of fried bread. All that greasy old bacon rind and dollops of brown sauce. Where're you going?'

'You rotten bloody ... ' Tosher bowed over to hawk into the hissing sea.

'Now what did I say?' Frank asked the shifting sky, enjoying his iron stomach.

The escort destroyers were low greyhounds off the starboard quarter, making smoke as they ran into the Straits. Light semaphored from a minesweeper and a 'stringbag' Swordfish made a turn towards the Rock of Gibraltar.

'Rotten ... rotten ...' Tosher drooled.

'Just trying to give you a taste of home,' Frank said. *Who am I kidding? We was lucky if we got a taste of goose, a new penny, a piece of coal and an orange in our stockings. Father Christmas never came to our house that I remember. What did us kids ever get when Christmas came around? Nothing but standing outside the pub with a glass of lemonade and an arrowroot biscuit while the old mother got stinking on gin and orange. And all the drunken old girls would nip out to give us a sloppy kiss, slip us the odd penny or two and give us a sip of their port and lemons to keep the cold out.*

Phyl said the old dad bought her a real doll's house one year. But it went to be popped at uncle's when the rent was due, and if she wanted to see it she had to go round and look in the pawnshop window. When it wasn't redeemed it disappeared and she never saw it again. That hurt her more than anything. Just knowing it was in the window was enough for her. But when it went ...

Frank wished he could smoke, but the wind burned cigarettes away too quickly, and going below to light up was out of the question. 'You all right, Tosh?'

'If you don't talk about ... food and that,' Tosher wiped scum from his mouth. 'When do we put into port?'

'Who ever tells us anything? One of the fish-head matelots said Alexandria, but they don't know any more than we do. Just be glad we're almost into the Mediterranean. It didn't ought to be as lumpy there.'

'Let's hope so. One of the blokes said we're all getting a Christmas card from the King and Queen. You reckon that's right?'

I'd rather have a pork pie and chips. 'We're supposed to get a cigarette ration, but with everybody feeling so humpty there's no chance.'

'I couldn't smoke anyway,' Tosher mumbled.

'Stop moaning. People pay fortunes, save half their lives for a sea cruise like this, and here you are getting one free and moaning about it.'

'Hang about, I think I'm going to ... ' Tosher bowed over the rail.

'Cough up, chicken. It might be an egg,' said Frank.

A destroyer *whooped* as it scythed past, making sounds similar to those coming from Tosher.

'And a merry Christmas to you too,' said Frank.

FIVE: DORIS

The Canadian soldier chewed gum and drank whisky chasers with his light ales. Emma Cooper wore her green hat and sang with a group around Mr Mason's piano, and Jack drank stout and mild as though he were alone in the smoke and noise of the Hope & Anchor.

'Come on, Jack love, sing up. We're a long time dead,' said Doris, winking at the Canadian as if they had been conspirators for a decade. She liked his drawl and his interest in her. He had bought the last three rounds and showed no sign of running out of money or generosity. With fellows like him around this war could get to be a lot more fun than she had first supposed.

'Another round here, miss,' said the Canadian. 'Another snort there, Doris? Jack? And what's your Mom drinking?'

'You'll get me tiddly,' said Doris, dimpling for effect, glad she had permed her hair that morning.

'Not you, Honey. Hardest head this side of Algonquin Park.'

'Is that far from here, Brandon?'

'Twopenny bus-ride from Canvey Island,' said Jack.

Brandon laughed. 'You're a real funny guy. Another of these pints, Jack?'

'He ain't funny. He's just being funny.' Doris accepted another gin and orange, frowning at Jack. *Why he's pulling a moody when this Brandon's buying three rounds to our one I just can't imagine. If it wasn't for me he wouldn't meet no-one. He ought to show willing just once in a while. I mean, it's bad enough him running off and leaving me at all hours of the day and night to mend his gaspipes or whatever he does.*

With Phyl gone he knows I'm alone in the house and I can't stand being on my own when there's a raid on. Of course I come out for a bit of company, he ought to understand that. But look at him, sitting there with a face like thunder 'cause I'm talking to Brandon. You'd think he was a German instead of a Canadian the way Jack's looking at him. It's not as though there's any harm in it. Mind you, Brandon does have lovely hair and his eyes wrinkle up like a cat's when he smiles with them lovely white teeth. And I bet he's lovely and smooth and ain't covered in hair like somebody not a million miles away. Jack's drinking his beer, so why don't he show a bit more life? Show willing. Sitting there beside Brandon he looks like an old rug left out in the weather. Anyway, it's his own fault if I have to find company where I can. When he does come home he's dead grumpy and tired and filthy-dirty, and he knows I can't bear hearing about how bad things are in the East End. I told him, let them as lives there take care of their own. He should transfer to this district, then it'd be easier for both of us. I don't want to hear about bombs and bombing. That's not for me. Ain't my war. 'Cheers, Brandon. Compliments of the season, ducks.'

'Flipping Merry Christmas,' said Jack.

'Here's how,' said Brandon, closing one eye in a long wink.

'How what?' Jack said, shrugging inside his jacket and rolling his eyes.

'You're being funny again, Jack,' Doris warned.

'Cheering up, ain't I?' Jack took another pint from Brandon and inhaled half of it, his eyes as humourless as splinters of mica.

'Funny cuts. Just 'cause I'm having fun you're jealous.'

'Me? I'm delirious. Who wouldn't be with Spam and chips for Christmas dinner? You and your Ma to look at when you've both been at the bevvy like drowning ferrets. You'll both have big heads from too much gin, and the chips'll be soggy. Not even a sprout or carrots to brighten it up. Blooming swedes that look like dead firelighters and taste like wet string. I've done my brain and pocket in to get you a decent present, and what did I get? Socks and underwear.'

'They're gold dust. You should be grateful.'

'Yeah, I'll think of you every time I sit down in the khazi.'

'Don't be crude.'

'You'd make Christ swear.'

'And don't blaspheme.'

'Don't give me that God stuff. Come the revolution, ugly-chops, we'll turn all the churches into picture palaces.'

'Showing all them bloody awful Russian films you make a fuss about, I suppose. Give me Gene Kelly and Fred Astaire any day.'

'You'd spend all your time in the pictures wouldn't you? If you had your way you'd have been born a flipping cinema seat in the three and nines.'

'And where's the fun with you rabbiting on about brotherhood and all that old political tonk? You and your bolshevism. Enough to turn a snake into a walking stick. And Brandon don't want to listen to all this.'

'Then bleeding Brandon can do the other thing, can't he?'

'Hey, Jack buddy ... '

'You ain't my buddy, so eff off out of it,' said Jack.

'Now ain't that sweet?' Doris sneered, wishing Brandon was bigger and Jack was a midget. 'You spoil everything. Take no notice, Brandon.'

'S'okay. What's Spam?'

'Tinned meat, ducks.'

'It's pink coloured, puke flavoured jellied armpits.' Jack called the barman. 'A pound's worth of mixed drinks, John. So long as I get change of a dollar.' He squinted at Doris. 'Jolly enough for you, girl?'

'Ha-flaming-ha.'

'D'you like sweet ham?'

Jack stared at the Canadian with suspicion. 'What's the catch?'

'What catch, it's a simple question, right?'

'It's simple all right.'

'Now, Jack,' said Doris. 'Brandon's trying to be nice. Ain't you, Brandon?'

The Canadian tweaked an earlobe. 'S'pose I am. I've got a five pound tinned ham, that's all. I thought maybe ... '

'How flipping much?'

'I thought,' said Brandon, 'that you and Doris might like to invite a stranger home for Christmas dinner. It would sure be nice to eat a home-cooked meal. I don't want to sell the ham to you.'

Jack swilled his beer around in his glass.

'You see where your bear's breath gets you, Jack?' Doris smiled at Brandon. 'You come home with us, ducks. We can put you up and everything. There's plenty of room with my sister away.'

'Hey, that's wonderful.'

'Yeah,' said Jack, watching Emma Cooper singing with her mouth all the way open, her green hat over one eye. 'She'll be in a right state in the morning.'

'Bless her, she's having a good time,' said Doris.

'I've got a bottle of Canadian Club in my duffle. 120° proof. A gift to the house of my English friends.'

'D'you play cards, Brandon?'

'Stud or draw, shuffle and deal. Just you name it, pal.'

'Hmmm,' said Jack. 'Sell us a deck of cards, John.'

Crosseyed John the barman wore a Warden's helmet with a sprig of mistletoe taped to it and the white berries bobbed as he talked. 'Found a mug have you? Or is that Frankie coming home?'

'Never you mind. Me and Brandon here'll find out who the mug is. Come along if you wanna lesson. Make it a decent school. You've got the three-ha'pence. Never knew a publican who didn't have a few bob in his bin and still cried poverty.'

Crosseyed John jerked his head from Jack to Doris. 'Who's put laughing boy in a good mood?'

'It's like living with a ruddy swinging door,' said Doris. 'Every time he opens his mouth another mood comes out.'

John's wall-eyed gaze took them all in. 'Penny a point?'

'Sure, friendly stakes,' said Brandon. 'This is gonna be more fun than tracking a marmalade cat through a roomful of rocking chairs.'

'Don't he talk nice?' said Doris. *I'll put Brandon downstairs in Phyllis's double bed. There must be a pair of Tommy's pyjamas around. He'll be comfy down there and Jack won't be forever tripping over him. He looks a bit like Robert Taylor in Camille, except he don't have a moustache and his hair ain't that black.* 'I'm playing.'

'I'll be down after closing.' John went off to ring last orders.

'Watch him when we're playing, Brandon,' said Jack, finishing his beer. 'John can see round corners.'

'Surely will.'

'Are you married, Brandon?'

'No, ma'am. Never ride one horse when there's a herd of mares on the homestead,' strong ale slurred Brandon's words. 'And your British girls are pretty and friendly.'

'Not this one ain't,' said Jack.

'He didn't mean nothing,' said Doris. 'Did you, Brandon?'

The Canadian laughed as the singers around the piano sang 'Silent Night' with more gusto than precision. 'No Ma'am.'

'Hmmm,' said Jack.

SIX: JACK

'I'm gone,' said crosseyed John.

'Your five bob and up five,' Jack pushed two half-crowns into the pot.

'I'm not playing silly buggers,' Doris threw her prial of twos in.

'Ten shillings, right?' Brandon skimmed a note onto the table.

'Ain't seeing me, eh?' Jack threw change for his last pound note. 'Then I'll turn you over.'

'Full house,' Brandon turned his cards. 'Aces over kings.'

'Three bullets and two fat dads,' said John. 'That's a bit healthy.'

'Too rich for me.' Jack lost his cards in the deck as Brandon scooped in the pot. *Drunk he may be, but this sod can play cards. I've only won one hand and John ain't had a look in all night. If this Brandon geezer's sharping he's going the right way about it.* He poured the last of the whisky into Brandon's glass. 'Your luck's in, my Canadian cocker.'

'Tasty one to win,' John looked at his watch. 'Another hour and every kid in the manor'll be opening their presents.'

Emma lay on the couch, snoring fitfully, the toes of her small fat feet pointing inward, her green hat clutched to her chest.

'Honest, Jack. You don't know when to stop,' said Doris, yawning behind her hand. 'At least there ain't been no raids, no sirens.' She tried not to see Brandon rake in the pot.

'Don't moo at me, Doris. My luck's gotta change soon.' Jack rolled and lit a cigarette. *She hates seeing me lose. Why she plays I don't know. She parts with money like it's glued to her fingers. The mean cow ain't so fond of this Brandon now he's won most of the poppy, is she? Now she's whining a different tune. If Phyl was here we'd be having sandwiches to soak up the ale. How this idle, mean cow and her can be sisters I don't know.* 'Your deal, John.'

'Let's make this the last one,' John collected the cards.

'Hold it until I've been to the little boys' room.' Brandon pushed back his chair and left the room.

'You know what to do,' said Jack.

'What?' said Doris.

'Never you mind. Get on with it, John.'

'Three hands worth?' asked John, rigging the deck with practised ease.

'Yeah. Move the luck around the table.'

'You're not ...' Doris started.

'Shut it. Go and keep him talking. Offer him a cup of cocoa or something,' said Jack. 'You want to be skint over the holiday?'

'No, but ... '

'Do it then.'

'On your head be it.' Doris went down the passage as the cistern flushed on the landing.

Jack closed the door and stood with his ear against it. 'Make it look natural, John. This geezer ain't no country berk.'

'How much you reckon he's got on him?'

'Enough for a few good drinks, that's for certain,' Jack heard Doris take Brandon into the kitchen.

'Ain't you taking a bit of a chance, like?' asked John, seeing that Jack had four sevens and Brandon could draw a flush.

Jack felt his neck muscles tighten as the whisky died in his stomach. 'Don't even think what you're thinking,' he said, seeing John blanch at the look on his face. 'You hear me?'

'No offence, Jack mate.'

'All right then.'

Twenty minutes later, Jack had won fourteen pounds ten shillings and John was up by eleven pounds twelve shillings and sixpence. Doris had won threepence. She moved her chair closer to Jack as Brandon said: 'That's a real relief I can tell you. I'd have hated to take you guys.'

'Hmmm,' said Jack. 'Only a game, ain't it?'

CHAPTER SIX

The British weakness for old dogs, aging actresses, and veteran statesmen is incorrigible ... and enough was said on the occasion of Chamberlain's death to make one feel that another woolly legend was in the process of being built up. In bars and buses, one heard people say mournfully, 'Ar,'e was too much of a gentleman to be up to their tricks, 'e was.' An unlovable personality, he had to wait to be dead to be loved by the nation, for some of the strangest reasons that ever didn't get engraved on a memorial tablet.

Mollie Panter-Downes *New Yorker*

When word came through of Taranto – a spectacular triumph for the Cinderella of the services, the Fleet Air Arm – Cockney newsdealers chanted with lugubrious relish, 'Eye-talian fleet done in! No more macaroni!'

Mollie Panter-Downes *New Yorker*

ONE: PHYLLIS

29 December 1940

Overnight rain had pocked the sand and the high sky was blue lacquer above the pewter sea.

'Come on, Phyl.' Sissie lit two cigarettes and took one side of the chemical toilet. 'Let's bury the dead.' She and Phyllis carried the brimming container out into the dunes, blowing cigarette smoke ahead of them.

'I hate this job, Sissie,' Phyllis said, starting to dig. 'Thank heavens there's nobody about.'

'I used to do ours at night until I tripped in the dark.'

'Your hair's growing out nice.'

'I still look like a freak. And it's no good you saying otherwise.'

'But we're still going into town?'

'Yeah, a promise is a promise, Phyl ducks. I even sleep in this turban so I don't catch sight of meself.'

'Your Asa didn't come on leave?'

'Nah, nor your Tommy, eh? Sometimes I feel like the last woman on earth. I miss London horrible. There ain't been no raids for over a week now. I wonder if it's all over?'

'Wouldn't it be lovely to go back, Sissie? Walk down Oxford Street and window-shop in Regent Street? Watch the fur coats go by, and have a pot of tea in Lyons Corner House?'

'Only makes you jealous, Phyl. I haven't had a new coat since I bought one off the tally man four years ago. Look at it, balder than I am.'

'You could dye it. Black maybe?'

'I would look choice, wouldn't I? With me hair like a Chinese puzzle and a black coat? They'd think I'd been to a mad funeral.'

'No they wouldn't.'

'How's your Harry's whooping cough?'

'Worse if anything. Sometimes he coughs so hard he knocks himself over. He holds his little hands to his head and coughs and coughs until he makes himself dizzy and tired, poor little mite.'

'Shame. My Stanley ain't drunk nothing stupid since the paraffin, but he do sniff so. I think he'll never lose that cold. Here, that's about deep enough.'

'Who's that whistling?'

'Mind, you nearly spilled it all over y'self.' Sissie supported the container as Phyllis's foot slipped.

'Sissie, it's soldiers.' Phyllis blushed scarlet, embarrassed to be caught emptying the toilet.

The soldiers waved and cat-called from a higher dune.

'What're they saying?'

'Don't listen. That filth would blister paint. They're them Durhams Mrs Wormold talked about. Remember the ones they billeted in the hotels in Weston-super-Mare when the Somersets moved out? The ones who stand at the windows naked and don't care who sees. That made old beanpole's hair stand up, I can tell you.'

'But look at the state of *them*, Sissie. They're naked, and in this weather. They're never going swimming.'

'They are too. He's a big one, ain't he? Look at the lunch on him. Makes my Asa look like he's got a little boy's finger.'

'Sissie, your mouth.'

'Only saying what you're thinking, Phyllis Penny. When did you last have a seeing-to from your Tommy? I miss it I can tell you. No ifs or buts.'

'It still ain't *polite*.'

'Polite, schmolite. At least Stanley ain't here to see it. It'd only give him ideas, and he gets enough of them all by himself. I caught him playing with himself, and he's only seven.'

'I'd cut my Harry's fingers off. Oh, they're coming this way.'

'Shall we wave?'

'Sissie Ackerman, you wouldn't.'

'Maybe not. But I'm tempted, ain't you?'

'Certainly not.' Phyllis tipped the container over the hole and shovelled in sand, ready to run.

Soldiers pounded past and floundered into the sea, their hard buttocks whiter than their torsos and arms.

'Where's their officers, I'd like to know?'

'In the oven right at the back. They'd have to put the whole regiment on a charge if they started. Them squaddies don't give a cold carrot for no one and who blames them? They went through that Dunkirk caper and a lot of their mates got killed. One of them S.S. regiments that don't take prisoners shot a bunch of them in a ditch, the cucks. They're soldiers, Phyl. Real men. They've got their knees browned and they want the chance of a real crack at the Hun. They ain't about to take no twaddle from peacetime officers when they ought to be over there,' Sissie pointed East, 'killing Germans in France. And I hope they exterminate the whole race, may God forgive me. I had relatives in Poland and Germany, and they've all disappeared into their dirty camps. And I'll tell you, if them animals come here none of us'll survive.'

'I thought it was all ... rumours.'

'Well it ain't,' said Sissie. 'Go on, mate,' she called to a soldier wearing only his ammunition boots. 'You get in there.'

'Come with us, darling. I'll scrub your back for you,' yelled the soldier.

'It'd take more than you, little legs,' Sissie bawled after him. 'Get that big bleeder to do it for you.'

'Sissie Ackerman!' Scandalised, Phyllis started back towards the chalet, her cheeks burning.

'Wait up, Phyl. Blige me, I was only funning.'

'Well it ain't funny. What happens if they think we're loose? They'll be staring in through the windows, making a nuisance of themselves.'

'You should think more of people. They're men ain't they? And I ain't had my share of male company in a long month of Sundays. Ask them nice and they'd empty your khazi for you. There's a couple of lads come over and do mine once a week. All they want to do is chat over a cup of tea. And they bring me the odd ounce of marge and tin of bully.'

'And you accept it?' Phyllis darted a look over her shoulder. The dunes were empty.

'I'd be daft not to. So they sit and look at me legs and chest, so what? It's as good for my morale as it is theirs, and it don't go no further.'

'Sissie, Sissie, you're a regular caution.'

'I'm honest, that's all. I wrote and told Asa about it, and he knows he can trust me.'

'But can you trust yourself?'

'That's a carthorse of a different colour, ain't it?' laughed Sissie, holding the lavatory door as Phyllis returned the container to its housing and charged it with chemicals. 'Yeah, I can trust meself – just about.'

'Come on, we can just make the nine o'clock bus. I'll get the boys' coats on.'

On the bus, Harry began to cough and couldn't stop. A woman complained and the bus conductor turned them off at the next stop.

'I know you, you long-faced sow,' Sissie told the woman as the bus pulled away. 'And you conductor. I've got your number don't you worry.'

'If you was my mother,' Stanley scolded, 'I'd *drink* something.'

'Hear that, you rat-faced enemy of the people?'

'Leave it, Sissie. It won't do no good.'

'If my Asa was here ... '

'Or my Tommy.'

The country lane enveloped them in silence. Sissie sighed and took Stanley's hand. 'Step out, chicken. There's three miles to go before you get a hot drink and a sit-down.'

Robert cried as Harry coughed into the hedgerow with his hands over his ears.

'Hurts Pillis, hurts ... '

'I know, love. I know ... '

TWO: HELEN

'There's this *woman* outside,' said Mrs Tolliver, her arms folded, her expression severe. 'And she's looking down her nose at everything. Told *me* I was her "good woman", and to tell *you* she was *here*. Now it ain't for me to say what I think, but if you asks me, she ain't what you might call suitable as a replacement helper. We can all do without all that snotty lahdie toffee from the likes of *her*.'

Helen fingered a throbbing temple. 'Then it's as well you kept your feelings to yourself, isn't it?'

'Yus, it *is*. And I told her you was too busy to be bothered with people just walking in off the street – large as life and twice as ugly – and coming the old madam with us W.V.S. ladies. Now *that* seemed to get right up her nose and she looks like her knicker elastic might just have got twisted.'

'Mrs Tolliver . . .'

'And she upset Nellie Posset. And you know she turns on the waterworks if you say boo to her.'

'Oh, dear,' Helen sighed. 'We've got all this clothing to sort and size, there are still three dogs and four cats in the Incident Inquiry Point, and sadly, two relatives who need to be ferried to the mortuary. A brouhaha now is the last thing any of us need today.'

'I told her that too. Where do I tell her to wait?'

'Nowhere. Have her come through here. And do say please?'

'I know my manners, Mrs L. But you're too soft by half,' Mrs Tolliver stamped out of the storeroom.

'Well,' Helen told the loaded racks, 'you make up for that.'

'In *there*,' Mrs Tolliver said from the passage. And then: 'If I've told you once, I've told you a thousand times, Nelly

Posset, all Red Cross parcels go in the store on pallets. And it's no good you bawling and pretending other-bleeding-wise. Now, blow your nose and cut along to the canteen for a cuppa tea. It'll settle you down, ducks.'

'Yes, Mrs Tolliver dear.'

'That's the ticket. And don't forget you don't put soap flakes anywhere near food. Stinks it up, don't it?'

Helen smiled behind her hand. Mrs Tolliver was a saint in dragon's weeds, and she bullied everyone with enormous affection.

'Who is that extraordinary woman? She'll have to be replaced.'

'Now look here,' Helen turned to stare into her mother's face, too shocked by the confrontation to find words. Mrs Caldercott was dressed in severe black and her gaunt face was thinner, her eyes more deeply set.

'Quite the grand mucky-muck, aren't we? Are all your people quite so disagreeably eccentric?'

'I'd like a thousand like her. Hullo, Mother.'

Mrs Caldercott stripped off her gloves and put them into her handbag. 'The Dowager Marchioness of Reading told me I should find you here. She and Sir Samuel Hoare are great chums of mine.'

'I know. Have you come to squabble, Mother?'

'No, my dear, to help. I've closed up the house and your father and I have taken a suite at the Savoy. Their shelter is the deepest and the most comfortable, and it's no fun in the country these days. Far too many people sitting out the war pretending to knit balaclavas for the armed forces, when all they're doing is hiding for the duration.'

'Isn't this something of a change of heart for you?'

'Consistency is the refuge of the mean-spirited, Helen. I like to keep busy. Now, where do I start?'

'If you're serious . . . ?'

'Deadly, my girl. Perhaps, as time passes, we might get to know each other a little better. I seem to have lost you along the way. My fault I am sure, but an effort from you would not go unnoticed.'

'Mother, it's dirty, discouraging and sometimes quite awful work we do here. It requires tact and patience, and above all, the ability to work with others who in other times ... '

'Would be quite beyond the pale, yes, I have been told. I take it that creature I happened upon outside is one such?'

'Mrs Tolliver, yes.'

'Then we'll start with her. Have her come in and introduce us formally. I'm sure she'll work under me very well.'

'No, Mother, that isn't how it is at all.'

A pencilled eyebrow rose up the powdered forehead. 'Oh?'

'If anything, she'll be telling you what to do.'

'Great good heavens,' Mrs Caldercott said. 'How are the mighty fallen indeed. You've become a rather hard young woman, and I don't know that I approve.'

'You have to know how things work down here, Mother. There isn't room for dissension or nepotism.'

Mrs Caldercott closed her eyes and took a deep breath.

'Mother, we have an admiral's wife, two wives of M.P.s, a retired schoolmistress, a Harley Street consultant, several housewives and a reformed prostitute. All of them rub along splendidly with Mrs Tolliver co-ordinating them. Without her I should have a very difficult time.'

'Will I be able to tell them apart?'

Helen smiled. 'Yes, I should think so.'

Mrs Tolliver appeared in the doorway. 'You all right, Mrs L? Them relatives are here. I'll have Mrs Dumpton drive them down the mortuary after they've had a cuppa. She don't take no nonsense from them at the Town Hall.'

'She's had that duty for the last three weeks,' said Helen. 'I think even her nerve is going after helping people to identify their next of kin.'

'Who else then, ducks?'

'Mrs Tolliver, I'd like you to meet my mother.'

'Never is.'

'And she is perfect for bullying officials.'

Mrs Tolliver nodded. 'I can believe that,' she said, holding out her hand. 'How do, Missus.'

'A cup of tea would be very nice,' said Mrs Caldercott. She eased off her shoes and rubbed her feet. 'The sirens were going when I came up through Leadenhall Street. There seem to be a lot of raiders overhead.'

Helen poured tea into a thick mug and spooned in condensed milk. 'Did you get lost? I asked you to go to the mortuary in Peckham.'

'I did do as I was asked. But when the cretinous fellow at the Town Hall refused to help those unfortunate people with money from the Lord Mayor's Fund, I tore him off a very large strip and went to see the Lord Mayor. One of my friends is his Personal Private Secretary, and he certainly put a flea into the ears of several pasty old dodderers down there. I think the way will be smoothed from here on in.'

'You didn't!' said Mrs Tolliver, impressed.

'Yes, Agnes, I most certainly did.'

Agnes, thought Helen, *Mrs Tolliver's Christian name is Agnes? What chemistry is working between these two women?*

'Well, good on you, ducks.'

'I also told the Medical Officer of Health he should simplify his official forms. Those things are designed to make the head spin.'

'What did he say to that?' asked Helen.

'Say? What could the fool say? Once he had filled one in for himself he saw the point. Is there a biscuit?'

'A Garibaldi,' said Mrs Tolliver.

'No, Agnes. Nothing of Italian origin will pass my lips.'

'They're never Eyetie?'

'Yes, and I'm surprised that a patriot like yourself would eat such *fascisti* provender.'

'Not no more I won't.' Mrs Tolliver dumped the biscuits in a waste-paper basket.

The drone of bombers rattled teaspoons in their saucers. The windows shook and the door rattled in its frame.

'It sounds like a heavy raid,' Helen said as shrapnel skittered across the road outside.

'That's as maybe,' Mrs Caldercott eased her hot feet back into her sensible shoes. 'But I have several urgent communiqués to deliver to the Town Hall before I take the mobile canteen out.'

'Wait until this passes, mother.'

Mrs Caldercott fixed her daughter with a hard glare. 'I'm sure the rain will hold off, Helen.'

'That isn't what I meant and you know it.'

'You sort out your knitting wool or tin cans or whatever you're currently engaged upon and leave my little chore to me.' She took her gloves from her handbag and snapped it closed. 'Oh yes, I think I can get hold of some army cooking stoves, Soya boilers they're called. I'm sure they'll be extremely useful when there's a major incident involving a great many rescue workers.'

'Yes, I imagine they would.' Helen watched her mother leave then shook her head. 'Impossible woman.'

'She'll do,' said Mrs Tolliver, 'so long as she's kept busy and don't have time to think lahdie.'

'Well, listen to *Agnes*,' said Helen, fear for her mother's safety making her snappy. 'It's a wonder you don't address *her* as Matilda.'

'Now that wouldn't be right and you know it, Mrs L. I wouldn't be comfortable and neither would she. Class is a swinging gate, ducks, and the harder you pushes against it, the harder it swings back at you. Take my tip, leave things as they are. I'm older than you are and I know. For all that things may look to be breaking down because we got to all pull together, they'll go right back to what they was when this war's over. You in your station, and me in mine. You see if I ain't right.'

Helen pointed a finger around her teacup. 'You're a clever, cunning old woman, Agnes.'

'Mrs Tolliver to you, ducks. Let's you and me keep things

right. If you don't show respect none of the others will.'

'Now I've got two harridans to bully me.'

'Not true, ducks. You'll come through with me behind you.'

'Hmmm,' said Helen. 'I wonder?'

'You mark my words, lovely girl.'

The sound of bombers drowned out everything else they might have said.

THREE: CHRISTOPHER

It was trying to rain.

Brigadier Marchbayne-Cleverly waved Christopher and Charlesworth into hard chairs. His office was a wooden shack next to an old quarry where the oolite sandstone lay in broken runs of stratum softened by clumps of rusty weeds and self-planted fern. Portraits of Winston Churchill and King George hung from nails behind the brigadier's desk, a small oil painting of Prince Albert stood on the shelf, his red telephone bore a 'Secure Line' sticker and his swivel chair creaked when he moved.

'Smoke if you've got them,' he said.

'Thank you, Brigadier.' Charlesworth lit a Craven A he did not want, his hangover heavier than the overcast.

'How quickly can the men be made ready to move?'

Christopher uncrossed a knee. 'Immediately, Sir. There are five men on compassionate leave and they're due back on the first. They can be advised of their new posting quite readily.'

The Brigadier lit his pipe and sighed in a cloud of fragrant Virginian tobacco. 'I want you both to keep this under your hats. The War House works in mysterious ways. Here I am, a Brigadier in command of a unit that has never had brigade status, and now that I'm being kicked upstairs, the regiment is being reorganised and will become a brigade.'

'Are we to congratulate you, Sir?'

'For getting a fatter pension? One scrap of bookish learning has got into the files and I'm to be in control of some "hush-hush" Balkans department. That means Whitehall.' The Brigadier poured whisky into three shot glasses. 'You need one, Neville. Lutyens here will join us to be polite.'

They drank and their glasses were recharged.

'I'm very sorry, Uncle,' Charlesworth fought nausea. 'What is to happen to us without you?'

'You'll re-train if you become volunteers. If your chaps are keen you'll carry them with you.'

'For what, Uncle?'

'Jumping out of aeroplanes or some such nonsense. It sounds highly dangerous to me,' the Brigadier allowed his monocle to fall onto his chest. 'I'm too long in the tooth for such activities, so perhaps it's as well I'm to be closeted with all the other old warhorses at the MoD.'

Christopher could hardly draw breath. Excitement bit the back of his throat more fiercely than the fiery malt he swallowed. 'Can you tell us anything more, Brigadier?'

'Only that your new commanding officer will arrive to take over the brigade in the New Year, and the Somersets as I know it will disappear. Those of your men who volunteer for parachute training will be sent to the Central Landing Establishment at R.A.F. Ringway near Manchester. Those of your chaps who don't make it through the training, which I understand is severe, will be "returned to unit" without stigma. They seem to be looking out for rather special sorts of chaps, half-bird, half-baked and completely mad. You two seem type-cast for the part.'

'Thank you, Uncle. It sounds . . . jolly?'

'I'd very much like to join the party,' said Christopher.

'Thought you both might. This is off the record, so not a word to anybody. Clear? Brigade, or South-Western

Command will make it all official in the fullness of time. Now cut along the pair of you, I have to pack.' The Brigadier shook hands with both men and said goodbye.

Outside, as they walked along the edge of the windswept quarry, Christopher danced on the spot, flushing finches from the undergrowth. 'Marvellous, eh, Neville? At last we can get to grips with something worthwhile.'

Charlesworth watched a bird in flight. 'Truly wondrous, old man. I happen to get airsick.'

FOUR: FRANK

The desert shimmered.

White-hot and desolate, it cast false horizons into the sky where refracted light layered the stifled air with shifting dunes and salt flats, liquid pennants of illusion that scalded the naked eye with brilliant apparitions.

Three Matilda tanks trundled through a herd of goats in the wadi below the ridge where Frank was doubled over with dysentery. He felt his stomach turn liquid and he voided painfully.

'Lose yourself, you little bludger.' An Australian soldier threw a rock at an Arab boy in soiled white robes who offered a bottle of lemonade for sale. The boy scurried away and the Australians climbed back into their 30cwt lorry and drove off after the tanks. The buzzing quiet came back and Tosher swore into it for something to do. Frank waited for his body to stop shaking. The sun lost heat as he started to shiver, too weak to pull up his trousers. He had laughed when Taggart went down with it, but now he sympathised, heartily convinced he would not live through the day. The desert was nothing like the pictures painted in P.C. Wren's *Beau Geste*. It stank and shimmered and hummed and everything that crept, crawled or flew seemed to have bitten him at some time or another. Frank bowed over himself, too miserable to care if the ammunition convoy left him behind.

Limey worked the bolt of his rifle, squinting into the haze.

'Stand to, Frank,' he said.

'You're joking,' Frank did not look up.

'What d'you think, Tosh?'

'Dunno, do I?' Tosher looked at Frank. 'Coop?'

'There's bloody hundreds of 'em.'

'Company for you then, ain't they?' Frank said, staring at his boots.

'They're Eyeties, got to be,' said Limey.

'Eyeties, my elbow.' Frank raised his head. Advancing through the heat haze of the dried river bottom were several hundred soldiers, light glinting on their weapons and buttons.

'Wasser,' one of them called. 'Wasser, amico mio.' He waved and started to trot forward.

'Do I fire in the air or what?'

'Wasser, wasser,' the cry became a chorus as the Italians mimed drinking.

Frank laughed and stood up, buttoning his trousers.

'What's funny, they're the enemy?'

'Then why ain't you dead?' Frank held his stomach. 'Give them some water, you berk. You're a hero, you just captured them all by yourself.'

'I am?' said Limey.

'Yeah, what a lovely way to end the year. We're bleeding heroes.' He walked to the lorry and pulled a jerry of water from the tailboard.

FIVE: TOMMY

Private Mifflin waited until Sergeant Trefoil had passed him before nipping out of the Company Office and across the barracks' square to the officers' lines. He found Tommy ironing Lieutenant Lutyens's shirts in the laundry room. Two other batmen buffed brass.

'Got a minute, Tommy?'

'Yeah, Miff, what's up?' Tommy spat on the iron and finished off a collar spear.

'Outside, son.' Private Mifflin said nothing more until they were out in the small vegetable garden. 'I've got some hard news. We're on the move again. Heard Trefoil talking to Brigade. There's some talk of us being volunteers for special duty.'

'Get off.'

'Straight gen.'

'You're serious.'

'Never more so, Tommy son.' Mifflin's eyes moved constantly, checking for eavesdroppers. 'That's why I reckon old Luytens and Charlesworth went over to the Brig's office this morning. He's given them forewarning.'

'Special duty, that mean we'll be going abroad?'

'Nope, north. Manchester. There's this special unit up there for jump training. I don't fancy the sound of it.'

'You mean over the sticks, like horses?' Tommy was confused.

'Parachute training, you berk. Out of aeroplanes, cocker.'

'Sounds handsome, don't it?'

'Yeah? That's how my old man copped it in the last war. He was an artillery spotter, right? They used to have a basket under a barrage balloon so they could see the enemy lines and zero in the guns. One of Richthofen's blokes flew over and shot the balloon down. Then he strafed the old man as he jumped. Shot him to ribbons. And I don't fancy going the same way.'

'It won't happen to you, Miff.'

'Bloody right it won't. They ain't getting me to volunteer for no parachuting.'

'Come on, Miff. We can't break up now, we're a team.'

Mifflin stared. 'You wanna do it?'

'Like a shot. Look around, you wanna be nothing special when we can get to join one the élite mobs? There's gotta be better pay, allowances and that. Let's get where the money is, right?'

'You reckon, do you?'

'Ain't them Airborne blokes the ones with the red berets with a horse on 'em? They're right smart.'

'This ain't toy soldiering, you know.'

'No, and I don't want none of that. If we're in this stupid war let's at least have a go at something a bit good. What d'you say?'

Mifflin shook his head. 'You've changed your tune, ain't you? What happened to that mouse who liked keeping his head down? Look at you now, ready to kick Hitler in the slats single-handed.'

'It'd make my Phyllis right proud.'

Mifflin looked at Tommy as if he had never seen him before. 'You've got more front than Woolworths, and there's one in every high street.'

'What d'you say, Miff?'

'All right, but if your bottle goes I'll kick it all over Christendom, you hear?'

Tommy's eyes sparkled. 'It won't, Miff. I won't let you down.'

'It ain't you I'm worried about, is it?' Mifflin shivered as if somebody had walked over his grave.

'We're on the move,' Tommy said, banners and martial

music in his mind's eye. He punched the air above his head. 'Now we'll see a change.'

'Oh blimey yeah,' said Mifflin, sweating coldly.

SIX: JACK

The sky in every direction was seared by fire, balling upward above the staring desolation of the ruined houses. A land mine fell a street away and the jet of hot blast flamed skywards, hurling brick, slate and concrete into the crimson overcast. Blast stirred Jack's hair and rocked the van on the mud-slicked road. The rubble that had been a dance hall smoked under his feet as he moved across it, listening for signs of life. More than a hundred bodies already lay on the pavement in the rain. Caked in clay and dust, they were the same colour as the road they lay in, the unreal hue of dirty marzipan.

An unexploded thermite bomb, the size and shape of a wine bottle, rolled away from his foot.

'Don't touch that, for Christ's sake,' said a Heavy Duty Rescue Worker. 'Gerry's started dropping some with explosive charges in them. We leave 'em to the army now. They'll have their work cut out tonight, though. I dunno how many hundreds of breadbaskets Gerry's dropped. This is the worst one yet.' A violet flash lit his face and his hollow eyes were very old.

'I know, mate,' said Jack. 'How many was in here?'

'More than two hundred, mostly young kids. The woman in the ticket office told us before she copped it. She had a railing through her gut, poor cow.'

'You see some sights.' Jack sniffed for escaping gas, the argument he and Doris had had that afternoon still fresh in his mind. He eased a floorboard away from a pile of rubble covering a stairwell and bricks fell into the void. *That must lead down to the cellar,* he thought, inching towards the lip of the hole. *She'd better have given that sodding Brandon his marching orders by the time I get home. He's been getting right up my snout with his dollar-lolly and flash ways and the way he's always turning up at odd hours when he thinks I might be on duty. Him keeping bloody Doris in nylons and grub we can't get, it's turned her stupid head. Them Canadians get more money than the Prime Minister. Still, I've won a good few bob off him since Christmas.*

Incendaries clattered down into the street and one skidded off the wall near Jack's head, singeing his hair as it flared alight. Somebody dropped a sandbag on it.

Jack flashed his torch into the hole and swallowed sudden bile. Bodies were huddled on the staircase in broken abandon. A young girl lay on a concrete joist, her naked legs flung apart, her broken arms hanging over the void. Her eyes flickered in the torchlight and her small, perfect breasts shone like pale marble. Jack's manhood stirred with unbidden desire, filling him with momentary self-disgust.

'Here's a live one, mister,' he called over his shoulder. *At least the gas main ain't fractured.* Dust spilled down the beam of his torch and dusted the girl's belly as the raft of wood he lay on shifted. 'Pull me back, I'm too heavy,' he said. 'Hold on down there, love. We'll get to you.' The girl's frightened eyes seemed to claw at his face.

'That's gonna be a sod of a job,' said the A.R.P. man. 'Easy as you come back, matey.'

Jack dry-swam backwards, hearing more rubble fall into the hole. He rolled over and stood up to see rescue workers approaching the broken staircase with ladders and scaffold poles, moving gingerly over the broken sprawl of brick and cement slabs and splintered woodwork. Firelight played on the ornamental mirrors on the one remaining wall and a battered drumkit stood on what had been the stage. A ragged velvet curtain flapped against the blackened bricks and a torn poster advertised a New Year's dance that would never now take place.

The girl's eyes and breasts overlaid the devastation and Jack could not blink them away.

'Go and get a cuppa, mate. We'll get her out,' said a Warden.

'Yeah,' Jack picked his way through the bodies and coiling hosepipes. Water spillage made the road treacherous as it turned the clay and dust to wet slime. Sweating auxiliary firemen directed their hoses into a burning church hall where the figure of Christ in a stained glass window glowed in the steam and flame as hard columns of water smashed over the flaming roof and freshets of muddied slurry ran from the gaping doorway. The heat banged out with each gout of flame in suffocating waves of humid, boiling discomfort. Motes of glowing soot spiralled in the turmoil and danced on the hot odorous air.

An old man and his wife sat on a wall watching their house smoulder, gutted by a single blast of high explosive. Ragged net curtains hung in the frameless windows and an aspidistra on a table were the miraculous survivors.

'Did anybody get out?' they asked Jack.

'A few.'

'They was a Sunday School group,' said the old woman, her white hair darkened by soot and plaster dust. 'It was their treat for good attendance, you see. Tea and buns and that. Now look at it. It's hard to believe there's a God anymore,' she buried her face into her husband's shoulder and he tried to keep his own chin from trembling.

There ain't. Jack did not voice the thought. *All you've got is your three score years and ten, ma, so make the best of this life. It's all you've got.*

A sailor and two airmen stood at the mobile canteen drinking tea and eating meat patties, all of them marked by blast dust. Glass shone in the sailor's hair.

The woman behind the counter drew tea from an urn and

passed Jack a cup. 'Here you are, my man,' she said.

'Ta, missus,' Jack ducked as bombs fell on the end of the street, gouging further holes in the waste. An oil bomb took out an entire warehouse in a ball of saffron glare. The walls folded outwards and debris bowled upwards and sideways, smacking into the road and hammering the ears as foul smoke rolled to envelop the rescue workers at the dance hall. Battered and deafened, Jack was skidded against the mobile canteen. His van had gone in the smoke and he realised that he had left Ken asleep inside.

Jack ran into the blinding smoke and was immediately disorientated. He stumbled against a fire appliance and was toppled by a run of hosepipes. His head slapped down onto the greasy road and he felt his own blood run out of his hair. His hands slipped in the mud and he could not get a knee under him. Chemicals seared his nose and eyes and he realised the warehouse was a medical wholesaler's. The toxic fumes made his head spin and terror gave him the strength to gain his feet and stumble back the way he had come. A fireman blundered into him and they fell together in a tangle of arms and legs. Incendiaries glowed in the poisoned fog and Jack kicked them aside as he scrambled upright. Debris fell all around him as walls weakened by the fresh blast toppled with lazy finality. A steel girder slammed down behind him, making the ground heave. He ran through the spray of a burst hydrant, groggily holding on to his dimming senses. There was more fog inside his head than drifted about him. His legs ran on, taking him away from the thunder and stench of destruction.

The smoke chopped off and Jack found himself free of it. He gulped the burned air, blowing filth from his clogged nostrils, spitting scum from his mouth. His face felt raw, scraped by the dull razors of lethal corrosive chemicals.

The woman was turning the driving wheel of the mobile canteen in an attempt to reverse. The tyre skidded clods of mudslick up into the faces of the airmen as they tried to push the canteen out of the boggy patch she had parked in.

Jack moved to help them, stamping his feet to bring the feeling back into his legs. There was a slow grind of movement that he sensed rather than saw. He started to turn toward it, his big arms raised to guard his head.

Then he was lying on his back with no feeling in any of his limbs. Curiosity prompted him to raise his head. The two airmen were trying to lift a heavy concrete pier from his crushed torso. Jack coughed blood.

'Don't bother, son,' he said, looking at the blazing night where burning flakes of shop-blind sailed like bright butterflies. *Funny, I know this is the end and it don't matter. There's no pain, no feeling of anything. I don't belong down here anymore. I'll just drift up with the flames and find my peace in the darkness. None of this is real anymore.*

The gaunt woman lifted his head and gently laid her folded coat under it.

'We'll have the ambulance along directly,' she said.

There's more toffee in your accent than in ten sweetshops. Jack tried to tell her not to dirty her coat even though she had a wardrobe full of them, but nothing would come from his mouth. The woman took his hand and her grip was as cool as the rain on his face. *Thanks missus, nothing like a bit of kindness to ease things along. Pity about that little girl in the cellar. It would have been nice to have got her out in one piece, but none of them would have lived through that last oil bomb. I hope it was quick for her. Pity there ain't no hereafter, I would have liked to see her again.*

'Hold on, chap,' said the woman.

Jack tried to smile. Can't missus. *You're all misty and it's getting real cold. Poor old Doris. Who'll hold her hand for her now I'm ... ?*

A last monumental door slammed in Jack's mind and he ceased to breath.

'He's gone,' one of the airmen said unnecessarily.

'I know,' said Mrs Caldercott. A tear rolled from her cheek

and plopped onto Jack's chin, merging with the spits of rain. She wiped it off anyway and continued to hold his hand.

SEVEN: DORIS

Her hand shook as she dabbed cologne behind her ears.

The dim overhead bulb laid shadows around her eyes and made her bleached hair look brittle, gave her skin harsh grain. *I can't look any more. I can see my mouth jerk every time a bomb falls, see the lines around my eyes deepen.* Doris shrugged on her dress, made a twirl to see that her stocking seams were straight and left the bedroom, turning on lights as she went. There were too many phantoms in the darkness, and with Phyllis evacuated, the entire lower floor was a black wedge of silence. She sat in the kitchen and put the kettle on the gas for the noise it made as it boiled.

The double crack of the door knocker made her jump, and she was down the stairs before she realised she had moved. Company, any company was preferable to solitude.

'Whisky,' said Brandon, a dark shadow against the searchlit sky.

'Jack's on duty.' Doris closed the door before too much light spilled into the roadway, convinced the German pilots and bombardiers could spot the glow of a cigarette.

'It's bad out there.' Brandon took off his greatcoat. 'Are you okay?'

'I'll be better with a drink inside me, Brandon love. We can play cards if you like.'

'Just a drink.'

They stood in the kitchen like the strangers they were, not looking at one another.

'So pour.'

'Yeah, sorry.' Doris clashed bottle against glass, slopping

whisky on the oilcloth. Brandon took her wrist to get her aim straight. His touch turned Doris's shakes to a shudder and she dared to look directly at the Canadian.

'You're really shook.'

Doris nodded, mute with fear.

Anti-aircraft guns boomed from the railway sidings and she knew tracers would be cutting the sky with yellow parabolas of phosphorus. She leaned in towards Brandon for the delusion of comfort, knowing it would not stop there but unable to prevent it, blaming Jack, blaming the war, blaming everything but her own lack of fibre.

'I'm here, honey.'

'He won't be back,' said Doris.

'No.' Brandon said. 'Drink up.'

'I want to be drunk.'

'Not too drunk?'

'Just ... enough.'

'Fine, honey, fine ... '

'He shouldn't leave me. He shouldn't.'

'No.' Brandon unbuttoned her collar and drew her dress down over her shoulders.

Not with the light on in the kitchen. In the dark where you won't see blemishes and how thin I am. Get it over quick so I can just be held. Gawd, his hands are like silk on me, not calloused and hard like ... Doris refused to frame Jack's name in her mind. Fear and need made it difficult to stand.

On the bed, Brandon's body bowed over her and his tongue travelled the length of her body, showing her things she had never dared to think of. He moved her so cleverly she found she was in positions that would have sickened her under different circumstances. She felt like a derelict house brought back to life by laughter and fresh paint. When her prudery made her shy away, Brandon brought her back with gentle insistence. Then, jogging to release, a million chrysanthemums of pleasure opened inside her and she fell into a great black pool of peace.

Over a shared cigarette she calmly listened to the crash of gunfire and thought of Jack.

Your fault, you bleeder, yours ...

EIGHT: HELEN

It was three o'clock in the morning and the raids had not diminished. The East End and the City of London was a carpet of flame. Not since the Great Fire of 1666 purged the city of plague and gave Sir Christopher Wren the opportunity to replace the gutted Gothic St Paul's with his masterpiece, and to build fifty-one other parish churches, had the capital suffered such a holocaust. Indiscriminate Luftwaffe bombing was now destroying much of that ancient splendour along with miles of slums and warehousing. The Guildhall was smashed, as were the peculiarly named churches of St. Lawrence Jewry, St. Brides', Fleet Street, St. Mary the Virgin, where Shakespeare had worshipped, All Hallows in Barking, the headquarters of Toc H, and St. Andrew by the Wardrobe, and many others, all gone in a single night. Only by a miracle had St. Paul's itself survived the fire raids that had destroyed Paternoster Square and flattened or gutted the area surrounding it.

In the East End the picture was worse, for it was there that the mass of people lived and the casualties were the highest, the many thousands bombed out and dispossessed of all they owned, however pitifully little it was.

The Rest Centre was packed with the shocked, the lost, the bereaved. Here they came to sit for a while whilst the W.V.S. and the A.R.P. did what they could for them. Indians, Jews, Catholics and Chinese mingled with their English counterparts, crammed together in the damp old building, most of them too shaken to talk in their various tongues.

Mrs Tolliver and Helen dispensed all they had until their shelves were empty and not a slice of bread nor a scrap of clothing was left. And still the refugees came.

A woman tugged Helen's sleeve as she helped to change a baby's nappy. Without looking up she said: 'Give your name to the Warden please.'

'It's me. Mother.'

Helen stared at the muddy dress, the straggling hair and the spattered stockings. 'Where's your coat ... your hat?' The question sounded foolish.

'Out there,' said Mrs Caldercott.

'Take over here, Nellie.' Mrs Tolliver took Mrs Caldercott's arm. 'Come in the office, ducks. You look done in.'

'I am rather ... tired.'

'Are you hurt?' asked Helen as they all threaded their way out of the Reception Area.

'Get her sat down first.' Mrs Tolliver closed the office door.

Mrs Caldercott sank into a chair, her face vague. 'I thought I'd never get back. It's all so changed. I've lost the mobile canteen. It just wasn't there any more when I went back for it.'

An ambulance and a fire appliance clanged past outside.

Mrs Tolliver rinsed a cloth under a tap and cleaned the worst of the mud from Mrs Caldercott's face and hands. The touch of water seemed to revive her. 'Thank you, Agnes. I'm quite all right.'

'Yes, ducks, of course you are.'

'How do they stand it? They are all so ... brave. Don't fret, I shan't break down, truly. He had such gentle eyes for such an ugly man. Brown and bright as Rags's.'

Helen shook her head at Mrs Tolliver's frown: 'Our spaniel.'

'Yes,' said Mrs Caldercott, 'just like dear Rags. I held his hand until he died. So peacefully, and I knew he didn't want me to be sorry for him. I suppose that's wicked of me, but it is what he wanted after all. Don't you think?'

'Yes, Mother, if that's what he wanted.'

'Yes,' Mrs Caldercott smiled and fell asleep.

Helen took off her mother's shoes and propped her feet on another chair. Mrs Tolliver covered her with her black coat.

Helen found herself sobbing. 'Can we take any more of this?'

The lightbulb swung on its wire as another stick of bombs fell nearby.

'Yes, ducks,' Mrs Tolliver said softly. 'We can take it. Ain't got no choice, have we?'

'Do you ever pray, Mrs T?'

'Me and God got an arrangement. I don't bother Him, He don't bother me. We talks when it's quiet, and we rubs along. There's just no point in asking for what you can't have, is there?'

'No,' Helen blew her nose. 'Let's get on, shall we?'

'Yes, love, best way.'

They left Mrs Caldercott to sleep and went out into the chaotic bustle of the Reception Area.

NINE: PHYLLIS

30 December 1940

Heavy drizzle swept over the mourners around the mass grave and turned their umbrellas into oiled black blooms. Rain fell on the rows of plain pine boxes and spattered the floral tributes with ochre mud. Grey vapour haloes made grey saints of those who stood bareheaded on the churned turf. A military band of young conscripts played brassy hymns, and when the Lord Mayor of London had delivered a short eulogy, an Anglican clergyman prayed into a microphone, much of what he said lost in the darting wind. A few people threw clods of dirt into the weeping trench before trooping away in sorrowing clumps.

'You're a good mate to come up with me, Sissie,' said Phyllis. 'You and young Stanley both.' She tucked Harry's scarf inside his coat collar and made him hold onto Robert's pram. 'Let's get the bus before we all die of pneumonia.'

'They've done 'em proud, Phyl. A lovely turn-out.'

'Pity they ain't so good to the living,' said Phyllis.

'Who's that soldier with your sister Doris?'

'Some Canadian, love. Nice, I don't think.' Phyllis would not look at Doris in her stately black, her veil concealing little of her theatrical sorrow. 'Jack's hardly cold and she's flaunting him all over the manor like she won him in a pub raffle.' She shook her head and shed rain.

'You gonna talk to her?'

'And say what? Who's your friend? Have a cuppa tea? As if Jack never happened?'

'Maybe you're right. She's having a good cry though.'

'She could always turn the tap on, don't let that fool you. Now she's whoring it with that Brandon she can go back to mother. They make a right pair with their stout and sniffles and self, self, self.'

'The old lady, your mother, didn't come then?'

'Her? Ma and funerals don't get along unless she's the star attraction. You should have seen her when my second dad died; she could give Greta Garbo lessons in the old sob stakes.'

'You get it said straight out, don't you?'

'Only way ducks. Then it don't fester. Let's get on home – *if* Hitler's left us one to go to. Look at this place. I played here as a kid and I wouldn't have known it but for the street names chalked on the barriers. Once there was a pub or a church on every corner, now there's just unexploded bombs and holes.'

They skirted a flooded bomb crater and trudged towards City Road.

On the trolleybus Phyllis said, 'I ain't going back to Somerset, Sissie.'

'What about the kids with all this bombing?'

'If we're together we can lump it. Only one thing frightens

me, and that's if I got hurt and couldn't get to them. If we all go together, all right. Just so's it ain't the other way, that's all.'

'You may have more bottle than a glassworks, Phyllis Penny, but if your brains was dynamite you wouldn't have enough to blow your hat off. Staying in London indeed,' Sissie said with force.

'That's me, Sissie, daft. But I'm staying all the same. Blige me, they've bombed Bristol almost flat, and that's only a spit and a jump from our billets. There ain't nowhere safe any more. So why not be where you knows you belongs and see it through with your own kind? Who's to take care of you or young Stanley out there in the wilds of no-place with no-one about? Here we all share what there is and go without what there ain't. In it together rain and shine.'

'And us, Ma,' Stanley said with a glottal sniff. 'Then I can collect shrapnel like other kids. There's only sand and sea in the country, and they talks funny down that school for 'vacuees. Can't rhyme or reason 'em.'

'Use your hankie, not your sleeve,' said Sissie. 'And don't interrupt when adults is talking. Seen and not heard, right?'

'Only if we can stay too.'

'Watch your lip.'

'And I wouldn't drink nothing funny no more, honest, Ma.'

'Listen to the little mensch,' said Sissie.

'No need crying, Ma.'

'I'm not neither.'

'I'm saying nothing.' Phyllis lit a Woodbine.

'Ain't you said enough already?'

'Only for myself. Your decision's yours, right? With this new training Tommy's doing I get extra allowances and such. Called "jump money" whatever that is when it's at home.'

'That's a new word for it.'

'It don't mean that neither, you and your mind.'

'Phyllis Penny, you're blushing.'

'You'd make a horse blush.'

They watched the traffic, busy with their own thoughts,

then Sissie said: 'My Asa would go potty if I come back to the Smoke.'

'If he cared that blooming much he'd be here with us, wouldn't he?' Stanley dodged a slap. 'Well he would,'

'Hold your clack, you snotty horror. If your dad *was* here you'd go across his knee in double-quick time, don't you worry about *that*, Stanley Ackerman.'

'Leave him be, Sissie. He's only a kid and don't understand. This war grows them up too fast anyway to my mind. Your dad'd be here if he could, Stanley. Just like Harry's dad would.'

'Millions'd believe you,' said Stanley, sulking with folded arms. 'Millions and me.'

They changed buses at Camden Town and caught a 41 to Hornsey.

There's bags of room at my place with easy knickers gone, Sissie. Tons. And we could share the rent,' said Phyllis, sensing the moment was right. 'Sleeping in my own bed last night brought home to me just how much I missed my old house and its bit of a garden. With Tommy drafted up north and Asa God knows where there's no point in staying down Somerset way, is there?'

'I'm thinking,' said Sissie.

Stanley mumbled, glazing the protective membrane on the window with his breath.

'I'll lose you overboard if you don't stow your clack, see if I don't,' said Sissie.

'Well, I've thought it all out,' said Phyllis. 'It just plain ain't right to be hiding away down in Somerset with our blokes doing their best to have a crack at Jerry. We gotta stand and face up to things however rotten bad they might get. Only way, Sissie. We're in this for a long time and ducking out won't get it done. Sounds daft said out loud, but it's gospel truth all the same. No waving flags, just standing our ground is all.'

'Who are you speechifying at, Phyllis Penny? I know when

I'm being got at. An upside-down boat ain't my idea of cosy living, you know?'

'Nobody said it was . . .'

'Think I don't miss Chapel Market and hot bagels on a Sunday? A bag of chips and cockles and nipping out to the pictures for a shilling's worth of romance and cowboys?'

'Nobody . . . '

'Well I do, don't I? Just as much as you and then some. You ain't so special superior, you know.'

'Who said anything of the kind?'

'Maybe nobody. But I don't like it, right?'

'Yes, Sissie.'

'Right then.'

'You go on back if it's right for you. Nobody's wrenching your arm out . . . '

'Ain't they? And who says I'm going back? Did I say I was going back?'

'No, but . . . '

'Well I'm staying, right? And I'll pay me and Stanley's way down to the last sixpence. You get that straight.'

Stanley threw his arms around his mother and nuzzled her face. 'I'll never drink nothing again, Ma. And I'll fetch horse manure for the garden and make my bed and everything.'

'And millions would believe you,' Sissie said, flushed and disconcerted by the enormity of her decision and her son's show of affection. 'He's never done that before, never.'

'I'll follow that coalman's horse for miles,' said Stanley, helping his mother from the bus. As they walked down Rathcoole Avenue Stanley held Harry's hand and pushed the pram as he enthused about collecting shrapnel and military badges.

'What a change,' Sissie marvelled.

Phyllis let them all into Number 63. 'Home,' she said and paused outside the kitchen door before throwing it open with a flourish. The table was dressed with crêpe paper and silver doilies and a small iced cake studded with angelica sat on a glass stand borrowed from a woman down the street.

A funeral and a birthday all in the same breath, thought Phyllis, striking a match. *Ma buried my sister Nelly and christened the surviving twin on the same day when I was Harry's age, so what's changed really? It had rained that day too. Smile for the boy.* 'Happy birthday, Harry.'

'Happy birthday, Harry,' they all chorused.

The boy's face was beatific as he stared at the cake with its five candles.

'Blow, ducks,' said Sissie. 'Make a wish.'

'Is Tommy and Jack and Uncle Frank coming 'cause it's my big birthday?'

'No ducks,' said Phyllis, a stone in her throat. 'They got to win the war first, ain't they? Maybe next year when you're six.' She reached for Sissie's hand as the sirens wailed alive.

'Then I'll be big enough to fight Germans,' Harry puffed his cheeks and blew hard. The flames went out and left the acrid smell of hot wax in the air.

Anti-aircraft fire came from the marshalling yards.

'Open your present, Harry.'

'Is it a gun?' said Harry. 'Bang.'

TEN: 1941

The bitter winter of attrition warmed into an easing Spring, but still the sirens wailed from dusk to dawn; still the Luftwaffe raids persisted. The previous September, when King George VI had announced the institution of the George Cross, a civilian decoration that ranked only second to the celebrated Victoria Cross, he said:

'To the men and women of the Air Raid Precaution Services I should like to say a special word of gratitude. The devotion of these civilian workers, firemen, salvage men, and many others in the face of grave and constant danger has won a new renown for the British name. These men and women are worthy partners of our armed forces and our police ... No less honour is due to all those who, night after night, endure discomfort, hardship and peril in their homes and shelters ... The walls of London may be battered, but the spirit of the Londoner stands resolute and undismayed.'

During April, whilst the Nazis gained control of Yugoslavia and Greece, a force of over 500 German bombers was claimed to have dropped in excess of 100,000 incendaries on the capital in a single night and in reprisal for Bomber Command's air attacks on Berlin. Although many R.A.F. night fighters were now fitted with the new and secret 'radiolocation' device, and were accounting for more and more enemy machines, the raids continued with massive ferocity until the end of May before petering out to solitary dashes by single raiders.

The heaviest of all air-raids came on the night of May 10th/11th, the first anniversary of the German invasion of France and the Low Countries. It was also the day that Hitler's deputy, Rudolph Hess, parachuted into the Scottish highlands on his comic opera 'peace mission'. His arrival leavened the grim war news with some badly needed humour, and as Molly Panter-Downes so aptly put it:

'A Nazi leader, catapulting down onto a Scottish moor, succeeded for several days last week in shifting the war into the key in which war rightly belongs – that of large-scale lunacy. The debt which the nation owes to Herr Hess showed in relaxed, smiling faces everywhere ... A London cinema audience roared when a newsreel commentator, anticipating further Nazi monkey business, said that even the arrival of Göring wouldn't surprise anyone, and added, "But I hope he brings his ration card."'

That night, with a full 'raider's moon' illuminating London, the Luftwaffe pounded the city. Amongst the 1,436 killed were the mayors of two London boroughs, and a further 1,792 civilians were gravely injured, but despite these numbers, the Government's cardboard coffins were never needed or used. The Houses of Parliament were severely damaged and the Commons' debating chamber so completely gutted that the House was forced to convene in the nearby Church House, conveniently kept ready for such an eventuality. The British Museum and Westminster Abbey, offices in Fleet Street and five hospitals were amongst the many public buildings that were hit or burned during the raid. It was destined to be the last great assault the German air force was to mount against the city, the cost had been too high and their planes were to be needed in another theatre of war, far to the east. By July the topic of Londoners' conversation had turned to food, clothes and rationing, and the surprise of finding the Russians as an ally. Not until June, 1944, was London to be threatened from the skies by the VI or 'doodlebug', but that *is* another story . . .